Colston's Phantom

Colston's Phantom

Brink of Death

A Psychological Horror

Fate's Eclipse Saga

Colston Alex Thief

The story that is about to unfold is a product of the author's imagination.

Any resemblance to actual persons, living or dead, or actual events is purely coincidental.

Colston's Phantom: Brink of Death A Psychological Horror
Fate’s Eclipse Saga 1
Imprint by DarkCold Industries
Publisher by Staten House
Distributed by Lulu.com

ISBN-13: 979-8-90243-525-9

Dedicated to

Caleb Hyles;
Whose voice gave life to Colston Driscoll

BLUEJAY;
For bringing Colston's song off the page

A Special Thanks to **Saoirse Finaly**;
To whom is My Kayra

TABLE OF CONTENTS

Chapter One: Five Years Later

We begin in the sleepy mountain town of Payholt, Idaho... Well, hold on, I am getting ahead of myself. Prior to sequestering ourselves in the story, let's take a moment to examine the state of the world, which serves as our backdrop. The situation is dire, as a pandemic is wreaking havoc. Areo Senilis, commonly known as Parched Fever, is a virus that initially presents as mild gastrointestinal irritation. After four days, it progresses to phase two, which is highly contagious and characterized by symptoms resembling the common cold, a rash across the abdomen, and weakness in the joints and muscles. During this phase, a high fever strikes the body within two days, and most people do not survive it. Discussions of lockdowns are circulating, instilling fear in the populace, while mask mandates and social distancing measures are enforced across much of the globe.

That is the global lens that now resides in the back of your mind as we zoom back into Payholt. There is nothing spectacular about this town, and its residents lead ordinary lives. With no intrusive neighbors, there is little gossip or rumor to spread. Payholt is spared from the clutches of tourism, allowing this quaint little town to maintain its harmony, rarely disrupted by outsiders. Who am I trying to deceive with such a description, setting a false sense of safety before the facade is shattered? Perhaps at first, it may seem that way. This book rests in your hands for a reason, waiting for the escape to begin. You may have been drawn in by the title or perhaps by the blurb on the back cover. You might expect the scent of blood to linger on the first page, only to be met with descriptions that do not directly connect to whoever Colston's Phantom is... or perhaps they do! Now these words are swirling in your mind, leaving you wondering and perhaps confused. What is the meaning? What role does this play in the narrative that follows? My answer: everything and nothing. As the story unfolds, subtle nuances may be overlooked, forming a larger picture that draws your attention away from the subtleties of these details. It is a combined effort of mine and Story crafting a journey where even the rests in between crescendos could lead to life or death.

An ominous fog lingers as we walk up the street, our eyes fixed straight ahead. There is nothing to see, so setting us to walk along this dark street feels like a waste of both your time and mine. We wait for Story to take command. The road bends to the left, and ahead of us, it juts out from the fog. The street clock, adorned with a large brass ring encircling its face, stands atop a tall brass post, inscribed with words around the ring. While it is visible to most of the town, it serves as a beacon toward the town's center.

As if following unspoken directions, logic suggests that we are poised to begin the story soon. We crane our necks and fix our eyes on the inscription, with nothing to see around us, yet the elegant black writing remains elusive, refusing to reveal its message. A strong wind blows against our left side, and the sound of swaying tree branches fills the air. Suddenly, the inscription rewrites itself just as something hits and clings to our legs. Aware of the sound of paper flapping in the wind, we are captivated by the new inscription: *He who for whom the clock ticks lies on the brink of death; only upon the final breath will relief from suffering come and new light dawn.*

The wind gusts again, causing the paper caught on our legs to flap loudly, drawing our eyes downward. The moment we grab the newspaper, the wind stops, leaving the ticking as the only sound.

In big, bold letters, it reads: **Trial of Abigail Sunderland Ended Friday.** The town of Payholt, Idaho, gained national notoriety due to the heinous actions of Ms. Sunderland that lasted for a period of nine years. Her charges are numerous, but to name a few: murder, conspiracy to commit murder, false imprisonment, and crimes against public safety. However, the identity of the survivor of her final attack, who contributed to her apprehension, has been kept from the public eye. During their testimony, they stated, "Abigail was good at making you feel comfortable while slowly and carefully sowing seeds of doubt until there was complete dependency. I was fortunate not to have reached that state of full dependency, so when she attempted to perform 'The Rite of Cherish Severance'... Read more on page 54.

Hmm... It is normal for even I not to know all the intricacies of Story's narrative. However, this seems like a significant element to be overlooked, doesn't it? I am apprehensive about what lies ahead, as it appears I have been excluded from Story's plot. I believed my role was secure, and with that said, beware, dear Sior Asumanove.

Bing! Bing! chimes the clock, startling us with its sudden loudness that seems to echo endlessly through the fog. I bid thee farewell as the narrator's perspective narrows even further...

The clock in the center of town chimed in the early hours of Monday, March 2, 2020. However, the chimes are unheard in the home of Colston and Kayra Driscoll.

Kayra lies awake, listening to her husband's erratic breathing. Her own heart begins to pound as she senses the underlying tension of what is to come. She glances at Colston in the soft light filtering into the bedroom, observing his large barrel chest trembling beneath the blanket, his head slowly rolling from side to side. She reaches under the blanket, attempting to find his hand as a way to comfort him. Colston's body twists and convulses suddenly. "Colston! Honey, come back to me!" Kayra shouts as he thrashes beside her in bed.

Colston moves as if he is trying to escape from someone who is on top of him.

"Damn it! Let me go!" he yells.

His body becomes still as her voice manages to loosen the grip of the nightmare, though it does not completely release him. Colston takes a deep breath, always apprehensive about opening his eyes after a nightmare, left to question his place in reality. He gently opens his eyes, and at the sight of his wife's face, a wave of calm washes over his mind. However, the glimmer of tears in her wide brown eyes fills him with sadness. He raises a hand and caresses Kayra's cheek.

"I am sorry," Colston says.

This phrase is as empty as a waterskin in the desert. Despite his genuine intentions, it has become nothing more than a bandage over the past five years.

Kayra leans into his hand and says, "Shhh, don't apologize." Her voice is soft and caring. "Trauma will always..." She pauses for a moment, contemplating her words. She raises her fingers to form air quotes. "'Attack,' if you will; the key is not to let it take control." She rests her head on his chest, finding strength in the rhythm of his heartbeat.

Colston stares at the ceiling, feeling the warm, gentle breath across his chest. "It's been five years," he says aloud, frustrated with himself.

The years of therapy have left him feeling lost and desperate for relief. His singing, along with the support from Kayra and Jordan, has provided him with some traction in this ongoing battle. Although he has never confided this to anyone, he remains bound and trapped in that bathroom. He may have escaped with his life, but a significant part of him remains locked away in that cell, intended to safeguard what he cherished during the ordeal. To this day, within his dreams, he pounds on the cell, yearning to feel whole once more.

Kayra looks at him and says, "It could be six months or ten years; trauma never truly leaves." She is trying to remind him that it is okay to feel scared at times; he is only human. "Do you need to talk to Todd?" This is a typical response after experiencing a nightmare.

Colston gently sits up, distancing himself from Kayra as he gets out of bed.

"No... No, I need something else," Colston says heavily, staring at the floor.

Kayra's heart leaps at the way he uttered those words, a mixture of fear and an overwhelming sense of defeat. She climbs out of bed and stands with him. "What is it?" she asks gently, yet with trepidation.

In this final year of nightmares, Kayra noticed a troubling shift in the effects it had on Colston. In the four years prior, Colston had transformed his nightmares into motivating forces that helped him overcome the heaviness that weighed on him. These nightmares have begun to wear him down, leaving him distant for two days or even longer. He would not eat, and the fear in his eyes was unmistakable. During these times, Kayra felt compelled to wait and watch, as he seemed so far removed from reality. Yet, when he eventually bounced back, he was strong, happy, and driven. To spare him further pain, she refrained from discussing those difficult days. Following his lead, she concealed her own fears, waiting to add to the pile with the next nightmare and the lingering days.

Colston sighs, still avoiding eye contact. "I want to go back to the house."

Kayra gasps and grips his hands. "Why?" Her mind is hijacked by vivid memories of the days when Colston was gone and the moment she found him.

Colston had always loved going above and beyond to create content for his channel. She was usually aware of his plans, but that year, she was not. She had left to gather supplies for his birthday the following day. When she returned twenty minutes later, she expected to find him still singing or editing, but instead, she discovered a note on the kitchen island.

Kayra,

Please don't worry. I have been scheming to make 'Colston's Creepy Covers' one of the best. I am perfectly fine and have a great team. I will return to you after this has run its course.

Love, Colston

Kayra had believed the contents of the note and even watched the upload later that day, witnessing the genuine fear that was in his eyes when the rag was placed over his mouth. It unsettled her, but she tried to dismiss it, reminding herself that Colston was merely acting to portray the fear of being kidnapped. However, the following day, his birthday, brought nothing from him. The last sentence of that note seemed to taunt her. She didn't want to overreact; however, when the *Ineffective* upload appeared the next day, she could not help but cry. The voice was not his, and seeing his hands bound made her heart ache for him. She did not listen to the entire song then, and she still hasn't five years later.

The next seven days were agonizing for Kayra. She wished he'd told her to alleviate her worries, as they seemed so real. She could not shake the feeling that something was very wrong. Colston, devoted to his craft, would have reached out to her despite his commitment to the act.

On the ninth day, an upload appeared, and the title brought her to her knees: *His Screams Echo, Unheard'*. She was very familiar with that song; it was Colston's warm-up track when he was preparing to perform a heavy metal cover. The song tells the story of a man who lacks confidence in his voice while dreaming of singing on stage until a strange, corrupt figure arrives to assist him. The man struggles to remain true to his own voice as the corruption spreads. Kayra didn't watch long enough to hear him start singing, which, in hindsight, might have saved him sooner. The first 30 seconds featured Colston standing in low light, hands bound, his poorly dressed body shivering. The golden mask that covered the upper portion of his face prevented Kayra from seeing his eyes. His captor loomed closely behind him, causing him to flinch, visibly terrified. Overwhelmed, Kayra stopped the video and screamed.

But... why the distance between uploads? Her phone rang, startling her and interrupting her train of thought. Without checking the caller ID, she answered, hoping to hear Colston's voice.

"Hey, Kayra, tell your guy to unsilence his phone. I need to let him know that the new upload gave me chills." The voice belonged to Jordan Youngblood, a fellow singer and close friend.

Kayra couldn't maintain her composure. "I am not with him! Jordan, I am scared!"

"Whoa, what do you mean you're scared?" Jordan asked, panic setting into his voice.

"I haven't heard from Colston in nine days," she said, tears streaming. "Please tell me I am overreacting!"

There was a pause, and during that moment, Kayra became convinced that something was seriously amiss.

"Kayra, if you don't hear from him personally within the next twenty-four hours, you need to call the police. I'll be there around eleven tomorrow," Jordan said.

"Can't I do it now? What happened in today's upload?"

"Kayra, either Colston has been taking acting classes, or he is genuinely singing for his life. Additionally, the fact that you have not heard from him is concerning," Jordan explained. "You can call the police if you want. You have every right to do so; I'll see you tomorrow."

Kayra sat in silence. She had dialed 911 several times throughout the day and night but never completed the call, always convincing herself that she was overreacting. Her emotions were running on overdrive simply because she was left in the dark about Colston's actions.

She fell asleep on the couch around one in the morning on the tenth day. Waking up at five with a headache and a stuffy nose, she prepared coffee and ate some dry cereal. All the while, she stared at her phone, anxiously waiting for that call and watching the minutes tick down to Jordan's arrival.

Idly picking at the tasteless cereal and sipping her coffee, she was startled when a call came through around nine o'clock. The number was unfamiliar; typically, she would have ignored such calls. What if it was Colston calling from an unknown number? She answered, "Hello?"

The only sound that came over the line was ragged breathing, followed by sobs, and then a desperate voice calling, "Kayra, Kayra, it's me!" This voice did not belong to Colston; it belonged to someone struggling to draw breath. Colston had sung yesterday or perhaps the day before. He was with a team, wasn't he? He was just running. Colston cherished his ability to sing as if it were his own child.

"Colston?" Kayra asked, her voice trembling.

"Yes, it is me. I was kidnapped, despite whatever you may have seen. It was not an act," Colston stated, very much struggling to remain awake.

"Where are you?" Kayra inquired.

"In a van, on the side of a remote mountain road north of t--" A coughing fit interrupted him.

Panic swept through Kayra's body as she listened to the deep, chesty coughs that left him gasping for air.

"I am coming; please stay on the phone," she begged, grabbing her keys off the counter and racing out the door.

"Kayra--I love yo-." Colston faded into unconsciousness.

Kayra paused halfway to the car, hearing the strained breathlessness in his words, and heard the phone drop.

"Colston! I LOVE YOU TOO! PLEASE HANG ON!" Kayra cried out as she pushed herself to move again. Why hadn't she trusted her instincts? She knew it was strange. Frustrated, she berated herself while following Colston's vague directions.

She called the police, and after learning that units had already been dispatched to the area, she called Jordan. The moment she heard Jordan answer, she exclaimed, "He was kidnapped!"

"What? Did he escape? Did the police find him?"

"He called me; he didn't sound well, and then he lost consciousness. I am on my way to the location he mentioned."

"Please be careful."

Kayra wanted to sob and was trying to adhere to the

speed limit. "Jordan," she said, sounding desperate.

"He is strong," he said. "Kayra, focus on driving. Call me once you've found him."

"I will." Kayra hung up and took a deep breath.

Kayra was on the four-lane highway, contemplating which of the numerous turn-offs into the forest was the correct one.

She noticed a thick column of smoke rising above the trees at the 49th turnoff leading toward Mirage Gap.

Turning onto the two-lane highway, she felt a deep unease at the absence of sirens. Gripping the steering wheel, her heart raced with every curve. Kayra had hoped she would not be the one to discover Colston.

She found it ironic that she was battling against her instincts, the truth.

Two miles down the road, the smoke became significantly more pronounced. As she rounded a bend, she spotted a white van parked on the side of the road, facing toward town.

"Oh my gosh!"

She parked behind the van and jumped out into the crisp, smoke-filled air. On unsteady legs, she approached the driver's side door. The window was tinted, and as she grasped the door handle, she braced herself for the worst. When she pulled the handle, a phone tumbled out, followed by Colston's arm, which flopped out alongside a strong smell of smoke. Kayra let out a sob. He was black and blue, covered in dried blood, and his shorts, along with the bottom edges of his sleeveless vest, showed signs of being burned. "Colston?!"

He remained still.

Kayra pulled herself up onto the runner and said, "Cole, come on, babe!" She interlaced her fingers with his left hand, which felt cold, and noticed that the skin on his wrist was rubbed raw. She folded his arm, pressing the back of his hand against her chest, and with her other hand, she felt his beating heart before gently rubbing his feverish face. "Colston, please."

The sirens were approaching. Kayra released his hand, allowing it to fall limply, and she cradled his face. "I am sorry; please stay with me."

Colston teetered on the brink of life and death. Exhausted, he had managed to escape, yet he could not allow himself to let go. He felt an overwhelming pull toward relief.

"NOOO!" he screamed in his mind as he pulled toward the source of the pain.

At that moment, he felt powerless against the pain, unable to compel his beaten body to continue fighting. He heard her calling him, and he summoned strength from deep within, pushing against the cold, the pain, and the fears that surged into his body with full force.

He took a deep, agonizing breath.

"Babe!" Kayra exclaimed.

He coughed and tried to suppress another fit of coughing. She didn't recoil; she just stared, waiting for his eyes to open.

Her heart fluttered when his eyes fluttered open. His once bright brown eyes had turned gray.

"Kayra?" His voice sounded distant.

"Yes, I'm here," she said gently.

Colston raised his shaky hand and brushed her cheek. "You're real?" Although it was a question, there was a sense of deep relief in his voice.

Kayra saw relief wash over his body. "Colston." Kayra was crying and terrified. "Help is on the way; you are safe." She softly kissed his cold, chapped lips, then watched as his eyes closed.

The terror of that day left a profound mark on her heart. They gaze into each other's eyes, having returned from the hold of their memories.

Colston is quite certain that the house isn't there anymore. "I simply have to." His words cut deeper than he intended.

Kayra doesn't back down from the heat of the moment; instead, she responds with care. "There's no need for you to return, please, honey."

Colston's gaze drifts away as he steps back from her and heads to the bathroom. After taking care of his business, he trudges back and pauses at the doorway.

He speaks slowly, "I have to confront that place. It was a real house, not just a figment of my imagination." Right now, unable to shake clear of what the police have been trying to hammer home.

Kayra rushes to him and embraces him. "Honey, it was real. Please don't give in to the lack of answers from the police. Only harm will come if you go back, especially right now, in your fragile state of mind."

"I need to confront the harsh reality that was my prison," Colston says, adding in his mind, *"is still my prison."*

Kayra tightens her embrace, her eyes squeezed shut as she attempts to shy away from the haunting image of Colston bruised and battered, unconscious in the front seat of the van.

"On one condition," she speaks slowly as she meets those distant eyes.

Colston stares in silence, torn between his desire to return and his overwhelming fear. His therapist has suggested this approach periodically over the years as an effective means of healing. He survived...*And what?* Colston often recites this question in his mind. He fears that when he sees the house or the location where it once stood, all the memories may come rushing back at once, and he might lack the strength to fight through. So why subject himself to that torment? He feels as though he is drowning without that portion that remains locked away. The house might be the key to liberating him once and for all.

"What is it?" he asks with an unsteady voice.

"I and Jordan go with you." Her statement is crisp in her resolve.

Colston looks at her, genuinely perplexed. "JD?"

Other than Kayra and his therapist, Jordan Youngblood is the only other person in his life with extensive but selective knowledge of what transpired. Both Kayra and Jordan have been his greatest cheerleaders, yet he feels he is failing them due to the persistent nightmares and their ongoing impact.

"Yes, Jordan. I do not want anything to happen that would prevent me from keeping you safe. I need to tell you the truth: when you isolate yourself, you become unreachable for days. Then you act as if nothing is wrong. I, I." Kayra speaks sharply, her voice trembling as tears well in her eyes, but she cannot finish her thought and buries her face in his chest.

Colston stands there, listening to his wife cry and numb to her words.

"Stop crying." The intended tone is lost in his strained throat, and this intense display of emotion irritates him.

A veil of darkness and terror has descended upon his mind, making everything once safe and calm feel distant. The monster within him feeds on this turmoil, its claws threatening to scratch at his already wounded heart. In his deteriorating state, the monster invades Colston's thoughts. He typically seeks refuge in his studio during these episodes because he fears for Kayra during them; he is not in control while he fights to maintain his sanity.

"Kayra," he says, struggling to keep his voice steady, which causes him physical pain. "I'm sorry. Please hold yourself together." He mentally berates himself for speaking to her like this.

Kayra feels his body tense in her embrace, and it frightens her, yet she doesn't pull away. She prays and hopes he can break through whatever he is facing in his mind.

"Colston, please fight." That's all she can think to say.

Her shoulders are gently pushed back, and she allows herself to be moved away. She feels and observes the tremor in his body.

"I... will... try to... be... better." The words are strained and thick.

As he collapses to his knees, Kayra gazes

into his eyes. Colston's look of apology is lost when his bright brown eyes appear to fade before flickering back to life. What is she witnessing?

"Better? No, Colston. Just let me in; leave the door ajar so I may peek in to see if you are okay. I have no problem leaving you be; just do not seal the door."

She cradles his face in her hands, tears streaming and his chin quivering. Leaning in to kiss him, she notices his eyes dulling once more. Terrified that he might fall unconscious, he not only kisses back but also embraces her. Making her heart leap with joy while simultaneously filling it with dread.

"I will try," he whispers.

They remain in that embrace for a while; for the moment, everything feels right and safe. The fear of what awaits them in the next moment is causing this one to linger.

Colston is exhausted and decides to return to bed. Although Kayra would love to join him, she can't. She cannot simply lie next to him, listening to his breathing and waiting. Kayra senses the tension; this situation feels different, and it frightens her. She realizes that she cannot handle this alone.

Kayra quietly leaves the room, where Colston is already snoring softly, and goes to the kitchen.

Means to an end; To satiate the demon: to silence the seething storm within. Means to an end; To satiate the demon: to silence the seething storm within. Means to an end; To satiate the demon: to silence the seething storm within. Means to an end; To satiate the demon: to silence the seething storm within. Means to an end; To satiate the demon: to silence the seething storm within. Means to an end; To satiate the demon: to silence the seething storm within. Means to an end; To satiate the demon: to silence the seething storm within. Means to an end; To satiate the demon: to silence the seething storm within. Means to an end; To satiate the demon: to silence the seething storm within. Means to an end; To satiate the demon: to silence the seething storm within. Means to an end; To satiate the demon: to silence the seething storm within. Means to an end; To satiate the demon: to silence the seething storm within. Means to an end; To satiate the demon: to silence the seething storm within. Means to an end; To satiate the demon: to silence the seething storm within. Means to an end; To satiate the demon: to silence the seething storm within. Means to an end; To satiate the demon: to silence the seething storm within.

Chapter Two: Second Nightmare

Jordan has done so much over the years to help Colston and Kayra. She needs him, but hesitation grips her fingers as she dials his number, weighed down by the heaviness she noticed in him during his last few visits.

Jordan answers with a yawn, "Kayra?"

She glances at the clock on the oven: 5:15 AM. Her face flushes with embarrassment. "JD, I am so sorry I was not paying attention to the time."

"It's fine. Was it another nightmare?" Jordan asks.

Shame fills Kayra; whenever she calls, it is about Colston and something that she needs help with.

"Jordan," she hesitates, unsure whether to let him go without revealing the truth or to apologize for only contacting him when she is struggling. Should she mention what Colston wants to do and ask for his help one last time? She ultimately decides on the latter. "Can you be here by tomorrow?"

"I can be there by 11 in the morning. Will that be okay? What happened?" Jordan asks, not in a hurry to get off the phone.

"That is fine. It was another nightmare even without his latest demand. There is something different, and I feel like I'm losing him."

There's a long pause from Jordan before a

sigh. "The last couple of times that I have worked with Colston, he's been fighting, doing his best to hide his internal struggle. I've noticed a change. I didn't know how to bring it up; it's hard to speak about such a difficult situation." He pauses again.

Kayra hears the phone shift from his mouth for a moment.

"What is he asking?" Jordan's voice is thick with emotion.

"He wants to go back to the house," she says in a low, worried tone. "Jordan, I saw the struggle in his eyes and felt his body tremble." She breaks after saying that.

"Kayra, please, for the sake of all of us, you need to build a bigger support system. I know Colston doesn't want the true nature of his situation to get out, but..." He stops, realizing he's trying to overstep Colston's wishes. Colston has been adamant about keeping the details of his kidnapping private. Yet Colston must understand the impact it has on Kayra and him. What about therapy? Again that feels like overstepping, but Kayra interrupts his thoughts.

"It only gets like this during these times, and they're becoming more frequent. But other than that, everything is perfectly fine," Kayra says, convincing herself of the facade.

"Everything is not fine. Colston is dealing with something that is wearing him down. Honestly, I don't think going back to the house will do him any good." Jordan says his voice is defensive.

Kayra, unfazed by the tone, responds.

"That's what I told him. So I set a condition: you and I have to go with him."

Jordan falls silent for a moment.

"Is Colston around?"

"He's sleeping."

"I'll start making my way to you soon. Hang in there, Kayra. See ya tomorrow."

"Bye, JD, thank you."

Kayra puts the phone down and rests her forehead on her arm.

Colston's restful sleep transforms into a very vivid nightmare...

Colston is walking along a warm, inviting path surrounded by lush trees, made even more lovely by the sun's rays filtering through and creating beautiful patterns. He is humming along to a tune in his head when suddenly the world morphs and contorts.

The warmth was swept away on a frigid breeze. As the path that bent and curled among the trees straightened and crumbled, the flowers and lush grass withered and died, lining the uneven path leading the way to a house left to face the elements alone. The melody in his mind vanished, swallowed by the fog of fear and the hint of a sweet odor. He felt himself start to lose balance, and in an attempt to steady himself, he realized that his wrists and ankles were bound with duct tape. But he didn't fall; a hand gripped painfully into his bare bicep. Colston hissed in pain.

"You have enough fat! You are fine!" the man said. "Now walk!"

The slow shuffle, like that of a man being led to the gallows, was the most spirit-breaking walk. Colston began to wonder at that point if this house was going to be his grave.

"Colston, breathe. Let go of your fear. I am here to help you." His voice was calm and sweet.

Upon reaching the threshold of the house, Colston finally managed to process what was said and formulate a response through fear and dizziness. "Help me with what?" His voice shook; he was in total disbelief that this was happening to him. He was a cover artist with a thicker build; this had to be a joke, a way to promote 'Colston's Creepy Covers'. Yes, there was a team behind this creating a realistic scenario, and to heighten the fear, he was left out of the plan.

He was halted, and his captor now stood in front of him. The hand gripping his bicep pinched his skin. The face of the man was obscured by a full-face mask reflecting Colston's image.

The other hand reached up and removed the mask, revealing a young, gentle, caring face, slightly rough around the edges, with sunken and dark eyes. Those eyes bore into Colston, filled with hope, care, and love. "I answered your call! You're struggling with the fear of failing; you're beautiful, yet you are lost, and that is what scares you. The thought of being lost forever. I can be your defender against that overwhelming sense." His voice was low and alluring, but the growing insanity in his eyes betrayed him with every word spoken.

Colston instinctively pulled away from the intensity.

The man's face twisted in the pain of betrayal before smoothing over again. He took a deep breath and moved back to Colston's left side. "Maybe a good night's sleep will help you realize this. Get moving!" He lifted Colston's bicep.

Colston shuffles forward and into the house. The air inside was stale and musty; the wooden floorboards were dusty, and there was rotting junk lining the walls, creating uncomfortable shapes in the fading light. He was led straight down a short, narrow hallway that creaked loudly as they entered. There was one door at the end to the right.

The man opened the door to a dark, rundown bathroom, dragged Colston inside, and sat him on the toilet. From his back pocket, he pulled out a flashlight and placed it on the counter, aiming the beam between them. Then he knelt before Colston, and he reached out towards his face.

Colston instinctively pulled away, watching as rage and betrayal flashed across the man's face. He saw the hand that was meant to caress his face flex and then relax. Colston wondered if he would be struck.

"I am here to save you!" The man screamed. The intensity of the voice rattled Colston as the echoes faded. He stared, realizing that this was no joke; this was a nightmare come true.

The man dropped his hand and glared at Colston. "This room is only for a little while." His voice was strained.

"What?" Colston questioned, dazed and confused. His heart was beating fast.

"I have a bedroom set up for you. Until I can trust that you won't run, this is your home." Colston felt a pang of terror. The way he said 'home' had forever stripped all the warmth and comfort from the word. "Once you sleep off your panic and understand that this is for your own good, conditions will improve." The man eyed Colston as he reached back with his left hand. When he brought his hand back into view, he was holding a straight-back knife.

Colston's mind swirled with alarm and panic, deepening the dizziness. The man released Colston's wrists and ankles; all the while, his eyes were daring him to make a move. Colston resisted the urge to shove the man and run; the odds were stacked against him. He had no idea where he was, and fear coursed through him, mixing with the remnants of the drug in his system. He couldn't trust his body and mind to work together, and he dreaded what would happen if he was caught.

In hindsight, he should have just run. The captor knelt there with his hands resting on top of Colston's wrists, seemingly watching him contemplate his position. A smirk appeared on the man's lips, making Colston's skin crawl.

"I knew you'd come around," he said; his voice was sickeningly sweet and patronizing. "Now sleep. I need to edit a video." He stood up.

Colston looked up and questioned, "What?"

"Oh, yes, everyone will know that you've been kidnapped. Now sleep; tomorrow we'll discuss the terms of your possible release." The smile on his face made Colston retreat as far as he could, his skin crawling with danger. The man left the bathroom with the flashlight, leaving Colston in complete darkness. He shook in fear at the sound of the deadbolt locking him in.

He thought to himself, *Tomorrow, at first light, I run!*

Kayra has drifted into a light doze at the counter.

Colston is tossing and turning, softly moaning in the bed. He is sweating.

The cold porcelain sides of the tub served as an uncomfortable bed. He could hear the wind whistling and felt intermediate drafts of cold flowing over the edge, caressing his poorly dressed body. Colston was prone to overheating, even in the winter, but what he was experiencing now was unsafe, and he needed to escape. If this treatment continued with the nights growing colder as October wore on, he dreaded to think of the consequences.

He crawled out of the tub and slowly got to his feet. He was sore, but his balance was intact, and the fog induced by the drug had cleared from his mind, though the fog of fear remained. That fear fueled his desire to devise a plan of escape.

There was not much to see in the dark, which made the faint outline of the door stand out more. He was thinking, but no good ideas came to him. He could attempt to bash through the door, but he didn't know how sturdy it was. He was a big guy, and fueled by panic and fear... He could vaguely recall the state of the house. Now was not the time for guesswork.

Then the sound of a generator kicked on, startling him out of his mind to listen. The generator drowned out most other sounds; he swore that he heard the ding of a microwave. If he could trust himself, he prayed that faint sound was indeed from a microwave. He made a plan and positioned himself so that when the door was opened, he'd be behind it.

Several minutes later, the generator fell silent, and seconds later, he could hear hollow footsteps approaching. Colston's heart pounded with each step. He heard the loud creak of the wood. He did his best to control his breathing. The aroma of food wafted under the door, reminding him that he hadn't eaten since lunchtime yesterday. He tried to ignore the terrible rumbling in his gut.

"Colston, you awake? I have breakfast for you." The man called sweetly through the door.

Colston held his hands at the left side of his face while leaning away from the door and let out an uncomfortable groan.

After the groan, Colston waited with bated breath, hoping to hear the sound of the deadbolt unlocking. The deadbolt was unlocked, and the door clicked open, and the door swung ajar.

"I am sorry about the accommodation, but so--" The rest was drowned out by screams as Colston rammed the door full force into the man before pulling it back open and stepping out. Steam rose from the food that now covered the man's face and chest.

Colston darted past him as the man collapsed against the wall, screaming and cursing. He barreled through the rotting front door, almost losing his balance but managing to keep upright. He had to reach the van, only allowing a brief second to worry that the keys might not be inside. Nevertheless, he ran around the front, but his left foot landed in a soft patch of dirt. Suddenly, he heard the sound of a motor revving from beneath the van. A rope looped around his ankle tightened and pulled until it pressed against the tire.

Colston fell screaming in surprise and pain. His left hand reached out, landing in front of the driver's side tire in another soft patch. He watched as another rope sprang free from the light covering of dirt, securing itself about his wrist and painfully wrenching it against the tire.

He was trapped, and his cries grew louder with fear and desperation. His plea for help was abruptly silenced when his captor covered his mouth with duct tape. The man moved back from under the front of the van and sat heavily on the ground and slammed the roll of duct tape beside him, looking disappointed at Colston, whose tears fell as he simply stared.

"Why?" His voice was low, struggling for control. "A year of work, Colston. A year of fucking WORK!" his voice echoed.

Colston lay there helpless.

His captor maneuvered onto his belly and wormed his way under the van until he was inches from Colston's face. "There is nothing to be afraid of. I understand you are scared, but," a hand caressed Colston's face, and a satisfied smile lit up the man's face. "I really, really don't want to hurt you. I want to help you. Should you test my patience... there will be hell to pay!" He got to his knees, hunched low to remain under the van, and said, "I hate seeing you like this, but I can't trust you."

Colston was taken by surprise by the sudden and solid hit to his solar plexus.

Colston is in a ball in the center of the bed, mouth open in a silent, breathless scream. Sweat, drool, and tears mix on the sheet. His body trembles in pain as the nightmare keeps a steady hold on his mind.

His vision faded for a moment, and he gasped for breath through the tape. His captor worked with uncanny speed to free him from the traps. Colston's wrists were taped together, and he was dragged along the ground. His left side scraped painfully as he was pulled from under the van.

"Please, stop!" he screamed into the tape. Colston was hauled to his feet as if he weighed nothing.

"Tape comes off once we're inside, but only from your mouth." The voice was sly and full of warnings. Colston was marched back down the path to the house, and with every step, his panic and worry grew. Had he just blown his only chance for escape? Shame welled up inside him, and tears fell.

The front door hung off kilter within the frame. Instead of going straight to the bathroom, his captor steered him to the left down a hallway lined with moving boxes and random junk. The hallway bent slightly left into an awkward three-way intersection. To his left, Colston was able to see the dirty kitchen with piles of dishes and dirt on the floor. Before he could see what was to his right, he was led through the doorway straight ahead, which opened up into a makeshift living room. A chair sat in the center of the room. Colston was led to it and seated.

"Stay!" His captor ordered as if speaking to a dog.

Colston looked away ashamed, but his eyes were drawn to something just inside a room to his right. He felt his ankles being tied to the legs of the chair. A long, narrow room stretched beyond his sight, and from the doorway was a camera on a tripod pointing into the room.

A camera! What for? He wondered. He felt the tight rope securing his right ankle to the chair leg.

His captor sighed and sat back on his heels, noticing Colston looking off to the right.

"You understand now!" his captor said, carefully removing the tape from Colston's mouth and pulling several strands of hair from his beard and mustache. Colston looked back into the man's sparkling blue eyes filled with so much hope. When Colston shook his head, he knew to expect some sort of backlash.

The sparkle dimmed slightly as the man placed a hand on Colston's taped wrists and squeezed. When Colston winced, he seemed to note the pain and removed his hand.

"I need you to see, Colston. You are suffering." He spoke with compassion, but Colston could hear the anger lurking beneath the kind facade. Colston understood that every time he opened his mouth to ask a question, he was treading into a minefield.

"What makes you think that I am struggling?" His voice was tired and low.

The man recoiled as if Colston had just slapped him. "Colston," he said, kneeling uncomfortably close, "It's in your videos, in your voice. You lack true belief in yourself. You are only beautiful when you can be stunning." The blue from the eyes faded into the dark orbs holding hellfire that seemed to burn into Colston's soul.

A small voice spoke to Colston's heart. *This man is so sincere that he doesn't recognize his own insanity! Be careful!* Colston nodded in agreement with the only thing that made sense in that moment.

The man interpreted Colston's nod as agreement. His eyes brightened to a vivid blue. "Good Colston!" The sheer childish happiness in his voice made Colston feel sick. An eager hand patted his bound wrists, and now his voice brimmed with confidence and poise. "Your voice is the only one worthy of my unwavering devotion. Your unyielding enthusiasm for acting and singing, all unimpeded by the lack of reception for your efforts, is truly motivating. But..." He stood up and began to pace.

Colston listened to a doting and inspired fan. Yet with his wrists bound and his ankles tied to the legs of a chair, combined with the man's previous dangerous behaviors. He firmly grasped that he was in for the fight of his life.

"Colston, my dearest Colston, the struggle has surfaced, and I must draw attention to it because it is drowning you." He crouched, placing his hands on Colston's thighs. "*American Idiot Medley* highlighted the terror that your subconscious was begging to express. The acting was too authentic to be a mere performance." His eyes flashed, daring Colston to argue the truth. He stood, keeping his gaze locked with Colston's. "You wanted to seek help but weren't sure how to go about it. You are convinced that you are fine when, in truth, you are just surviving. Waiting for that breakthrough, I am the one to guide you."

Colston stared at him, his heart ignited by the words. Fear transformed into defiance as he protected his voice. "You do realize that I was *performing* to the song? That was my. Conviction. To. My. Damn. Art!" Colston dared to thrust his bound fists toward his captor.

The man reacted by grabbing a hold of Colston just above the tape. Colston watched as the bright, hopeful blue of the man's eyes shifted to dark, hateful spheres.

"NO!" he roared.

Colston was yanked into the air and spun around. When he was released, he flew a short distance and crashed into the wall. The chair was crushed between the wall and Colston's back. He let out a yelp as he hit the ground, landing heavily on his left shoulder with a sickening crunch and a jolt of pain. A groan escaped his lips as he rolled onto his back.

"That is a false conviction!" his captor screamed, advancing on Colston until he stood over him, feet on either side, grabbing him by the bound wrists. Pulling Colston's fists up against his chest, lifting Colston's back off the ground in the process with one hand while poking at his bare chest with the other. "Your mind has tricked you! I only did as you asked, to save you, and this is how you thank me? Your heart is struggling against your mind, setting you up to fail! You need saving. You can't deny when you were singing *Die to the Fire*. You weren't contemplating ending it all because the struggle was becoming too great. You were singing *Hell Upon Your Doorstep* when I claimed you. I am a blessing disguised as your hell!" He let Colston drop back to the floor and stepped away, running his hand down his face in exasperation.

Colston lay among the splinters, his left shoulder surely dislocated. He was too stunned by the declaration to speak, to cry, or to move as the terror firmly wrapped itself around his soul. He needed to escape and fast; this man was insane and would no doubt kill him.

"Colston, you need to wise up." The man crouched. "People know that you are kidnapped." Colston's heart jumped in extreme fear, and his captor smirked, "But you and them have known that. The clues have been there."

Colston's eyes widened. "You've been hijacking my videos!"

For the past two and a half months, Colston had been trying to figure out who was adding bizarre, creepy elements to the ends of his videos. Despite working with the support team from Collective Creative Entertainment to put an end to it, their efforts were ultimately in vain. This situation was worrisome and downright unsettling. However, he couldn't deny the buzz it was generating for October and the creepy covers. Seeing others get excited was contagious and sparked his own enthusiasm.

His captor extended his arms. The blue in his eyes flickered back momentarily before fading again. "'Colston's Creepy Covers' is going to be a spectacle. You are singing for your life!"

Silence enveloped them as their eyes locked. Colston was too overcome by fear to speak while his captor waited for the response of approval.

Overcome with emotion, Colston cried, "Please stop this! You can be my teacher, my editor! Just let me go!"

The man lunged forward and gripped Colston's vest at the neck. The urge to choke Colston was evident in his entire demeanor.

"Bribery is the fastest way to piss me off!" He spat through clenched teeth. He yanked the fabric to the side and pressed it against Colston's throat. "You bribing me is NOT going to save you from yourself!"

"What do you want?!"

Chapter Three: Let Me Go

Colston silently cries as he is trapped in this nightmare. The thin sheet has gotten wrapped around his neck, and he desperately pulls at it. While simultaneously in the nightmare, his vest was being pushed to his throat.

"WHAT DO YOU WANT?!" The scream is filled with desperation that echoes through the stillness of the house.

Kayra is jolted from a gentle snooze so violently that the stool tips over, spilling her onto the floor. She sits there in a daze; her mind refusing to accept that scream came from Colston; it is hard to deny as it sounded like him. The raw desperation in that scream was chilling. She tries to convince herself that she had been starting to go into a bad dream, no doubt a result of her sleeping slumped on the counter.

From the bedroom, she hears the most awful guttural cry she's ever heard, "NOOO!!" Kayra scrambles to her feet and rushes to the bedroom.

Colston had awakened himself during his last cry and freed himself from the sheet. He lies in the center of the bed, breathing heavily, drenched in sweat, and unsure of reality. He hears footsteps approaching. His mind is a hectic mess while his body aches. His eyes shining with diminishing hope, he focuses on the open door. His heart pounds in his chest, anxiety mounting as he tries to convince himself that those footsteps belong to Kayra. He wants to call out but fears the voice that might respond. Even more terrifying would be to discover that his bedroom and, by extension, the last five years of his life are illusions created by his feverish, dying mind.

When Kayra appears in the doorway, her eyes wide with concern, Colston lays his head back on the mattress. All the tension releases as he realizes he is safe. The lingering residue of the two back-to-back nightmares has left him fractured.

"Kayra." He sobs.

"My gosh." She kneels by the bed, grasping his clammy, shaking hand. "Cole, I--" she struggles to find the words.

She is terrified. Two nightmares in a row, the scream, and now she is watching the bright brown eyes fade to gray. "Baby?" she asks, panicked.

Kayra sounds distant as the veil of despair thickens. He looks at his wife and speaks, absently, "I need to go to my studio." He slides out of bed opposite Kayra, but their interlacing fingers remain locked above the sheets.

Kayra, on her knees, pleads, "Colston, please, come back to me."

Colston leans over the bed. "I'll try." The claws are trying to tear him apart.

"That's not good enough!" Kayra stands and shouts in defense.

"That's all I can give," Colston replies weakly and in a monotone voice. This is the only grace he is allotted; everything else is tainted with vitriol, which he refuses to unleash. He'd rather drive a kitchen knife into his own chest than allow that to happen.

Kayra's eyes search her husband's empty gaze. She senses him starting to pull away. Tightening her grip, she holds his wrist with her other hand, her eyes pleading.

Colston looks at her with bleak eyes. "Pl-please," he stammers as the cold starts to encircle his heart. "I--don't want--you-to see th-this." His body trembles.

"What is this? What is happening?" Kayra asks, panic coursing. She leaps over the bed and catches Colston's collapsing body. "Cole, please!" Her hand instinctively falls to his chest, wincing slightly at the small scar above his heart, but she feels his heartbeat once more. "Babe?" she cradles him.

Colston knows he lies in a loving and warm embrace. Understanding these are real feelings he longs to experience, he feels lost in the grip of his impending danger. Day by day, his fight wanes, and he is unsure how much longer he can hold on for.

"Ka," his voice trembles as he clenches his teeth and strains his neck, pulling at the painful knot in his throat. "Let--me--go." The moment the words leave his mouth, he regrets them.

He wants to feel her embrace and know that his wife is truly there. While the other implication of the phrase is another very disgraceful and real desire, driven by shame and fear.

Kayra stares at him, her eyes pleading. "I am not letting go." Her voice is firm as she searches the emptiness of his gaze for that spark of life that is Colston. "I will fight for you and with you."

His eyes reveal no change, and he lets out a painful grunt, dropping his head. "It's--been--five--years!" he says, breathlessly.

Kayra begins to understand; she knows only parts of what happened along with how she found him. She places her hand under his moist, bearded chin and gently lifts it. "I don't think your answer is at the house."

Colston starts to shake his head. She gently holds his face. "You are searching for closure. Proof that the man is real. Babe, that is how he is still keeping you trapped."

"I--want to--stop re--remembering." Colston pleads, "L-let me g-go, reclaim--my fire."

Kayra simply nods and releases him. She sits on the floor, hugging her knees to her chest, staring blankly at the wall. Fear envelops her mind as she recalls his retelling of the day of the fire. He had finally shared it two weeks into their marriage. Kayra wanted to know how he escaped.

Colston woke up, blinking several times in disbelief as he took his first conscious breath, slowly... waiting. He expected to feel his lungs fail to draw in air and his brain to remind him that he was alive and now awake only to inform him his body was failing. However, the breath completed its cycle; his lungs continued to pump oxygen throughout his body. *Thankful...* he thought. Yet he remained unconvinced that he didn't have a stab wound. He slowly and painfully lifted his wrists toward his chest; when numb fingers made contact, they tingled, and he gradually slid them over his chest. This lasted about thirty seconds before the pain and overall weakness became overwhelming, forcing him to drop his wrists to his lap. When they landed, a wave of pins and needles surged throughout his body. He had stared death in the face, yet he still existed in this nightmare.

He forced his body to move again, blindly searching for the blanket. If that cruel person couldn't finish him off, he wasn't about to succumb to the elements without an all-out battle. He started to cough, pausing his search for the blanket as he lay there, waiting for his breathing to stabilize. A song surfaced in his mind from a band known for only sleeper hits, Fragment of Embers, which portrayed hope in the face of tragedy. It is one of Colston's comfort bands, yet he has never covered one of their songs. The song that surfaced was *My Dying Lament;* he was unable to see the irony. As he closed his eyes and focused on his breathing, he felt a connection to this song, reclaiming his voice. He had to sing free from the weight of punishment and just let his emotions guide. Singing was the last thing in the world that he wanted to do, which was so painful to admit, let alone feel, but it was sing or die.

"Bleeding from this wound, feeling so much pain,
My heart, it aches as tears fall like rain.
Do I fight to see your warm eyes once more?
Or embrace the cold. and walk through death's door.
Contemplating life and death in this moment of despair
I see your face before me, but you're not really there.
The love we had is slipping through my fingers.
As I lie here bleeding, with shattered dreams that linger,
My love, it hurts; it's tearing me apart.
Should I push forward? Let hope ignite my heart.
Or should I surrender to the icy embrace?

Now I'm in a dark place.
The memories of us haunt me like a ghost.
I'm torn between living and giving up the most.
But in the end, I'll hold on to a sliver of hope.
And fight to see your warm eyes again; I refuse to elope.
My love, it hurts; it's tearing me apart.
I'll push forward, letting hope ignite my heart.
I won't surrender to the icy encase.
I'll find love's warm embrace."

He ended with his eyes closed in prayer. This prayer was not for strength but for forgiveness, for taking his gift for granted. It hurt him to feel nothing while singing. When songs are meant to elicit emotion from the listener, that cannot be achieved effectively if the singer lacks feeling.

His eyes snapped open as a new smell assaulted his nose. Was it smoke? At that moment, the door was kicked in.

"Colston, time to go!" said the man as he rushed to him.

Colston saw the knife and closed his eyes. When he felt his hands fall free, he opened his eyes to find the man's once emotionless gaze now filled with fear and compassion.

Colston was pulled to his feet, but he lacked strength to stand on his own. "It's alright, Colston; I got you."

They reached the threshold of the bathroom, and the fire licked across their path. "We're going to need to move fast, or we're going to burn to death," the man said while allowing Colston to lean on him completely.

"O...okay," Colston struggled to speak, preparing his battered body to help as much as he could.

They waded through the fire. Colston's eyes were locked on the door, the adrenaline pumping. This was life or death, and the door seemed so far away. The fire felt painfully hot against his numb body, and he could feel the bones grinding in his ankle. The smoke rose around them, making it hard for him to breathe. He felt his body wanting to cave, but by the grace of God, he kept putting one foot in front of the other.

A loud crack echoed above. The man removed Colston's arm from around his shoulders and pressed keys into his hand. "You are an hour north of town!" He then shoved Colston toward the door.

Colston yelled in surprise and pain, falling toward the door that seemed so distant. He threw himself forward, crashing through the door and colliding with the frozen ground. A loud crash came from behind him, accompanied by a painful cry.

Colston scrambled to the van, using all of his strength to stay awake and keep moving. He was free, tears streaming as he climbed into the van. Without looking back, he drove onto the road.

He drove for a short distance before having to stop. There was a phone in the ashtray. He grabbed it and turned it on, full battery. He immediately dialed 911. After informing the authorities of the situation, he called Kayra, feeling himself fading.

"Hello?" Her voice came over the line.

After Colston had opened up, he appeared visibly lighter, yet burdened. Though, still very selective when it came to sharing with her and Jordan from then on. At first, she understood his guarded nature, but now Colston clings to it, suffering alone, which is harming him. Perhaps with Jordan's presence here, they can encourage him to release what weighs him down. What she already knows is horrifying and terrifying: Colston has become a shadow of his former self. She worries about the back-to-back nightmares and hopes they don't take Colston away for good.

Colston kneels in his studio, silently weeping.

"Why won't he leave me alone?" Colston screams in his mind.

He is freezing, reaching through the bars of that damnable cell. Trying to grasp the warmth of life, the light of hope, and the confidence to endure this trial. Yet it always remains just out of reach. He pulls at the bars with such fierce desperation, causing the dry skin on his hands to crack and bleed.

"Please! For the love of God! I am dying!" he screams in his mind. *"Why am I being punished?!"*

His shaky hand lifts to his chest, feeling his pounding heart. "My heart beats; at times, I wish it would stop, to be spared of moments like these." He clenches his fingers on his chest as if trying to rip his own heart out. "How shameful the thought! What does it mean? I am deserving of the torment if I don't face it with strength. Only can I cower beneath the weight." Colston lets out a shaky breath and collapses to his side. "I tire of this; when I am the furthest from the nightmare, it reappears, starting this cycle of wishing to 'cease breathing' all over again. It is always stronger than the last, making resisting the urge that much harder." He takes a deep breath; the air is cold. An audible sob escapes his lips, "LET ME GO!" He screams into the room and weeps into the carpet.

Moments later, there is panicked knocking

at the door.

Colston continues undisturbed, "Why help me to survive? You clearly didn't care about me!"

He continues to cry his words, pleading for release from the black ice that keeps him forever trapped. He sees the man only as a creature with the fires of hell in his eyes. That creature broke him, allowing the venom that spewed from those lips to poison his subconscious.

"Colston! Please, open the door! Babe!" Kayra cries through the door.

Colston hears her clearly, and when he fails to move to let her in. A voice speaks within Colston's mind.

"This is where you need to be. Present."

"I have failed," he says, defeated, listening to Kayra sob through the locked door. "I have locked her out once again."

"You can't shoulder this alone for much longer."

"I--can't--tell--them--about--that," He takes a breath; the cold is once again taking hold. "I don't want her to know."

"A word of advice: this will kill you."

Colston immediately questions how they will view him afterward. He forces himself to his feet but suddenly feels sick to his stomach. The terror and shame threaten to overwhelm him, driving him toward the unthinkable. He stands an arm's and a half length from the door, about to tell Kayra that he is coming, when the most terrifying thought halts him. A sentence spoken by his therapist after a year of sessions: *"Perhaps he used the fire to cover his tracks."* Though he has heard this before, it hits him with such force that he cascades to his hands and knees. "HE IS DEAD!" he screams. He clings to the belief that the man managed to crawl out of the house after part of the ceiling collapsed and died somewhere in the woods, where animals found the body. But another thought emerges, challenging that belief and aligning with his therapist's insights, a notion he despises even more. *"It was all planned, and this is how my captor is still 'helping' me."*

All the hair on his arms and the back of his neck stands on end. His mind is filled with the menacing laughter of his captor, as his heart is rapidly encased in ice, then spears outwardly in sharp spikes. Colston screams and collapses to his chest.

"COLSTON, PLEASE!" The doorknob rattles. "OPEN THE DOOR!"

In pain and trembling, Colston takes the key from his pocket and slides it under the door.

Kayra feels the key slide under her toes. Dropping to her knees, she grabs the key and unlocks the door. When she opens it, she finds Colston sobbing on the floor.

"Honey!" She immediately shuffles in, lying beside him and taking his hand.

His grip on her hand reveals the trembling strength still within him.

"I am sorry," Colston says, those heavy words hanging between them.

Kayra squeezes his hand. "You opened the door; there's no need to apologize."

"You deserve so much better." Colston replies; his resolve is strong as he lifts his head off the carpet. "This must be a nightmare for you. I love you, but I know this is hurting--"

Kayra gently places her fingertips on his lips. "Indeed, I do hurt. I hate that this happened to you. But you are trying ninety-five percent of the time. I see Colston Driscoll, the energetic, passionate singer, and my husband and best friend. The other four percent is when that struggle takes hold. That... This Colston frightens me because I am merely a stranger to him. Me being here right now is all I could ask for."

Colston exhales deeply, lays his head back down, and grips her hand again. He shouldn't have been surprised by her response to his acknowledgment of her pain and his invitation for her to walk away from the marriage. Kayra is just as committed to them as he is to his voice, a truth he should have recognized as tears of shame fell knowing he was going to commit the unthinkable the moment she left. Now that he understands she is willing to fight, he knows he must fight too for her as well as for himself.

"I love you so much," he says, filled with relief and deep shame.

"I love you too. Can I make one request?" she asks.

"Anything." Colston breathes.

"Never ask me to let you go again," Kayra replies.

Colston rolls to his side and draws her into his chest. "I will never ask that of you again."

They ended up sleeping on the floor in each other's arms, enjoying a dreamless and restful sleep.

Suddenly, they are awakened by knocking on their front door. Colston keeps his eyes closed, holding Kayra's body close while nestling his face in her neck. "I believe someone is at the door."

Kayra lets out a soft moan as she turns in his embrace, cuddling against his bare chest. "Let them knock. I don't want to move." She replies, nestling her head under his chin.

Colston smiles opening his eyes, shifting to kiss her head. They hear a phone ringing from the bedroom.

"My love, that's your phone." Colston whispers.

She snuggles close, saying, "I want to stay in your arms."

Colston holds her tight. "My arms are your shelter whenever you desire." He feels a pang of sadness, regretting almost sacrificing her love.

"Love..."

The knocks become more insistent, followed by a distant voice. "Colston? Kayra? Is everything alright?"

"Is that Jordan?" Colston asks.

Kayra opens her eyes and looks at him. "Yes, it is." She replies, reluctantly pulling away. Noticing his confusion and panic, she pauses mid-sit-up. "Cole? You okay?" she asks, rubbing the side of his face.

He searches his memory for any recent conversation with Jordan, trying to recall a song he was supposed to practice for an upcoming recording session. When nothing comes to mind, he remembers their last discussion, a month ago, casually talking about the online concert in April with the idea that they would be on the duet bill. Focusing back on Kayra, he says, "I will be." He offers a genuine smile. "I'll be out in a moment."

She kisses his cheek. "You sure?" Kayra asks, getting to her feet.

"I am sure." He replies, sitting up.

Another knock prompts Kayra to leave the room. She makes her way to the front door, peering out the front window to see the glow of dawn on the horizon. She is astonished that they slept on the floor for so long. A smile spreads across her face at the closeness she now feels, realizing that Colston has let go of his worries about her stubbornness and the possibility of her leaving him.

Colston's phone pings with a message from the living room as Kayra unlocks and opens the door, "Jordan!"

Jordan Youngblood looks up from slipping his phone into his pocket and flipping his long blond 80s rocker-style hair back, revealing his clean face. His blue eyes shine with tears he knows he won't be able to hide.

Kayra immediately embraces him, sensing the tension. When Jordan hugs her back, it's one of relief. She whispers apologetically,

"I'm so sorry. We crashed after an emotional night."

"It's fine," Jordan replies after they pull apart, trying his best to calm down. As he enters the house, he wipes away the lingering tears, doing his utmost to leave his worries outside. "Where's Colston?" He asks, knowing that seeing him will ease his remaining anxiety.

"Right here, JD." Colston says, walking down the hall toward them, now wearing a shirt.

Jordan turns and immediately opens his arms to embrace Colston. He is two inches taller than him and is leaner and more muscular than Colston, who is robust. Jordan fights a breakdown as he hugs him.

Kayra watches as Jordan's worry fades away; she smiles at this. She had been concerned that Jordan might be growing tired of these types of visits, but seeing him with Colston eases her mind, knowing Jordan cares about him just as much as she does.

In the tight embrace, Colston can't shake the thought that he is starting down the final path, remembering what the voice said last night. He is aware of the conditions Kayra set in order for him to go back to the house; however, he didn't expect Jordan to arrive so quickly. It is a thirteen-hour drive from Dryad's Cove, Washington, and Jordan had his own commitments. They have all silently agreed to ending this once and for all.

The hug breaks, and there's a long silence among them; each is unsure of how to begin this trek.

Colston finally speaks, voicing his original worry. "It's great to see you, but I must admit. If we planned to sing, I can't today." He rubs the back of his neck nervously.

Jordan gently shakes his head. "Cole, that's not why I am here. You've been drowning, and I'm here reaching to pull you to the surface."

Colston bows his head, feeling every single ice spear within the hollowness of his chest cavity. "No," he whimpers.

"We want to help you," Jordan says.

"I can't," Colston replies weakly as his stomach rumbles.

Colston turns and walks around the kitchen island, feeling the cold seep in. He focuses on Kayra's words from last night: he will never be alone with these nightmares. Tears escaped from his eyes because of Jordan's words; with all the relief, it amounts to nothing. Jordan's presence meant he was going to the house today. As much as he wants just to rip the band-aid off and face it, he fears the truth. The truth might set him free or utterly destroy him.

"Colston?"

"I am sorry; I didn't mean to," Jordan says, approaching Colston, who is standing at the closed refrigerator.

"Don't apologize," Colston replies, turning to face his friend. "I understand that I will never be truly alone in this mess. Even though I've withheld a great deal from both of you, it's comforting to know what I have shared isn't just my burden to bear." Colston pauses, trying to fend off the cold that threatens to overwhelm him. Absently, he lifts his hand to his heart.

The panic on Jordan's face is instant, his voice full of concern. "Colston?" He opens his arms, ready to catch him.

Colston tries to shake off the worry by waving his hand dismissively. "The--cold--is ever persistent." He takes deep breaths.

"Colston, sit down; I will make us something to eat," Kayra says.

Jordan looks at Kayra, struck by her calmness while Colston struggles. He then glances back at Colston. "Cold?" He instinctively touches Colston's bare arm; it's warm.

Colston doesn't shy away, though he feels a twinge of hurt.

"It's the ever present cold of that nightmare. It has pierced my heart, always trying to overwhelm me, and fighting it hurts." Colston explains. He had always tried to battle the cold while singing with Jordan, seeking normalcy. But now coming clean, he feels a mix of shame and relief.

Colston and Jordan have taken a seat at the counter. Jordan feels ashamed for jumping straight into the reason for his visit and still can't shake the troubling scenarios from his mind.

"JD?" Colston asks, noticing Jordan's distant gaze. "Are you okay?"

Jordan looks at Colston, but his eyes seem unfocused. "When no one answered..." Jordan pauses, his voice sounding far away.

"My mind panicked. I am trying to forget them...I can't stop thinking about them." He drops his head, fighting back tears.

Kayra reaches across the counter, resting her hand on his arm. "They didn't happen. Everything is fine." She reassures him, understanding how the worst thoughts can linger.

"You can tell us, or if you need to, you can rest knowing that everything is fine." Colston suggests.

Jordan shakes his head. "I don't want to say..." He takes a deep breath. "On a happier note! Colston, I saw that you not only made the duet bill for the concert but also the solo bill!" His tone shifts, and he sounds genuinely excited for Colston managing to push aside the troubling thoughts.

Colston wants to respond in kind but is cut off.

Chapter Four: Unscheduled Therapy

"I am here to help you! You're losing your soul!" the voice of his captor roars in his head. Colston clamps his hands to the sides of his head, losing control and folding in on himself, his eyes shut tight.

"Colston?!" Jordan asks, panicking.

"Baby, come back, please!" Kayra rushes to him. A hand falls on his shoulder, and he flinches.

"For you to understand that you are drowning in fear and hiding it, stop hiding it! Kill that fear and sing. If you don't, I will make you scream!"

Colston slides off the stool and drops to his knees, crying as more of the poison surfaces and wreaks havoc. Jordan and Kayra watch, while their cries and pleas go unheard. Colston's body trembles, and his breathing is heavy.

"IT WAS NEVER FALSE CONVICTION!" Colston cries out, flopping backward.

"Cole!" Jordan yells, catching him before his head hits the tiles.

Kayra grabs his hand. "Colston?" Her voice is soft.

This shocks and scares Jordan. Colston is not well; this is beyond the help of normal counseling or even a support group. He needs medication, or perhaps a few days in an institution. This is not normal and is highly reactive. He has been concerned for Kayra, and now he is extremely concerned for her and Colston's well-being; now he understands the urgency behind the calls. Jordan loves him, and what Colston endured was undoubtedly traumatic, but this display was dangerous, not just for him but for those around him.

"Jordan, I am sorry you had to see that," Colston says, his voice coming back from somewhere far away and sounding annoyed. He desperately needs to isolate. When a voice on the edge of his hearing sounds, "The amount that isolating helped yesterday." Colston's heart drops; that voice is right.

"It's alright; I'm kind of glad I got to," Jordan replies semi-honestly.

Colston's phone starts to ring from the living room. Kayra squeezes his hand and then leaves to get the phone.

Jordan helps Colston to his feet. Colston notices a new fear in Jordan's eyes. "I believe this is a result of wanting to go to the house." Colston says this, hoping it didn't mean anything else.

"Then why go, man?" Jordan says, exasperated.

Colston's sad attempt to argue is cut off.

"Colston," Kayra rushes to him, "It's Todd."

Colston takes the phone, looking perplexed and taken aback by the coincidental timing.

"Todd?"

"Colston, I hope my call finds you well."

"Truth is actually quite the opposite,"

Colston says, feeling his mind swirl.

"Oh, well, I'm going out of town for a week. I'd like you to come down at 1 PM to meet my replacement. While here, we can talk about what's been going on." Todd's voice is deep and rough like sandpaper.

"Okay, see you soon."

Colston hangs up and looks at Kayra and Jordan. "Todd wants me to go see him at one o'clock. He's leaving for a week and has a replacement set up for me to meet." His voice is soft and unsettling. "I'm going to shower."

Both Kayra and Jordan are not alarmed by this. Colston often feels this way before meeting Todd, and it lasts for the remainder of the day. There's a fifty percent chance of a nightmare that night, leading to a ten percent chance of an emergency session and more time in isolation.

As he prepares for the shower, he thinks about this replacement and how much he will have to reiterate just to help them understand what he's going through. The thought of arguing with Todd crosses his mind while the warm water cascades down his body. Disputing Todd would be like persuading a brick wall to move. Todd is one of the best trauma therapists in the area and has a very particular approach to his treatment.

"I am not your friend; I am here to help you work through this difficult time. I work closely with the police, and they handed me your file." Todd had said this during his visit to Colston in the hospital a couple of days after his escape. Todd also mentioned that after two years, Colston would be ready to move on to another therapist because of Todd's strict code of conduct. He focuses on stabilizing clients, helping them feel comfortable and capable within their own minds before handing them over to a more personable therapist.

"It's been five years; who is failing whom?"

Jordan sits at the counter yawning for the fifteenth time in the last ten minutes, ignoring his desperate need for sleep. "Kayra, what is different?" he finally asks, breaking the unbearably tense silence.

Kayra bows her head as she prepares to fry up bacon and eggs. Without turning, she replies, "I've heard him yell, plead, and beg over the years. But this: 'Dammit! Let me go!' sounded... absolute. Now there's a heaviness that looms over us. I understand why he isolates himself. I saw the extreme physical effects and the emptiness..." she shivers thinking about it. "The emptiness in his entire being was frightening to behold." As she fries the bacon and eggs, she adds, "Now, with the double nightmares and his persistence to return to the house, I can't help but harbor the idea that this all is going to end loudly."

"What does that mean?" Jordan asks.

Kayra sighs and moves to where she can glance down the hall toward the closed bedroom door. Upon seeing it closed and moving back around the island, she eyes Jordan speaking gravely, "You know what he did last night after he let me into his studio? He gave me an out."

Jordan's eyes widen. He recalls Colston apologizing after coming out of the flashback. "He is aware of the impact it has on us." Jordan states realizing this awareness is almost more painful than ignorance.

"Yes, and he's agitated that he's still experiencing these setbacks. He's reaching his limit, and that scares me. He'll snap, drawing unwanted attention. I dread to think about what he might do."

Jordan contemplates for a moment, but before he can respond, Kayra continues.

"I am grateful you came, and once we have overcome this heaviness. I will look for alternative ways of helping; of course, you are always welcome here." Kayra says heavily but strongly. She sets a platter of food down in front of Jordan, who gently places his hand on hers.

"Kayra," his fear of being left to the wayside clear in his eyes. "When I said you need a bigger support system, in no way did I mean that I wished to wipe my hands clean. I just think it's important to find someone trustworthy for you and Colston. If you need immediate help, they can be there until I arrive."

Kayra's eyes well up with tears, and her heart feels lighter. "Really?"

"I have worked with many artists before and after meeting Colston. I have yet to meet someone who sings like him. He injected new life into my own work and my overall feelings about life. I fear for him... for the both of you. We are here for him, and this won't defeat him." Tears streamed down both their faces.

Then she says something that strikes him hard. "We can only help him so much. The mind knows its limits, and when those are reached, there is nothing that can be done. No amount of pills, kind words, or discussions will help. Of course, we can always hope. When the body is sick, it reacts, vomiting or heating up. The mind, however, is harsher when it comes to releasing what it doesn't want."

Kayra takes a piece of bacon and bites into it as Colston enters the kitchen.

"Hey, babe." Kayra greets him, holding out a plate for him, "Here."

"Thanks," Colston takes the plate and begins eating, doing his best to hide the fact that he is forcing himself to eat. To distract, he says, "JD, did Kayra tell you that she won a flash fiction writing contest?" Colston glances up and catches Kayra blushing deeply.

Jordan leans back in his seat. "She didn't. Kayra, that's fantastic news."

Kayra looks at her husband, who is staring at his plate. "Cole?" The tone carries a hint of betrayal.

He looks up and takes her hand. "My love, I know you don't want attention, but I want to celebrate you just as you do for me."

Kayra shakes her head. "There's a reason why you've never seen it or why Jordan didn't hear of it. Why did I enter it in a contest? Even if first place was a hundred dollars, I had to express the truth, dressing it up as fiction; only those involved will know."

Jordan and Colston know exactly what she means by 'the truth'. Jordan, regardless of the subject, wants to commemorate her art. "Flash fiction isn't easy to begin with, especially in the way you used it. Don't downplay this accomplishment." He glances at Colston, "We are very proud of you." Jordan smiles, and Colston nods.

Kayra feels shaky but smiles shyly, "Thanks. Just don't go promoting it or looking for it. Please." She holds an unwavering gaze at both of them.

"We promise, love." Colston kisses her hand and then releases it.

"I've known you for how long? And I'm just now finding out that you dabble in the arts." Jordan says.

She blushes again. "It's a hobby, one that I made Colston swear to keep secret."

"I hold the spotlight, and she creates in the shadows," Colston says. "Sometimes when I am so excited for her that I want to give her the spotlight." He checks the time: 10:35.

"Your voice deserves that light."

Colston counters, "Your words deserve the light too."

Kayra shakes her head. Then she says something that she has always been afraid to say. "You could always remove your voice from the light."

Colston understands it is merely a suggestion, but in his current mental state, he reacts strongly. "No," he whimpers. "Please, don't ask me to do that." Tears flowing freely down his face.

In his mind, the glow within the cell brightens, sending him to his knees as he shakily clutches the bars. In reality, he releases a strained breath. He feels a hand on his right cheek.

"Honey, I'm sorry." Kayra says, noticing his trembling body.

"Love, it's fine; you're trying to help. But I can't abandon my voice, or he will have won, leaving me lost and unfulfilled." He thinks about revealing something to them. Again he glances at the time: 11:11. Time moves quickly, but not quickly enough, he sighs. "Kayra, do you remember that first dinner with my parents after I was released from the hospital?"

"Yeah," Kayra replies, trying to sound brave, though the memory still weighs heavily on her. "You fell in the kitchen."

Colston shakes his head. "I didn't just fall." His voice is low and full of shame.

Fear grows on Kayra's face. "Please tell us." She urges while moving a stool to sit across from him and holding his hand. She glances at Jordan, who, despite being tired, remains focused.

"We all know that my mom can be a bit possessive being the only child. I was afraid of how she'd act following the kidnapping. By the time of the dinner, three weeks after my hospital stay and nearly a month after my escape, I was focused on healing." He drops his head.

Jordan then puts a reassuring hand on his back. "Cole, physical pain heals much faster than mental. There is no need to feel ashamed."

"I just want to leave it behind; why can't I?" He asks even though he knows the reason he can't let go. He hasn't fully escaped. "Anyway, we agreed to go to dinner as a reason to get out of the house. There wasn't much conversation as I had barred talks about what happened. When dinner was served, I started to tremble as Mom set the plate in front of me. Kayra had refused to sit across from me at the table, which upset Mom while Dad had to remind her that Kayra was more of a comfort to me. Seeing me tremble, Kayra gripped my hand, and it was difficult to keep myself composed, fighting back tears and the urge to leave. Somehow, I managed to maintain control. The meal was tense; I could feel everyone's eyes on me. Halfway through, I set my fork down and announced that I planned to record a song for my channel before the year ended. I wanted to break the tension so badly. I must admit I felt deep fear and shame after making the announcement; there was no turning back. Dad looked at me with pure joy while I felt small under Mom's disapproving gaze. I wanted to leave right then as my body braced to be hit. I grabbed my crutches and excused myself to the kitchen. Once in the large, bright kitchen, I was able to breathe. I walked over to the center island, trying to keep it together, reminding myself that they were family and meant no harm, just expressing concern. I questioned if I was moving too fast in returning to singing. I just needed to get my life back on track, knowing that if I didn't soon, I might never be able to. The door to my right opened. I turned to see it was Mom. I told her I was fine. Then she said, 'Why give the world your voice when the world did this to you?' She lunged at me, grabbing my shirt. I was so stunned that I just stared at her. 'My boy, I can protect you.' I took a step back and tripped over my crutch. She watched me fall with a harsh look, which immediately changed to a kind expression the moment Kayra and Dad rushed in." Colston stops as he shudders at the memory.

Jordan is flabbergasted, and Kayra is equally troubled. "Why didn't you tell me the truth?" Kayra asks.

"Because I knew I could control my future encounters with her, also with the help of Dad. I also didn't want to hear, 'She's your mom, and she's just concerned.' We had more pressing matters; I didn't want family drama." Colston replies. "I need to get ready to go." He stands up, leaving his partially eaten meal.

Kayra follows his movements and embraces him. "Colston, has she done anything else since?" Kayra asks seriously, "Please, don't hide this from me. You might be her son. But you are my husband; I have every right to protect you."

Colston swells with warmth and tightens the embrace. "Two other times in the last five years," he whispers, his voice wavering. When they pull apart, his eyes are growing distant. "You guys want to meet me afterward."

"You intend to go to the house?" Kayra asks sadly.

"I am,"

"Buddy, please, could we talk about this? Your life is important!" Jordan pleads, still grappling with the bombshell that was just dropped.

Colston turns and moves toward Jordan, who stands at his approach. "My life, important or not, I need----to----do----this." He embraces Jordan.

As he grabs his keys and wallet before heading out, Colston thinks about how he truly owes Jordan his life.

Colston drives toward the center of town. The day is pleasant, yet the streets are empty. The masks and social distancing mandate in effect for the past week have seemingly locked down the town out of fear. He feels even more isolated, as he would enjoy people-watching, seeing the smiling, content faces moving freely throughout the day. Tears trickle from his eyes; his strength is waning. He has slid down to the floor of his mind, resting against the cold bars of that cell. He can't give up on himself, but he reflects on the shameful number of times he's nearly succumbed under the weight of the past. He hears in his voice the struggle to sound unburdened. His reserve of hope is draining at an alarming rate as he struggles to regain his sense of self fast; he needs answers.

Pulling into the parking lot of the

three-story building, he sits and gazes up at it troubled.

The time reads 12:45. He reaches into the center console and grabs his paper mask. With a deep breath, he exits the truck and heads towards the building. On the door, there are a few notices:

Masks required
One adult for child patients
Adult patients alone.

And another

Ask your provider for
Info on Telehealth

Colston dons the mask and then immediately rips it off. His eyes are closed, and his left hand braces against the rough brick siding. A memory floods Colston's mind: his captor crouching over him, sliding a gold upper face mask onto his face.

Colston takes deep, shaky breaths and mentally refocuses on the present. Opening his eyes, he sees the glass-pane door with the notices, reassuring himself that he is safe. After another moment, he puts on the mask again, and the flashback does not return.

He opens the door and heads to the second floor. This building's owner rents out suites or sections to private practices, almost all of which are mental health-oriented, giving the interior a calm feel with quiet, brightly lit hallways.

Colston walks the narrow halls and climbs the stairs to the second floor, then proceeds down a few more corridors. When he reaches the suite of Healthy Minds, Better Lives, he peeks through the window. Inside the dimly lit reception area, he sees Todd talking to a woman.

Colston hesitates to enter the office at first, not wanting to intrude on someone else's personal matters. Todd spots him lurking and waves him in. Colston opens the door.

"Colston, welcome," Todd greets him brusquely.

The difference between the hallway and the reception area is striking; it shifts from bright and calm to overbearing and cold.

Colston approaches the pair, and the woman glances at him with an inscrutable expression.

"Before we step into the office and start the session, I want you to meet my replacement," Todd says, pointing to the stern-looking woman. "This is Melody Dakota."

The woman offers him the most forced smile he has ever seen. Colston, who had removed his mask, gives a half-hearted smile, already disliking this situation to the point of questioning Todd's choice of replacement.

He asks, his voice unsteady, "How much does Melody know?"

"I know enough to be able to help you," she replies. Her voice is pleasant, but her annoyance, like sharp bits of glass, keeps her tone high.

Colston nods politely, feeling judged.

"Shall we go talk about what happened?" Todd asks.

"Um..." Colston replies, trying to steady himself against the cold.

Todd extends out his arm, directing Colston toward the room. His calm demeanor grows more resentful with every second that Colston hesitates.

"Colston?" Todd's voice sharpens.

The tone prompts Colston to walk toward the room with his head bowed. Upon entering, he is greeted by Todd's space, chilly and dimly lit with yellow light. He takes a seat in the corner chair, while Todd and Melody sit on the couch near the door.

"So, Colston, a nightmare again?"

"Yes... And frankly," Colston avoids eye contact and takes a deep breath, "I have reached my limit. So, per your suggestion, I am going to the house."

Colston doesn't notice, but Todd perks up. "Really? I don't want credit if the results are barren," he quickly adds, "You going alone?"

"N-no, Ka--Kay--." Colston stutters.

"Kayra, your wife." Todd clarifies.

Colston nods. "And--JD."

"Probably for the best." Todd replies in a bored tone.

"Two--night--mares. An----hour----apart." Colston blurts out confused. He knows he won't find help here, but a small part of him wonders if he might be too resistant.

"That's a first. If I recall correctly, in the first several months post-escape, you had nightly nightmares, but never two so close. What were they about?"

Colston looks up and, in a split-second decision, chooses to lie again. "Waking--up in the--van. Then, my-first----escape--attempt."

Todd gently shakes his head. "You waking up in the van," he sighs and leans forward, his eyes fixed on Colston. "Let's walk through it again. And, Colston, for your own sake, see the truth."

Colston closes his eyes and takes a deep breath. "I woke up. My mind in a fog with my wrists and ankles bound with duct tape."

"It was just duct tape; did you try more than once to break out of it?" Todd interjects, his voice cutting into the memory like an insufferable instructor.

Colston flinches at the phrasing more than Todd's tone. He stares at Todd hurt. What truth could there be besides the fact he couldn't escape? It seems to Colston that Todd is just as fed up as he is. He keeps calm, mainly to maintain some semblance of control. "I--I tried; of course I did. I tried to bite through the tape around my wrists, but it wouldn't rip. I tried to reach my ankles, but I just... couldn't." Defeat and resignation set deep, weighing heavily on him, the cold seeping in once again, taking all it can. Is this what Todd wants? For him to admit he is a failure and he got what he deserved?

"So you started to call for help, thus drawing him to you." Todd's voice lacks gentleness. "We've been over this moment several times. A pivotal moment with an underlying truth, one that you have yet to grasp, or perhaps you have and are refusing to acknowledge. The icy grip of the entire ordeal is strong enough to make it a living nightmare. He has managed to imprint himself onto every word you sing, as you've described over the years. Thus, whether you want it or not, it has tainted your music where your soul resides."

Colston glances up, desperately trying not to draw parallels between Todd and his captor in this moment. He struggles to suppress his defiant nature when his voice and music are under attack; Todd is trying to help, and he needs to accept this assistance, unlike when he was with his captor.

"At that moment, I was at my strongest, only dazed by the drug in my system, confused and scared by the situation. I could have tried harder to escape; it would have been the best outcome for me." The defeat in Colston's voice is clear, made more defined by the brand on his soul.

"Adrenaline would have kicked in, regardless of the drug numbing your body, propelling you to fight." Todd says, raising an eyebrow.

"I know," Colston replies. "Adrenaline was there, but the drug was overwhelming."

"Only overwhelming because you allowed it." Todd interjects.

Colston stops mid-thought. "What?" This is the sharpest tone he has ever dared to use toward Todd. "No! That... I... can't be hearing this right now." He leaps to his feet, drawing a gasp out of Melody, while

Todd merely straightens up in his seat. "I hope that visiting the house will unlock something!" He pats his chest, tears streaming down his face as he collapses to his knees. "I'm tired of fighting for my life!"

"Colston! Get back in your seat!" Todd raises his voice, sending an unwanted wave of comparison through Colston's mind.

Colston's defiance surges, and he stares into Todd's tired, aging eyes, shaking his head. "No, I am done feeling trapped and incomplete!"

"Incomplete?" Todd questions, letting it linger for a moment before continuing with his gaze steady on Colston. "I pushed your buttons; I'm sorry for that. But something is keeping you trapped." His voice lacks kindness.

For once, Colston appreciates Todd's indifferent attitude, which spares him from being accused of hiding something due to fear of the truth.

"I didn't ask for this to happen." Colston says, lowering his head as he sits back on his feet.

"Then why are you still in its icy grip?" Todd challenges, leaning closer. "Colston, look at me." When Colston meets his gaze, Todd is a few inches away from him. "Honesty now, Colston. I have directed your aggression at me. Do you want to harm me?"

"No," Colston replies, maintaining Todd's gaze.

"Colston! Do you want to harm me?"

"No!" Colston declares. "What would that

yield? It would only allow the torment to turn me into a monster."

"Dammit! COLSTON! I am right here and caused you pain; you could take it out on me!" Todd watches Colston recoil.

"NO!" Colston holds steady, but tears stream, confusion overwhelming him. His mind is blank, nearly shattering as he clings to his truth. He didn't wish to harm Todd, just to leave the vicinity.

He flinches at the voice of his captor raging in his head, *"FOUR SONGS TO TELL THE STORY. SING SO HONEST IN HEART, AND YOU'LL SURVIVE!"* He fought then with his resilience; right now, he battles the same.

"Stop this now!" Melody shouts.

Todd leans back, and Colston retreats to his chair feeling heavy and deflated. *I never asked for this!* He cries in his mind. He lifts his hands to his face and shakes his head.

Todd again shifts to the edge of his seat, closing the gap. At an uncomfortable distance, he briefly catches Colston's eyes and says, "We'll leave this here; we're getting close."

Those words encase Colston's mind in fear and panic. Todd pulls back, claps his hands together, and says, "This is an off-the-record session since it only lasted twenty minutes. With you going to the house today, you will need to visit with Melody tomorrow. Colston, I implore you not to wait until Friday. What you are going to endure upon returning will be intense, but it's necessary for healing. It will be worth it."

Colston nods, feeling completely drained. While staring at the floor, he whispers, "I'm going to go."

He rises and exits the suite. Once in the hallway, he feels the warm air caress his cold skin, pausing as his balance falters. He steadies himself physically to barely be able to support his mental instability.

I was not asking for help! His mind cries out again.

His legs threaten to buckle with every step. Stumbling down the hall, his mind is still lost in the memory of the fog he experienced when he woke up in that van. He had been holding out a note when the man covered his mouth and nose with a rag. Out of pure fear and panic, he inhaled deeply, allowing the sweet aroma to pull him into unconsciousness. He remembers trying to break the tape; there was panic in that moment, but the tape held. He glances at his wrists; he can faintly see the three-inch rings. He had pulled and twisted at the tape for days, but its grip remained firm.

He lumbers down the stairs, his mental anguish on full display, not caring who sees. Leaning on the railing, trembling and screaming in his mind, *"What are we getting close to? Why? Oh God, why did he push me to say that I wanted to harm him?"*

On the first floor, and as fast as his shaky legs will allow him, he rushes out the door. Stumbling and gasping for breath in the openness, sobbing as he makes his way to the truck. He has never left a session feeling so broken and scared. Never had he felt so alone in this pain; he understood that he failed himself, so he deserves this torment!

He climbs into the truck and sits there staring at his phone resting in the cup holder. When he slumps onto the steering wheel, wailing.

After about ten minutes, he composes himself; he then belts, each word dripping with pain and emotion:

"I put on a brave face, but inside I'm falling apart. The weight of these emotions are tearing me apart. I long to break free from this cycle of pain. But the fear holds me back; I'm struggling in vain. I am strong; I am not weak. But why do I feel so scared and meek? The turmoil inside, the battles I can't beat. I long for peace, but all I feel is defeat. Let this not be my swan song. Let hope rise and carry me along. Confusion fades; fear is gone. I am strong, and this is not my swan song."

Falling back against the seat, he feels a weight lift off his shoulders, carried away by the words. Yet he feels drained in his resolve to fight on, to which he sees no end.

He picks up his phone and calls Kayra.

"Hi, love." Her soft, loving voice warms and comforts him.

"Hi, are you and JD ready to come pick me up?" He asks as steadily as he can.

"Really? You didn't have a full session?" Kayra's voice is filled with concern.

"It was an intense twenty minutes," Colston admits.

Kayra sighs. *"We are on our way. I love you."*

"I love you too."

Colston puts the phone back in the cup holder and lays his head back. A few minutes later, he drifts off to sleep, hoping for some relief.

Chapter Five: The Engagement

On April 6th, 2016, Colston stood outside his truck, staring at the home of Kylie and Savion Rhavin. Gripping his cane in his left hand, he felt more nervous than he had at any convention performance; this was a life commitment to someone beyond just his voice. Was he right for Kayra? Could he provide her with a comfortable, happy life?

Taking a deep breath, he limped toward the front door. As he stepped up onto the screened-in porch, the door swung open.

"Yo, my boy, what brings you to our door unannounced and without my daughter at your side?" Savion asked cheerfully.

A nervous smile broke over Colston's mouth. "Mr. Rhavin, I have come to ask your permission for your daughter, Kayra Shirah Rhavin's, hand in marriage." He delivered the statement as formally as he could.

Despite the fact that they had already lived together for six years, he felt immense relief in finally posing that burning question. A question that burned brighter than the nightmares for the past four weeks, allowing him to achieve restful nights of sleep and regain a semblance of life before the kidnapping. Todd hasn't been able to get much out of him in terms of starting to process and work through what happened. Which seemed to piss him off. Colston often wondered, *Why?* Shouldn't the fact that he felt the poison was far away be something to celebrate? With his mind no longer drowning in painful memories, real improvement came during physical therapy for his ankle. At this rate, he'll be free of the cane by summer.

Savion straightened up and wore a careful smile, matching Colston's distinguished demeanor as he posed the life-changing question, "Colston, my shared son, I would be delighted to give you my permission." He extended his hand.

Colston took Savion's hand, and as they shook hands, he was gently pulled into a hug. As a happy squeal came from the other side of the door. Colston and Savion shared a chuckle, pulling apart when Kylie appeared and embraced Colston. Once the embrace ended, Kylie cradled Colston's face in her hands; her smile and tears assured him he had made the right choice.

"My son! You're finally going to propose to your girl?"

Colston glanced behind Kylie and saw his dad.

"Dad? What are you doing here?" Colston asked.

A quick glance passed between Savion and Elliot.

Savion replied, "A bit of home improvement."

"I see. And to answer your question, Dad, yes, I am going to propose tonight."

"Well, alright." Savion chuckled.

Kylie clung to her husband's arm. "She's

going to be so happy!" she said with delight.

Colston smiled, "Let's hope."

All three of the parents looked at Colston with hopeful smiles.

His dad moved around the pair and put his arm around Colston. "You have nothing to fear, son."

Colston nodded. "Thanks for the vote of confidence. Make sure that your phones are close by tonight." He added, "I am going to get going."

"Go get her, pal."

Colston nodded and turned to head back to the truck. Butterflies started to flutter in his stomach. He was more excited about surprising Kayra than nervous about her saying no. Unlike their parents, he didn't want to be overly confident given the baggage he carried. The very reason Colston wanted to marry her was that she had been so patient and caring as he endured the torment.

She was saving him every day.

He started up the truck and grabbed his phone. He texted Jordan, *"JD, I am proposing to Kayra tonight."*

A grin spread across his face as he shifted the truck into gear and pulled onto the road.

A few minutes later, his phone rang. He picked it up and blindly answered it.

"My guy!" Jordan exclaimed happily. *"It is about bloody time!"* He laughed.

Colston joined in the laughter. "Yeah, I know; I just needed to make sure it was the right time."

"Oh, bud, you can never know that. You

have nothing to worry about. Kayra loves you; that's undeniable." Jordan reassured him.

Colston smiled shyly. "I might be jumping the gun here, but if all goes well, would you be my best man?"

There was a pause as he heard a small hitch of emotion from the other line. *"Really?"*

Colston was surprised by Jordan's reaction. "JD, not just because of the last few months. You've boosted my confidence, and I have had a blast singing with you for the past eight years."

"Brother, I'd be honored." Jordan said, *"I'll eagerly await Kayra's phone call."*

"Yes."

Colston hung up. He was nearly home and needed to kill or make a believable excuse for his ear to ear grin.

As he pulled up to the house, he took a breath, reached into the center console, and pulled out a blue felt ring box. He stepped out and tucked the box into a deep pocket of his cargo jeans. Grabbing his phone and keys, he glanced at the cane. He closed the door and walked inside.

"Kayra, I'm home!" he called cheerfully.

"My songbird!" she replied from the living room, rounding the corner and stopped. "Your cane?"

Colston stood with his arms open wide, smiling. "If I take it easy and start walking without the cane, I should be free of it by the summer," he said.

Kayra ran to him and gently jumped into his arms. Colston held her tight as she kissed his lips.

"I love you so much," Colston said.

She just wrapped herself around him even more.

Colston wanted to propose right then, but he wanted this moment to be special.

"Hey, let's go to dinner," he suggested.

She nodded and resumed standing, "Where?" she asked, her eyes shining with love.

"How about Comfort Crescendo Craves?"

"Sounds great."

He took her by the hand and led her out the door.

Even on a Monday evening, Comfort Crescendo Craves was packed, and music filled the dining room. Unfortunately, the karaoke singer was off-pitch.

Colston opened the door with Kayra on his arm.

"Hey!" someone shouted, pointing at Colston.

Many heads turned in his direction.

"It's Colston Driscoll!"

"An actual singer has arrived!"

Colston smiled and gave a small wave. He then realized this would be the first live crowd he would perform for since the kidnapping. Fear tensed his body for the first time in weeks. It didn't linger long; Kayra responded by holding him close and placing a hand on his chest. Colston gently patted the hand.

The host approached and asked, "Welcome. Two tonight?"

"Yes, and we intend to sing karaoke." Colston replied. There was no cost for karaoke. They just wanted to gauge how many additional moving bodies there might be in the dining room.

The host nodded, grabbed two menus, and led them into the dining room. A chant of Colston's name had begun to fill the space. Hearing that filled him with happiness and a sense of purpose, even though he still felt incomplete. The impact of his voice was undeniable. He was still working up to a cover a week; for now, it was a cover every two weeks.

They were seated at a table for two that was in the center of the room. Colston ignored the chanting and eyes on him as he pulled out Kayra's seat.

Before she sat down, she leaned in and whispered with a smile, "Give them a song, lest thee wish a mob to form."

Colston smiled, kissed her, and walked toward the mic, trying his hardest to make the limp less noticeable.

The dining room erupted into cheers.

"Hello!" Colston said into the mic, waiting for the crowd to quiet down. He slowly drank in the atmosphere, feeling composed. He looked at Kayra, her beautiful smile and loving gaze mixed with a hint of concern. He returned to her broken and beaten, yet she looked at him with love. Colston didn't understand why.

"Thank you for that. Let's get this party started!" he said, as the cheering led him to the music selector, where he chose, *My Songs Know What You Did In The Dark (Light Em Up)* by Fall Out Boy.

He wanted to get his body moving, feeling the nerves and excitement coursing through him. For Colston, this was not just an engagement; this was a triumph over life's trials and tribulations. He prayed his ankle wouldn't buckle during the performance.

Before he started the song, he spoke into the mic, "If you know the song, sing and join me as we dance." He pressed play and stood with his back to the crowd, hearing their excitement rise.

When he began to sing, he spun around on his right foot to face them. Bringing the song to life with his power and emotions, his body moved with words that flowed out of him. The music lifted him, and he experienced a release; he believed that he would never feel again. The crowd was as connected to his performance as he was to the music. There was something incredibly gratifying in a live performance. The energy from the crowd replenished his ever-dwindling reserve.

As he reached a brief pause before a long note, he called out, "Let's finish strong!"

When he started the long note hold, about ten people rushed to the dance floor, providing the background vocals and dancing around him. Colston emerged from the long note into the last run of the chorus. The room buzzed with electric energy, leading to a powerful finish.

The dining room erupted in a standing ovation. He bowed and said, "Thank you so much. Your energy is insane." He placed the mic in its holder and rejoined Kayra, who was beaming.

Their hands clasped immediately as Colston sat down.

"That was amazing!" Kayra said.

Colston beamed, still a bit out of breath. "Thanks."

A cup of warm tea awaited him, his preferred drink after singing.

"I didn't know how much I missed watching you perform." Kayra said, rubbing the side of his hand with her thumb.

"To be honest, I never thought I'd be able to do it."

"Oh, babe, it's a part of you. When you don't think and just dive in," she pointed to the stage. "You perform."

"You two ready to order?" the server asked, raising their voice to be heard over the new singer.

Colston looked at Kayra and squeezed her hand gently.

"I'll have the chicken salad and lobster tail," she ordered, glancing at Colston for approval.

Colston nodded and added, "And a glass of wine to match the lobster."

Kayra's eyes widened with wonder. "Hon, that isn't necessary."

"Nonsense, it is necessary." Colston replied, feeling his heart nearly pound out of his chest.

"Sir?"

"I will have the BBQ bacon burger with crisp-cut fries."

"And the glass of wine is still a go?" the server asked.

"Yes," Colston said.

"Alright, we'll have those out soon," the server said, walking away after collecting the menus.

"I was invited to a girl's night in two weeks. With Abigail, Lucy, and Sadie." Kayra said, sounding a bit disheartened.

"Hey, look at me," Colston said, interlacing his fingers with hers as her eyes met his. "I know they don't think highly of me, but they were your best friends. Having them invite you to a girl's night is a good step in the right direction."

"You think so?" she asked shyly.

"Of course, I think it's a good idea to give them a chance at least," Colston said, then added, noticing the worry that was still lingering on her face, "If you don't want to, that is fine too. Do what makes you comfortable." He took a sip of his tea.

For the first time since Colston sat down, they released their hands. Kayra sipped her lemonade.

Colston couldn't wait anymore; he jumped to his feet and made his way to the vacant microphone, locking eyes with Kayra's wide gaze.

"I hope you all will indulge me for a moment," Colston addressed the dining room, doing his best to keep his voice steady.

The room fell silent with all eyes on him in wonder and excitement. "Kayra, can you join me?" he asked, extending his hand toward her.

She blushed as light applause encouraged her, and Kayra got up to join Colston.

"Kayra, I am still amazed that you chose

me. As your songbird, I flit within the shine of your eyes. Fear and stress leave my heart when you are near; the darkest corners of my mind are illuminated when your arms are around me." Colston struggled to maintain his composure, his gaze locked on the glistening eyes of the love of his life. "Kayra Shirah Rhavin," he said, dropping to one knee. "Will you marry me?" He pulled the box out of his pocket and opened it.

The room held its breath. Kayra could feel her heart beating out of her chest. The only sound was the deep, nervous breathing from the man on a bent knee before her, asking for the life commitment. She took the mic from his hand and recited with tears of pure happiness, "Every note you sing becomes an invitation rare, drawing me closer into your ethereal lair. My heart beats in time to each delicate sound, longing to be near you when love is finally found. Colston Zamir Driscoll, yes, I will marry you." Kayra said, aware of the applause filling the room, but it was distant.

Colston spoke, his voice trembling, and he shared that tremor with Kayra as she extended her left hand. "I promise to keep you safe and love you for the rest of our lives." As the ring slid onto her finger, he stood up, and they embraced while the world's sounds returned to normal. They turned to face the room, with Kayra's arms wrapped around Colston's chest, one of his arms resting on her shoulders. He waved, and they returned to their table.

Once seated, Kayra admired the ring, a

simple gold band with a jade stone cut in the shape of a heart. It was so beautiful that she couldn't contain her tears of joy.

"Chicken salad and lobster tail?" the server announced, startling Kayra out of her head.

"Um, yes," she replied, thumbing her tears away.

The server set the plate down with a smile and said, "Congratulations; you've got yourself a splendid-looking man."

Kayra glanced up and caught Colston's eyes. "Thank you; he's wonderful."

Colston smiled as his food was served. Instead of the glass of wine, they were gifted the entire bottle.

"Thanks; you guys are too kind," Colston said.

"It's not every day we get a proposal here, and with a local celebrity," the server remarked before leaving them.

Kayra reached for Colston's hand with her newly adorned one.

"Words cannot accurately describe how I feel, Colston. I----this," Kayra struggled to express.

His words were soft and reassuring. "Sometimes, words fail us, perhaps because the right words have yet to be discovered to capture the feelings we hold in our hearts." Colston continued comforting her, "Silence will not cause my heart any worry. I see the truth in your eyes." He reached across the table and caressed her cheek.

She mouthed, "I love you."

"I love you too," Colston replied.

Over the next thirty minutes, they ate their meals while listening to karaoke singers cycle through.

Kayra kept stealing glances at Colston; her heart soared. He was hers, and she was his. They already belonged to each other in their hearts and in the eyes of their parents. Now it would be official.

"Cole?"

He looked up at her, his eyes holding hints of that sparkle, which had begun to show throughout the past few weeks. The sparkle had been stolen by the man who kidnapped him. Despite the lack of wholeness in his eyes, Kayra remained steadfast by his side, undeterred in her love. It was simply a new side of him that she had to understand. She felt fortunate to still have him.

"How long have you been planning this?" she asked, curiosity evident in her voice.

A momentary flash of pain crossed his eyes.

Colston fought against pain that flared up with her question, pushing it down as he refused to let the torment affect him.

"I was actually going to propose on my birthday last year." He watched as sadness washed over her face.

She reached across the table and caressed his cheek, letting the touch convey her feelings. Colston leaned into her hand.

He opened his mouth to speak but hesitated, worried about the pressure it might place on her to know that thoughts of her had kept him alive during his captivity.

"I need to share the news with my folks,"

Kayra said.

"Then let's get out of here." Colston replied. He stopped a passing server and asked, "Could we get the bill, please?" The server nodded and hurried off.

Moments later, the manager approached their table. "Mr. Driscoll, soon-to-be Mrs. Driscoll, your meals and the bottle of wine are on the house," he said it with a smile.

"No, please, let me pay for the meal," Colston insisted.

"I won't accept any payment from you. Perhaps you could sing another song? If it won't spoil your engagement?" he asks, mainly looking at Kayra.

"I guess I could," Colston said, glancing at Kayra.

Kayra was beaming at the prospect of seeing Colston perform again. "Go on, babe," she encouraged.

Colston stood and extended his hand to Kayra. "I would love for you to join me."

Kayra blushed and took his hand. The manager announced, "Give it up once more for the newly engaged!"

Colston led Kayra to the front as the room cheered for them. When they reached the stage, Colston pulled Kayra close and whispered, "The song is going to be, *When You Say Nothing At All*."

She nodded and watched him go to the music selector, her heart pounding. As the song began, the room fell silent. When Colston was close enough, she planted her hand over his heart, feeling its strong and steady beat chase any lingering fears away.

He smiled as the words flowed from him, placing a hand over hers. They swayed together, lost in each other's eyes. She was terrified she'd wake up realizing that this was all a dream, a cruel joke played by fate. His voice deepened the moment. The warmth of his hand on hers, the desire to be married to this man, a fantasy now on the verge of reality. His soft voice, the soft fabric beneath her fingertips, and the rhythm of his heart against her palm never faded within the threat of a closing dream, anchored in reality; tears streamed down his face, and her own fell in response.

The song ended, and the room erupted in cheers as Colston and Kayra smiled and cried.

"Thank you so much for being a part of this special moment; you were fantastic." Colston said, putting down the microphone.

They returned to the table to gather their belongings and head out. While walking to the truck, Kayra called her mom on a video chat, holding her ring in front of the camera. Kylie only said, "H," before the rest of the word was drowned out by her squeal of happiness. "Oh my goodness! That ring is gorgeous!"

Colston had opened the door for Kayra, and she flipped the camera to include both of them in the frame.

"A truly beautiful couple," Kylie remarked fondly.

Colston felt his cheeks get warm. "Aww."

"Now, Colston, take care of my girl." She urged playfully.

"Yes, ma'am, I will take good care of

her." Colston replied, looking at Kayra. She caressed his cheek and kissed him with a smile.

"Whoa, kids!" That was Savion's voice.

They both giggled as they kissed. Turning, they saw not only Savion and Kylie's faces but also the faces of Colston's parents.

Colston was not surprised by this but avoided holding his gaze because he saw the underlying anger in his mom's eyes.

Kayra laughed. "What's going on there?"

"You two are what is going on! Show us that fabulous ring."

Kayra held up her hand in front of the camera and glanced at Colston, who held a slight look of guilt in his eyes.

As the parents admired the ring, Kayra smiled and asked, "You couldn't keep it to yourself?"

"Not when I asked for permission before arriving home." Colston admitted.

"We're just as happy for you two," Kylie added. "So, hosting dinner and waiting together to share the good news just made the most sense."

Kayra climbed into the truck, answering questions about where it happened. Colston stepped off the curb onto his left foot, and the fatigue of the day caused his ankle to buckle under that last weight-bearing step. Colston quickly jumped, switching feet and cringing in pain as he leaned on the truck while limping to his door.

Once inside, he felt the pins-and-needles sensation in his ankle. He leaned his head back, and the intensity grew to a near-teeth-bared level.

Kayra placed a hand on his arm, striving to hide her worry from the parents. Colston looked at her and patted her hand reassuringly.

"Right, I'll come by tomorrow to show it off in person. But we have other people to call."

"Congratulations!" a chorus of voices chimed.

"Bye!" Kayra and Colston said in unison.

Kayra ended the video call and turned her full attention on Colston. "What's wrong?"

"It's just my ankle," he replied, rolling his head to smile at her. "I overworked it."

"You need me to drive?" Kayra asked.

"No, I can drive. The pain isn't that bad. Tomorrow may be a different story." Colston said as he straightened up.

"Alright, want me to call JD?"

Colston smiled as he started the truck. She did the same with Jordan as she had with her mom.

"Is that the ring?" Jordan asked.

"Yes, it is!" Kayra turned the camera to face her.

"So happy for you two," Jordan said.

"Thank you!"

"Could I come down in a few days to celebrate with you, if that is okay?"

"Of course! We'd be more than happy to have you." Kayra replied.

"Cool, I'll let you two enjoy your engagement. I'll see you on Wednesday."

Kayra hung up and set the phone down and

interlaced her fingers with Colston's.

"So you're happy?" Colston asked.

"Babe, I'm ecstatic."

"I'm sorry, I can't come with you today." Colston said.

Kayra was helping Colston settle into his recliner. His ankle was swollen and causing him significant pain, which he was concealing. It was important for him to keep it iced and elevated. "It's fine, hon. But are you sure you don't want me to stay?" she asked for the tenth time.

Colston smirked and reached for her hand. "Babe," She took his hand and perched on the arm of the recliner. "I will be fine. I am a big boy. Don't let me keep you from going out."

Kayra blushed and took a deep breath. "I know this question may come up, even though we haven't been engaged for twenty-four hours yet. When will our wedding date be?"

Colston looked at her, holding her hand in both of his. "I don't want a long engagement." Colston replied.

Kayra ran her other hand through his hair. "I agree. How about this? You say the month, and I'll say the day."

Colston smiled and, without missing a beat, said, "June."

Kayra thought for a moment. "Fifth."

"It's our date." Colston said, reaching up to place his hand on the back of her neck and gently pulling her in for a kiss.

Kayra sat at the dining room table at her

parents' house feeling downcast. When the topic of bridesmaids arose, she realized she didn't have any friends she would consider for her wedding party. The few she might have chosen didn't like Colston, and she had been in limited contact with them for four years. However, there was a glimmer of hope after telling Colston about being invited to a girls' night and him mentioning that their attitudes might have changed over the years.

"You could have your cousins be your bridesmaids," Kylie suggested. "It really doesn't matter who is in your party. What matters is you and Colston becoming united."

As much as her mom was right, she still wanted to try. Kayra smiled and said, "I am still going to try to rekindle the friendship."

Kylie sighed. "Just be careful, please. I am not going to stop you; just be cautious."

Kayra nodded. Her mom never liked those girls, believing they were delusional and pretentious. They seemed to think the world revolved around having the perfect man and dressing in high fashion for attention. Their callous attitudes often drove away anyone with dignity and self-respect, yet Kayra remained resilient to their behavior. Her mom and dad always warned caution but never denied her hanging out with them.

Her parents were thrilled when she formed a friendship with Colston, easing their worry that Kayra wasn't brainwashed by the girls and was still an individual.

Kayra hugged her mom goodbye and walked out to her car. She pulled out her phone and sent a text to Abigail: *"Abbs, I have some news I want to share with you."*

Abigail was typing instantly. Anxiety washed over Kayra, seeing that. *"We are at the mall! Come and join us!"*

Though nervous, Kayra texted back, *"On my way!"* She figured it'd be good to get the awkwardness out of the way before staying a night together.

While driving, she called Colston.

"Hello, babe." Colston said, sounding a bit out of breath.

"Are you up and about when you need to be resting?" Kayra asked, masking her anxiety with love and care.

"I can't just sit idly all day. I am walking with the cane." Colston admitted.

He failed to catch the hint of anxiety that was present in Kayra's voice.

"Alright, please take care of yourself. By the way, I am on my way to the mall to meet with Abigail," she said, trying to sound hopeful.

"Really? That is great to hear! Have fun. What would you like for dinner tonight?"

"I am not going to be that long," Kayra replied.

She glanced at the time; it was barely one o'clock.

"Kay, if you girls hit it off, don't be in a rush to get home." He said gently.

She couldn't help but smile at that. "I hope it goes that well." Kayra remained skeptical about any change.

"It will. Have fun; I love you," Colston reassured her sweetly.

"I love you too, bye."

That brief exchange left a smile on her face and boosted her confidence a little.

At the mall, she checked her reflection and felt disheartened again. She had no makeup on, her hair was in a ponytail, and she was dressed in olive green cargo pants, a plain t-shirt, and sneakers.

The group's near-daily routine would be to go to the mall and pick out the most lazily dressed girl and comment on her outfit. Kayra never engaged; instead, she always sympathized, and even though the comments were never directed at the faces of those targeted. She often wondered if they sensed they were under scrutiny. Then they would search for the wealthiest and most handsome-looking man. While they hunted for the perfect suitor, Kayra was asked for her 'realist' views, which drove her insane. She was searching for her own lone stable boy, gentle and pure of heart; however, that was regarded as a fairy tale and unsustainable as the world values money and looks. Her argument was, *'It becomes an investment, hoping to use the man as your own piggy bank. That is why you can't keep a relationship: there's no love or respect.'*

"What am I doing?" She asked herself in the rearview mirror. She considered just going home and naming her cousins as bridesmaids. Shame settled in the pit of her stomach; she realized she had no one outside of family or Colston's friends to invite to her wedding. She always held out hope that Abigail would come around because she was lovely and caring in her own way, even if Kayra never shared her ideology. She never felt ostracized.

She pulled out the keys and stepped out of the car. A sense of pride washed over her as she looked at the ring on her finger. "I can do this," she whispered.

She texted Abigail.

"We are in the food court." Abigail texted immediately.

Kayra made her way toward the food court, trying to loosen her gait as she entered the busy mall. The food court was on the second floor, accessible by an escalator just after entering and walking through the main concourse.

"KAYRA!" The high-pitched scream was full of delight. Kayra jumped, and all heads in the area turned toward them.

A woman was running daintily toward her, which was completely out of character. Abigail wore tight white jeans and a leaf-green ruffled layered top, her long blond hair flowing out behind her. Her makeup, an attempt to enhance her stunning glow, only succeeded in making her look artificial. Kayra stepped aside from the escalator in time to be enveloped in an embrace. For a moment, she hesitated before returning the hug; although it was tight, it felt distant. It had been almost a year since they last saw each other. When they hugged, it had been a lean-in style, so no filth got on Abigail's clothes.

Abigail broke the embrace and held Kayra at arm's length, hands on her shoulders, eyeing her once over.

"You are absolutely glowing; too bad your outfit doesn't match." She said, satisfied.

Kayra made sure her ring was clearly visible.

An audible gasp escaped Abigail's lips as she grabbed Kayra's hand in both of hers. "Now I understand the reason behind the laid-back style of dress. This is absolutely beautiful."

"Thank you; I got it last night."

Abigail scrutinized Kayra. "No--is this your engagement ring?"

Kayra beamed, "It is!"

"Oh my gosh! Oh my gosh!" Abigail tilted her head, giving a side-eye questioning look. "Who is the lucky guy?"

There was a ping of disappointment in the question, but Kayra announced proudly, "Colston Driscoll!"

A flash of disgust crossed Abigail's face, and she shook her head. "I'm sorry." Her voice was sincere.

Kayra was taken aback. "What?" That was all she could manage to say.

Abigail knelt before Kayra, daring a dirt stain on her pristine white pants, holding Kayra's left hand in both of hers. Kayra watched in shock.

"Kayra, my behavior has been utterly disgraceful. I should have never treated you or Colston with such disrespect. Before you accept my apology, I'd like to formally meet and apologize to Colston."

With tears of happiness, Kayra pulled her up into a hug. This one felt much closer.

"So is that a yes?" Abigail asked.

"Yes."

Abigail broke the hug and took Kayra by the hand, leading her toward the table near the center of the food court. Lucy and Sadie sat there watching in confusion as they approached.

"What was that display?" Sadie asked. "You just risked soiling your pants." Her hand covered her mouth, horror evident on her face.

"Look!" Abigail squealed with delight, thrusting Kayra's hand forward. "She's engaged!"

There was an abhorrent chorus of shrieking that followed. Kayra wanted to hide feeling the anger and annoyance directed at them.

Kayra folded her fingers to keep the ring from sliding off. "Hey, just look. Please!" she ordered firmly.

Lucy and Sadie backed away with their hands behind their backs, looking embarrassed.

"Sooo, where is your delicious arm candy?" Sadie asked, scanning the food court.

"He's not here." Kayra replied.

"What a strong, independent woman!" Lucy said, swaying slightly. "Of course, I'd be showing off my catch."

"Speaking of catch, who is *he*?" Sadie asked.

Kayra felt two sets of eyes fixed on her, filled with wide-eyed curiosity. A swell of confidence and pride surged within her. No amount of scornful looks or harsh words aimed at her fiancé would deter her.

"Colston Driscoll," she said firmly.

They recoiled, expressions shifting from happiness and envy to outright repulsion.

Abigail wrapped her arms around Kayra, urging her to hide from the hostile stares against her shoulder. Kayra did so, even though it wasn't necessary; she appreciated Abigail's display of care.

"Hey, this is no way to act," Abigail scolded. "We've moved past this. Kayra has found a man who loves her, and she loves him back. Meanwhile, we're still searching. Perhaps Kayra has the cheat code to holding down a relationship."

Kayra peeked out and noticed Lucy's head had bowed, while Sadie remained repulsed. When their eyes met, Sadie said coldly, "Well, there should be a body type code."

Kayra lifted her head from Abigail's shoulder, staring daggers at Sadie. "Do not body shame, my Colston."

"Sadie Lancaster!" Abigail exclaimed at a volume that made everyone nearby quickly move away. "You are doing us dirty with comments such as that. Kayra is a crucial member of this group. Her willingness to remain hardhearted in her own ideals while tolerating our stubbornness creates harmony."

Lucy looked up with narrow eyes. "Our dynamic hasn't changed since Kayra has been off playing fairy-tale with the tavern's busboy." Her voice dripped with jealousy.

Kayra felt her emotions rising; the disrespect toward Colston was just too much, making her just want to go home and lay in his arms. She pulled away from Abigail and ran, disregarding how it might appear.

She was halfway to the front doors when someone grabbed her hand. "Kayra, please." Abigail pleaded, breathless.

Kayra stopped and faced her, crying into Abigail's shoulder, "I can't handle this. I thought it would be nice to try to have the group back in my life. I will no longer sit by and allow this type of shame and ridicule, especially when it's directed toward my husband." Kayra said.

Abigail gently rubbed her back. "Forget about them. They don't understand the value I see in you."

Kayra looked at her. "Really?"

"Yes! Now, hows 'bout a trip to your house?"

Kayra stared in surprise. "You really want to meet Colston?"

Abigail nodded with a warm smile.

"Let me call Colston to make sure he isn't working."

"Come back up to the food court afterward." Abigail walked toward the escalator with a certain swagger that set off alarm bells in Kayra's mind.

She ignored them, remaining in a state of indifference. Abigail came after her and showed genuine concern and expressed a willingness to meet Colston. However, Abigail's ideology was a significant part of her identity. Could Kayra still put up with it without destroying the harmony or herself? As she watched Abigail disappear from view, she asked herself, *Is it worth it?* There was absolute glee with the idea of having Abigail back in her life, but there was a package deal involved. A small voice urged her, *Stand tall and firm. Harmony doesn't mean sacrificing your self-respect or hiding your hurt. While the effort could be worth it, remain on your toes. People like Abigail will come and go, with lessons and trials. They will stick around if they're meant to. At the ending, you will be safe and comfortable in the arms of your husband; he will be your constant.*

Kayra pulled out her phone. Finding comfort and confidence in those words, she took a few calming breaths and dialed Colston.

"Hello, love." Colston answered, his voice enveloping her with warmth and making her reconsider her decision.

"Hi, are you up for a guest?" she asked, trying to sound gleeful instead of dejected.

"Sure, I might be singing. But it's just practice because I discovered a song request," Colston replied, playfully, a smile evident in his voice.

Kayra blushed; he had found her song request that she had left in his studio that morning. "Is that right? Well, Abigail and I will be that way shortly."

"See you soon. Love you."

"Love you too."

Kayra pocketed her phone and hesitated about moving forward. She gave herself a little pep talk: *"Girl, come on. She's willing to meet and apologize to Colston. That's worth giving this friendship another try, right? Remember, you can walk away at any time, and you don't owe anyone an explanation."* With newfound confidence, Kayra took a step toward the escalator, gently fiddling with her ring as she ascended. What she saw was unsettling: Lucy and Sadie sat there with their heads lowered while Abigail stood leaning over them, her finger pointing and waving as she spoke. Thankfully, her words were not loud, but Kayra dared not move any closer to avoid overhearing.

Abigail glanced Kayra's way, then turned back toward the others before straightening up. She pivoted on her heel and headed toward Kayra while the other two sat looking chastened.

Abigail wore a smile, but there was something about it that sent a chill down Kayra's back. Was she really that satisfied with herself for scolding her friends like disobedient children in public?

Did Kayra truly want this kind of unnecessary drama in her life? Did she want Colston exposed to it?

"So what's the verdict?" Abigail asked.

"It's a yes," she replied with a cheerful smile, still ignoring the extremely loud alarm bell in her mind. She began to worry about how easily she was masking her discomfort, which seemed to grow the longer she spent with Abigail.

Abigail hooked her arm around Kayra's. "Then let's go!"

Kayra mutely nodded. They left the mall and walked to Kayra's blue Toyota Corolla.

As they walked, Abigail talked about the

desire for a possible change in her current job position, expressing frustration that her needs weren't being met quickly enough. When Kayra unlocked the car, Abigail stopped and tightened her grip on Kayra's arm, "This yours?" She gasped.

"Yes, my last year's birthday gift from Colston." Kayra replied.

Abigail's eyes widened. A quick flash of envy crossed her face, but it was replaced by sorrow. "I am sorry; I placed Colston so low on my totem pole." She trailed off, looking ashamed.

Kayra struggled to respond, settling instead for, "Shall we get going? I will bring you back to your car after."

Abigail immediately released her arm and skipped to the passenger side while Kayra continued to the driver's side.

During the ride to the house, Abigail tried her best to be respectable and not outright ask about Colston's earnings from the Collective Creative platform. Kayra sidestepped the numbers and spoke instead about the hard work and passion that Colston had invested over the years.

Abigail grew extremely fidgety trying to hold her tongue. Kayra felt a surge of hope. "Hey, thank you."

Abigail looked up, shocked. "What? Why? I've done nothing."

"You are." Kayra had tears in her eyes as she grabbed Abigail's hand.

As Kayra pulled onto her street, she began to slow down.

"No, now you are joshing with me!"

Abigail exclaimed, squeezing Kayra's hand.

Kayra anticipated this reaction; the last house that she had visited was the shared trailer home that she and Colston had when they first started dating. This neighborhood, while not overtly affluent, was noticeably upscale.

"Like I said, hard work and dedication will get you places." She pulled up next to Colston's truck. "Ready?" she asked, shutting off the car.

For the first time since the hug after coming up the escalator, Abigail's confidence faltered. The worry was clear on her face. "Is he going to yell at me?" She was showing the vulnerable side.

"My Colston does not yell unless it's necessary. He was happy when I told him you had invited me to a girls' night."

"Really?"

Kayra nodded and stepped out of the car with Abigail following suit.

When Kayra opened the front door, Colston's voice singing the chorus of *I Wanna Grow Old with You* by Westlife filtered out. Her heart leapt, and she fought back tears of happiness.

"I'll go get him." Kayra said.

She walked down the hall and waited for the song to end before knocking.

"Babe?"

The door was unlocked and opened, revealing a smiling Colston. "Hi."

"We've got company."

Colston nodded, and not trying to hide his injury, leaned on his cane as he limped into the hall.

"You must be Abigail," he said cheerfully.

She nodded and hesitantly stepped forward, extending her hand. "You must be Colston." Her voice was quiet.

"Indeed, I am," he replied, shaking her hand.

Abigail swallowed her pride. "Colston, I am sorry. I spoke ill of you behind your back. I want to have Kayra back in my life, but I need to clear the air between us first." Her voice trembled.

Colston smiled, clearly impressed. "Consider the air clear; all I ask is that Kayra is safe and comfortable when you two are out together." Colston requested.

"I can keep that promise." Abigail said.

The Demon never cared: the storm deepening. The Demon never cared: the storm deepening.

Chapter Six: Back to the House

"Colston! YOU CAN'T GET AWAY!"

He sprinted into the forest.

"YOU'RE GOING TO REGRET THIS WHEN I CATCH YOU!"

A cold wind enveloped him...

The nightmare slips in at the end as he lies between the state of wakefulness and sleep; he is stripped of that sense of calm that he had gained after remembering the time of his and Kayra's engagement; he despises this state. During that time, he had focused entirely on Kayra and their engagement. The nightmare was the furthest from his memory, though, closer in proximity to the days of captivity as opposed to now. Five years later, he feels its suffocating grip more than ever. Despite his happiness and dedication, he struggles to escape the memories of what has been lost. *Why can't I retrieve what I locked away to keep safe?* As he gazes out the windshield, the oppressive sky mirrors his internal turmoil, amplifying his sense of despair. He cannot even look up for solace in the brightness or warmth of the sun. Does he not deserve such simple pleasures? Not after last night; he feels he has earned this absence of light. What lesson is he meant to learn from this experience? One thing he has come to understand is that to ensure survival, one must outlast. However, no matter the outcome, the mind suffers immensely, leaving the victor questioning everything.

Kayra, his beloved wife, is his anchor. He offered her an escape last night; she will never realize that this simple gesture saved him from himself.

He hears a car pull up beside his truck and hopes that he can maintain his composure when he sees Kayra and Jordan. Wanting to forget about the session, he glances over and spots Kayra. Although he grins at her smiling face, he doesn't truly feel it. He rolls down his window.

"Colston, baby," she says in a somber tone, "are you certain you want to go through with this?"

Colston feels dejected. What is happening to his ability to conceal his internal struggle? A thought crosses his mind: What if he never concealed it as well as he believed?

"I need to do this. I... I..." Colston struggles to explain, mainly because he doesn't want them to realize he's missing a significant part of himself. "I hope it provides the closure I am seeking."

Jordan leans close to Kayra to peer up at Colston. "Buddy, we hope so too. Come on, Cole, we're in this together."

"I must warn you; I don't know what state this experience will leave me in."

Kayra extends her hand out of the window, and Colston reaches out to grasp it.

"It will be okay; we will be here for you."

Jordan opens the door and steps out. "Come on, let's go."

Colston, not letting go of Kayra's hand, says, "I'll take the back, please."

Jordan simply nods and settles back down.

Colston then releases Kayra's hand, rolls up the window, and turns off the truck. Before stepping out, he realizes that this moment could save him or utterly destroy him. He is willingly heading to the birthplace of this never-ending, heart-freezing, mind-numbing nightmare. He prays for the inner strength to endure the pain that is undoubtedly about to come and for the ability to resist succumbing to the insanity.

He steps out onto unsteady legs, bracing himself against his door and Kayra's car.

"Oh, babe," her voice is soft.

He shuts the door and locks it, always keeping his left hand on the car as he climbs in.

Jordan looks back and gives him a reassuring pat on the knee.

"Are you going to be alright with the replacement?" Kayra asks as she backs the car up.

Within Colston's chest, a deep, hollow feeling swells with anxiety and fear. Ignoring it, he remains in control; he answers truthfully, "I didn't get a good vibe from her. There was no kindness or understanding." Colston feels sick after making that statement. He realizes he is passing harsh judgment without giving her a fair chance, but he knows his limit has been reached, and what is or isn't present at the house will determine his next step.

"Really, why would Todd have someone like that?" Kayra asks.

"Todd is a very arduous person, not one to sugarcoat things for the sake of others' feelings or mental well-being. Melody complements that well," Colston states.

"So, he has one of those personalities that is an 'acquired taste' type?" Jordan asks.

Colston shrugs and nods silently.

They are still very much in town; Colston is trying to convince himself that they are merely driving. However, the known destination complicates that notion. He wonders if it would be better for him to be asleep during the drive, as a bubble of emotions within his chest is steadily intensifying with the cold becoming nearly unbearable. He attempts to speak, but his voice has already abandoned him, overwhelmed by fear and fueling his panic. Once his key to survival, his voice has now become a means of releasing his pain. It is so easily silenced, and he is hurtling headlong toward that dreaded place.

A positive sign, right? He's attempting to view this optimistically while he is still capable. Despite Todd's relentless push toward the brink of insanity, perhaps the answer has been at the house all along. The fear of confronting his prison may have prevented him from unlocking that cage and freeing himself. He struggles to push through, striving to express his thoughts so he can regain a sense of control within the nightmare.

"Colston?" Kayra asks, her voice slightly louder. She has been trying to get his attention for the past five minutes.

Colston hunches forward and lets out a strained gasp.

"Cole?" Jordan asks, panic clear in his voice as he places a hand on Colston's shoulder and gently pushes him back. When Jordan meets Colston's gaze, he pulls away sharply.

Kayra glances at him, noticing his expression of fear and confusion. She checks the rearview mirror but sees nothing alarming. Nevertheless, this does not alleviate her stress.

Jordan observes the color change in Colston's eyes, shifting from the vibrant brown eyes so full of life to a color that could have been interpreted as steel gray.

"What's happening?" Jordan whispers; unfortunately, Kayra overhears him.

"Baby?" she asks, glancing at her husband through the rearview mirror.

Colston glances at her, allowing her to see the change in his eye color as well as the pained expression on his face. She places a reassuring hand on Jordan's shoulder and says, "Let's pull over for a moment."

"Might be for the best." Jordan whispers.

Kayra pulls into a gas station. Colston's gray eyes are fixed on Jordan, filled now with pleading and pain.

"We don't have to go," Jordan says, hoping to restore some color to Colston's eyes. Ever since his kidnapping, Colston's once vibrant and rich brown eyes have dulled significantly. This is a painful reality that Jordan has come to accept; Colston may never be the same. It breaks Jordan's heart to witness his close friend's decline while he continues to fight so hard. He feels torn between two choices: convincing Colston to seek alternative means of finding relief, even if it means enduring a slow deterioration, or allowing him to confront the place where it all happened, risking the chance of watching him die under the painful truth. Jordan would choose the first option, determined just to be there to inject happiness and courage for both Colston and Kayra while things are sorted out.

However, when Colston's eyes widen and his chin quivers, "I----have--to----do----this." He gasps, struggling, "I----I'm----sor----ry."

Kayra turns around and says, "Honey, please." She can't bear to listen to his struggle.

The gray eyes fixate on her, conveying the same pleading and pained expression. She reaches out and grasps his hand, only to recoil as its icy chill sends a shiver through her.

"Sor-sorry." Colston stammers, gulping. "I-am-t-trying-to-fight."

Kayra reaches for his hand, and this time, Jordan takes Colston's other hand.

Jordan is left speechless. "How is his hand so cold?"

Kayra lowers her head and quietly responds, "I don't know, but I hate it." She gazes at Colston and adds, "We're here; you are not alone. But, hon," she leans in to caress his face, "you are not well, and we have no idea what awaits you at that place. Can't we take a day or two to think it over?"

Colston's chest swells with fear as he shakes his head. "I------can't----wait------an--y----longer." Tears stream down his face; he feels as though he is dying. This buildup is suffocating him, and he desperately needs to release it, for better or for worse. His eyes dart to the gas station. "Drinks--and snacks." Colston is beyond frustrated that his speech has been reduced to that of a young child.

Hands are released as they exit the car. Kayra quickly rushes to Colston's side and takes his hand in hers. The warmth of her touch contrasts sharply with his freezing hand. He holds her hand tightly, not to cause her pain, but to concentrate on the sensation.

Jordan opens the door and allows the other two to enter first.

Colston leads them to the cold cases, where Kayra briefly releases his hand to grab a lemonade for herself. Colston and Jordan select sparkling water. Jordan turns and notices a child, likely eight or nine years old, excitedly pointing at Colston. The mom looks nervously at Jordan. He smiles and raises a hand, signaling for them to wait a moment. Then, he places his hand on Colston's shoulder, leans in close, and quietly whispers, "Cole, buddy, there's a young fan."

Colston immediately reaches up and places

his hand on Jordan's hand resting on his shoulder, taking a few deep breaths to regain control. Kayra has just returned to Colston, who has his eyes closed, while Jordan is left feeling the immense fight surging. After an intense several seconds of suppressing everything, Colston looks up at Kayra and Jordan, his eyes regaining their color and warmth returning to his skin. As he glances over his shoulder and his gaze lands on the boy, who adopts the starstruck expression: wide eyes, slack-jawed, and a slight, uncontrollable tremor in his knees. Colson looks at the mother, whose eyes seem to silently ask if her son can approach him.

Colston turns and smiles, a blend of forced and genuine warmth, as he begins walking toward the pair. Halfway there, the boy rushes the rest of the distance to meet him.

"I love your voice!" the boy exclaims enthusiastically.

"Jake!" the mother scolds. "I apologize; he's just excited."

"It's fine; I'm honored you like my voice," Colston says, summoning every ounce of strength to suppress his inner turmoil. Hoping to provide the boy with an enjoyable experience, Colston poses the only question that he can clearly retrieve from his mind, "What is your favorite cover?"

The boy ponders for a moment, exclaiming, "*Hellfire* and *Die to the Fire*!" A wide smile spreads across Jake's face.

"Both of those are excellent covers; thank you."

Kayra can feel the struggle emanating, but fortunately, neither the boy nor the mother senses anything.

"Do you mind if we take a picture?" the mother asks.

"Of course," Colston replies cheerfully.

Jordan and Kayra move aside, allowing Jake to happily stand next to Colston. He gently places his hand on the boy's shoulder.

"Thank you for this moment," Jake says.

"You are very welcome." Colston smiles for the photo.

He finds himself reveling in this moment, a poignant reminder of what it once was and an even stronger reminder of the significance of his decision not to reveal the truth. He didn't want to see the worry that he constantly sees in Kayra and Jordan's eyes; in the eyes of his fans. Let the music dominate.

The picture has been taken, and the mother beckons for Jake. He takes a hesitant step away from Colston, his eyes wide and his mouth working, but his voice fails him.

"You have something else to ask or say?" Colston inquires warmly.

"How did you escape?" This question is posed with genuine innocence.

Colston's knee buckles. "A miracle," he breathes, as his right hand plants on the ground.

Jake appears to be on the verge of tears.

"So sorry," the mother says in a panic, taking her son by the hand and pulling him toward the door.

The moment Colston dropped to his knee,

Kayra looked horrified and locked eyes with Jordan. The question that lurked was, "Is this the beginning of the end?"

"Jordan, hand me the drinks. Could you go out to the car with Cole?" Kayra asks shakily.

"Of course," Jordan says, handing the drinks to Kayra, then helping Colston to his feet.

Then he and Colston walk out the door. Colston keeps his head down, lost in thought about that question and pondering how many others have asked it. The videos remain on the channel, and after *'His Screams Echoes, Unheard'*, he didn't upload again until mid-December.

Jordan is walking beside Colston, his heart thumping. He recalled the earlier conversation with Kayra about Colston's potential snap. He can't shake the thought that the final piece Colston is withholding is the source of the intense manifestation. Coaxing it out is going to be challenging, as the fear is tightly wrapped around Colston's soul. Why did he feel the need to guard it so fiercely?

"Colston!"

Jordan gazes across the parking lot and notices the same boy again, attempting to escape from his mother. Upon closer inspection, Jordan is able to see that the child is crying.

"I want to apologize, please!"

Colston, pulled from his thoughts and back to reality, stops and looks toward Jake. He then glances at Jordan, noting Jordan's concern, and nods in acknowledgment.

Together, they approach Jake and his mother, who immediately ceases squirming. The mother has a firm grip on her son's shoulder, clearly horrified by his behavior. However, she recognizes that Jake feels remorseful, and with Colston approaching them once again, she ultimately decides to postpone punishing her son. Colston and Jordan join them in an empty parking space.

"Don't cry; you did nothing wrong," Colston reassures Jake.

"I am sorry," he says, standing with his head bowed and appearing small. "I didn't mean to hurt you. Pl-please, don't stop singing." He sniffs as a tear falls onto the pavement.

Colston is flabbergasted by Jake's awareness. Now, he desperately wants to lift that burden from Jake's shoulders. Colston willingly kneels this time.

"Jake, for this alone, your mom ought to be proud." He looks at her as he speaks, and she smiles. Colston shifts his gaze back to Jake. At that moment, Jake is looking up, tears streaming. "Listen, you didn't hurt me, okay? And even if you did, I wouldn't stop singing. I would sing to prove that I am strong."

The young boy's eyes gleam with understanding.

"Can I hug you?"

"Of course," Jake melts into Colston's embrace. It only lasts a few seconds, but Colston could feel the impact.

Colston stands after the embrace and

shakes the mother's hand, who appears equally flabbergasted and embarrassed. She says nothing and simply wears an awkward smile.

Kayra has set the bag of drinks in the car and turns to see Jordan and Colston approaching her. Just then, she notices Colston nearly stumble, prompting Jordan to throw Colston's arm over his shoulders for support. Concerned, Kayra rushes over to them, positioning herself under Colston's right arm and placing a hand on his chest. She dislikes the lack of color in his face and the weakness of his heartbeat. "Are you really sure you want to go?"

"I need----to," his chest heaves.

"Buddy, please think about this. You are drained; we are not about to watch you die," Jordan says.

Kayra, horrified, firmly smacks Jordan on the back. They exchange glances from around the front of Colston.

"I am----dying----all----the----same. Babe, I----am----trying." Colston says, feeling Kayra fold into his chest. "I----need to----face this,----and I need----closure."

They are standing outside the car. Kayra cradles his face and says, "You aren't dying. We can try medication and seek other psychological help. This is not taking you away from me... no more than it already has."

Colston places his hands over hers and gives her a sad, knowing look. "I refuse to mask this with meds when all I want is to understand who he was." Once again, he is lying and wonders if God is punishing him for such.

"Do you really believe that knowing the guy's name will provide that kind of relief?" Jordan asks.

Colston drops his head and his hands. "I----don't----know. I----know----that----he----was suf--fering------too."

Jordan and Kayra exchange glances. "I'll drive," Jordan says, turning to Colston. "On our way, if something comes up that scares you, talk, just talk. It doesn't need to make sense; just don't get lost in your mind. We can't help you there, okay?"

Colston gazes into the weary eyes of his best friend, sensing the genuine concern and fear; he nods in response to the request.

"Alright," Jordan sighs, "let's go."

Kayra sits in the back with Colston, feeling an overwhelming fear of letting him go.

For most of the drive, silence prevails. On the four-lane highway, the trees in the woods grow increasingly dense. Colston senses a swirling wind in his mind, and a deep, hollow sensation settles in his chest.

"My phantom was so convinced that he saw me begging for help during my performances. I was concealing my true self because I feared failure." Colston says unexpectedly, startling himself.

He feels both pairs of eyes fall upon him as he wonders, *Why... did I just call my captor? My tormentor? My phantom?*

"Phantom?" Kayra inquires.

"I don't know; I don't particularly like it. But it just... fits."

"It painfully does, as he haunts you," Jordan says. "Colston, you don't think he died in the fire, do you?"

Colston feels his blood run cold as he catches Jordan's eyes in the rearview mirror. Did Jordan just hit the nail on the head? Is this truly his fear, not finding closure at the house, but rather discovering that he is still alive? "No, he had to----have------died. He pushed me------out------before------some of the house------came down on----top----of------him." A pang of guilt lands hard in his chest, which confuses him. He leans forward. "He couldn't have used the fire to cover his tracks." He whispers quickly to himself, "I heard him scream." Colston exclaims in a panic, and with his next breath, he begins to sing *My Dying Lament*.

"Babe, that was hauntingly beautiful. That was the song you sang on the day of the fire, right?" Kayra asks.

"Yes, from the band Fragment of Embers. Honestly, I sang that song for no other reason than to distract myself from dying. Exhausted by everything, and for the first time ever in my life, I had to coax the song out. I was alone, not pressured to sing, and free of the fear of being beaten." Tears of guilt and shame stream down his face as he shows his weakness, having pulled himself back from the brink of death just days prior.

"Cole, why do you feel the need to hide the fact that you wished for death? We won't blame you; you went through hell, and you're still fucking here. Buddy, please don't sell yourself short just because you wanted to die," Jordan says, barely able to keep his voice from breaking.

"My reality while in the hands of the phantom is a nightmare for only the two of us to understand. It was sheer insanity, yet it indelibly marked my soul. Not because I believed it, but due to the fear and torment that accompanied it."

Jordan makes the turn at the 49th exit.

Kayra tightens her grip on Colston, anxious that he might fade away at any moment. She can feel his heart pounding.

Colston is straining his eyes to see between the trees, straightening up, with Kayra still attached to his side.

The air in the car is thick with tension as Colston holds his breath. Two miles down the road, he finally sees it. His resolve shatters like a brittle branch, and a wave of fresh fear washes over him. Through the trees, he glimpses...walls.

"Stop!" Colston shouts.

Jordan is so startled that he slams on the brakes. Kayra lets out a shriek and pulls away from Colston.

The car skids to a halt just before turning down the driveway. Colston, now in a trance-like state, says, "I'm going to walk."

He opens the door and steps out into the crisp mountain air, moving at a steady pace down the driveway.

Jordan and Kayra follow, uncertain of what to expect.

Following the driveway as it bends to the left, the charred skeletal remains come into view for Colston. He stops and drops to his knees, his breath catching in his throat.

"Colston?!" Kayra exclaims as she and Jordan swoop in to help.

"No... Give... me... space!" he demands.

He stands and pushes forward, his mind a whirlwind and his body numb. He walks with his head down and arrives at the head of the path, recalling his first entrance into the house. His wrists and ankles were bound; this was one of the longest walks of his life. He was uncertain whether he would be able to walk out again.

He looks up through the doorway, staring down the narrow hallway, to the entrance of that dark hole that was his prison.

The icy spears within his chest twist and turn. "OUT OF ALL THE THINGS THAT ARE LEFT STANDING, IT IS THAT HORRID HOLE!" Colston screams, extending his hand toward it.

Jordan is holding Kayra, listening as the fading echoes of Colston's scream dissolve into silence. Jordan wants to stop Colston. This method of seeking closure is the worst kind of punishment. Kayra perceives so much in that scream: pain, fear, release, and an absoluteness that unsettles her.

"Colston, are you satisfied?" Jordan asks earnestly.

Colston whips his head around, still pointing at the hole. "See that? That is here!" He taps his head with his other hand. "My prison: cold, dark, and powerless!"

"Honey, please, you are not trapped there anymore," Kayra pleads, stepping away from Jordan. "This place can't hurt you anymore;

please, Colston, let go!" She begins to approach her husband.

"I can't!" Colston cries. "Not until I..."

A gust of wind sweeps through the house, stirring up dust and small fragments of debris. Colston notices something brilliantly white fluttering against the dark doorway of the bathroom, causing him to abruptly stop talking as a flashback floods his mind.

He opened his eyes after a sleepless drift, his mind racing with fear and unable to formulate any ideas for escape. Around him on the floor, he noticed a few battery-operated tea lights, a thin blanket covering his legs, a tray of food, and a jug of water. The tray was positioned beside his right side, making it easier to reach. However, he didn't reach for it; instead, he stared at it, captivated by something that stood out vibrantly against the dim light and in sickening contrast to the rest of the food. It was a slice of cake, clean and perfectly placed in the left-hand corner. The white frosting adorned the white cake, topped with colorful sprinkles. Colston was dumbfounded; despite the cake's delicious and visually appealing appearance, a hollowness in his gut dissuaded him from even touching the tray. Yet, hunger prevailed, and he grabbed the single piece of breaded chicken, dipping it into the mashed potatoes. Just before the food reached his lips, he finally registered the lack of warmth in it. He stared off for a moment, the food in his hands becoming squished. The man must have entered while he was asleep, covered him with the blanket, and left food for him along with the lights. Colston was by no means comfortable enough to have been in such a deep sleep that he wouldn't have heard the man.

His eyes then focused on something just outside the boundary of light at his feet. He leaned forward and grabbed the objects. Colston retrieved a gold upper face mask with eye holes shaded blue, along with a note featuring elegant, piercing handwriting. He brought the paper closer to a candle to read it.

Happy Birthday, Colston!
On your channel, it is currently 'Colston's Creepy Covers', and we are
Committed to delivering quality content.
Wear the mask while you sing today, and free yourself from this cage.
Which you have locked yourself in, and by extension, you have Locked me in as well.
I will help you. I will teach you to free your voice and reach new heights.
So, Colston, I'd advise you to fix what needs to be fixed within yourself.
Or remain locked here with me forever.

He lets out a whimper as he refocuses on the world around him. His hands are clasped with his wife's, and her eyes are fixed on him. "Kayra, you shouldn't be here," he says. He doesn't want the horror of this place to touch her, and he is uncertain whether he can refrain from lashing out at her.

Kayra reaches up to caress his face, but he pulls away from her, leaving Kayra frozen in heartbreak. He backs into Jordan, and Colston turns to shove him away, using his forearm against Jordan's chest.

He stumbles backward a few steps but remains on his feet. "Whoa, Colston," Jordan exclaims, shocked.

Colston is shaking and backing up toward the rubble. "I'm sorry," he cries.

"My love, please, let's just go. Let's leave this place behind," Kayra pleads with him.

"Something is among the rubble," he explains, glancing back at the debris just two feet away.

"Trash, Colston, that is what it is!" Kayra shouts. "You're just torturing yourself even more."

"Kay, I am trying to free myself. Believe me," he says, remaining still.

"You're going to get yourself killed by going in there. Is that what you want?" Jordan asks, attempting to reason with him.

Another gust of wind blows, and the sky darkens with ominous storm clouds.

"Let me just go get that thing," Colston says.

"What are you expecting to find?" Jordan yells. "It's nothing but trash blown in by the wind."

Colston observes their pain, yet he feels no emotion as he is driven to enter the rubble. It is incredibly foolish and reckless, but he turns and wades into the wreckage, being cautious with his foot placement to avoid destabilizing what remains standing. Although witnessing the collapse would be the greatest thing to watch for Colston, he is nonetheless venturing into the mess. He survived this place once, and he doesn't intend to get himself killed over something that could have been avoided.

His eyes are fixed on the white thing, which he can discern as a sheet of paper. Hoping it is merely trash, a voice interjects, *"Colston, what else could this possibly be?"*

The terror that rips through him with that question is unsettling. What is he hoping to find? He can only pray for forgiveness after this foolish and trivial trek. He does not enjoy testing their patience, but he must uncover something from this cursed place. He is not prepared to die.

He mutters under his breath, "I have no idea."

His heart pounds fiercely in his chest, drowning out all other sounds, as he focuses intently on the paper and the doorway.

'YOU CALLOUS SON OF A BITCH!!' These words resonate with his heartbeat. *'Please, I beg you, let me go!'*

Gripping the paper, Colston is suddenly overwhelmed by the pungent smell of smoke, and his body is engulfed in searing heat. He closes his eyes, the agony of the external flames clashing with the icy terror of his mind overshadowing the beating he endured here.

Once the moment passes, he finds his body drenched in sweat and chilled by the light breeze. Suddenly, he is filled with terror at the sight of the paper in his hand; it is new amidst the five-year-old charred remains of the house.

My Dearest Colston,
You remain the means to an end.
I sacrificed my all to save you.
When the fire separated us, the timing was not right.
I have waited patiently for the moment you returned to our shared place.
Showing me that you are prepared to become truly stunning.
Finally freeing us!

Upon the first line, in his mind, his dying self, pleading for relief, is wrenched away from the bars of the cell that confines his light and warmth. He is cast aside.

Colston can't believe what he has just read; he feels trapped, staring at the paper. Breathing heavily, he grips the sides of his head and screams, "NOOOOO!"

Jordan and Kayra watch Colston go into the rubble, hoping it won't collapse on him. Their silence is shattered by Colston's distressing scream, followed by his sudden collapse to the ground. The feeling of exasperation they initially felt is replaced by worry and concern.

"Colston!"

"Kayra, go get the car! I'll get Colston."

Jordan sprints down the path, reaching the rubble. He vaults into it and moves quickly. "Cole? Come on, bud," he pleads. Upon reaching Colston, he immediately drops to his knees beside him and gently attempts to wake him. "Wake up, please!" He places his fingers against Colston's neck; his pulse is alarmingly quick. Jordan then notices a piece of paper clenched in Colston's hand.

"Colston! Jordan, what's wrong?" Kayra screams as she jumps out of the car, her eyes fixed on Colston lying in the rubble.

"Stay out there!" Jordan shouts as he frees the paper.

After reading the note, he looks around and then back at Colston, who is still unconscious.

"Oh, God," he whispers. "Cole, I promise he will not get to you." He pockets the note, then picks up Colston and carries him out of the rubble. Upon reaching Kayra, he reaches into his pocket and hands the note to her before gently laying Colston in the backseat. Leaving the back door open, he goes back to check on Kayra, who is leaning against the front of the car with the note held tightly in her hands.

"Kay?" Jordan asks, shivering.

"We can't let this deranged man take him again."

Jordan pulls her into an embrace and reassures her, "We won't. Come on, let's get out of here."

Chapter Seven: Glimmer of Hope

Kayra walks into the living room, arms folded and wearing one of Colston's sweatshirts. "I figured you'd gone to bed," she says, stepping into Colston's chair and settling down.

Jordan replies, tiredly yet warmly, "I figured you would have stayed with Colston."

Kayra lowers her head. "I shouted and completely disregarded him, breaking my promise to myself about what he needs to do to help himself. Of course, I'll show care while allowing him the space, but..."

"Kayra," Jordan leans forward on the couch, "I'm right there with you. There was no way we were going to let him get himself killed over a piece of trash."

"That's the thing! IT wasn't trash." Kayra exclaimed, curling up into herself. After tossing the note onto the table, she silently weeps into Colston's sweatshirt. "Those aren't empty words." Remembering the note left for her on the day of the kidnapping, a note intended to mislead her, which continues to haunt Kayra. This new note, however, conveyed his true intentions, leaving her feeling increasingly helpless. Overwhelmed by dread and a desperate desire to keep Colston safe, she feels as though her efforts might be futile. Tears fall, she looks at Jordan and says, "JD... I can't lose him."

Jordan moves from the couch and kneels in front of her. "Kayra," he pauses, struggling to offer her genuine reassurance. He could speak endlessly to help soothe her worries, but he cannot escape his own fear. The events of the past twenty-four hours, including his becoming privy to extreme displays following flashbacks, the unsettling change in eye color, and now with this brazen move from the kidnapper, have left him in disarray. This is real life, yet it feels like a horror movie. Left in the wake of a plot point, surrounded by the shattered remnants of understanding, which were already scarce to begin with. Among the rubble, he vowed that he wouldn't allow Colston to be taken again. He meant it, but the fleeting hope feels demoralizing. He shakes his head, dispelling such soul-crushing thoughts. "You can't let him get to you, too. Colston is safe now, and we will be here. Our guy needs us to be strong and to reassure him that he will not be taken again."

Kayra stares in terror. "I have seen the struggle countless times, and I wait for the final. I want my husband back; that man took something from us."

"He took Colston's sense of self, and Colston has been fighting to regain it." Jordan pauses. "We should try contacting the police."

Kayra lowers her head and says, "We should..."

"Kayra, what's wrong?" Jordan asks.

"We haven't spoken to the police in a

year and a half," Kayra says in a low tone.

Jordan wearily shifts to sit down completely on the floor.

"Colston wanted to find out if they had any information, as there had been no updates from the police. When Colston returned, he was devastated. However, he didn't share what had happened, and I never pressed him for details."

Both Kayra and Jordan yawn.

"The spare bedroom is all set for you," Kayra says as she stands and helps Jordan to his feet.

"Yes, sleep," Jordan says.

Colston lies awake, unfortunately, alone, which only heightens his anxiety that Kayra is extremely angry with him. The mere fact that he is still breathing feels astonishing. When he had screamed, he felt lightheaded, his heart fluttered, and he lost consciousness before hitting the ground.

What on earth was he thinking? Going back! What relief did he expect to find? A sense of peace? He lets out a small, sorrowful chuckle at the mere idea of peace. For Colston, that sense of tranquility would have come if he had died after his second escape attempt. A sharp pain pierces his chest. He is taking the second chance for granted, disregarding God and the talent bestowed upon him. He rolls onto his side and pulls his legs up.

Somewhere deep inside, did he know that the phantom wasn't truly dead? He stares into the darkness, still struggling to comprehend why he cannot mentally free himself. For the past five years, he has been battling against the steel-barred door of that cage. Instead of the door bursting open and gaining the warmth and hope back. He now finds himself miles from the door, and his body is nearly too weak to push forward. His mind is questioning the cost of such a struggle, especially with the phantom alive and seeming apt to claim him once more.

The door slowly creaks open, causing Colston to freeze momentarily. He quickly relaxes as he watches Kayra enter the room.

Kayra gazes toward the bed and can make out Colston's form beneath the blanket; he lies on his left side. "Colston?" Her voice is cautious and soft. "Baby, you awake?"

Colston remains still but replies in the same tone, "I am, love."

Kayra moves into the room, closes the door, and takes off Colston's sweatshirt before getting into bed.

Colston is startled by where she climbs in and, at the same time, immensely relieved that she chooses his side. That allows her to nestle into his arms and snuggle against his chest. Colston immediately wraps his arms around her, feeling a surge of joy; however, she whispers, "I am sorry," causing a wave of fear to slice through his joy.

Taken aback, he whispers, "Why are you apologizing?" When it should be him doing the apologizing.

Kayra, listening to his voice and feeling his embrace, is finding it difficult to stay awake. "I shouted at you without considering what you needed to do."

Colston hears the emotion in her voice. "Honey, no," he says, holding her close and kissing her forehead. "You were worried for my safety. I wish it had been trash, and I could have just dealt with the repercussions of being irresponsible."

"Enough talk about that. No doubt, a nightmare will haunt you tonight, and the uncertainty of tomorrow is daunting. But, Colston, just hold me." She kisses his lips, and he deepens the kiss.

She runs her hand over his bare chest, her fingers grazing the scar above his heart. The sight of the scar always makes her shudder, a reaction that Colston feels strongly. He gently breaks the kiss and places his hand over hers, pressing it against his chest. "Pay no heed to the scar, but to the beating heart 'neath. That beating heart loves thee."

"My love, my songbird, my world, thee hath stolen the words from my very lips. My love and desire for you are boundless." Kayra rolls over, pressing her back against his chest. She intertwines their fingers and folds his arms across her chest. He gently rests his chin on her neck.

"I love you, Colston."

"I love you too, my Kayra."

Sleep swiftly separates them from one another.

Hand in hand, Kayra and Colston walk, bathed in sunlight, with the sound of birds chirping all around them. Their faces beam like teenagers sharing shy, awkward glances filled with deep affection. As they approach the street clock, they pause in a small grass patch.

Colston turns to face Kayra and runs his fingers through her hair.

"The time does tick; oh, how I wish it would stop. Time, spare my love, I beg of thee." Kayra's voice echoes all around them.

A voice responds, resonating and emanating from the direction of the clock, "Some people's destinies are to suffer for their actions, while a rare few are destined to suffer at the hands of others!"

At each word spoken, marks appear on Colston: raw skin on his wrists and bruises on his face and arms. He remains on his feet, running his fingers through Kayra's hair, while tears cascade down his cheeks and his breathing becomes heavy. Once the last word was spoken, Colston's body arched forward, and he screamed in pain.

Kayra feels the intense heat against his back as she guides his trembling body to the ground.

He reaches up and touches her face. "Love, please, let me die!"

"No! I love you. I can't live without you," she says, gazing into his pain-filled eyes.

The voice erupts in laughter, causing the ground to tremble. Colston cries out as blood spills from his mouth. The earth splits open and engulfs him.

Kayra wakes up. against Colston's chest.

"Kayra, come on, baby," he says, his voice soft and caring, yet tinged with a hint of disquiet.

She bursts into tears and tightly embraces Colston, trembling.

"It was just a dream," he whispers, attempting to dispel the fear.

She gazes at him in the light of the new dawn. Something about her expression sends chills down Colston's spine. He runs his fingers through her hair and asks, "Did I do this in front of the street clock?"

Kayra gasps and nods, now staring at him terrified.

"We shared the same dream," Colston gasps, running his hand to her chest. "I don't know what it means, but I'm here, right here."

Kayra clings to her troubling question: *If not now, then when? When he is unreachable and susceptible to the question?* She ignores her mind berating her weakness.

Colston witnesses another wave of tears run down her face as she buries her face against his chest. "Kayra?"

"I can't lose you. How can I stop it so you don't feel like you are fighting for your life?"

The phrasing catches Colston off guard; it is the same phrasing he used with Todd in yesterday's session. Honestly, he cannot answer without instilling more fear in her. In the dream, he begged for death, and without any light in the deepening darkness of his mind, he struggles to suppress his desire for it to become a reality.

He closes his eyes in an attempt to center himself. As hopeless as this all seems, he understands there is light that will guide him to the conclusion he wants, free from the nightmare and still breathing.

"Colston, why don't you and Jordan sing today?" Kayra suggests.

Colston opens his eyes; he considers the distraction, aware that someone is lurking outside, preparing to abduct him once more. The police have proven ineffective in this matter, and the thought of confiding in Melody feels equally futile. Perhaps a day of creativity will provide some good. "Will you be okay?" Colston asks.

She snuggles into him and whispers, "Just don't get lost in your thoughts."

"I'll try," Colston says, finding it easy to envision creating with Jordan.

"We'll take this new information day by day," Kayra says quickly, as her emotions threaten to overwhelm her.

The aroma of coffee wafts into the bedroom.

"It seems our guest is awake." Colston kisses her on the forehead and slides out of bed, walking around to the dresser. Kayra rolls into the warmth of the spot that his body had just vacated, fighting tears.

Colston puts on a shirt and notices that Kayra is still in bed. He sits down beside her and gently rubs her back. "Baby, are you okay?"

Kayra turns to face her husband, noticing the pain in his eyes. She sits up and gently cradles his face. "I want you to get better.

I can see the added weight. Please, how can I help?"

"I--must...keep pushing----forward." He gasps as the fleeting moment of peace drains away, and his chest heaves. "If... I... allow it... to be. It's... going to... kill... me. Don't... give... up on... me." He leans in and kisses her.

She returns the kiss and wraps her arms around him.

He forces everything back down. "I might need to talk to Melody," he says, shivering as he recalls yesterday's events. A thought suddenly comes to him, and he concentrates on it. Although she may have appeared hardhearted, she had shouted at Todd to stop grilling him.

Kayra sees a glimmer of light enter Colston's eyes. "Babe?" There is hope in her voice.

Colston hears the hope in his wife's voice. He is hesitant to embrace the notion that maybe Melody might be different; nonetheless, in the spirit of pushing forward, he feels compelled to at least see her and keep Kayra's hope alive that he will overcome this challenge. Colston decides to tell the truth, despite being uncertain of Melody's resolve. "She did give me hope, albeit a small amount. I am scared, though." His anxiety mounts as he contemplates the idea of going. He wants to share with Kayra what Todd did yesterday, but he is reluctant to cause her any worry.

He extends his hand to her; she accepts it, and he assists her in getting out of bed.

She slips back into his sweatshirt, and hand in hand, they leave the room.

Jordan is sitting at the island with a bowl of cereal in front of him and an empty coffee mug beside him. He turns and sees them. "How are you feeling, bud?" he asks, aware that it is a loaded question.

Colston looks at Jordan, attempting to maintain a hopeful expression, but the cold quickly begins to take its toll. He says, "I'm fine; would you like to sing with me before I go talk to Melody? I might have a solo in the concert, but you and I have a duet." Colston is ready to forgo this week's cover song in order to practice with Jordan.

"Really? Okay! What song?" Jordan asks excitedly.

"I have a challenging idea: we perform a duet using two different songs." Colston notices Jordan's curious and confused expression. "Stay with me. The melodies of these songs mirror each other; we may need to fine-tune the lyrics to align with what I envision in my head. If we hash out the lyrics and create a vocal guide, I can send it to Decklin to begin the mixing."

"My guy, if you believe we can accomplish this before April, I am completely on board." Jordan says with a smile, "What are the songs?"

"*Wind's Melody* and *My Dying Lament*, both by Fragment of Embers."

The coffee pot dings, prompting Kayra to move from Colston to prepare two mugs of coffee.

"*My Dying Lament*, the one you sang

yesterday?" Jordan asks cautiously.

"Yes, I hope you don't mind if I take that song."

"Not at all, Cole. So, mine is *Wind's Melody*?" Jordan asks, grabbing his phone to look it up.

"Yes," Colston replies as Kayra places a mug of coffee in front of him and then reaches for Jordan's.

"Thank you so much, Kay," Jordan says with a smile.

Kayra smiles as she pours Jordan's coffee; there is something comforting about hearing the two of them discuss any upcoming project. The weight of the unknown feels less burdensome.

Colston is seated next to Jordan, and they are playing songs on their phones one after another.

"Once I finish my cereal, we can go to your office. Sorry, Kayra," Jordan says.

Kayra looks at him, dumbfounded. "When have I ever asked you to move your work to the office?" Her tone is not sharp, just serious.

Jordan is at a loss for words and looks away, pondering why he made that statement. "You're right, Kayra. I don't know why I said that. I've been shut down so often recently that I feel like I need to be in a designated work area," he sighs.

For the past six months, he has been doing collabs with other artists. Jordan enjoys when the creative process begins outside of the traditional work environment, as it fosters a more relaxed atmosphere.

However, whenever he and the artist he is collaborating with gain momentum, they are often asked to move into the studio. The tones of these requests are frequently unkind, as if those around him are growing weary of his presence.

Kayra reaches out and takes his hand. "Anywhere in this house is open for you to create. It fuels my creativity and brings me joy," she says.

Jordan pats her hand and nods, "Alright."

Right then, Colston's phone rings, cutting off the music and startling all three of them. Colston stares at the caller ID, feeling a wave of emotion wash over him as he sees the name: Healthy Minds, Better Lives Counseling. He swallows hard and reminds himself to keep pushing forward. He answers shakily, "Hello."

Kayra is instantly concerned by the quiver in his voice.

"Hello, Mr. Driscoll, this is Melody Dakota. I understand that it is your responsibility to arrange an emergency session. Mr. Driscoll, I cannot stop thinking about what happened yesterday; I feel terrible for not intervening sooner." Her warm and compassionate voice struck him like a ton of bricks.

"W...why...w...were...you s...so...co...cold?" Colston asks, desperate to understand.

"Per Todd's instructions, he did not want his code of conduct compromised by my personality. After meeting with all twenty of his clients, I found that you, Mr. Driscoll

caused the most concern. I need to see you as soon as possible. How about in an hour and a half, at 11:30?"

"Today?" Colston questions, looking at Jordan.

Jordan places a reassuring hand on Colston's shoulder and nods toward the phone.

"Mr. Driscoll, I apologize if I seem intrusive or if you feel hesitant. I understand that you are tired of facing this alone, and distractions can be exhausting. May I ask, did you visit the house?" The question is posed in a completely non-judgmental manner, filled with sincerity.

Colston could have broken down in loud sobs over that, but he holds it in, allowing the tears to flow freely.

Kayra grasps Colston's other hand and shares a look of great concern with Jordan.

"I did and didn't find what I hoped for," Colston says, concerned that he might be falling into another false sense of security with someone he is meant to trust.

"Okay, I can promise you that I won't leave you high and dry."

Colston takes a deep breath. "Alright, see you soon," he says, clearly indicating to Melody that this is his final attempt to save himself.

The line disconnects, leaving Colston staring at Jordan and Kayra. "We'll have to put our plan on hold for a couple of hours. But Jordan, I beg you, get me singing," Colston pleads, still wary of Melody's promise.

Jordan realizes the desperation in

Colston and says, "Of course, Cole, even if I have to sing to you until you feel the drive to sing with me."

Colston stands and embraces him tightly.

Jordan matches the tightness while sharing a concerned glance with Kayra.

She silently prays for Colston's strength, sensing his waning hope that people can truly help him.

Colston, after hugging Jordan, turns to Kayra. "Love, I am going to need you to drive," he says before pulling her into his arms.

"Of course, sweetheart. If necessary, we can return later for your truck. It cannot remain in that parking lot for another night."

Colston rests his head against her shoulder, overwhelmed by a torrent of emotions. He is torn between the urge to cry and the desire to numb himself to it all. Fearful of experiencing any potential relief, he dreads the inevitable disappointment that would follow. He gently releases Kayra and says, "I'm going to get ready." Turning to Jordan, he adds, "JD, you know the studio is always open to you."

Jordan nods and takes a sip of his coffee. Colston grabs his cup and heads to the bedroom. Meanwhile, Kayra relaxes in the sunroom with her mug, waiting for Colston.

The fear of the unknown hangs heavily in the house, leaving an unsettling feeling in everyone's stomach. Jordan and Kayra are waiting and watching Colston, hoping to provide the support he needs while also serving as a constant reminder that he will be okay.

Colston sits on the bed, cradling his mug in his hands, staring blankly at the floor, unsure of what to do next. He can't continue living like this for much longer; he doesn't want to end it all prematurely. However, if the torment of the nightmares persists, he may be forced to spare himself from having to endure whatever the phantom has planned for him. He has fought for five years, and he is exhausted. He knows this struggle has changed him; he feels the burn of the poison every time he sings. All he wants is for the nightmares to release their grip on him. *First, you must let go.* His own voice echoes in his mind, startling him slightly. "This has too many interpretations," Colston whispers to his cooling coffee. *Yet, there is only one interpretation, one that you are most fearful of.*

Colston shakes his head in response, sips his coffee, then stands up and grabs clean clothes from the dresser.

Kayra is sitting in the sunroom, which is notably devoid of sunlight, and can't shake the feeling that she is being watched. She wants to leave the room, but thoughts of Colston compel her to endure her discomfort. This is her creative space, and she refuses to be driven out. The three large windows overlook their large backyard, the primary feature that sold her on this house. The yard is enclosed by a privacy fence, with the top of the 6-foot fence barely visible above the large leafy bushes that line the fence. *Come on, Kayra, breathe. Don't let the paranoia get to you.* She is attempting to calm her nerves, but it is difficult knowing that someone is intent on taking Colston again. She understands that if that man succeeds, she may never see him again. Perhaps she could persuade Colston to report it to the police once more. With the new note in conjunction with the previous one, there might be a chance they would take it seriously and increase patrols on their street.

"Kay?" The gentle voice of Colston breaks her thoughts.

She tilts her head back and looks up at him, noticing that he has been crying. Rising to her feet and standing before him, she gently runs her hands over his face. "Baby, I am so sorry," she leans into his chest; she feels his arms wrap around her.

Colston says bleakly, "Ready to go?"

"Yeah,"

They bid Jordan goodbye, as Colston grabs the note off the coffee table and places it in his wallet before they leave the house.

Once Kayra pulls onto the road, Colston catches glimpses of the clock through the gaps between the trees.

"Hon, before we go to the therapist, could you drive by the clock?" Colston asks.

Kayra shoots him a worried glance and asks, "Why?"

"We shared a dream--"

"Nightmare more like it. Colston, please stop doing this. There is going to be nothing there."

That seems to have woken him up. Shaking his head, he says, "You're right; I'm sorry. I guess I'm just scared about this session."

"Honey, listen to me: if this session with Melody doesn't help, I want you to seek out another therapist, one who will actually help you. I am tired of seeing you looking so lost. Yes, revisiting trauma is difficult, but you should feel as though you are making progress." She says, glancing at his chest before briefly meeting his eyes.

"Kay," he says, taking hold of her hand. "It was not your fault." His voice is soft.

Kayra's eyes begin to blur as she squeezes his hand. "It is the only visible mark, and it's over your heart..." Tears stream down her face.

"Babe, pull over; let me drive," Colston offers.

"Cole, what was said in the dream, you recall?" she asks tearfully.

Colston knows exactly what she is referring to: "A rare few are destined to suffer at the hands of others." He sighs.

"Why did it have to be you? I want to save you. Will you ever tell me the full truth about what happened in that house? Baby, the way you screamed... I have never heard anything like that come from a living being." Kayra has pulled over and is holding his face, her eyes pleading.

"I honestly don't know." He holds her gaze. "I'd prefer that you draw your own conclusions about what transpired based on the condition in which you found me and what I have shared with you."

"Why?" she whispers, her voice barely audible as her hands gently trace his face. "That is not going to help you! When I opened that door, I thought you were..." She stammers, refusing to say what she had thought.

Colston takes her hands and holds them between them. "In that moment, I was closer to death, but I just couldn't let go. I don't want to share what I keep close to my chest because I'm ashamed that I failed to escape," he says.

Feeling Kayra's death grip and hearing the sound of her choked emotions, "You did escape," she whispers.

"Physically, yes, but mentally..."

"Cole, he can't get you again."

Colston is not going to tell her that there is no way to stop him. "I know; I hate this because I feel like I am just in a larger cell," he says. "I understand that it is wrong to wish death upon someone." He sighs and shakes his head.

Kayra returns one hand to the steering wheel, getting back on the road and holding the back of his hand against her wet cheek. She then pulls into the parking lot and parks next to his truck.

He leans over and, with his free hand, brushes away her tears. "I'm here, babe; I am right here," he says before kissing her.

She kisses him, yet the tears continue to flow.

"Rest; I'll be back." He gently pulls away and leaves the car.

He gazes up at the building, a revolting

sensation settling in his gut. It has been less than twenty-four hours since his last visit. His knees tremble, and his shoulders feel heavy. Can he trust that Melody won't leave him gasping for air as the poison finally overwhelms him? Can he endure the weight of scrutiny? A look he has encountered so often from others that it has led him to question the validity of his own truth. His stomach churns once more with anxiety.

He hears the car door open. "Colston, are you okay?" Kayra asks after watching him stand there for five minutes, staring at the building.

Colston wants to collapse. "I----can't----do----this!" He cries.

Kayra notices a few people walking by turn their heads at Colston's cry. She quickly shuts the door and rushes to his side, immediately grasping his hand. "Together."

Colston gazes at her, his chest heaving and his face streaked with tears. He swallows hard, closing his eyes for a moment to gather his wits. "To--get----her," he stammers.

Hand in hand, the husband and wife take their first step in unison. Colston continues to question how Kayra could still love him.

Kayra pulls the door open, and Colston holds it ajar with his other hand while guiding her under his arm and inside. Their hands remain intertwined.

As Colston climbs the stairs, he feels his mouth dry out and hears the phantom's laughter echoing in his head, triggering a headache. He pleads silently for it to stop.

"Cole?" Kayra asks, alarmed, as he leans against the wall, shaking.

Kayra wonders if this is what happens every time he comes here. If so, she now understands the weariness and lost expression in his eyes. She just wants to take him home. "Honey, I am so sorry. You haven't received any help from Todd; instead, he's made you even more withdrawn."

Colston looks at her with a fearful truth. "He----has----traumatized------me."

"Let's go home and figure out something else," Kayra says.

The hopelessness in Colston's eyes is palpable. "As------much----as----it----hurts----I----need to----try."

The door to the stairwell opens, and a soft, pleasant voice calls down, "Mr. Driscoll, I am glad you came."

Colston looks up from his position halfway up the first flight of stairs, fearfully anticipating the switch that might occur once they are alone. "Col--Colston. This----is----my----wife, Ka--Kayra."

Melody rushes down to meet them, genuine concern etched on her face. "Let's move up to the landing," she says.

Kayra briefly releases his hand to readjust her arm beneath his, their forearms pressing together and their hands clasped. "I've got you, babe."

Colston can't get his legs to move, and it feels as though his mind is splitting open. "I------want------relief!" The words escape his cold throat as he painfully inhales the frigid air, which causes him to cough.

Melody stands on the step above him. "Colston, I want you to go somewhere in your mind, a place where you feel most at peace. It doesn't have to be a location you can visit in real life, but it certainly can be. Just make sure it's a place that belongs to you." Melody's gentle voice guides Colston into a state of tranquility, a calm he has only ever experienced with Kayra, Jordan, and his father.

Riding this state of tranquility, he reflects on where he feels the most at peace. The answer is simple: it is the place that brings him the greatest joy. He takes a few deep breaths to immerse himself in that moment, envisioning, "I am on a stage, ready to captivate an audience with my voice. However--" Colston is about to reveal that with every note sung, a burning sensation ignites in his throat.

"No, Colston, just be present. Whatever is troubling you, try not to focus on it," Melody says. She then turns to Kayra, "This is also how you can help him; sometimes he just needs a reminder that a place like that exists and that he can go there whenever he needs to." Her tone is not condescending in her explanation. "Mrs. Driscoll, I want to be transparent with you. Yesterday's meeting was not the smoothest, and I want to apologize to both of you."

Colston hears that, and his knees buckle.

"Whoa!" Kayra exclaims, trying to support Colston.

"Colston, can we please move up to the

landing?" Melody asks, reaching around his shoulder.

Colston reestablishes himself in reality, sobbing, but he easily ascends the four steps to the landing.

"Colston, talk to me. What happened?" Melody asks, noticing that Kayra has not let go of his hand this entire time.

"You just vetted my story I told yesterday. Instead of leaving me to appear as though I'm in the wrong." He speaks with a tremor in his voice.

Melody is nearly reduced to tears by that sentiment. "I can see that your wife loves you deeply and is protective of you. I want her to know this as well as you. My role here is to help you."

"Thank you!" Kayra says.

Melody nods at Kayra. "Colston, can we move upstairs?"

Colston nods, straightening his posture, and shows no intention of letting go of Kayra. He walks with a lighter step, feeling confident for the first time in a long while.

Climbing the stairs, relief fills the Driscolls with every step; someone is finally going to help. Upon reaching the suite, Colston quickly notes the brightly lit reception area. Melody opens the door and leads them into the suite.

"Mrs. Driscoll, you can sit out here," Melody says. "Shall we go to the room?"

Colston can sense the open door to his right; he avoids looking at it, not wanting that dark, cold room to extinguish his hopefulness. He kisses Kayra and holds her hand as she sits down in one of the five chairs around the room. Kayra pats his hand, noticing his hesitation. "Love, breathe. If it becomes too overwhelming, I will be right out here."

Melody appears on Colston's left. "If at any time you feel overwhelmed, we can stop; I promise."

Colston takes a deep breath and turns to face the room. He freezes in fear, yet simultaneously experiences a sense of defiant relief. The room before him is bright and inviting. He gazes at Melody, his eyes filled with concern.

"Colston, don't worry. It will be okay." Her voice is gentle.

"You sure?" Colston asks.

She steps in front of him, her eyes filled with sadness. "Colston, I want to express my thoughts freely. I have met all of Todd's twenty clients, and he is not as strict with them as he is with you. Currently, all of them are within the first year of Todd's two-year rule, except for you, who are approaching five years."

Colston lowers his head. "It makes it sound like I don't want to get better, when I truly do!" he exclaims, with a primal intensity.

"There is no doubt that you want to rid yourself of the memory of your kidnapping. I have a theory, but please keep in mind that each therapist has their own methods of helping and should not criticize others' approaches. However, things aren't adding up. Correct me if I am wrong, but the police have written off your kidnapping as a hoax, correct?"

Colston gazes at her, rendered speechless as he attempts to clear his mind in order to avoid disrupting this dream.

Melody observes the fear of acceptance reflected in Colston's eyes, while simultaneously sensing his desperate desire to embrace the knowledge that someone, an outsider, is genuinely on his side. She strives to maintain her composure, even as she feels the urge to vent about Todd. It is essential for her to remain professional. "He's trying to pressure you into conceding to the less-than-stellar evidence suggesting that you are responsible for this. He aims to assist the police department by forcing you to admit that it was merely a creative stunt that went awry."

Colston shakes his head; it makes sense, but it is not true.

"Frankly, by doing this, Todd is just as irrational as the fan who abducted you.

Colston lets out a strangled breath and says, "Thank you."

Melody nods and gestures toward the room. Her demeanor is gentle, not forceful. Colston stands there; he finally feels heard. "I am sorry; this gentle way is a nice change."

"No need to apologize."

Colston begins to move his body. As he enters the bright, warm room, he sits down heavily and wipes away his lingering tears.

They sit in a long silence until Melody gently breaks it with this. "So before I share some ways to help yourself, what did you find at the house?"

He rubs his hands together while staring at the floor. "I found that most of it----was--burned----but----the walls----that----made my cell still----stood." He takes a deep breath and taps his head, looking up. "This--is me fi--fighting----that cold----that dark. What I----had--hoped to gain, I got----the opposite."

He grabs his wallet from his pocket and pulls out the note. "I found this----in the--rubble----in front of the hole."

He hands the note over.

Melody takes the paper and reads it. After a moment, she looks up and says, "This paper is new."

Colston nods.

"Is this from your kidnapper?"

Colston nods once more and dryly states, "My phantom lives."

"Phantom? Why give him that name?" This question is posed not as a challenge but rather as a search for deeper understanding.

Colston breathes a sigh of relief and takes a moment to reflect on why he decided to personify him as the phantom. Colston voices his thought process, saying, "On the way to the house, my friend Jordan urged me to speak so I wouldn't isolate myself in the nightmare. When I spoke, 'My Phantom' just rolled off my tongue." Tears of anger well in Colston's eyes. "Why--why can I not call him what he truly is--my captor, my tormentor?" His fists are clenched together, trembling slightly. He looks up at Melody; anger and pain are evident, but there is a dangerous desperation in his gaze.

Melody holds his gaze. "Your mind is trying to help you. Referring to him as your captor or tormentor gives him power and leverage over you. Calling him 'phantom' is a way for you to reclaim that power." The light in her eyes and the tone of her voice suggest that Colston should be celebrating.

Yes, he ought to be, as this marks the first time in five years. He feels as though he has taken his first step toward actual recovery rather than merely masking his struggles. However, in his mind, he is dragging his body toward the cell door.

"Colston, what is on your mind?" Her voice is gentle.

"You have restored my hope after all," he says, dropping his head in frustration. "I still have a ton to do."

"You just need to remember that you are fighting and that you are on the right path."

"He's going to come for me again," Colston says.

He sees Melody glance at the paper once more, then back at him before saying, "Alert the police." However, the moment these words leave her lips, she realizes how futile this action is.

"That's not going to stop him. I just hope nobody gets harmed in the process," he says.

"Think he'll try publicly this time?"

"To some extent, I feel as though I must always be on guard. Thus, wearing me down and making me vulnerable to an easy takeover. I can't shake the thought that my constant fighting may ultimately lead to my demise."

"Do you really believe he would go to such extremes, even after all this time?"

"I might sound crazy, but if the insane side is in full control, I am as good as dead. If the rational, 'fan' part of him is in control, I may have a chance."

He waits for the disapproving look from Melody that would label him as a crazy person. Instead, he receives a look of understanding; he struggles to speak through his building emotions, "I looked upon both sides over the course of those ten days, the dark eyes that were alight with the fire of hell. It was rare to see the bright blue of childish wonder." His voice is filled with resignation.

Melody cocks her head and says, "Colston, if you expect help, you can't have already given up on yourself."

"It----is------hard," Colston begins, his lungs filled with fury. "I was under his control for ten days; everything about him is etched into my memory." He takes a cold breath, causing his teeth to tingle with sensitivity. "After----the--------fire------ he became a--------phantom. Leaving----me-- with------nothing."

Melody observes Colston descending into a self-destructive spiral; she must loosen the noose around his neck. "He may have slipped into the shadows and embarked on a long con, but he has made a mistake," Melody says, a hint of a smile playing on her lips.

Colston gazes at her, his heart leaping from its hollow depths, curious about what she might see.

She hands the note back and says, "He told you that you'd be together. You will be ready, even if you are weary from waiting. He's in this to feel in control. If you meet him on level ground, you'll throw him off balance."

Colston cast her a weary glance. "He knows I'll fight and has had five years to prepare. The first time, he prepared for a year and taunted me for three months leading up to the day."

"Taunted you? How?" Melody asks, now questioning the validity of Todd's claims.

"He hijacked my videos and added creepy messages at the end. We couldn't identify the source; I made changes to my channel, but it didn't stop. He waited until Kayra had left for the store to sneak in and caught me off guard while I was singing." Colston's stomach feels hollow. "I am not a fighter; in the physical sense, violence is not my nature. But it is in his." He shivers and shakes his head, reaching up to the sides of his head. "Pl----eas, I want------the------memories, night----mares to------stop."

"Take a moment to go to your happy place and breathe. Afterward, I will introduce another tool, but this one will require a bit more energy."

Colston nods and concentrates on his breathing to calm his mind, just enough to visualize a dark, empty stage. The more he attempts to create, the sharper and deeper the cold becomes. "I can only envision an empty stage."

"Are you strong in that place?"

"For the moment," Colston says. "Is it meant to get easier with practice? What if I don't want to do this for the rest of my life?"

"You are going to have to trust me."

"How am I supposed to do that when I will only be meeting with you for four more sessions?" he questions.

"I was going to save this until after the session, but you are not going back to Todd; I am taking over your treatment." She pauses, noticing a sudden dark shift in Colston. He went from shivering and looking lost yet hopeful to sitting straight up with an expression of fearful defiance. "Colston?" she asks cautiously.

Colston remains unresponsive, his gaze unwavering. Internally, he is paralyzed by fear; he is bound and unable to move, while a tiny voice attempts to break through the terror, urging him, "Cole, she is trying to help you. She just phrased it poorly. Don't shut her out; be honest. She is your last chance at actual survival!"

He struggles against the bonds that tighten with every movement he makes, the breath being squeezed from his lungs and the phantom's laughter drowning out any thoughts of escape.

"COLSTON!" The panicked voice of Kayra cuts through the chaos, freeing him from his binds and silencing the laughter.

He finds himself on the floor, staring up at the ceiling, with Melody and Kayra looking down at him. His heart races in his chest.

"Sorry," he says breathlessly as he attempts to sit up.

"No, stay lying down. At least until your heart rate returns to normal. Are you feeling any pain?" Melody asks.

Colston assesses himself; he is aware of Kayra's hand resting on his chest and the other gripping his right hand. He shifts slightly to gauge any pain. "No pain," he says, attempting to relax in order to slow his racing heart.

"What happened?" Kayra asks.

Melody looks at Colston, the fear in her eyes evident. "I triggered an extreme fear response, and I am truly sorry. Colston, are you afraid of the repercussions from Todd?"

"No," he replies effortlessly. "It was------the------phrasing. The feeling of being tossed around and having no control over what happens to me."

The light of understanding illuminates Melody's eyes. "My gosh, of course, that is my fault for assuming. Right after I asked you to trust me. I'm going to touch your wrist to check your pulse; is that okay?"

Colston nods and rests his head on the floor.

"I am sorry; I did slightly panic when your eyes rolled back into your head," Melody says as she begins to count.

"It's fine, and we are both grateful that you brought Kayra in here." Colston says, looking at Kayra.

"Yes,"

"Colston, would you like to sit up slowly?" Melody asks, sliding her hand under his left shoulder blade. Kayra shifts her hand from his chest to support his right shoulder.

He sits up almost entirely on his own. Keeping his breathing steady.

Melody asks, "Kayra, do you want to stand in front? Let's get him standing up. Are you ready, Colston?"

He is holding both of Kayra's hands. "On your own time, Cole," she says.

"Let's go," Colston says.

They help him to his feet; he experiences a brief moment of lightheadedness, but it quickly subsides.

"Alright?" Melody asks.

Colston nods.

"I think we should call it; I don't want to overdo it. I don't mean to leave you hanging, but seeing you pass out is a clear sign that we should take a step back."

"Could you please email me the other tools you were planning to show me? I would like to have more resources to rely on," Colston asks.

"Gladly," she says, offering a smile.

"Thank you, and yes, I want to continue working with you." He gazes at Kayra. "I finally see the light through the nightmare."

They shake hands with Melody. Colston exits the room, feeling his ground solidifying. He feels Kayra squeezing his hand. Outside the suite, Colston stops and pulls Kayra in front of him. "Are you okay?" he asks, gently stroking her cheek.

"It terrified me to see you on the floor, unresponsive, Colston." She grabs his hand, which was gently stroking her cheek, and looks him directly in the eyes. "We are meant to grow old together, dying hours apart. I want a longer life with you."

Colston, despite the assistance Melody is providing, is struggling to fully promise a complete life. However, he wants to instill hope in her. "We are going to be okay," Colston whispers with genuine sincerity.

"Really?" Kayra asks, her eyes shining with hope.

"Yes," Colston seals it with a kiss.

Chapter Eight: The Burden of Truths

After convincing Kayra that he is fit to drive, Colston gets behind the wheel of his truck and heads home, reflecting on the session. He feels a renewed sense of control and support, and he is grateful to have met Melody.

Pulling into the driveway, he steps out and meets Kayra on the opposite side of the truck. Together, they walk toward the house.

Upon opening the door, they are greeted by the sound of Jordan singing in Colston's studio. Colston and Kayra exchange smiles, make their way to the kitchen island, and sit down to listen.

Jordan is in Colston's studio practicing *Wind's Melody*. It is proving to be very difficult. The soft, haunting melody and the simple tempo, not even the lyrics, are the problem. Instead, it is Jordan's inability to let go of his worries. He can't get through the second verse without being reduced to tears, his throat tightening, and making it impossible for him to continue. He stands alone in Colston's studio, acutely aware that Colston is alive, yet his mind relentlessly tortures him.

"Enfolding me gently, embracing my soul. Coaxing out my melody and making me whole. In the depths of sorrow," he pauses, his throat tightening with emotion.

He slides the headphones off and stands hunched over, his hands resting on the desk.

"He's not dead!" He yells in his mind.

Then his own voice speaks in a studious and hardhearted way, *"Yet, you are watching him die, slowly driven to madness, unable to prevent it from happening."*

"Shut up!" Jordan's entire body trembles. *"I will be here to ensure he knows that he is not alone."*

"Ha, and risk your livelihood? Doubtful. Additionally, you do not bear the burden that Colston does. You weren't there. He can share his experience, and you can demonstrate your understanding. However, it ultimately comes down to this: in the end, it is Colston who must overcome this challenge. It is not your responsibility."

"STOP IT!" Jordan screams in his mind, while on the outside, he has knocked over the microphone.

"Jordan!" Colston exclaims, his voice laced with concern as he walks in, having noticed the absence of singing.

Jordan turns to face Colston, his eyes filled with tears and an overwhelming sense of remorse. However, before he can even begin to explain himself, he notices a familiar glow in Colston's features, one he hasn't seen since the kidnapping.

Colston walks over to Jordan and places a reassuring hand on his shoulder.

"Hey, buddy, sit down." Colston invites gently.

"I'm sorry," Jordan apologizes meekly as he takes a seat.

"Don't worry about that," Colston says, shutting the door before sitting down in the secondary chair. "JD, you came here to help me. Buddy," Colston takes a deep breath, and his eyes shift to the downed microphone. "What is wrong?"

Jordan lowers his head. "Nothing, the song is harder than I expected," he lies.

Colston shouldn't be surprised by this. The ominous sense of impending death makes the truth even more difficult to accept. Colston realizes that he should not be privy to their truths while he has not fully disclosed his own.

While Colston sits in silence, stewing in the lie he was just fed without hesitation or even ensuring it made sense, Jordan endures the harsh criticism of his own cold voice. It mocks him, saying, *"Gosh, Jordan, do you really think Colston is dense? A singer is struggling with a song, poor baby. Your best friend is suffering under his mental strain, and you can't put forth a convincing lie to conceal your truth. You could simply talk about the weather, as you always do. But you will remain fearful, and it will begin to show; it already has. Be honest and open with him; nothing you say can hurt him more than what he is already facing."*

Jordan screams in his mind to silence the voice, *"HE IS VULNERABLE! I NEED TO PROTECT HIM!"*

"Jordan!?" Colston yells in alarm as blood begins to flow from Jordan's nose. "Kayra!" Colston rushes to support Jordan's trembling body and gently lowers him to the ground.

"Colston, what is it?" Kayra asks as she rushes into the room.

Colston turns, panic evident on his face, with Jordan's blood smeared on his shoulder. "He started bleeding from his nose and shaking," he says, turning back to Jordan. "Jordan, come on," Colston pleads.

"I'll call--" Kayra begins.

"I need to protect you," Jordan whispers as his body stops shaking, and tears mix with the blood.

"What?" Colston asks, his voice trembling.

Kayra rushes out to retrieve a damp cloth for Jordan.

Jordan, with blurry vision, gazes at Colston. "I don't want my truth to destroy you," he says, his face crumpling and his chin quivering. "I know you saw through my lie, but please don't ask me to reveal it. Just... please, Colston."

"Okay, I won't," Colston says, shocked.

Kayra returns with a warm rag. Kneeling beside Colston, she hands the rag to Jordan. "Here, JD."

Colston feels as though he has been kicked in the chest. "JD, you don't need to protect me from that," he whispers.

Kayra looks at them in confusion and asks, "What is it?"

"The truth you are clinging to is destroying you, Colston!" Jordan exclaims in desperation as he sits up. Colston remains motionless. "I don't want to add to our pain; we will endure together, but in silence. Let the music dominate." Jordan's face crumples once more, and he breaks into heavy sobs.

Colston pulls him into a hug, and Kayra joins the embrace. "How long can we hold out?" she whispers.

"We'll have to open up sometime," Jordan says. "When we do, we'll lay it all out."

"I think that is for the best," Kayra says.

"Let me review the emails that Melody will send me. For now, I want to savor this small victory," Colston states, expressing his peace.

The embrace is broken, and Kayra leaves from them.

"So, what song are you going to sing for the solo portion of the concert?" Jordan asks, eager to change the subject.

Colston chuckles, "Let's get you cleaned up first." He stands and extends his hand to Jordan.

Jordan simply stares. "Is this what you do daily?" He takes hold of Colston's hand.

"Yes, it's not a nice feeling," Colston says as he helps Jordan to his feet. "You eventually get used to it."

"I don't want to get used to it," Jordan says, not immediately letting go of Colston as he feels a bit unsteady. "How do you sing with this pressure?"

"You don't have to; you can tell me. It won't hurt," Colston says, using music to break through Jordan's defenses. He takes a deep breath. *"This is not the end; just let us win. I'll hold you as you fall; you always were there for me. What is it that weighs heavy? What are you feeling? We've been through too much now. Don't let it crush."* Colston pauses, realizing that this conversation is a two-way street.

"Did you just relyric, His Theme, from Undertale?" Jordan asks, smiling in disbelief and comfort.

"Yeah, how was it?"

"You hit heartstring chords." He sighs, "I am terrified of losing you. Every time Kayra called after a nightmare or whenever we got together to sing, I could see that struggle; that man stole so much from you. I can't shake the feeling that I am watching you fade away."

Colston flinches at the final line, not for any other reason than its truth.

"You'd be correct," he states bluntly, "but it has been halved and will continue to diminish further."

"How can I help?" Jordan asks.

"Just don't give up on me," Colston says.

"Not a chance, brother."

They leave the room, and Colston takes the rag to the laundry room, where he removes his shirt. He then goes to his bedroom and grabs a fresh one, throwing it on as he walks down the hall. He finds Jordan in the kitchen and, glancing to his right, sees Kayra sitting in the sunroom. He walks to the sunroom and wraps his arms around her.

"Hi, babe," she says with a smile. "Aren't you going to sing?"

"Jordan is cleaning up and getting some water," Colston says. "Are you alright?" She feels tense in his arms.

Kayra contemplates confiding in Colston about her increasing discomfort. She tilts her head upward and smiles, saying, "Yes, love. I'm just tired."

"Then rest, babe; maybe later we'll go out for dinner."

Kayra turns in her chair and gives a concerned look. "You think it's safe to go out?"

Colston moves around and kneels in front of her. "Baby, yes, this is how I fight back: by getting out and refusing to let him keep me trapped in any aspect of my life." He runs his fingers through her hair and whispers, "I refuse to allow you to be confined." Tears begin to well in the corners of his eyes. "You have beauty to share with the world, and by the love of God, I will not let it go to waste."

Kayra caresses his tear-soaked cheeks and says, "I am scared."

"Trust me, it will be fine... Please, trust me." He gently pulls her in for a kiss.

"Okay, Colston," she says, running her hand down his chest and around his back as they stand up. "You sing, and I will rest."

"Okay."

Kayra leaves the sunroom and walks past Jordan. "You alright?"

"I am. Are you?"

Kayra doesn't respond verbally; she allows the heavy silence to speak for her. Jordan offers her a hug, and while in the embrace, she whispers, "Thank you for being here."

Kayra pulls away and heads to the living

room to lie on the couch. Jordan notices Colston gazing out over the yard.

"Cole?" he asks, taking a few steps toward the sunroom.

Colston turns to Jordan and says, "JD, I think Kayra and I need to leave... We need to move." His voice is breathless.

Jordan joins Colston in the sunroom. "Have you discussed this with Kayra?"

"No, I just... This place is filled with so much bullshit. The situation with Abigail and my own issues; I want to provide her with a better life. I want to start fresh." Colston gazes at Jordan. "I have had eyes on me for the past five years, and by extension, so have Kayra and you."

Jordan shakes his head. "We'll figure this out together. For now, let's get lost in song." He pats Colston on the shoulder.

Colston nods and turns to leave the sunroom. "I have a surprise for my solo performance at the concert."

"Really?" Jordan asks.

"An original song," Colston says, feeling a flush of heat in his cheeks due to a mix of excitement and anxiety.

Jordan is grinning at the news; he has been waiting for years for Colston to write his own music. The way he injects new life into covers is remarkable. Now, he gets to experience the joy and excitement of sharing his own stories. "How long have you been working on this?"

"About four months now." Colston says.

Entering the studio, Jordan takes the secondary chair, allowing Colston full access to the computer. As Colston opens the document containing the lyrics, he asks, "Why aren't you on the solo bill this year? For the past seven years of this concert, you've always been included." He turns to face his friend, who meets his gaze.

Jordan isn't going to withhold this from Colston out of fear that his head might explode. "I relinquished my spot to you," he says.

"What? Why? I made it onto the duet bill; that is great enough for me," Colston says.

Jordan shakes his head. "I am tired of the beauty contest. The struggle you have endured for the past five years. Yet, you sing; that is truly inspiring. However, those who listen have no idea of that struggle. Kayra and I do."

Colston, in tears, examines himself, his barrel chest giving him an unsightly, round appearance. However, he never allowed that to affect him. Suddenly, a rush of memories floods his mind, his mother force-feeding him microwaveable meals before his father arrived home, only for her to insist he eat dinner afterward. If he vomited, he would be scolded and spanked before being sent to bed. Colston cherished the moments he spent at school, as they provided an escape from that treatment.

He suddenly reels back at the memory. "What the hell?" he asks himself.

"Colston?" Jordan asks, his voice filled with concern.

Colston effortlessly breaks free from the forgotten memory, stating, "Everyone has their own tastes. I don't fit the flavor profile for most. However, I am grateful for the 2 million subscribers I have on my channel."

"I initiated the fight; your voice deserves to be heard."

Colston simply nods and replies, "Thank you. Should I stick to a cover, then?" He genuinely appreciates what Jordan is doing for him, but he feels Jordan is beginning to cross the line of wrestling control from him. To prevent an outburst, Colston decides to end the conversation.

"Hell, no! Give them a surprise. Make them regret not inviting you sooner."

"Oh, stop it," Colston says, playfully. "I am not the only singer out there."

"I know, but the way you infuse each song you sing with new life is truly remarkable."

He blushes and says, "You give me way too much credit. Anyway, the song is called *That Line*. The story revolves around our struggle toward the ever-pressing line. This line, which varies for each individual, represents the end of the fight. The concern is how much of ourselves remains once that line is crossed and the fighting ceases."

Jordan raises an eyebrow and asks, "Can I have a sample?"

"Sure, I don't have the complete instrumental. I outsourced it to Decklin last week. However, I do have verses one and two, as well as the first chorus."

Jordan smiles as Colston picks up the microphone and adjusts the output settings for both the speakers and headphones, ensuring that Jordan has the full experience.

Colston begins the track, coming in on a count of five and starting with a purposeful half-breath and tremble in his voice. *"My heart beats within my bruised chest, beating fierce and strong; I am not yet finished. The line beckons; wearily, my legs press on. No time to wonder what awaits once that line is bridged. My wish is lessons learned remain.*

I fight; I fight for my life. I'm always left puzzled, with my life on the line. Drawing in a pained breath, I scream fire!

Flames rapidly wane low, threatening a bitter chill to creep within. That fire, my spark, my youth, and strength to face the world. Chasing dreams with reckless abandon, the weight of the world threatening but never slowing my stride. That line looms; am I about to surrender my flame? Am I ready to? Why the long, drawn-out fight?" Colston extends the final note for a few seconds because the next run of the chorus is meant to come in underneath.

Jordan is left speechless as a tear of pride trickles down his cheek. Colston lets out a long sigh and turns to him. "Well?"

"Holy shit, Cole! They are going to love it. However, for the few of us who know, that line better not be in your sights."

Colston chooses not to tell the truth; this line represents the meeting that is inescapable. "I left you on a cliffhanger."

"I know. I want to be able to follow that song with our mashup." Jordan pauses, slipping into thought. "The amount of times I have been blindsided by double-edged lyrics is one thing. I wonder if the phenomenon with the two songs was intentional or accidental."

Colston pauses to reflect on his words. "Oh, how my story is portrayed as a tragedy, while yours is depicted as hope amidst tragedy. Yet, they unfold differently by the end of the song."

"Yes, and they complement each other better than I expected; their melodies do, at least," Jordan says.

"I like to think they did it intentionally. Subverting the audience's expectations can be effective when executed properly. These two songs achieve this perfectly and both convey a sense of hope."

Jordan abruptly breaks eye contact, struggling to hold back tears.

Colston places his hand on his shoulder and says, "Don't hide; we are fighting together."

Jordan looks at Colston and says, "How can I still fear that you are dying? You are right here in front of me."

"How is it that I am still trapped in that cold nightmare? I am here with you, free and warm. In our----moments----of cl----clarity----it seeks----to----destroy." Colston closes his eyes and clenches his fists in frustration.

"Cole?"

"I'm fine; I----have----a lot--of----work." Colston says, noting that the urge to isolate is growing. He envisions the stage in his mind, still empty and now growing cold. "Let's get... out of here... and go to dinner." Colston opens his eyes.

"What? Are you sure?" Jordan asks.

Colston experiences a strong sense of déjà vu. "Yes, I want----to--celebrate----this----small yet impor---tant victory."

Jordan nods, and they exit the room.

Colston enters the living room and finds Kayra sleeping peacefully on the couch. He quietly kneels beside her, brushing her cheek gently. "Sorry to wake you, honey," he whispers.

Eyes still closed, she smiles and takes his hand. "I wouldn't want to be awakened by anyone else."

She opens her eyes, and his gaze reveals his emotions. "Colston, are you okay?"

His head drops in dejection. "Let's go to dinner." The effort required to keep the cold at bay is immense.

Kayra sits up and pulls him onto the couch. "Alright, baby," she says, looking up at Jordan with a smile. "What was that song?"

Jordan sighs, "Oh, that wasn't mine. That was all this guy." He gestures toward Colston.

"What? An original?" Kayra exclaims with delight.

"Indeed,"

Kayra pulls him into a kiss and then asks, "So, where are we going?"

"Comfort Crescendo Craves?" Colston proposes.

This restaurant holds countless happy memories for the three of them, and Colston believes it will provide a pleasant escape.

Jordan extends his hand to Colston, who takes it and allows himself to be pulled to his feet. "One hundred percent yes," Jordan says. His most treasured memory originates from that place. Twelve years ago, after a convention in Oklahoma, Jordan was taking the scenic route home. While passing through Payholt, Idaho, he stopped for a bite to eat and heard Colston for the first time. At that time, Colston was nineteen and had just reached 1,000 subscribers on his channel, while Jordan had 32,000 and was already familiar with Colston's work. Both were cover artists, and Colston was rapidly gaining popularity. At twenty-four, Jordan was astounded by how Colston brought the song to life, making it feel like he was hearing it for the first time. Jordan had planned to eat and perhaps sing a song or two before getting back on the road, but it turned into a four-hour singing session and the beginning of a very strong friendship.

Kayra smiles and nods.

They climb into Colston's truck and drive into town. It is nearly five o'clock, and the restaurant is bustling with activity. Despite the escalating pandemic, business continues as usual, with everyone striving to maintain a sense of normalcy. The atmosphere inside is almost as bleak as it is outside. Colston intensely fights off the biting cold and looming spiral of hopelessness that is feeding off the world around him.

Colston is positioned on Kayra's left side, while Jordan is on her right.

"Welcome! Three tonight?" the masked server asks.

"Yes," Colston replies.

"Do you intend to do karaoke?"

"Yes," Kayra replies.

Colston and Jordan smile at Kayra. Heads begin to turn, curious about who is bold enough to sing at a time like this. Excited whispers of Colston and Jordan's names start to fill the dining room.

"Okay, come this way."

They follow the server to a table in the back corner near the microphone, which is currently unoccupied.

Kayra slides into the rounded booth first, with the guys flanking her.

"It looks like we'll have to break the dam," Jordan says, gesturing toward the microphone while ignoring the eyes that are blatantly fixed on him.

Colston nods as he removes his mask.

"My name is Neil, and I'll--" The young server pauses mid-introduction, his eyes darting between Colston and Jordan. "I apologize; I'll be your server tonight. May I take your drink orders?" Neil is starstruck.

Colston smiles and says, "I would like a raspberry tonic water, please."

"Sure thing, Mr. Driscoll."

"And for you, Mrs. Driscoll?"

"Um, a lemonade, please."

"Coming right up. And for you, Mr. Youngblood."

Jordan smiles and responds, "I'll just have water, thank you."

"Alright, I will be back in a moment."

"I'll be right back," Jordan says.

Colston nods as he casually flips through the menu, although he does not have a strong appetite.

Jordan approaches the music selector. Ever since Colston suggested this place, this song called out to Jordan. *Whispers in the Dark* by Skillet. They collaborated on this track years ago.

He set it to go after the next random song so he could inform Colston.

Neil is currently bringing the drinks.

Colston requests a few more minutes to review the menu. As Jordan slides back into the booth, he mentions, "The song following this one is *Whispers in the Dark.*"

"You want to burst the dam wide open," Colston smiles. "Hon, if you're hungry, feel free to order. I might need to sing to work up an appetite."

"I also might not be able to eat a full meal," Jordan says.

"Me too." She looks up at Neil. "Perhaps we could hold off for a while, if that's alright?"

"Yes, might I suggest the family-sized plate of nachos?"

The three exchange a silent nod as Colston kisses Kayra before moving toward the stage. He takes his place at the microphone just moments before their song begins.

Shaking off the nerves, he reminds himself to trust his voice and Jordan. Performing in front of crowds is in their blood. Colston sings the first verse and chorus.

Kayra observes as the eyes of the room are drawn to her husband, who captivates everyone with his voice. Through his voice, he creates an atmosphere that is free of worry.

Jordan sings the second verse and chorus, and people are rocking along.

During the instrumental, Colston and Jordan enthusiastically play air guitars, while the dining room erupts in applause. The dreariness is dispelled, allowing everyone to relax for a moment.

Together, they sing the final run of the chorus. As thunderous applause erupts, they bow and return to their seats.

"That was great!" Colston exclaims, filled with pure exhilaration.

"Please, sing *Plagues!*" a young voice cries out.

The room falls silent as Colston and Jordan exchange glances.

"Can we have a second microphone?" Jordan asks.

This is a performance piece.

The room erupts into applause as a second microphone is added to the stage, and Colston and Jordan take their positions. Colston portrays Moses, while Jordan plays Ramses.

The emotions of the characters are vividly portrayed. The trust between Colston and Jordan is undeniable; one can easily lose themselves in the performance while the other adeptly follows.

After the applause subsides, Colston addresses the audience, saying, "Thank you so much. We are going to eat now." This was met with another round of applause.

"Wow, these people are really into it," Jordan says, smiling from ear to ear.

"How many professional singers simply

show up at a karaoke bar and perform?" Kayra asks.

Colston smiles shyly as he serves himself a small portion from the larger plate.

"Kayra, I have been thinking. I believe it would benefit both of us if we moved, don't you think?" Colston inquires.

"Would it be out of town or out of state?" She asks, dragging a chip through a mixture of cheese, olives, tomatoes, and guacamole before popping it into her mouth.

Colston finishes chewing and swallows. "What would you rather do?"

Kayra looks at him, her eyes filled with love and a longing to start anew. "I want to leave the state," she says, tears welling up in her eyes.

Colston nods and grabs her hand reassuringly. "I completely agree. What do you think of the West Coast, particularly around Dryad's Cove?" He casts a sly glance in Jordan's direction.

Jordan reacts dramatically. "You want to invade my stomping ground." He chomps down on a chip.

Colston smiles, "More like neighbors to enhance our musical capabilities. Together, we would be unstoppable.

Jordan licks the grease off his fingers. "Hmmm, alright." He chuckles heartily. "I love this idea!"

Neil approaches their table and quickly says, "Mr. Driscoll, this was left for you." He places a folded piece of paper beside Colston's arm and hurries off before Colston can thank him.

"So do I. Next week, we can start looking for places." Colston distractedly grabs the paper and opens it without looking at it yet. "I would love to be able to move in two months' time. Unless this pandi--" He glances at the paper.

Colston's mind is abruptly stripped of its calm and plunged into darkness and burning cold. His heart skips a beat as his throat constricts, leaving him struggling to breathe.

Kayra and Jordan spring into action, doing their best to avoid drawing attention. Jordan shifts and gently nudges Colston aside. He places his hand on Colston's arm and realizes he is freezing. Panic begins to set in for Jordan as he glances over at Kayra. She has taken the note from his hands and is visibly overwhelmed by fear.

A special request for My Colston: for old times' sake, I wish for him to sing *Ineffective*.

"Colston, please come back," Kayra pleads, gently shaking him.

Colston is already gone, trapped in his own mind, powerless to stop it.

The question, "What do you want?" left Colston's lips in a moment of pure desperation.

His captor's eyes flickered between love and hate, a tension heightened by the looming threat of being choked with his own vest.

"What do I want?" he swooped in close to whisper.

Colston shifted uncomfortably as the man moved again, demonstrating his remarkable speed and strength. The vest was shifted away from his throat, and as the man straightened up, Colston was pulled to his feet.

"What do I want?" he repeated, his voice a decibel louder. He pulled Colston close by his vest. "I want you to sing! But with reckless abandon. You have been conditioned to believe that practice makes perfect. It is the fear of failure, the fear of rejection, and the fear of fading into the shadows."

The last line came softly, and a hand reached out to caress his face, but Colston immediately jerked his head away.

"Don't touch me!" Colston growled.

Colston's back slammed against the wall, and he groaned as he once again found himself breathless.

"I don't care what you want! Now, Colston, listen." A hand firmly cupped the side of his face. "I have prepared four songs for you to sing. Trust your voice; believe in yourself."

Colston regains his awareness; he is still seated at the table in the restaurant. The paper is no longer in his hands.

"Colston, let's go," Jordan whispers to his right.

"He's here," Colston says, his voice trembling.

"That's why we need to go," Jordan pleads.

"Please, honey."

Colston, though terrified, must demonstrate to the phantom that he will not back down.

"I----need--to----sing--a--song." Colston says.

Kayra gently runs her hands down his face and cradles it. "You don't! Let's go home and call the police," she says.

"Sweetheart, please, I--need to. He's--going----to----come for----me; he's just wearing me down."

The fear in Kayra's eyes makes him wish he hadn't been so blunt.

"Just----don't----take----your----eyes off--of--me." He says, then looks at Jordan. "Could you set the song to *This is Gospel* by Panic! At The Disco and wait for my cue?"

Jordan's heart leaps with fear as he holds Colston's gaze for a moment, hoping for a telepathic connection. *"Any song but that one. Please!"* When Colston doesn't suggest another song, Jordan looks around and says, "We'll be here."

Colston nods as he approaches the stage. He flashes back to the moment just before singing the second song, which was *His Screams Echo, Unheard* by Steel Enigma.

The final waiting game was brutal on Colston's stress and anxiety levels due to the uncertainty that awaited him after the performance. Despite his efforts to push it from his mind, the overwhelming dread gnawed at him. He could not endure another cold night, another beating, or another song; he had to take a stand.

"Colston! Time to sing!" The voice of his captor echoed through the cold house, piercing his very soul. He struggled to stave off the breakdown that loomed. No amount of pleading, begging, or tears would save him. He understood that this was a do-or-die moment. As the bathroom door swung open, Colston locked eyes with his captor, holding steady.

The person, that monstrous presence, stood over him, holding his gaze with equally weary eyes. He remained at the door, crouching down, maintaining eye contact, and the venom that seeped from him made Colston's heart skip a beat. "You know that you are going to die here?"

Deep down, Colston was a wreck; that part of him he had locked away. Fear gnawed at his heart, tears streamed down his face, and his mind raced with thoughts of everything he would be missing. On the outside, he responded calmly, "I know; however, I will die knowing that you did nothing to change me."

He stands with the microphone in his hand, tears of fear, anger, and absolution streaming down his face. The room is silent. This song is his declaration, singing to reclaim his life. He glances at Jordan and nods to signal the beginning of the song.

The moment the song begins, the audience erupts, rallying around Colston as the room closes in on him. The words flow powerfully from his lips, and he must trust his voice with every line he sings. The sound begins to fade, and his vision blurs, barely managing to hold himself together and continue singing. He is conveying to the phantom that he will fight, that he and his voice belong to no one but himself. The final run of the chorus escapes his lips. He hears nothing; his heart pounds against his numb chest, and his mind... His mind is there, trapped: bound, cold, sick, and dying. The last note transforms into an anguished shout.

Kayra and Jordan rush in, unable to endure this any longer. The room is enveloped in stunned silence. Jordan grabs the microphone while Kayra attempts to get Colston to focus on her. She gently lifts his head, gazing into his vacant, unblinking eyes.

Jordan is trying to shield him from the increasingly restless audience. "We need to go!" Jordan exclaims.

"Cole?!" Kayra exclaims, rubbing his cold face. "Please, I need you to come back."

She receives nothing, not even a flicker of emotion in his eyes.

Jordan observes Kayra's increasing desperation.

"Hey, what is going on?" This voice rises above the others, filled with annoyance.

"Sorry," Jordan says as he wraps an arm around Colston and scans the room for a back door.

"Hey, get this act together and entertain us!" The voice calls out again, this time accompanied by others.

Jordan turns, still shielding Colston. "My friend and I came to have fun; however, the last song was painful for him. I ask for your patience," Jordan pleads with the crowd.

He redirects his attention to Colston and attempts to take a step, guiding him to the back, away from the public's gaze.

"Jordan, watch out!" a young, familiar voice calls out.

Jordan whips his head around in time to see a burly-looking cowboy trying to grab him. He jumps beside Colston to evade the man's grasp, then leaps back to shield Colston and Kayra. Jordan throws his slender frame against the burly man, who simply takes a measured step back.

"Colston, we need to go!" Kayra screams

as the burly man punches Jordan in the face.

Colston's eyes shift to see Jordan crumple to the floor, and several screams erupt throughout the room.

Colston steps back until he is parallel to Jordan, spins Kayra so her back is against his chest, and wraps his arms around her. "Sir, please, we are just going to leave!" he proclaims, exposing his back.

"The hell you are!" the man roars. "We paid for dinner and entertainment."

"Jed, sit your ass down! You know damn well you don't pay for entertainment. Leave them alone; the police are on their way," the manager yells from the kitchen door.

"Good, that little shit on the floor needs to be locked up."

Before Colston or Kayra can protest, the manager speaks again, "No, Jed, they are coming for you, and don't you dare claim self-defense. I, along with everyone in this establishment, witnessed what happened."

Kayra, still protected by Colston, moves to check on Jordan. Colston shifts his body slightly to maintain his position between them as much as possible.

"Oh, well, if I'm going to jail," Jed says as he grabs Colston by the back of his shirt.

Colston is instantly filled with anger. He spins around to confront Jed, who is twice his size.

"Keep your hands off me!" His voice is deep and resonant, filled with frustration. "Leave my family alone!"

Jed's expression softens, and he takes a

step back.

Kayra wakes Jordan as Colston drops heavily beside him and asks, "JD, are you okay?"

"I got hit in the face," Jordan says, his voice filled with pain and indignation. He is unable to open his eyes.

"Shhh, just rest," Kayra says.

Kayra places a hand on Colston's, but he pulls away sharply. Startled, she watches as he gets up and walks away.

"Cole? Colston!" Kayra calls out.

Chapter Nine: Poison Runneth Over

Colston pushes out of the restaurant and onto the street, his hands buried deep in his pockets as he turns left, seeking solace. He becomes aware of how irresponsible this behavior is. Is he wanting to be taken?

They must be getting tired of this... because I sure as hell am.

He walks beneath the weight of his actions. Driven by shame and guilt, he faces yet another public display. He has concealed this darkness for so long, and now he is beginning to falter. Why?

He had observed the frustration in Kayra's eyes and heard it in Jordan's voice.

So, Colston, big boy, you walked out. Accomplishing what?

Colston pauses mid-step. *Am I succumbing to the madness?* This wonder further deepens the despair that he may never had control. He resumes walking, contemplating the words that lingered at the edge of his hearing.

"Accomplishing what?" he asks aloud.

The only person who can provide an answer to him is him. By being out here, he is achieving nothing. Instead, he is likely causing more stress and anger for Kayra and Jordan. His desire for solace cannot be found in this place, as the source of his misery lies within.

He hears the sound of approaching cars

behind him. Glancing back, he sees a police car and an ambulance.

"I should go back," he whispers, yet he continues walking along the quiet street. Tears fall, blurring his vision as he presses on.

You fought back tonight. Again, that voice lingers at the edge of his hearing.

"Fight? Ha, what a laugh! No, fighting is what I have been doing. Fighting the urge to end it all because I see no light at the end of the tunnel. Consider this," he catechizes to the empty streets. *Oh, God, I am losing it.* He stares at his feet as he walks, and when he speaks, it is out loud. "Considering it took the phantom a year to plan to take me the first time, and for three months prior, he taunted and warned me." Colston pauses and looks around; he is alone. "Now it has been five years, and he waited for me to go to the house." This time, he stops walking, his ear cocked, waiting. He stands five blocks from the restaurant, in front of a dark barbershop. He sighs, hoping to hear that voice again, but it is just him. "Why would he wait at the house? Why would he think that I would go back?" Tears fall, and he shudders in fear and disgust. As he recalls Todd's comment about how he allowed the drug to overwhelm him, his shoulders grow heavy. He whispers to the sidewalk, "I went back to find a way to escape. NOT because I felt I belonged there."

His hands move to his chest as he closes his eyes. Through tears, he prays for the strength to continue the fight. "Please, my

God, I have glimpsed the light at the end of this struggle. Though the path is long and arduous, filled with more cold and darkness, I long for it to be over. I wish for an end to this suffering, or... grant me the freedom I seek and take me into your loving arms." He lets out a sob; he's at the end and is leaving it all in God's hands.

What is to gain?

"I don't know!" he screams in his mind. *"Why did he choose me to take?"*

"COLSTON!" he hears the panicked echoes of Kayra.

"Why couldn't he have just killed me?" he whispers, turning and allowing his back to hit the wall of the barbershop as he slides to the ground. "This existence is not living; it is merely waiting for the next breakdown. I am always wondering if this one will finally do me in," he breathes. "If I had tried harder before I entered that house, before he could infect me with his poison."

"COLSTON!" Kayra's voice grows nearer.

He wonders... hopes his heart will just cease beating, releasing him.

"I don't want to be a disappointment anymore!" He clutches his chest. "God, am I supposed to keep going?"

"OH GOD!"

Colston hears the footsteps approaching.

"Okay, my God, I hear you loud and clear," he whispers as Kayra kneels beside him.

"Colston?" Her voice is soft and cautious.

"I am so sorry. How is Jordan?" Colston

asks.

"He's on his way to the hospital. The bridge of his nose and his eyes are swollen; nothing is broken, or so they hope," Kayra explains.

Colston lets out a sob; the guilt is weighing heavy. "Can we go see him?"

"With the new restrictions, we cannot," Kayra says.

"I am so sorry. Are you okay?" He opens his arms, and Kayra easily folds into him.

"Babe," Kayra says, her voice trembling with fear. Another public display, and his kidnapper was so close. "You were gone." Her voice is quiet.

Kayra witnessed the moment Colston disappeared. As he read the note, the self-assured Colston vanished.

Colston looks at Kayra and whispers, "What do you mean?"

"When I looked into your eyes, you were not there. I have seen your eyes fade, but tonight, there was nothing. Colston, please tell me, where did you go?" Kayra asks.

Colston sighs, "I should have just said no, left, and embraced my newfound confidence. But I couldn't... I couldn't let him win." He takes a shaky breath. "I--tried," he says, his jaw clenched tightly as he strains his neck. The cold is creeping in, and he struggles to resist it.

Kayra, nestled under his arm, rests her head on his chest. She can feel the growing chill that has echoed in his voice over the years. It is the same cold she felt when she first touched him after ten long days apart.

At that moment, his heart was beating strongly, providing her with the strength to comfort him as he faced the brink of death. Now, it instills in her the confidence to urge, "Go on, let me in," Kayra pleads softly.

"When the paper came across, *Ineffective*, the first song he made me sing was a subtle reminder that I was useless without him and powerless against his desires. That----bold----move had angered me then, and tonight I proceeded to bite off more than I could chew." Colston pauses, his breath trembling. He just wants to stop. And accomplishing nothing. He swallows hard. "By switching the songs, I demonstrated that I am not afraid. However, when Jordan started the song, I was immediately transported back to that place, bound, cold, and sick. I knew very well that after the second song was sung, I was on borrowed time. Though the song was different, it still represented a blatant disregard. The lyrics tonight were a battle cry, and I know I am inviting trouble. What you witnessed was me fighting to regain control, not just to maintain it." Colston stops; he is exhausted.

"Babe?" There are unmistakable tears in her voice. She will never comprehend the strength he exerts to cope with what that man did. It terrifies her to wait and wonder. "I want to save you."

Colston holds her tight and says, "I love the help."

They sit quietly for a moment, allowing the gentle breeze to swirl around them.

"Let's go home," Kayra says, squeezing

Colston's body.

He rubs her back. "Let's drive by the hospital first," Colston says. He feels he needs to at least try to check on Jordan.

"Okay," Kayra replies.

They help each other up and begin heading toward the truck. When they hear the click-clacking sound of rapidly approaching heels coming from their right. Colston's hand locks with Kayra's as a breathless yet frantic voice calls out, "Mrs. Driscoll? Kayra Driscoll?"

Kayra, feeling confused, slows their walk to a stop. They turn to observe the woman with red curly hair framing her tan face, dressed in business attire and carrying a binder.

"Yes?" Kayra asks shakily, gripping Colston's hand for stability.

The woman halts just short of Kayra, her words rushing out rapidly. "The quote 'survivor of Ms. Sunderland's final attack' unquote and the author of the flash fiction, The Scar I Left Upon His Chest by Lila Everhart." She hurls the binder at Kayra's feet. Papers scatter at their feet, and Colston envelops Kayra, who stands frozen in place.

"Leave us!" Colston demands.

Kayra, peering over Colston's shoulder, can still see the frantic eyes of the woman.

The woman points at Kayra and declares, "The Coven of Pulchritudinous stands, though wounded. In due time, your betrayal will be claimed and left putrid among the life you sow!"

"LEAVE US!" Colston yells as he sweeps Kayra into his arms.

Kayra buries her face against his neck, sobbing, "I thought it was over. How did she find out who I was?"

"Shhh, they won't come anywhere near you. We can report this to the police."

"It's not fair!" She drapes her arms over his shoulders.

"It is the way of the world, I'm afraid. Let's go see Jordan and then head home."

Kayra remains in Colston's arms all the way to the truck, feeling anxious and questioning whether her identity being discovered has put Colston in greater danger.

Colston opens the passenger side door and sets Kayra inside. As he pulls away, he notices that she is silently crying. She locks her fingers behind his neck and says, "I am so sorry, Colston. I...I shouldn't have published that story. I've put you in even more danger."

Colston pulls her back against him, gently rubbing her back. "You have done no such thing." He speaks with confidence in that statement.

Kayra looks him in the face. "How?"

Colston cradles her face and says, "If they truly wanted to take action, they would have shown up in numbers." He runs his hand through her hair and adds, "As long as I draw breath, they won't steal you from me."

Kayra plants a kiss on his lips and whispers, "We need to move as soon as possible."

"We will," Colston says, as Kayra adjusts

herself in the seat, allowing him to close the door.

At the hospital, Colston enters alone. Kayra, who is dozing, assures him that she will be fine.

The spacious lobby is bustling with activity, yet it is not overcrowded. He approaches the front desk.

The nurse at the desk is looking ragged. "Can I help you?" Her voice is kind yet fatigued.

"A man named Jordan Youngblood came in, and I would like to check on how he is doing."

The nurse sits down at the computer and asks, "And who are you?"

"I am Colston Driscoll. Jordan is a friend and a guest in my home."

"Mr. Youngblood is in room 406 on the fourth level for non-emergency observation. You may visit him, but only for a brief moment."

"Okay, thank you." Colston heads to the elevator before she can change her mind.

He takes out his phone and calls Kayra.

"Colston?" Kayra replies wearily.

"I'm going to see Jordan."

"Oh, you get to see him? Should I join you?" she asks.

"I think I just got lucky; best not push it." Colston steps into the elevator, saying, "I'll be out in a moment. I love you."

"I love you too."

Colston hangs up and begins to contemplate what he will say to Jordan.

Stepping out of the elevator, a doctor rushes past Colston, who spins to avoid a collision. The doctor says nothing as the elevator doors close. Colston shakes his head and continues toward Jordan's room.

He stands in front of room 406, bracing himself for the angry words he knows he deserves. Gently, he knocks and opens the door. "Jordan?" Colston peeks into the room. Jordan is lying on the bed, a bandage covering his eyes. As Colston fully enters, a wave of shame wells up inside him. He slowly approaches the bed, and as he gets closer, he realizes that Jordan is breathing heavily.

"Jordan? Hey, it's Colston."

"Cole?" His voice is choked with emotion as he reaches out with a trembling hand.

Colston grips it. "What is wrong?" he asks gently.

"Colston, please don't go anywhere alone," Jordan pleads, reaching with his other hand to uncover his eyes.

Colston's heart sinks at his words. He notices that Jordan's eyes are nearly swollen shut. "Jordan, I am so sorry. I shouldn't have left you lying on the floor."

He shakes his head, which triggers a deep throb in the center of his skull. With the hand not holding Colston's, he rubs his temple in an attempt to alleviate the pain, but to no avail.

"No," he says, squeezing Colston's hand. "He came here! Cole..."

Colston stares at Jordan's swollen face, unsure of how to respond to this information, "He won't do anything to you, JD, I promise," he reassures, though the phantom did get to him. He then thinks, *I need to get to Kayra.*

"He won't harm me or Kayra. Only if..."

"I will go with him quietly," Colston says. "How long ago was he here?"

"You need to report this. If he gets to you... he'll..." Jordan stares at the blurry form of Colston. "He claimed he is the only one who can truly save you from yourself, and this time, when you fight, he'll kill you." He grips Colston's hand tighter. "He left five minutes before you arrived."

Colston sits on the bed, contemplating whether there is any point in trying to lead a normal life, not that his life has truly been normal.

"Say something," Jordan urges.

"I am going to fight. He is insane. I need to go to Kayra..." He considers revealing to Jordan what happened to Kayra. He sighs, "Kayra was discovered to be the last survivor of Abigail."

Jordan gazes at the ceiling, his teeth clenched in pain. He says, "You have been fighting." Then he turns back to Colston. "What? Are you freaking serious?"

Colston shakes his head slowly and says, "Jordan, we are just a phone call away, but I need to return to Kayra."

"Go, but please, Cole, don't give up."

"I won't, JD. I have you, Kayra, and I still have songs to sing."

"Damn right."

Kayra is snoozing in the truck. She hears the driver's door handle being pulled, followed by a gentle knock. Without glancing, she unlocks the door. As it opens, Kayra, feeling utterly exhausted, instinctively extends her hand, allowing Colston to interlace his fingers with hers.

The hand that grips hers is not the thick hand of her husband. Her eyes snap open, and she sees her own frightened reflection in a full-face mask.

"Make a sound; Colston dies tonight," the voice declares.

Kayra stares, still gripping the gloved hand of the man who stole her husband.

"Kayra, the best thing you can do, not just for yourself but for Colston, is to leave him. He belongs to me; his voice soothes the burns of life. I do not wish to harm my dearest Colston; he has so much to offer. You may give him life, but I see what he can become, and that potential cannot be achieved while he is divided. If you truly love this man, you will let him go." He steps out of the truck and walks into the night.

Kayra is left frozen in fear; a folded piece of paper rests in the palm of her hand. Her eyes are fixed on the empty driver's seat, the door ajar. Tears slide down her cheeks as the overwhelming fear leaves her gasping for breath.

"Colston," she whimpers, "I can't let him go. He's mine."

Moments later, Colston dashes around the open door, calling out, "Kayra?" His voice is filled with panic.

Kayra drops the paper and scrambles over the center console into his arms.

Colston holds her as she trembles so violently that she can barely speak. "He! He... here!"

Colston's anger flares. "God...Did he hurt you?"

Kayra cradles his face in her hands; her 'no' is not audible.

"Did no one see?" Colston asks. This creep has gotten to both people who mean the world to him.

"He threatened to kill you tonight if I made a sound."

Colston's eyes drift away from Kayra, yet his face remains cradled in her hands. "He got to Jordan, too," he says.

"What? Is he?"

"No, Jordan is fine. Just a warning: when I fight, I am dead. But you and he will be safe."

Kayra hugs him again, not wanting to repeat what the man told her, as the words continue to gnaw at her.

Colston gently places a hand on the back of her head and breaks down, saying, "I'm sorry!" He understands that this apology holds little significance in the grand scheme of things; it is the only thing he can think to express.

"He left a piece of paper in my hand." Kayra moves back over the console and picks up the paper from the floorboard.

Colston climbs laboriously into the truck.

Kayra reads the words on the front to herself.

The Driscoll Defender's Important Note to My Dearest Colston

Kayra feels a wave of sickness accompanied by a pang of jealousy as she reads this. Colston takes the note, glances at it with a look of despair, and then opens it. With his right hand, he gently takes hold of Kayra's hand and reads the note aloud. All the while hearing the cold yet passionate assuredness of the phantom.

"My dearest Colston, your display of strength was admirable tonight; however, it was very disrespectful. I'll let this slide, but understand, Colston, that this is the last time. The first was at the house. I had set the house on fire and was coming to kill you because I could no longer tolerate your lack of respect and genuine conviction. However, when I heard you singing so freely and purely, your pain and sadness resonating so clearly, I would have preferred to stab myself rather than confront my near mistake. I realized my near mistake. I realized. My. Near. Mistake. Colston, it is time for you to recognize yours. Soon, Colston, soon."

Colston concludes by tossing it onto the floor. He leans his head back against the headrest, finding it hard to catch his breath. The phantom had intended to kill him, but it was not for the reasons he had assumed. It was because he couldn't handle the fight, not because that was the plan all along.

"What do we do now?" Kayra asks, feeling numb.

"We go home," he says, dazed by the new cognizance.

Colston pulls into the driveway but remains seated in the car, not making any move to get out.

"Cole?" Kayra asks, gently rubbing his arm.

Colston reaches into his pocket, pulls out his phone, and checks his emails. Desperate for assistance, he notices an email from Melody sent three hours ago. The subject line reads: Help to Lessen the Impact of Flashbacks.

Colston pats Kayra's arm. "Melody sent some things, but before that, we need to inform the police that your identity has been compromised," he says.

Kayra picks up the note from the floorboard. "What about you? Is this not worth anything?"

"They don't care!" Colston exclaims, his voice rising above a calm tone.

Kayra remains steadfast, tears spill, as the hand that has been resting on her arm intertwines with his hand. "They have to! It's their duty to protect."

"I am on my own, Ka. The last time I went in, they outright told me to stop pretending and to man up," Colston repeats with a shudder.

Kayra is taken aback by this revelation, her anger rising at the blatant disregard for the physical evidence. Then something clicks, and with it comes a rush of hope. "Cole, if I report that my identity has been compromised, they will have to protect both of us because you are my husband."

"It could work. Do you want to go to the

police station?"

"Yes, perhaps then we can get some sleep," Kayra says, yawning.

Colston follows closely with a yawn of his own. He then puts the truck in reverse and pulls out onto the road.

Kayra folds the note and places it in the glove box. "I wanna burn it," Kayra folds herself up, haunted by the cool assurance.

"Honey, I am sorry," Colston says.

"Baby, why? Are we being punished?" Kayra asks as the woman's words sink in.

"I don't know," Colston says. He couldn't allow himself to linger on that train of thought for fear of going insane. "Babe, I'm sure God will protect us and grant us guidance," he adds.

"What about Jordan? He's in the hospital because I needed help!" Kayra says, swallowing hard and looking at Colston in utter horror.

Colston's eyes remain fixed on the road, and his hand never pulls away from Kayra's. He feels numb.

As they pull into the parking lot of the police station, he glances at Kayra, who wears a fearful expression. "Let's take care of this first, then we can go home," he says, his voice calm and reassuring.

"Cole... What if they ask me to leave you?"

"We'll worry about that bridge when we come to it." Colston kisses the back of her hand. "Shall we go inside?"

Kayra shakes her head. "No, Colston. I just want to go home." Her mind is a whirlwind of panic, filled with the woman's words and the phantom's warning to leave Colston to him.

"Kay," he says, folding the hand that held hers against his chest. He then reaches over and caresses her cheek. "We need to inform them. In case I am unable to protect you and Jordan is in the hospital, there are too many variables at play that are beyond our control. They promised you complete anonymity during and after the trial."

She squeezes his hand and leans into his touch. "Complete anonymity for both of us! Christ, Cole, you do remember what happened, right?"

Colston nods and gently rubs her cheek with his thumb. "Yes, of course, I remember. The impact on you is more significant."

She bursts into sobs, placing her other hand on his cheek. "How can you say that?! Honey, your life has value. You've stared death in the face and have been on the brink of death. Please, fight for your own sanity."

Colston feels her shudder when she mentions death in connection with him. This causes his heart to tremble. "Honey, please," he says, his voice shaking. "My sanity remains intact knowing that you are safe."

Kayra spies an officer approaching the truck. "I'd die without you at my side," she whispers, leaning into him as much as she can with the center console between them.

Colston holds her, feeling pangs of guilt. A single knuckle thump on his window startles him, prompting him to turn and look outside.

The man, dressed in a police uniform, looks annoyed, tired, and somewhat concerned. "Mr. Driscoll," he says with an exasperated sigh, "roll down the window."

Colston presses the button to roll down the window while still holding onto Kayra.

The officer casts a disapproving glance at Colston before shifting his gaze to Kayra, whose face is buried in Colston's chest. Colston watches the officer, trying to determine whom he should address first.

"Alright," the officer begins, glancing back at Colston. "We honestly didn't expect to see you on our doorstep again, ironically, the day after Todd leaves town. He informed us that your appearances around here might increase. Not only that, but the public is becoming aware of your instability. You are treading on thin ice; your case of crying wolf is closed. We don't have time to pursue the ravings of a desperate, failing singer."

Colston feels incredibly small, further driving home the fear that he is on his own without a buffer between himself and the phantom.

Kayra pops up and gazes at the officer. Her face, streaked with tears and contorted in anguish, reflects her shock at the words she has just heard directed at her husband.

"Ma'am, is your husband causing you distress?" The officer asks in a much friendlier tone.

Kayra feels Colston's strength fading as it drains from his body. She quickly comes to his defense, stating, "My husband is a great, caring, and honest man. Since you are leaving him out in the cold, we are done here." As she settles back into her seat, she turns to him and says, "Let's just go, Colston."

Colston doesn't want Kayra to feel as hopeless as he does. He turns to the officer and says in the strongest voice he can muster at that moment, "We were approached tonight by a woman who claims to have discovered Kayra's identity as the 'survivor of Ms. Sunderland's final attack.'"

The officer's demeanor changes immediately, disregarding the fact Colston made the statement, and looks right past to address Kayra, asking, "Is this true?" The urgency in his voice instantly irritates Kayra.

"Yes," she says sharply, gripping Colston's hand.

"I would like you to come inside to provide an official statement and to consider entering witness protection. This situation extends deeper and further than just here and with Ms. Sunderland."

Colston beats Kayra to the question, "Were you ever going to inform us?"

"Believe it or not, we prefer to avoid causing stress when it is unnecessary," he replies sharply, still gazing at Kayra. "We believed we had concealed her identity effectively, but some people are quite determined."

Kayra hugs Colston's arm and rests her head on his shoulder, her heart pounding with anger and hurt. "His life is just as important as mine!" she yells tearfully.

The officer sighs, "With all due respect,

the coven poses an extreme danger to the women it brainwashes. Mr. Driscoll," he casts a cynical glance toward Colston, "was fortunate to have survived." He turns his attention back to Kayra. "Your struggle to escape was extraordinary, placing you among the 1 percent of women who manage to do so. Mrs. Driscoll, I urge you to consider witness protection."

"I am not leaving my husband," she says.

"If he loves you, he will let you go," the officer says, eyeing Colston.

"NOOO!" Kayra cries, tugging at Colston's shirt.

The officer is taken aback by her reaction to his statement. Colston allows himself to be drawn toward her, wrapping her in his arms. "I'm right here."

She cries into his chest, "Don't let me go! Please!"

"Never." Colston says, looking toward the officer. "We are going to leave now." He rolls up the window and focuses on comforting his wife.

"How can they do this to you?" She cries.

Colston is at a loss for words on that one. "I don't know, but that is why I believe moving is our best option right now."

Kayra looks him in the eyes and says, "What about therapy? You found someone who cares."

"I am sure we could meet over telehealth, and we could correspond via email," Colston says.

"Speaking of emails, she sent one. Let's read it here and then go home. I just want to lie in your arms."

Colston nods, and Kayra loosens her grip on him just enough for him to retrieve his phone from his pocket. With his right elbow resting on the center console and Kayra leaning against his shoulder, he gently rests his cheek against her head as they read the email together.

I hope this email finds you well, Colston. I know I mentioned two techniques; I will share one here, and we will cover the other in the next session.

This technique is called Survival to Observation. When flashbacks occur, you enter survival mode because they feel just as real as the day they happened. We need to train your brain to understand that you are no longer in that moment and that those experiences cannot hurt you anymore. It will take time, practice, and energy to effectively implement this technique.

During a flashback, you essentially awaken and detach yourself from the experience, becoming an observer of yourself. This shift can cause the flashback to pause or become distorted. Once this occurs, your mind will release you.

Also, this can be achievable in dreams, but it requires significantly more effort, as there are additional layers to navigate in order to reach your conscious mind.

If you wish to practice, I suggest lying down and having your wife present before allowing thoughts to flood your mind.

I hope this information is helpful, and I wish you the best of luck.

Sincerely, Melody Dakota

Colston and Kayra finished reading the email, both feeling relieved to receive helpful information for a change.

"Let's go home," Kayra says.

They lay in bed, feeling gutted by the night they had just experienced. Colston feels queasy knowing that Jordan is at the hospital, wondering if he is safe. He stares at the ceiling, feeling Kayra toss and turn beside him.

While in the grasp of the phantom, he faced death twice. He fought against the phantom but ultimately lost consciousness both times, overwhelmed by pain and/or fright. Yet, the phantom spared his life; why? A chilling thought crossed Colston's mind: Did the phantom want to witness his reaction when the final blow was struck?

He shivers as Kayra rolls back against him, lightly tracing her fingers across his bare chest. Colston gently places his hand over hers, flattening it against his chest. "Love, we need to sleep," he says.

Kayra nestles her face into his neck and whispers, half-asleep, "You are mine; he can't have you."

Colston, tears welling in his eyes, drifts off to sleep.

He was left to awkwardly crawl to the tub after being pushed to the floor just inside the door. His broken ankle caused his movements to be slow, and his sick body throbbed with heat. Upon reaching the tub, he braced his forearms on the edge to pull himself up and lean into the corner. When the tape finally broke, fresh fear washed over him, but it was quickly replaced by relief as the cold air caressed his raw skin. He wrapped his sore, cold body in the blankets and drifted off to sleep before worry could deny him rest.

An anguished scream pierced the cold, silent house, jolting Colston from a dreamless slumber. Groggy and loath to fully awaken, he relished the warmth enveloping him and the freedom of his unbound wrists.

The sound of running footsteps echoed, accompanied by his captor roaring, "NOOOO!"

Colston's heart pounded in his chest as his eyes remained fixed on the door. He braced himself for another beating, hoping the man would snap out of his frenzied rage before he was killed.

The door was kicked open, and his captor barreled in. He seized the edge of the blanket and yanked it forcefully, nearly ripping it in half. Colston slid away from the tub with such speed that the back of his head struck the floor.

"YOU CALLOUS SON OF A BITCH!!"

Colston shielded himself as best as he could. "PLEASE, STOP!" he begged. His body could endure little more of being a punching bag.

To Colston's shock and disbelief, he did. That malevolent man loomed over him, panting and failing to recognize Colston as a fellow human being. This man was at the end of his rope, and Colston was the one who had driven him there.

Colston's world was spinning, and he felt nauseous. "Please, I beg you, let me go!" He knew it was futile.

The man's face dipped close, his lips contorting into a snarl. He seemed to be gnashing his teeth on words. Colston shut his eyes against the terrifying visage just inches from his own and attempted to turn away. A hand seized his face, forcing it back. "Look upon me!" he shouted, shaking Colston's face. "LOOK UPON THE INSANITY YOU BIRTHED!!!"

Colston's ears were ringing as he opened his eyes. Staring into the void, "I--did what you asked," he said.

"NO! You have made a mockery of me. That song was meant to illustrate you and me right now! But you changed the lyrics, and I don't know how. You don't look like a metalhead, yet in those altered lyrics, you've ensured that the third song will never be reached! You were dealt into my hands, and I accept that responsibility." He punched Colston in the chest.

Colston groaned as he successfully managed to roll onto his side and curl himself up.

The man leaned in close to his ear and whispered, "Why can't you accept your place and learn?"

Colston's eyes were tightly shut. The pain coursing through his body was overwhelming, not just physically but mentally as well. He longed for it to end before he succumbed to the madness.

His captor had left, and Colston was afraid to move.

"Wrists together, NOW!" he bellowed, storming back into the room.

Colston followed the instructions. After his wrists were bound, he was forced onto his back once again.

"Open your fucking eyes!"

He opened his eyes to see the man pull a straight-back knife from his back pocket. Then, he crashed one knee down onto Colston's shin. Colston howled in pain, but his cry was abruptly silenced when a hand covered his mouth.

"I brought you here to save you!" Colston felt the sharp tip dance across his bare chest. "Because I love you." The man let out a sob. "But with you fighting me and being so ungrateful for such a helping hand... I... I am okay being the one who kills you!" he screamed.

Colston shut his eyes and let out a cry as the hand covering his mouth pressed harder...

Colston knows that this is where he lost consciousness. He stares at the frozen image from behind the phantom. Before he can manage to wake up, he is startled when the picture resumes movement. The phantom looks up and smiles, while the screams of Survival Colston are muffled by a hand, and his eyes fill with panic.

"Shhh, it's for the best," the phantom says to Observation Colston before turning back to the other.

He watches himself yell into the hand as the phantom retracts the knife. He is unable to move or speak; all he can do is observe.

The phantom thrusts the knife into Colston's ribcage. Both versions of Colston's breath are snatched away; the observer Colston collapses to the floor, while survival Colston's eyes remain fixed on his captor. As he witnesses the mixture of great satisfaction and absolute horror in the monster's eyes, tears stream down his face while the creature caresses him. Colston's eyes slowly close.

Observation Colston, having just witnessed the remnants of himself die. He watches as the phantom stands and looks down at him, "Soon!" The phantom exclaims, raising the knife before dropping to his knees beside Colston.

Colston screams to awaken himself.

He wakes up, his body trembling and his mind reeling. He gazes at Kayra's peaceful, sleeping face. Sitting up, he rubs his face and glances at the bedside clock, which reads 3:24. He has only been asleep for an hour; he should try to return to sleep. However, he doubts he can, so he quietly gets up and makes his way to his studio.

He feels violated and helpless. There is currently no information available about this man; however, there are messages laying out his intentions, and he has visited Kayra and Jordan. His intent is not to threaten their lives, but rather to exert control by threatening his own.

He gently strikes his desk, numbed by the relentless cold that has become a constant presence. Now, fueled by anger, he realizes he must allow this rage to dissipate before he is compelled to act impulsively.

"What am I to do?" Colston asks aloud.

The meeting is inevitable; it's merely a question of when. For the sake of his life, he needs a plan.

"Was there ever a plan?" He dismisses that voice, which echoes from somewhere deep within his troubled mind, as he reflects on the session and attempts to recall what Melody had said.

"I need sleep," he whispers. "If I don't, I won't have the strength to defend myself." The thought of finding himself in a similar situation again sends a shiver down his spine, and he shakes the idea away.

Days of torture, which were used for entertainment, would not have been torture if he had simply relented and expressed gratitude.

Colston leaves the room and retrieves his wallet. He pulls out the note he found at the house. With that in hand, he heads to his truck to grab the other one.

On his way back to the studio, he hears Kayra calling out for him. He drops the papers and rushes to the room, asking, "Babe?"

Kayra looks frantic as she sees Colston

appear in the doorway, and she jumps out of bed. They meet in the center of the room, where Kayra wraps her arms around the back of his shoulders. "I can't." She weeps into his shoulder.

"You can't what?" Colston asks gently.

"Keep watching as you slowly die," Kayra says with great effort.

Colston feels a sharp pain at the words. "I understand." That is all he could manage to say.

"I am so sorry, Colston," Kayra says gently as she pulls away. "If he comes, I'm going to get you killed!"

"No, hon," he says, unsure of where to go because, unless by some miracle, he is going to die. "Kayra, don't let go." He takes her hands in his. "I need you; having you by my side gives me the strength to try to find a way to survive this." Colston realizes the weight he has just placed on her shoulders. "But it does not make you responsible if something happens. I am fighting for a normal life with you, and that keeps me from going completely insane." He bows his head. "If you need to leave, I understand, and I will still fight to be with you."

Kayra gently lifts his head and gazes longingly into her husband's eyes. "You are so brave and strong. I don't want to abandon you; I love you and see that constant struggle. It's one that you tried to shield me from, but I insisted on knowing." She reflected on the man from before and felt a deep fear at how untouchable he seemed.

"Colston, come back to bed and just hold

me," Kayra says.

Colston nods, and they climb back into bed. With the rhythm of their heartbeats and the safety found in each other's arms, sleep quickly follows.

Kayra falls asleep, pleading with God for strength.

Chapter Ten: The Final Boon

Kayra drifts away from the comfort of Colston's embrace and the feeling of his warm breath gently caressing her neck. Descending into her restless mind conjures a hellish landscape that robs her of both sleep and a sense of safety.

She stands alone on the grassy patch in front of the street clock, watching the hands spin wildly. A gloved hand slips into her left hand, and her body tenses with a mix of fear and anger. She cannot speak, nor can she tear her gaze away from the whirling hands. The other gloved hand gently sweeps her hair over her shoulder and rubs the back of her neck. Tears begin to trickle as whispered words from the night echo in her ear: "Colston dies tonight." "He is mine." "My dearest Colston." "If you love this man, you will let him go."

She trembles, yearning to scream, but her mouth remains sealed. The spinning hands blur further amidst the cascade of tears.

The same deep, resonating voice from the shared dream with Colston now envelops Kayra, causing the world to shudder. *"Suffering at the hands of others doesn't have to be shared. Hearts can be drawn together yet pulled apart once a limit is reached. Be deluded and suffer alongside, or be cowardly and abandon, to leave it all behind."*

Kayra hears the words as another hand slides into her right, slender in frame. The other hand gently grips Kayra by the chin, turning her head effortlessly, leaving Kayra unable to resist. Face to face with Abigail, whose eyes are dark and sunken, she smiles wildly. "Kayra," her voice echoes. "Poor tortured soul, I knew this would become of you. Yet, you locked me away, and now you are forever trapped in the shadows. Do what you need to do."

The presence of Abigail and the phantom fades. When the hands of the clock align at 12:00, the world shudders once more with the thunderous boom of the clock. Kayra is thrown to the ground, gasping and crying. Her hope is dwindling, and the questions are beginning to overwhelm her mind. The more she struggles, the more lost and hopeless she feels. The pain in her chest is so intense that she screams, her fingers digging into the grass.

"Kayra?"

She looks up and sees Colston. A sensation of splitting in two overwhelms her as something inside snaps. Her eyes are wild, her arms push her off the ground, and her legs propel her forward...

Her eyes snap open, locking onto Colston, who is sleeping peacefully beside her. She moves like a predator stalking its prey, carefully yet swiftly.

He softly moans in response to her movements. Kayra's heart races, fearful that he might wake up. She glances toward the door and then down at her fists, clenched and trembling. As words caress her mind, *Long, drawn-out, with the risk of him fighting back, or quick and painless.* The voice in her head is Abigail's. A small voice screams and pleads to be heard: *Just leave! There is no need to kill him! You are still deeply in love with him!* But that voice is swiftly silenced, leaving Kayra standing by the bed, staring down at the slumbering man. She glances at her fists again, then folds her left hand around her right fist and slides her right knee onto the bed.

Colston grunts in his sleep and shifts onto his back. Kayra's wild eyes fixate on the scar on his chest. She raises her fists; in her mind, she thinks, *I am suffering! It's not my fault!*

She brings her fists down onto Colston's chest with all the force she can muster.

Her fists do not linger on his chest as he remains motionless; only a single gasp of air escapes. She straightens up, her expression revealing dissatisfaction.

Abigail speaks up again. *Too clean, Kay. Blood needs to be spilled.*

Kayra, with her wild eyes and fists still clenched, turns and, without checking to see if he is still breathing, stalks out of the room.

She feels a slight urge to glance into the open door of Colston's studio. Instead of peering inside, she tramples over the scattered papers and closes the door, further severing that connection.

Into the kitchen, she glides, oblivious to her surroundings, focused solely on her task. She stops at the knife block, her right hand fiercely clawing at her left, which remains clenched in a fist.

TAKE THAT DAMN RING OFF! THEN GO PLUNGE THE KNIFE INTO HIS HEART!

Kayra cowers in response to Abigail's head-splitting command. That whisper, that dying whisper, screams its final message: *Kayra, that man loves you, and you love him. His voice envelops you in warmth, and his arms provide a sense of safety. Wake up! Before you destroy your world! WAKE UP, KAYRA!*

Kayra turns her head toward the hall, where her gaze lands on a large picture adorning the back wall. The photograph captures Kayra and Colston on their wedding day, their foreheads pressed together with the setting sun illuminating the scene behind them. Beneath the image, an inscription reads, *Today two hearts beat as one; forever one, never to be torn.*

Kayra collapses to the floor, shaking uncontrollably. She stares at her left hand, where the back is covered in scratch marks. Some are quite prominent, but none are bleeding. However, her palm of her left hand has several droplets of blood.

"No, no, did I just kill Colston?" Her voice is barely audible. Her mind is flooded with memories of the battles Colston has fought. She weeps, "I was afraid of this. Lord, please, I am not brave enough to enter our shared bedroom. Give me a sign so I know that my husband is alive!" She bows her head and clasps her hands together.

She suddenly feels light as her stress

and worries melt away. A voice fills her with warmth and comfort: *"My daughter, thee must grow deaf to this siren of death. The love thy give is strong and can survive. He dost draw the breaths of life, even though danger still surrounds."*

Kayra sits on the floor, gazing at her wedding ring. "I am sorry, my love!" Similar to her having no courage to go into the bedroom, she lacks the strength to remove her wedding and engagement rings. Even when she is out of her mind, her devotion to Colston remains steadfast. "I can't be trusted around him," She says to the empty kitchen, "I need to clear my mind." This comes out in a trance-like state as her eyes remain fixed on the wedding photo.

She pulls herself up using the counter, quickly realizing that she needs to go to the bedroom for a fresh pair of clothes. All she can do is pray that he stays asleep because she can't face him, not after what she did. She'll give herself two days, then return to confront him.

With tears in her eyes, she begins to walk toward the hall but stops when she notices the papers on the floor. She picks them up and slips them into her pocket. Quietly, she makes her way toward the room, feeling immense relief upon hearing him snoring. Nevertheless, she avoids looking at the bed, fearing that she might lose control of herself once again.

That tiny voice then questions, *What makes you think a few days will make it better?*

Kayra shakes her head and replies, *"It just will... it has to. What he is facing, I can't let him face it alone."*

But doesn't he need you at this moment?

She replies while pulling out a fresh pair of clothes from the drawer, *"I struck him with the intent to kill. I need to ensure that Abigail's influence on me doesn't resurface like that again."*

How?

Kayra pauses at the door, clothes cradled in her arms, and listens as Colston emits a snorting gasp before his gentle snoring resumes. Battling the urge to turn back, knowing that if she does, she won't be able to leave, she reminds herself that she must go for his safety. With a sigh, she walks away from the bedroom.

You need to tell him about what just happened; it may be beneficial to both of you, sharing.

Kayra nearly collapses in the hallway at the thought, *"Abigail is locked up; the stress triggered the conditioning, allowing her to take over. I know it wasn't her, but..."* Kayra pauses, hearing a phlegmy cough from Colston.

She goes to the kitchen and writes a note.

Colston, you are my world; sometimes we become angry at the world. Thus, doing damage to it before rebuilding, so before any more damage is done, I must flee. I will come back to you once I have rid myself of my anger.

Love, Kayra.

P.S. Please send me a text once you see this and let me know that you are okay.

An hour later, Colston awakens, engulfed in a great deal of pain. "Kayra?" he calls out, noticing her side of the bed is empty, but his voice is barely above a whisper. He tries again, but this time it is even quieter than before. His vision is doubled as he scans the room, and his heart is skipping in his chest. He knows he must get up to check if Kayra is in the house. Slowly, he sits up, tears streaming from the pain and fear. Where is Kayra? Is he having a heart attack?

A gasping sob escapes him; the thought of dying alone is terrifying. He gets on his feet, fighting the urge to pass out. He takes five careful, unsteady steps until he reaches the bedroom door, where he braces himself and cries out for Kayra once more. Using the wall for support, he stumbles down the hall. He is sweating, shaking, and dizzy. Colston is on the verge of collapsing, weakness coursing through him.

He cannot allow himself to succumb to weakness while alone in the house. He notices his phone on the counter, accompanied by a piece of paper. His ability to remain upright relies entirely on the wall for support. The three steps from the wall to the counter feel like a mile to Colston, given his unsteady state. His vision is distorted, and his heart pounds, intensifying the throbbing in his head. He needs Kayra; something is seriously wrong.

He attempts to take his first step away from the wall but immediately crumples to his hands and knees. The impact jars his chest, causing him to cry out, and he tastes a metallic flavor in his mouth. He must crawl to the counter, feeling frightened and desperately wanting to lie down in hopes that it will ease the pain. He hopes Kayra has gone out shopping or something and will return soon. He is uncertain how long he can remain awake. Reaching up to the seat of the stool for support, he begins to push himself up, flexing his chest. A cough escapes him, spraying blood onto the back of the island as he cries out Kayra's name. He throws his right hand onto the counter, gripping the paper before collapsing back to the floor. Painfully and wearily, he positions himself against the island. Gasping, trembling, and filled with fear, it takes him ten minutes to focus his vision on the writing.

He cannot comprehend the PS due to tears of guilt and pain; he has no one to blame but himself. Is this his reparation? He has inflicted enough suffering on those he loves that it would be better if he were no longer here. He leaves the paper stained with blood and crawls back to the bedroom.

"Please, let me die before he breaks in again," he whispers to the emptiness before closing and locking the door.

Kayra is parked in the hospital parking lot, looking over the notes. She is not just looking at two notes, but three. Kayra has retained the note that was left for her on the table the day of Colston's kidnapping. That haunting line, 'I will return to you after this has run its course', she recalls the final line from the note she left for him and shivers.

"'Means to an end.' What does that mean?" Kayra stares at the solitary phrase. The rest, though completely insane, makes sense. What does he want? The thought terrifies her, and she wishes it would simply vanish.

She gazes up at the hospital. Once again, she finds herself fleeing to Jordan, feeling ashamed, but he is the only person she trusts. He needs to know that she was visited too... and that she must confess what just happened.

It has been four hours since she left, and she has received nothing from Colston. The clock reads 11:20 AM, and Colston never sleeps past nine. Although she requested in her note that he text her, he won't out of respect. She is beginning to contemplate confronting him; this silence is unbearable. How could he ever trust her again?

She places the notes in her pocket and puts on her paper face mask. Exiting the car, she heads inside. The atmosphere is bustling, with people hurrying about. Before anyone can stop her, she purposefully runs to the elevator. She enters one alongside a young doctor, who is too preoccupied with his clipboard to notice her.

Kayra watches the numbers count up to four. Once the door opens, she hurries out and heads toward Jordan's room. Standing outside room 406, she takes a moment to compose herself. Then, she gently knocks and opens the door.

"JD?"

Jordan is lying at an angle; the swelling in his face has decreased. He can see clearly, but moving his eyes is painful. He is fortunate to have escaped without any fractures or hemorrhaging.

"Kayra?" His voice is filled with concern, turning to outright worry when Kayra shuts the door without Colston. "Where is Colston?"

"He's at home." As those words leave her lips, the realization strikes her like a ton of bricks. She had been so consumed by the fear of exposing that she had tried to kill him, leaving him all alone once more. "What have I done?"

Jordan is doing his best to remain composed, primarily to avoid inflicting pain on himself; however, he also reads that Kayra is clearly in distress.

"Kayra, what happened?"

"When Colston was here with you, his kidnapper visited me. He told me that the best thing I could do was to leave Colston."

Jordan sighs as she approaches him. "He left this for Colston," she says. Kayra reads it aloud to him, trying to spare his eyes from strain.

"Kayra, why? Why have you left him alone?" Jordan asks. "He is a man, not a phantom. Colston needs you, Kayra. I know this is frightening. If you abandon him now, we are playing into the kidnappers' hands." He is trying to reason with her.

She starts to cry, "I tried to kill him!" She says, kneeling beside the bed.

"What? What did you do?" Jordan asks,

panic evident in his voice.

"I slammed my fists down on his chest, but when he didn't wake up, I went for a knife. I managed to snap out of it before I could grab it," Kayra cries.

"Did you check on him before you left?" Jordan asks, his voice filled with concern.

"I heard him snoring, and he let out a cough before I left," Kayra says, feeling ashamed.

"Kay," Jordan says, grabbing her hand. "You should have woken him; he should have awakened right after you hit him." He struggles to hold back his tears. "How long ago did you leave?"

"Four hours ago." Kayra feels unwell; a part of her still wants to stay at a hotel. And do what? To wallow in self-pity while Colston confronted that man for ten days and has been struggling for five years? He has never laid a hand on her. After confronting her past, she loses control and is ready to leave and hide. "I can't face him, and I don't want to be alone when I return to the house."

Jordan closes his eyes for a moment to alleviate the throbbing pain, but his anxiety only intensifies. "Have a police officer meet you at the house."

Kayra can barely hear Jordan as she scolds herself in her mind. How could she have almost allowed Abigail to ruin her marriage again? She can sense Abigail laughing at her. The near-deadly combination of trauma is causing her to realize the focus is centered on the presence of Colston and the push to leave or rid his presence completely. But both would leave her empty of him in her life; there have been countless times when she looked into his eyes and saw the desire to end the pain. She suppresses her fear of rejection because she loves Colston, and he needs her to stand by him.

"I should be out tomorrow, but please don't abandon him."

"I'm not going to," she says, hurrying out the door.

Jordan wishes to follow her and help her. He reclines his head against the pillow, hoping that the next person he sees will be Colston.

Kayra runs to the car. How could she have been so stupid? This is how he was taken five years ago; she had left to go shopping. At that time, she was completely unaware of the danger. She hopes he is safe and that he will forgive her for her moment of weakness.

She takes out her cell phone and calls Colston.

Colston's phone rings in the kitchen, but the call goes unanswered.

"No, no! Come on, baby!" She calls again, but she receives the same result.

She dials 911.

"911, what is your emergency?"

"My name is Kayra Driscoll, and I am concerned about my husband, Colston. I fear that something may have happened to him. He is not answering his phone, and he is home alone."

"Okay, Mrs. Driscoll. Where are you, and how long has he been silent?"

"About four hours. I was visiting a friend in the hospital. I'm on my way home now, but I don't want to be alone in case something has happened."

"Please provide me with your address and wait for the officer. Has your husband been violent or experienced suicidal ideations in the past?"

"God, no!" The tremors in her hand make it difficult for her to hold the phone. She lets out a sob and adds that she is about five minutes away from her home, following the address.

"Ma'am, I recommend that you wait for the officer for your safety."

Kayra thanks her, drops the phone, and prays tearfully for Colston to be alright.

She pulls up to the house and steps out of the car as the sounds of sirens draw nearer.

"What am I doing? He's my husband." Still, she hesitates to enter the house. She cannot bear the thought of discovering Colston alone.

She glances down the street; there is still no police car in sight. She looks at the house, her heart pounding in her chest.

"Your husband may be dying," a voice whispers in her heart.

Kayra hears a car approaching, accompanied by the piercing sound of sirens. Still, she stands there, her heart racing as she fights the urge to run to the house just yet. *"Kayra! What are you doing?"*

Tears welling in her eyes; she isn't strong enough. She prays that nothing terrible has happened.

The police car pulls up to the curb, and the sirens are turned off. The moment Kayra sees the lone officer begin to exit the vehicle, she runs toward the house.

"Hey! Mrs. Driscoll, stop!" the officer shouts.

Kayra doesn't hear the door shut, but she hears the sound of someone running up behind her. At the door, she leads with a trembling hand to grip the knob; however, due to the weakness in her hand, she fails to turn it, resulting in her painfully bashing her shoulder against the door.

She lets out a whimper as the footsteps behind her grow closer. She forces herself to turn the doorknob.

"Mrs. Driscoll, please stop." The voice is right behind her.

"I should never have left!" She turns the knob and stumbles inside. "COLSTON!"

Hoping for a response but receiving nothing but eerie silence, her legs threaten to buckle as her gaze lands on the note lying on the floor, smeared with blood. "COLSTON! PLEASE, BABE!" She cries out, feeling a gentle hand rest on her shoulder, which she quickly shakes off. She then heads toward the studio, but her eyes are drawn to the closed bedroom door. She moves with wide, unsteady steps; the bedroom door is only closed when they are inside.

"Colston?" she asks gently as she reaches for the doorknob. It is locked, and Kayra's breathing quickens in panic. "Colston!" she calls out, striking the door with her open hand. "Please, open the door!"

"Move aside," the officer commands. Kayra steps aside but remains close. "Cols--Mr. Driscoll, open the door; this is the police."

Kayra barely notices the slip-up, as there is no response from the bedroom.

The officer looks at her and asks a question that he seems almost regretful asking, "Are there any weapons in there?"

Kayra screams in horror, "No!"

The officer nods and drives his shoulder into the door, causing it to swing open. As he rushes inside, an audible gasp escapes him. Kayra looks past him and sees Colston face down on the floor.

She collapses just outside the bedroom, her eyes fixed on his lifeless form. The officer gently rolls Colston onto his back and checks for a pulse. A thin trail of dried blood runs from the left corner of his mouth.

The officer grips his walkie-talkie and relays, "I need an ambulance at the Driscolls' residence for Colston Driscoll. He has bruising on his chest, signs of internal bleeding, and his heart is racing. I need to speak with his wife and attempt to wake Colston." He glances back at Kayra and adds, "He's alive, but he may be bleeding internally." His expression reveals his fear.

Kayra crawls toward her husband.

"Mr. Driscoll?" the officer asks nervously. "Can you wake up?"

"Officer, can you provide a clear determination of whether the patient is exhibiting symptoms of Parched Fever?" dispatch asks.

Kayra doesn't notice the officer's frustrated sigh as she concentrates on Colston. She places one hand on his chest, pushing aside the guilt that arises when she sees the bruise alongside the scar, to feel his rapid yet trembling heartbeat. With her other hand, she grasps his hand, whispering, "Colston, come back to me." Her voice mirrors the quivering she feels in his chest. She cannot shake the image of him, battered and barely alive, in the front of that van.

His eyes remain closed.

Kayra has not heard the officer ask the same question more than once.

"Mrs. Driscoll, could you please answer my question so I can get help here?" His commanding tone startles Kayra back to reality. She looks at the officer, who asks again, "In the last two days, has Colston experienced cold like symptoms or extended weakness in the legs and/or arms?" He can determine that there are no signs of a rash across his abdomen.

Kayra replies, "No."

Just as a soft groan escapes from Colston.

Kayra glances back at Colston as she hears the officer report, "The patient is not exhibiting symptoms of the virus. Get an ambulance here immediately."

"Colston, can you open your eyes for me, sweetheart?" Kayra gently urges.

Colston weakly squeezes Kayra's hand.

"Ka--yra?" Colston asks breathlessly, yet his eyes remain closed.

Kayra gasps, and a new wave of tears

cascades down her cheeks.

"Cols-Mr. Driscoll," the officer says, visibly annoyed with himself for his lack of professionalism. "Can you open your eyes?"

Colston's grip tightens as he takes several deep breaths, his head gradually rolling from side to side.

Kayra's hand, which rests on his chest, moves to his face, gently rubbing his cheek. "Come back to me, please, Colston," she lays against his chest, whispering, "I am so sorry."

The officer is observing this sensitive moment, feeling both awkward and intrusive.

Colston's eyes opened, tears running. "I thought that was it."

"Mr. Driscoll, could you please explain what happened?"

Colston is not surprised by the officer's presence at all.

When Colston recounts the moment he woke up, his narrative is slow, shaky, and airy. "When I finally reached the room, I locked the door because I was alone. As I attempted to make it to the bed, I felt as though my heart was going to explode from how hard it was pounding, and the world was spinning so fast, then suddenly, nothing."

Kayra is silently sobbing against him, and the officer listens before taking a moment to ask the next question. Colston, despite his disoriented state, can see and hear the officer's struggle to maintain professionalism. This offers him great comfort while simultaneously instilling a sense of anxiety.

"Why did you feel the need to lock the door?" the officer asks.

"Could you help me sit up?" Colston asks, feeling uncomfortable.

"I'd rather wait for the paramedics before attempting to move you any further."

Colston nods in understanding. He sighs and gently squeezes Kayra's hand. "Officer, how long have you been on the force?" he asks.

This question confuses the officer; however, he responds without appearing offended. "Three years," he replies.

"Why did I feel the need to lock the door? Five years ago, I was kidnapped while alone in the house, recording a song. As of two days ago, my kidnapper, whose identity remains unknown and whom I believed had died in the house fire that helped secure my escape, has reappeared with the intention of taking me again." Colston says.

The officer gazes at both of them with an expression of profound sadness. He is compelled to break eye contact. "I must apologize for my lack of professionalism. According to protocol, I should not have answered this call, as it constitutes a conflict of interest."

"What does that mean?" Kayra asks softly.

The officer reestablishes eye contact and says, "I actively watch Colston's channel."

The rest of his thought is interrupted by his radio: *"Officer Acarus, we are attempting to dispatch an ambulance to your location as soon as possible. What is the status of the patient?"*

"Mr. Driscoll is awake and speaking; I had to roll him onto his back. No other movements have been attempted," he reports.

"Good. Radio back if he passes out again or if his breathing or talking changes. ETA: 20 minutes for that ambulance."

"Copy that over and out."

Kayra is now sitting up, still holding Colston's hand.

He stares at Colston. "That wasn't staged?" he asks quietly.

"It was not," Colston confirms. "He held me for ten days in an abandoned house in the woods." He is doing his best to remain calm.

"Why wasn't there anything on the news about it?" he asks, confused.

Kayra gently stops Colston, saying, "Rest, hon." She continues the explanation, "It was set up by the person who took him, making it appear as though it was intended for the October event on the channel. Afterward, he wished not to disclose the truth to the public. That being said, we would appreciate your discretion regarding the truth."

"Scout's Honor," Acarus responds immediately. "I'd prefer to leave it at that as well; it would hurt my daughter."

Colston's gaze shifts from the ceiling to the officer. He lets out a gasp, "Are you indifferent toward what your colleagues have labeled content creators, my 'kind of creatures'?" Colston's trust remains guarded.

Acarus maintains eye contact. "At the beginning of my time on the force, I subscribed to that mindset. It wasn't until a year and a half ago that my daughter changed my way of thinking. Your voice saved the life of my third youngest child."

Colston smiles shyly and calmly offers, "I just added to the strength that was already within her."

The officer's expression shifts to one of shock as he sits down fully on the floor.

Kayra, concerned for the officer, reaches out and touches his shoulder while still interlaced with Colston. "Sir?"

"Oliver, please. Once again, I must apologize for this."

Colston wishes to move, but he feels lightheaded, so he remains on his back. "You don't need to."

Oliver looks up, and he is crying, "I said she was guided to your voice by God. It is through your voice that she will find guidance. Your statement just now confirmed that my daughter is following a good person."

Colston awkwardly extends his left hand, intending to shake Oliver's. Oliver reaches out and grips Colston's hand. As Colston's heart races, he lets out a cry, sending more droplets of blood flying from his mouth before he loses consciousness.

"Colston?" Oliver asks, quickly checking his pulse.

"Babe? No, wake up!" Kayra cries.

"His heart is racing." He reaches for the radio to report the change as the sound of approaching sirens grows louder.

Oliver gets up and rushes out of the room. Kayra immediately kisses Colston on the lips. "Please, hang on," she pleads, lying against him and gently rubbing his face. "I am sorry; don't leave me."

Hearing footsteps approaching down the hall, Kayra pulls away as the paramedic takes her place to attend to Colston. Oliver and Kayra step into the hallway.

"I will ensure that Colston's case receives another review," Oliver states firmly.

Kayra gazes with renewed hope that her husband's life will be saved.

"Mrs. What struck him?" The paramedic asks bluntly, with a hint of accusation in his tone.

Kayra turns her gaze away from Oliver and toward the paramedic, who is kneeling beside Colston and placing an oxygen mask over his mouth and nose. "Um... I..." Kayra stammers, panicking at the thought of being separated from Colston's side.

The paramedic gestures to his partner to monitor Colston's vital signs as he stands up. "Mrs. Driscoll, we need the truth so we can properly treat him," he says, his tone cold and forceful.

With her head bowed, she says, "I struck him. The stress of the night caused me to depersonalize, and all my aggression was directed at Colston." Tears leak from her eyes as she looks toward Colston.

"Officer, she's all yours. We need to get him to the hospital."

Oliver steps forward and says, "Do not prevent her from visiting him in the hospital. I observed her behavior and sensed nothing amiss."

The paramedic gets in Oliver's face and says harshly, "Then why didn't you know the truth?"

"Be----cause." Colston says, breathless and muffled, as he holds out his trembling hand.

Kayra moves to grab it, but she is blocked by the paramedic.

"Jeff," Oliver says.

"Please, my------wife------is------my------strength." Colston says.

"Jeff, go get the stretcher; there is no need for this pissing contest," says the paramedic in charge of Colston's vitals.

"Then what is the fucking point of domestic laws if they are completely overlooked?" He brushes past Oliver and strides down the hall.

Kayra hesitates to reach for Colston's hand. He was right; she is the reason Colston is severely injured.

"Kayra, it's------okay." He says, his trembling hand still extended.

"Cole, he is right; he is trying to protect you. I struck you hard enough to cause damage. You are in danger when you are around me."

"Well, Jeff is in quite a foul mood," Oliver says.

The other paramedic looks at Oliver and says, "Can it, Ollie! The day's been full, and it's barely noon."

The room is filled with a tense silence.

"Coming through!" Jeff announces.

Kayra and Oliver move to the side in the bedroom.

"Alright, Colston, I'm going to help you sit up slowly, okay? Please let me know if you feel lightheaded or experience anything unusual."

Colston nods, frustrated by his inability to manage on his own. The mere thought of sitting up independently makes him feel lightheaded. As he feels hands supporting his shoulders, Jeff begins to lift him. Suddenly, he experiences a sharp pain from something bursting in his chest and cries out. Jeff paused, asking, "What is it?"

"Some------thing------popped." Colston says as he fades into unconsciousness.

"Colston?" Jeff asks.

"His blood pressure has dropped," his partner reports.

"Prepare the backboard, Jeff says, guiding Colston flat onto his back.

"Colston? What happened?" Kayra asks, doing her best to remain composed.

Jeff let out a loud sigh. "Something popped in his chest. It could be nothing, or..." He gently rolls Colston onto his right side as his partner slides the backboard under him. "Mrs. This, the act you're putting on? You can drop it; I see right through you." After securing Colston, he stands ready to lift him, meeting Kayra's hurt and tearful gaze.

"I would never willingly hurt my husband," she states emphatically.

Jeff turns, leaving his partner prepared to pick up the board at Colston's feet. He faces Kayra and says, "That is what they all say. Then a call comes through reporting that a death has happened."

"Jesus Christ, stop it," Oliver says, gently pulling Kayra back.

He turns to Oliver once more, saying, "We've seen it more than enough times. Why are you convinced that this is not a ticking time bomb?"

"It just won't! Now, get Colston to the hospital and do not prohibit a wife from being with her husband in his time of need."

"Even though it is her fault," Jeff concedes, but not without delivering one final jab. "Blood on your hands."

Kayra watches as they lift Colston from the floor onto the stretcher, desperately wanting to lie against him and plead for forgiveness.

Colston lets out a moan, rolling his head toward Kayra as he opens his eyes. She looks terrified. "Kay," he says, his voice muffled by the mask. He wiggles and flexes his left hand, feeling the strap across his forearm.

Kayra, despite the risk of further irritating Jeff, rushes to his side. Gripping Colston's hand with one hand and caressing his face with the other, she notices that the bruising on his chest is now much more prominent. "Forgive me, honey!"

Colston nods, and they exchange a meaningful glance.

"Alright, Colston, we need to get going. Your wife can meet us at the hospital." Jeff's voice is softer.

"I love you," Colston says.

"I love you too."

Kayra is left standing in her bedroom as

her husband is wheeled away.

"I am sorry you had to endure that," Oliver says, apologizing for Jeff's behavior.

She doesn't look away from the hall as they turn the corner and exit the house. "It is no different from the treatment that Colston receives from the police," she whispers.

"Before I take my leave, once Colston is discharged from the hospital, could he come to the police station? And Mrs. Driscoll, once you ensure that Colston is settled, could you come down to start the process of reopening the case?" Oliver asks.

"Yes," she replies, gazing at him, "you might want to speak with Jordan Youngblood, who is at the hospital following an altercation with Jed. Additionally, consider reaching out to Melody Dakota from Healthy Mind Better Lives."

Oliver nods and walks out.

Before heading out to the car, Kayra goes to the kitchen to retrieve Colston's phone and makes a call to Melody. She leaves a message. "This is Kayra Driscoll calling on behalf of my husband. He has sustained an injury that will require him to stay in the hospital overnight. Please, once you receive this message, I would appreciate a call back. Thank you."

"Colston, what triggered such a deadly reaction from your wife?" Brad, the partner, asks. Jeff chose to drive.

The mask is removed so he can speak. "A lot happened last night. I don't blame her."

"That is a clear indication that you did something and are too afraid to admit it, letting your wife take the blame." Brad's voice is bleak and going right for the throat.

Colston is struck with astonishment by the overwhelming lack of care and the assumptions people make. "We are all guilty of experiencing trauma and becoming overwhelmed by it at times," he reflects, wishing he were home right now.

"Yes, I am certain that she is simply exhausted by your fabricated trauma. We were all informed by Todd before he left town. Boy, howdy, did he accurately predict everything."

Colston lies there, feeling utterly dejected. Todd has turned not only the police against him but also the healthcare system as well. He somewhat wishes for the phantom to appear. Perhaps with his death, he will finally be believed. He is doing his best to remain calm so his heart doesn't feel like it's going to explode.

Kayra had just pulled into the hospital parking lot when Colston's phone rang. She answers it, "Hello."

A warm voice replies, *"Hi, Mrs. Driscoll. This is Melody. Is Colston alright? Are you okay?"*

Kayra feels emotional just with the genuine care. "I hurt him, and I'm afraid of losing him. So much happened last night." She dumps.

"Whoa, Mrs. Driscoll, take a few deep

breaths," Melody instructs gently. *"What happened? How did you hurt Colston?"*

"I was out of my mind with aggression and stress. I slammed my fists against his chest while he slept. I managed to regain control before I grabbed a knife." She feels nauseous and despises herself for being so weak under pressure.

There is a pause from Melody.

"I could hear Abigail Sunderland's voice stringing me like a puppet. She nearly convinced me to kill Colston four years ago."

"Okay, so this episode was triggered by stress rather than by Colston directly."

"Indirectly, trauma aggravating trauma, along with other variables that contribute to the hopelessness."

"Hey, everything will be okay. I will stop by in the morning. After I see Colston, I will call you. I have another session, so just hang in there."

The call disconnects. Kayra pockets both phones and steps out of the car, staring at the building, feeling numb. Why are they being punished? That question burns within her; Colston just wants to sing, and she wants to write and love him. So why are they being cast into the open flame, forced to believe they are not being burned? She takes a deep breath and reflects, *"I saw the look on Abigail's face when she received her life sentence. I know she can't hurt me, nor can her followers. They are all words and no action. Colston doesn't have that luxury; a face burned into his memory. Yet, he remains elusive to the rest of the world. This man is all action. It is up to me to make it harder for him to get anywhere near Colston. I know who harmed me; Colston doesn't. Lord, I shall take steps to avoid becoming overwhelmed. Please keep my love safe. Amen."*

Kayra makes her way into the hospital to see Jordan and hopes to find Colston before heading to the police station. As she enters the hospital, she takes in the slight chaos of the lobby. The reception desk is overwhelmed, allowing Kayra to slip into the elevator unnoticed. She has no idea where Colston is, but she wants to reassure Jordan that Colston is safe and here.

"Kayra, where is Colston?" Jordan's eyes filled with tears as he saw Kayra without Colston and noticed her downcast expression.

Kayra approaches him and says, "Hey, he's fine; he's here. He was in and out of consciousness, but he's here."

The relief that washes over Jordan is immense. "I want to see him."

"Tomorrow, right now, you both need to focus on recovery."

"I am fine; there is pain, but the concern about a concussion has long since passed. I remain at the doctor's behest. I just need to see Colston."

"I will inform you of the room number as soon as I find out. However, I need to go to the police station right now."

"What?" Jordan asks.

"Hopefully to reopen his case. You might get visited by an officer as well."

Jordan nods, "Be careful."

"I will."

She is leaving for the police station.

Not before she checks her phone and sees a message from Theodore: *"Ms. Walters, I have the check ready."*

Kayra smiles. This has been one of the hardest secrets to keep from Colston, but now it is about to pay off.

Chapter Eleven: Had Enough

Jordan lies in silence with his eyes closed. He isn't tired; he simply feels more at ease in the dark. He could have been released, but this is worrisome for the doctors.

There is a knock on the door, and it carefully opens, revealing an officer. "Mr. Youngblood?" the officer asks, drawing Jordan from the darkness.

"Yes?" Jordan replies, his heart sinking slightly, though Kayra had warned him.

The officer steps further into the room, retrieving his notepad from his breast pocket. "I am Officer Oliver Acarus, and I am here of my own accord, hoping to find justice for Colston Driscoll. Were you ever questioned after he was found?"

"I was not. I had just arrived in town shortly after he was found." The effort of thinking causes him a headache; he is willing to endure the pain if it means helping Colston. "I knew Colston enjoyed doing creepy things for October. It wasn't until the second upload that I had an overwhelming sense that something was wrong or perhaps his acting was just that convincing. I couldn't reach Colston, so I called Kayra, and that's when I discovered she hadn't been in contact with him for nine days." Jordan pauses and lays his head flat.

"I apologize if this is putting a strain on your injury," Oliver says softly.

Jordan simply dismisses the concern, saying, "I just want Colston's torment to end."

"I am trying to convince the detectives that they are not pursuing a ghost." Oliver replies sullenly.

"Colston was kidnapped, and his spirit was broken by that man. To see someone in uniform stepping up means everything to us," Jordan says.

Oliver feels a surge of disquiet, threatening his composure. He clears his throat and moves on to the next question, "What happened last night?"

Jordan provides a clear account of last night's events, detailing Colston's transformation after the note arrived at their table. He describes how deeply he retreated into his mind, becoming unresponsive. "I was lying here with a cooling pack over my eyes when the man entered. He covered my mouth with a gloved hand and whispered that if I alerted anyone, Colston would die that night. His voice was full of confidence as he assured me that both Kayra and I would be safe as long as Colston goes with him quietly, and he is prepared to kill him if he resists." As he recalls this moment, tears well up in his eyes. That voice sent chills down his spine.

"Did you get a look at him?"

Jordan takes a pained breath and replies, "No, my eyes were covered; I was in too much pain and just plain scared. I am sorry."

"Hey, shhh," Oliver says, stepping closer to the bed and placing a comforting hand on

Jordan's shoulder. "It's fine. I'm just trying to get an angle on this man."

"Right after the man left, Colston arrived. While Colston was with me, the man visited Kayra and left a note with her."

"He likes to leave notes. What did it say? If you can remember."

"Kayra read it to me; it mentioned that this would be the last he'd allow disrespect to slide. He had set the house on fire and was going to kill Colston when he heard him singing." Jordan's head is throbbing, and his vision is shaky.

Oliver notices Jordan's pain. "Rest now; I'll see about speaking to Kayra and Colston," he says. He is perplexed by the man's behavior. Naturally, he is not permitted to access the case files, which he may never see, as the detectives are working to have them sealed, a decision that only he seems to be attempting to prevent. He bids Jordan goodbye and leaves.

Colston lies in a hospital bed, utterly bored, and it has only been an hour and a half. He has avoided surgery, as the bleeding was caused by ruptured blood vessels that will heal on their own.

There is a knock on the door, and Oliver peeks in. "Sorry to disturb you, Mr. Driscoll. May I come in and ask you a few questions?"

"Sure, but only if you address me as Colston," he says with an easy smile.

Oliver nods and enters the room. "I just finished visiting Mr. Youngblood. I'm getting the details of what happened last night. He described how, when you sang in response to the note, you went deep into your mind and became unresponsive."

Colston immediately folds in on himself, and the laughter of the phantom fills his mind. "What----are----you----asking?"

The change in demeanor is startling to Oliver. "Is it that triggering?"

"Yes, when----the------idea----of re------membering those------ten------days." Colston says, struggling to pull himself into observation. He feels like a failure, unable to escape the memories of five years ago.

"Okay, Colston, I have one more thing to ask. When he saw Jordan, he said that if you fight, he'll kill you, but as long as you go quietly, Kayra and Jordan will be safe. However, in the note he left with Kayra, it stated along the lines of he had set the house on fire and was going to kill you but couldn't go through with it when he heard you singing. So my question is, what does he really want with you?"

Colston simply shakes his head and says, "I don't know. He's just insane."

"Okay, I am going to track down Kayra; I think she's at the station, and I'll try reaching out to Ms. Dakota."

"Thank you for not viewing this as a lost cause," Colston says, feeling a sense of relief, though he hears the warning sirens urging him not to get too comfortable. Colston can't help but feel grateful; he has faced opposition from many people of influence against him. Being able to rely on someone is a godsend because he grows weary of being on his own.

"Every case has a way to solve it. Some just require more digging than others. Get some rest, Colston." He turns to leave.

"Wait," Colston says, and when Oliver turns, he continues, "Your daughter, whom you mentioned earlier. What is her name?"

Oliver smiles. "Amber," he says, and leaves the room.

Colston reclines his head and dozes for a few hours.

When he wakes up, he wishes for Kayra, but he finds himself alone. He reaches into the left back pocket of his shorts and pulls out his notepad and pen. Propping himself up, he begins to write. His mind is in a whirlwind of emotions, making him feel isolated in this mess. So he writes:

I am alone in this nightmare, one that I didn't ask for. I must catch the phantom off guard as he believes he is wearing me down. But how?

Colston sets down the pen and rests his chin on his folded hands. He feels adrift. Wishing Kayra were here, as he attempts to ground himself. Just as he reaches for the pen again, the world begins to shift. He closes his eyes and takes a few deep breaths. *"I will rest after I get this out, please!"* he silently pleads with his body to align with his mind.

My mind beats my weary body, tired from the strain of the ordeal that refuses to let go. My wrists, still bound, yet not by tape but by the relentless fear. Free as I am, he still keeps me. I wait for the creak of the wood and him to break through my weak defenses. I must see the fire in his eyes extinguished, the insanity erased. There, among the cooling embers, the key to my cage. My warmth, my hope. To feel whole again.

Colston writes, still having found no way to help himself. He looks out the window and sees the sun beginning to set, painting the sky deep purple and red.

A knock on his door draws his attention as a nurse enters and announces, "I need to take your vitals."

Colston nods and lays back, closing his notepad.

"How are you feeling this evening?" she asks while putting on the blood pressure cuff.

"Alright," Colston replies, only half lying.

"Blood pressure is high: 134 over 83, temperature 90, pulse 101, and rate 20." As she puts away the equipment, she adds, "Okay, Colston, I'm going to get you another blanket, and I'll hook you up to a saline drip. I want you to rest for an hour; try to sleep."

Colston nods and lowers the bed to a more comfortable position. His eyes are already heavy.

A few minutes later, a different nurse enters, carrying a heavy blanket over one arm and pushing an IV tray.

"Colston, I have a blanket for you," the nurse says kindly and quietly. Colston's restful state is interrupted, triggered by the simple statement.

"Colston," the man called coaxingly, "I have another blanket for you." Colston briefly gazed into the eerily lit spheres but found it difficult to maintain that gaze. "It's your fault," the man hissed, tapping Colston's left cheek. "If you say it and truly mean it, your accommodations can change."

The nurse's expression shifts from calm to worried. "Colston? What is it?"

The flashback is brief but leaves Colston feeling uneasy. "So--sorry, a----flashback," he says.

"What kind of flashback?" The nurse lays the blanket over him.

He lies on his right side, instinctively pulling his legs up and drawing the blanket to his shoulders. As the effects of the flashback fade, he realizes he has been careless once again.

"I'd rather not talk about it." Colston says.

The nurse nods. "Alright, I am going to need your arm for just a moment."

Colston slides his arm out from under the blanket. For a moment, his bare arm feels the chill from the bathroom, but as the nurse touches it, warmth spreads instantly.

He lies back, fighting tears.

"You're going to feel a little pinch," he warns.

Colston feels it but is unaffected, staring at the ceiling and waiting for the nurse to leave.

"Alright, Colston." The nurse slides the arm back under the blanket. "Just relax, okay?"

When he hears the door close, he allows tears to fall.

Kayra leaves the police station feeling extremely depressed, confused, and angry. The interviewing detective, Conright, tried to explain that Colston was being manipulative, using his situation to overshadow what happened to her with Abigail. She was urged to consider this carefully: why hadn't Colston opened up about it? Whenever Kayra attempted to explain, she was shut down and told that Colston was afraid of the real truth coming out. They didn't even look at the notes indicating his kidnapper's reappearance.

Kayra shut it down after four hours of receiving no signs of help. Colston is neither lying nor exaggerating his trauma.

Sitting in her car, she tries to compose herself. The sun has set, and it may be a long shot, but she needs to see Colston after being turned away earlier.

Before she can go to him, however, she has some business to attend to. While sitting in her car fighting back tears, she hears soft knocking on her window. The sudden noise nearly makes her fumble her phone. She looks up to see Oliver standing there looking both anxious and assured.

She rolls down her window. "Why weren't you there?" she asks, her emotions getting the better of her. "I just spent four hours listening to them paint Colston as a manipulator, insisting it was a stunt gone wrong. It's all a show, and he was in on it!"

Before Oliver can reply, another detective exits the station and announces, "Officer Acarus, the captain wants you in his office now for allegedly stepping outside your jurisdiction."

Oliver gives Kayra a sincere look of apology before turning to return to the station. Kayra witnesses Oliver hand off a notebook to the other detective before they both disappear inside.

Frustrated with how people are treating Colston, Kayra draws her attention back to her phone and texts, *"Theo, sorry it's late. Could I possibly snag that check from you?"*

"Of course, I am still at my office."

"Be there in ten."

Kayra puts down her phone and freshens up. She's not in the mood for questions; she just hopes this won't hurt Colston too badly.

Kayra pulls up to a building that houses several storefronts. The headlights illuminate the name, *Theo's Odes.* Theodore, tall, lanky, and bald, leans in the open doorway, wearing a smile and playfully waving a check. Kayra smiles, feeling guilty as she turns off the lights. Theodore walks toward the driver's side, and Kayra rolls down the window. He leans against the edge with his arms folded.

"Evening, Laura," The check dangles from his fingers inside the car.

"After this, it will no longer be Laura Walters, at least to you." Kayra replies quietly.

Theodore pulls back in shock. "Taking the money and running?" he teases.

Kayra stares at him, stunned and slightly annoyed by his playful tone, then shakes her head. She breaks eye contact, guilt rising to a near uncomfortable level, and replies, "No, I have not been honest with you."

"Here," he smiles softly, urging her to take the check. "Then my hunch was right?"

Kayra briefly glances at him before shifting her eyes to the check. The amount is fifteen thousand dollars and made out to Kayra Driscoll. "How?" Kayra asks.

Three years ago, Kayra had started writing poetry to cope with her father's death. She wanted to surprise Colston with a getaway, so she used a pen name the entire time.

"I watch CCE and stumbled across Colston's channel through your engagement announcement video. You seemed genuinely happy, not trying to escape an abusive husband."

Tears well up at the mention of that title in relation to Colston; it's beyond painful. "I did this to help my mom and to surprise Colston with a getaway," she confesses.

"Wait here," Theodore says, then he turns and runs back into the store.

Kayra is in shock over the amount.

Theodore comes running back with a stack of books in his arms, exclaiming, "A gift!" He smiles and passes the stack through the window.

Kayra smiles and thanks him, setting them in the passenger seat without looking at them.

"No, look at them," he urges gently.

Confused she does. The cover is a glossy blue with gold flowers surrounding the title *Lament for a Father's Comfort*. They bear Kayra's real name.

She gasps, tears filling her eyes.

"Given the personal nature of the collection. Not to worry, that stack alone bears your name." He offers reassuringly.

"Thank you. I need to go share this with my husband."

She shifts the car back onto the road and heads to the hospital. The moment of joy is fleeting as her mind becomes overwhelmed by the events of the last four hours and the reason she is visiting her husband in the hospital. She feels torn between her trust and love for Colston and the police's trained perspectives, which make her question everything, a feeling she despises yet finds hard to ignore as it encroaches on her gut feelings.

Before she enters the hospital, she stows her books in the trunk, then with one tucked under her arm. Enters the hospital unaware of the tears streaming down her face.

"Ma'am, are you okay?" An older nurse asks her gently, easily recognizing Kayra.

"I need to visit my husband, Colston Driscoll."

The nurse offers a sad, sympathetic smile and seems about to speak but then closes her mouth, placing a hand on Kayra's shoulder. "Come with me."

She guides Kayra through the sparsely populated lobby and into an elevator.

"Mrs. Driscoll I'm Elnore, and I'm responsible for monitoring your husband tonight. Due to the new restrictions related to the virus, visiting hours have long since ended. However, considering who your husband is and the briefing we received when Todd departed town, there are several of us who genuinely care. To be frank, you don't seem fit to drive, so I'm allowing you to stay with him. Perhaps you can assist if he has another flashback, as he is reluctant to discuss them."

Elnore's words fill her with a sense of dread but also relief that good people still exist. "How many has he had?" Kayra asks softly.

"One that has been noted. So these flashbacks are normal?"

"They are persistent, yes." Kayra replies.

"I won't press for the story behind them. I just need to know if they've made him violent toward you or himself." She says gently.

"No," she replies, shivering but managing to keep her voice calm. "But they are wearing on him."

The elevator opens. "Go see your husband, room 308: I'll go grab a cot for you."

"Thank you."

Kayra rushes down the hall to his room.

She sends a text to Jordan with Colston's floor and room number. Then she steadies herself and opens the door. Colston is asleep under a heavy blanket; his right arm is exposed with an IV port in his arm, but nothing is connected to it.

She longs to be in his arms. She is doing her best to ignore the relentless reprimand for her desire to defend her love and the truth that Colston is not manipulative. She walks over to her lightly snoring husband, and before intertwining her fingers with his outstretched hand, she places her poetry book on the floor.

He instantly folds his hand around hers. "Kayra?" His voice is groggy.

"Yes, love, I didn't mean to wake you. I just wanted to hold you."

His eyes slowly open, and a smile spreads across his lips. "I'd rather wake up to you than anything."

A soft knock sounds at the door. Kayra moves aside so Colston can see who it is, but she doesn't let go of his hand.

Elnore and another person enter the room. "Colston, can I take your order for dinner?" the other asks.

"Um... " He isn't really hungry. "A salad and--" he says, shaking the hand that holds Kayra's.

"Chicken strips, please." Kayra responds.

"Drinks?"

"Hot tea, please." Colston replies.

"Water is fine for me, thanks."

Elnore sets down a cot and leaves them alone.

Kayra sits on the bed, unsure of what to tell Colston first. Whether it's the good or the bad, she is grateful to be here and can look into his eyes, seeing nothing but love for her.

He reaches up and tucks her hair behind her ear. "Sweetheart, please don't let this consume you."

"You're in a hospital bed because of me. How could it not?" Kayra asks, squeezing his hand.

He moves their intertwined hands and places them over his heart, resisting cringing in pain at the touch. "I'm alive;

I'm with you, and nothing will change that."

"How did I get so lucky?"

She leans down to the floor and grabs her book. When she hands it to him, Colston looks at her with a mix of confusion and happiness. "Kayra?" he asks, his mouth agape.

She smiles, "I've been doing this in secret for the last two years. I wanted to surprise you."

Colston sits up and embraces her. "I'm so proud of you. Also, I know that Savion is too."

Kayra then reaches into her pocket and pulls out the check. "Half for my mom, and the other half to whisk us away on a vacation or to help with moving."

Colston stares at the amount and hugs her tighter. "I'm sorry."

Kayra pulls away and gazes at him in wonder, "What? Why?"

"I missed it; I was caught up in my own stuff. I didn't see your own passion pouring out."

She runs her hands gently down his face and speaks lovingly, "You missed it because I hid it from you, only writing when you were in your studio or late at night while you were sleeping. You're not mad?"

"Congratulations! Once I'm out of here, we'll celebrate properly. Honey, why would I ever be angry at you for this?"

Kayra shrugs. "It could be seen as a betrayal since I did it without you knowing."

Colston cups her face. "I would never feel betrayed by this. If anything, I'm amazed you kept it a secret for so long." He kisses her.

She kisses and embraces him, "These are special for the family. The public knows me as Laura Walters."

Colston understands the reasoning behind that. Kayra pulls out his phone and hands it to him. "You should let your dad know you're in the hospital," she suggests.

Colston shakes his head. "I'll tell him when I get out and some of my strength has returned."

Kayra stares at him with curiosity and a hint of fear. She decides it's not the right moment to ask questions. Lying down beside him, he opens the book.

Jordan is having his eyes tested.

"Alright, Jordan, there is no swelling. Is there any pain when you move your eyes?"

"A little when I try to look far left and right, but it's nothing I can't handle."

"Good! Do you notice any blurriness or dark spots?"

"No, but could I walk the hallways for a bit and assess how I feel afterward? I want to make sure that I am fit to make the drive home in a few days."

"That's not a bad idea. I'll return in three hours for your one AM vitals, and if you're not asleep, I'll take your report. You might be able to leave here tomorrow. However, regarding your drive home, you may need to plan for a two-day trip just until you're one hundred percent."

"Alright," Jordan smiles and slowly gets out of bed.

"Do you want someone with you, just in case?"

"I'll be slow," Jordan reassures him.

"Okay, have a nice walk."

Jordan nods and allows him to leave before attempting to fully stand. This time, he does so without relying on the wall he typically uses when going to the bathroom. He stands tall, letting his legs adjust. Once steady, he walks to the door. There is a slight weakness in his legs, but now that he is standing and walking for more than just a few seconds, his head begins to pound.

He opens the door and enters the hallway. It is quiet as he walks toward the elevator. He wants to check on Colston, his best friend and singing partner. He doesn't want him to dwell on what happened; he needs to focus on getting better and building his strength to fight.

The throbbing behind his eyes is intense, and he is just a few feet from his room. He continues concentrating on the floor and room number that Kayra sent. He could check the message again, but looking at his phone isn't wise in his current state.

He reaches the elevator without being stopped and presses the down button. As he waits, his head pounds. When the door opens, he steps inside. As the elevator descends, the pressure makes his eyes throb. He closes his eyes and tips his head back to ease the pain and to keep his meal of hamburger, chips, grapes, and soda settled in his stomach.

The elevator stops on the third floor.

Jordan steps out into another empty hallway.

"Sir, can I help you?" A strong but tired voice sounds from Jordan's left.

He turns slowly and sees a doctor approaching him. "I'm just out for a walk," Jordan replies, not wanting to reveal that he is visiting another patient.

"You need to go back to your floor," the doctor says.

"Doc I'm sorry; I just want to ensure I can go home tomorrow. I'm taking the elevator and then walking the stairs to see how my injury holds up," Jordan explains. "I won't be here long," he adds.

The doctor sighs, "I'll hold you to that," he says, stepping into the elevator.

Jordan desperately needs to sit but continues shuffling toward room 308. He glances at the sign with an arrow pointing right to rooms 305-308. He walks to the right, straining his tired eyes to read the room number 307. Turning left, he walks a few feet until he sees the door on the left side of the hall; the plaque reads 308. He thinks he hears Kayra.

He knocks and opens the door. "Colston?" he asks as he peeks inside.

Colston is sitting up and slowly eating his salad. He had no appetite before ordering, but after hearing what Kayra endured at the police station, he feels like vomiting.

"Jordan?" Colston looks up at the door.

Kayra gets off the bed and rushes to the door. "JD, what are you doing?"

Jordan gently grabs her by the arm,

saying, "I needed to see Colston, and I need to sit down."

"Come on," Kayra replies, leading him to the bed.

Seeing how pale Colston is, Jordan asks, "Are you alright?" as he sits on the bed.

"Tired and sore. You don't look too terrible yourself." Colston says, trying to lighten the mood.

"I got off lucky, but I am definitely hanging up my boxing gloves."

Silence follows as no one wants to discuss the obvious elephants in the room. Colston lets out a sigh. "I am sorry. You two are getting hurt and traumatized because I wasn't strong enough when it could have made a difference."

"Don't you dare blame yourself," Jordan says, reaching for and gripping one of Colston's hands. "This!" he points to his face. "Is the result of an asshole. Don't beat yourself up over something you couldn't control."

Kayra grips his other hand and holds his gaze. "We love you and are willing to endure the hurt with you. Sure, I had a major hiccup, but I've let go of my fear and won't be swayed from your side again."

Tears slide down Colston's cheeks; he struggles to find the right words. He feels grateful but unworthy of such sentiments. Both Jordan and Kayra move closer and embrace Colston.

There is a knock on the door, and Elnore enters. "Um, excuse me, Mr. Youngblood. You are not supposed to be here. I assure you that Mr. Driscoll will pull through. Now, if you could please return to your room." She is gentle yet firm.

"Stay strong," he whispers before pulling away from the embrace.

Colston nods.

"I'll help him back to his room," Kayra says.

"Thank you." Elnore replies, starting to take Colston's vitals.

"Alright, Colston, just relax. This will only take a second."

Colston nods and feels the cuff squeeze and then release.

"Looking good, blood pressure 122 over 78, temp is 97.9, pulse 93, rate is 17. It seems you've escaped another saline drip."

"Good," Colston says, his voice airy.

"Alright, I shouldn't have to do that again tonight," Elnore says before leaving Colston alone.

He reaches for his notepad again.

I drink from the cup of poison, wanting so badly to seal my lips against the burning liquid. I know it is bad; it is killing me, yet I swallow down the insanity, delaying death a bit longer. Dead by poison or dead by his hand, there is no escaping. A loophole there must be in this fate's design. I can't be destined to meet my end like this; I must take back control... but how?

At that moment, Kayra returns.

"Is Jordan okay?" Colston asks, feeling sleep settle in.

"He is in pain; he hopes to be released tomorrow," Kayra replies, walking over to Colston and gently running her fingers through his hair. "Babe, you should sleep."

Colston yawns, "Yeah, you're right."

"I'll be here." Kayra assures him.

The following morning, Friday at 8:10,

Jordan is still trying to sleep off the headache he gave himself last night. A loud knock jolts him awake. The door opens to reveal a well-dressed man.

"Mr. Youngblood, I am Detective Barnet. I need to ask you some cleanup questions that Officer Acarus inquired about yesterday about the Colston Driscoll alleged kidnapping case five years ago."

Jordan clearly detects the condescension in the detective's voice, which irritates him.

"Alleged? No, it happened. You saw the bruises on his body and the condition he was found in. But you don't see the lasting effects this has on him mentally and in his job." Jordan says, shaking with anger, causing his head to spin. "And the man is back!"

"Yes, I have the notes from the officer. But let me ask some clarifying questions with our investigative skills. Why come to you? Why not just take him?" The detective asks carelessly.

"I don't know!" Jordan exclaims, clenching his fists in the sheets. "How can you be apathetic toward the people you're meant to protect?"

"And how convenient that he came in here and you didn't notice." The detective steps forward aggressively, a sly smile forming on his lips. "If this man were here, someone would have spotted him, or the camera would have caught him." The detective is now inches away from Jordan.

Jordan stares at the detective with fear

and anger. "What are you suggesting, sir?" he asks shakily, his head pounding.

The detective smirks and steps back slightly. "Colston shows up here ten minutes after the supposed kidnapper. Then, five minutes after Colston left the cameras' view, the alleged kidnapper appeared to Kayra and vanished into the night. After that, Colston arrived."

"I don't want to hear this! Colston is a victim of kidnapping!" he cries out.

"Are you sure about that?" The detective turns and walks out.

Jordan stares at the door, shell-shocked. *"Colston is a victim, not..."* The pounding in his head intensifies, and he leans back and passes out.

Colston wakes up gently and finds Kayra sitting on the cot, looking out the window. It is an overcast day, and there seems to be a threat of rain.

"Kayra?" Colston asks.

Kayra turns her head and smiles. "Babe." She gets up and walks over to him. "How are you?"

"I'm okay," Colston replies, taking her hand. "Hon, I am so sorry. I wish I had been there yesterday."

"I should have had better control over myself. In my fear and stress, I let her brainwashing take over," Kayra whispers sadly.

Colston shakes his head. "Kayra I know she hurt you, and your silence about that time is you trying not to overwhelm me. But honey, when I help you or praise your accomplishments, it keeps me grounded. You can tell me. I want this to be over so badly. I just want to know who he is so we can live a normal life."

Kayra kneels beside the bed and softly says, "I will be by your side. I love you dearly. Soon I'll share my truth because it hurts to keep it from you. I want you to be a little stronger before I do."

"Thank you; I love you too."

Kayra leans in and kisses him.

The door swings open, and Kayra looks up while Colston glances over his shoulder. Standing there is the same detective who was just speaking with Jordan. In one hand, he holds a folder, and in the other, he displays his badge.

Kayra stands firm, gripping Colston's hand for stability. This is the detective who called out Oliver yesterday at the police station. "Could this please wait, sir?" Kayra pleads.

The man looks at her and gestures with the hand holding the badge. "Mrs. Driscoll, this can't wait. There is nothing going on, and if you had listened to my partner yesterday, you would consider severing your marriage and entering witness protection." His gaze shifts to Colston. "If Mr. Driscoll understood the trouble he could face; he would feel a mental relief after dropping the act and admitting that his kidnapping never happened!" the man declares.

Colston stares, breath stolen from his lungs, feeling very small. He is petrified;

his mind is shattered. The hopeful expectation of protection by the police has vanished, leaving him exposed. His thoughts are trapped in a cold cage where he hears the phantom's laughter echoing endlessly.

"It did happen." Colston's voice trembles like a child caught with his hand in the cookie jar.

The man approaches with an expression of apathy. He slams a folder down on the tray that holds Colston's notepad and a cup half full of water, spilling it along Colston's back.

"Hey!" Kayra exclaims.

Colston squeezes her hand.

"There is no evidence of another person!"

Colston rolls onto his back, the cold water soaking his gown and the waistband of his shorts.

"Just look at the videos on my channel! You can clearly see him snatching me and then standing behind me as I sang!" His voice remains quiet.

The detective slams his hand down, "ALL AN ACT! YOU PAID HIM OFF!"

Colston is ripped back into his memories.

His captor punched the floor. "YOU HAVE NO CHOICE!" He lunged forward, roughly grabbing Colston's hair, yanking his head back, and striking him across the face. Colston gasped in pain, his eyes watering as the man twisted his head and restrained his struggling body, making him realize that fighting was futile and that the man was in control. "I didn't want to do this. It's your fault."

Colston experiences no respite, shifting

from a nightmare to being accused of orchestrating it all.

"The house was abandoned; among the ashes, there was no sign of anyone else. You set it up too cleanly! Here is some indisputable proof that falsifies your statement. The van was purchased two weeks before the alleged kidnapping. It was bought from Larson's Marketplace. Although the van was never registered, we tracked down the seller. He described the buyer as bulky, wearing a full-face mask and paying in cash, which contradicts your description of him as skinny. It was signed off by the 'Driscoll Defender.'" The folder opens, revealing pictures that support his claims. He leans in close to Colston, triggering another flashback.

"You might be a tormented angel, but you're acting like a SPOILED CHILD throwing a fucking temper tantrum! It may be your 26th birthday; however, this is not your party!" His voice lost its calm halfway through.

"It's not normal for me to be kidnapped and used for entertainment." Colston shot back.

The man placed a hand on his chest and caressed his face. Colston shifted sharply, "Don't touch me!" The man fell fully on top of him.

Quickly correcting himself and remaining crouched over Colston. He slapped him."You don't have to act anymore! You can be your true self with me, Colston." He slapped him again.

"I'm not going to sing for you!" Colston retorted.

What the detective was saying went

unheard by Colston, who was still caught up in the berating.

"STOP!" Colston yells, fed up with the situation.

The detective jumps back but smirks, "Just tell the truth!"

"Leave me alone! I know what happened to me, and IT DID happen!" Colston raises his voice. His heart begins to pound as he squeezes Kayra's hand to help calm himself.

Kayra's other hand rests on his chest, feeling the rapid beats.

"Colston!" A voice of a woman calls as she rushes into the room.

It is Melody. Kayra watches as Colston passes out. "Colston!"

"Detective!" Melody shouts.

The detective points at Kayra. "He's faking it to escape the truth." He places a heavy hand on Colston's shoulder.

Kayra immediately pushes it away. He stares at her as if she had slapped him.

"This conduct is unacceptable! I was informed that this interview would take place at the station under the assumption of reopening his case. In reality, you're trying to convince Colston that he is delusional."

The detective steps away from Colston, glaring at Melody and speaking sharply, "Are you his lawyer?"

"His therapist," Melody replies.

"Then, sweetheart, how about you mind your own business? If you intend to defend this delusional content creator," the detective retorts.

"His passing out is not an admission of

guilt!" Melody insists.

"Then what the hell do you call it?" The detective challenges angrily.

"This man is in the hospital after fainting due to heart problems! Do you really think he would let himself die rather than drop the charade?"

The detective stares at her with narrow eyes. "I trust the evidence, and it all points to him faking it!"

"To whose benefit? Certainly not his or his wife's!" She glances at Kayra, who has her hands over Colston's ears. "Leave!" Melody orders.

The detective moves to collect the folder and pictures, adding one last remark. "Even you are lying to yourself; he is here because his wife attacked him in his sleep!"

Kayra is trying to wake Colston while watching the detective leave the room. Melody approaches the bed and offers her hand to Kayra. "I'm sorry about this. I don't know why it's happening."

Kayra shakes Melody's hand with her other hand, unwilling to let go of Colston.

Means to and end. Pain and misery to follow. Why even bother?

Means to and end. Pain and misery to follow. Why even bother?

Means to and end. Pain and misery to follow. Why even bother?

Means to and end. Pain and misery to follow. Why even bother?

Means to and end. Pain and misery to follow. Why even bother?

Means to and end. Pain and misery to follow. Why even bother?

Means to and end. Pain and misery to follow. Why even bother?

Means to and end. Pain and misery to follow. Why even bother?

Means to and end. Pain and misery to follow. Why even bother?

Means to and end. Pain and misery to follow. Why even bother?

Means to and end. Pain and misery to follow. Why even bother?

Means to and end. Pain and misery to follow. Why even bother?

Means to and end. Pain and misery to follow. Why even bother?

Means to and end. Pain and misery to follow. Why even bother?

Means to and end. Pain and misery to follow. Why even bother?

Means to and end. Pain and misery to follow. Why even bother?

Means to and end. Pain and misery to follow. Why even bother?

Means to and end. Pain and misery to follow. Why even bother?

Means to and end. Pain and misery to follow. Why even bother?

Means to and end. Pain and misery to follow. Why even bother?

Means to and end. Pain and misery to follow. Why even bother?

Means to and end. Pain and misery to follow. Why even bother?

Means to and end. Pain and misery to follow. Why even bother?

Means to and end. Pain and misery to follow. Why even bother?

Chapter Twelve: Closing In

Melody quickly notices the loss of color in Kayra's face and feels the weakness in her handshake. "Kayra, are you okay?" She asks, moving around the bed to ensure she can catch her if she falls.

Kayra stares fixedly at Colston's still face, waiting for her voice to return. To her relief, the murderous voice does not speak; instead, the cool, reassuring voice of the phantom washes over her like a freezing wave, reinforcing the need to leave Colston. She hears Melody but cannot respond. The hand gripping Colston's hand tightens in fearful desperation as she lowers her face to his neck. "Please, babe," she weeps. "I am not going to leave you, but..." She whispers in his ear, "I am afraid for you."

Colston hears her words echo in the darkness where he lies seeking reprieve from pain and suffering. He likes it here, but he is not ready to let go. He forces himself back to the pain, hoping to avoid hearing the detective yelling at him. Soft voices drift in, accompanied by the rustling of chairs or something with substantial heft.

"Why was Todd able to turn everyone against me?" Colston asks on the verge of tears, completely devastated. He rolls his head to see Kayra and Melody sitting on the cot next to his bed.

"This is a case of victim blaming. Law enforcement has been unable to uncover anything to support your claims. To save face, they shift the blame onto the victim. In most cases, this leaves the victim feeling helpless and unable to relax. In your situation with Todd, he is trying to make you buckle under constant pressure and scrutiny."

"He--has--revealed--himself," Colston says, looking at Kayra. "He--got--close." He pauses, struggling to compose himself, overwhelmed with emotion.

Kayra places her hand on his chest and whispers, "Shh, babe." She looks at Melody. "How is this treatment legal?"

"It is not," Melody replies bluntly. "And unfortunately, I believe that if we could find any physical proof against this man, they would do everything in their power to suggest it was all a social media stunt. Not necessarily a failure but that the trauma behind it is fake."

"The walls continue to close in, and I am on my own. Without the support I have, I'd be dead. But he's out there waiting, and I have no shield."

Kayra grips his shoulder, saying, "We need to just leave."

Colston gazes at her and pulls her close, rubbing her cheek with his thumb. "Honey, as much as I want to cut and run, I don't want to give them the satisfaction of driving me out of town with their misconduct. I also don't want him to follow us when we move." This is Colston's way of beginning the mental preparations to confront the phantom, which seems like a grim undertaking. But he needs to end this once and for all just to feel relief from this pain.

"How long can you endure this?" Kayra asks pleadingly, gently resting her head on his chest. "You can't wait forever. Prepared as I am to stand at your side, I utterly refuse to watch you slip away from this."

"It----won't----be for----ever." He replies, rubbing her back.

"He's right; this man has waited five years, and now that he has made himself known, it shouldn't be long before he makes his move," Melody adds.

Kayra lifts her head off of her husband's chest but replaces it with her hand, gaining strength and reassurance in its rhythm. She gazes directly at Melody. "I am not going to wait for him to be taken again--or worse. That man's brashness mixed with calculated words and an absolutely assured tone is frightening. The police have told me to leave him." Tears spill down her cheeks, feeling Colston's hand cover hers. "'If you love this man, you'll let him go.' 'Free yourself from this manipulator and sever your marriage.' I now have to wait for the man who frightened my songbird to return to his life, knowing that this man once considered killing him." She stops and lies beside Colston.

He holds her tightly and says, "Jordan---we need---to check---on--him. I---don't---want him--alone--if that--detective g--got to--him." He swallows hard, and with a quiver to his chin.

Melody listens intently, observing that Colston is facing someone far too clever for his own good, and it seems this person intends to follow through on his threats. She wants to understand the last bit but takes in the toll of this emotional turmoil and decides to wait on seeking understanding.

"Where is your friend?" she asks.

"Here. In room 406, Jordan Youngblood. " Kayra answers before Colston can respond, wanting to avoid listening to his struggle and snuggling against him for warmth while being mindful of his sore chest.

"I'll go see him and try to have him moved down here," Melody says.

Colston looks at her, his trembling hand outstretched, wheezing, "Don't----get----yourself--in trouble." Panic fills his voice and his eyes.

Melody offers a reassuring smile. "I am here to help people. Colston, you're caught in a rut, pinned between injustice and the desire for healing. There is strength in you, but you can only endure for so long before losing hope. You have Kayra, Jordan, and me pulling you out of that rut."

"You are our miracle," Kayra says.

"Far from it; I just provide a different perspective to help the miracle that is Colston to thrive. I'm going to go now."

Colston lays his head back, his mind swirling with vivid thoughts. His moribund self dragging his almost useless body toward the cage door while also seeing his enduring self in the bathroom, wrists bound and wrapped in a comforter, facing torment as the fire creeps ever closer, eager to consume him.

Kayra notices his breathing pattern

change; he is dreaming. She stays close, hoping to provide him comfort and hope in the dream.

"Babe, you are not alone," she whispers.

The door opens, and a male nurse enters with the vital machine.

Melody knocks on the door of room 406 and slowly opens it. She finds Jordan lying in bed with a damp rag over his eyes.

"Mr. Youngblood?" she asks.

Jordan doesn't move but replies sharply, "If you are not a doctor or a nurse, I have no desire to talk."

Melody senses the pain. "I understand, but I am here to help your friend Colston."

Jordan carefully lifts his head, and the cloth falls away. His eyes are red and puffy. "Are you truly here to help, or are you just going to blame him?"

Melody shakes her head and steps fully into the room. "I'm Melody, his therapist. I'm here to ensure Colston's safety as we help him navigate these emotional traumas."

"So you know that he is a victim of kidnapping, and his kidnapper plans to reclaim him?"

"Yes."

The relief he feels is immense, yet that hesitation to trust remains. "How could they ignore the beating he endured or that he nearly froze to death? How could they think he allowed it to happen?"

"His kidnapper is playing a calculated game, ensuring everyone knows their place. When he thinks Colston is most vulnerable, he'll strike. What did he tell you last night?"

Jordan takes a breath, fighting his emotions. "I want to stop thinking Colston is dead; it's like my mind has already written him off, and I hate it! That... That evil person stole in here last night to tell me; if Colston resists, he's dead; he can save him from himself. Yet, left me unharmed... physically. Why?" He feels some relief in divulging his haunting truth, free of deadly consequence, even though, Colston knows.

"Mr. Youngblood, the uncertainty of the situation and the fear of death are causing your mind to prepare for the worst-case scenario. We will ensure that nothing happens." Melody continues, as Jordan's hardhearted voice laughs mockingly. "To him, Colston's life is the ultimate price. By not threatening you directly and by using Colston, he's further isolating him. He maintains control by keeping you safe, as it offers hope for Colston while in captivity. People who love him still want him to fight. If Colston resists, it will only lead to pain. However, it would take a lot for him to outright kill Colston. He'd likely allow him to die by other means."

Jordan looks defeated. "Then you haven't read the latest note, the one he boldly placed in Kayra's hand!"

"What note?" Melody asks curiously.

"The maniac started the fire at the house and intended to kill him. When he heard Colston singing, he saved him instead. If he gets him, we'll never see him again!"

This knowledge confuses Melody with everything else she knows. However, if this man, steadfast in his fabricated conviction, is met with resistance long enough, the outcome will be deadly.

The hesitation in Melody's response is not the reassurance he wanted. "We have to do something!" Jordan pleads, grappling with the pain of his injury and the thought of losing Colston to this maniac.

"Mr. Youngblood I came up here to see if I could have you moved to Colston's room so we could work something out together." Melody says.

"Jordan, please, I'll come regardless of what the doctors say."

"Jordan, your health is just as important as Colston's." Melody replies.

He pauses halfway out of bed, and with a look of pure love, says, "I have watched that man slip and slide on the brink for the last five years. The struggle is evident in his eyes and voice as he sings. This fight is draining the life out of him. I will no longer sit idly by and let it happen." Jordan's voice trembles with emotion.

Melody smiles. "Then let's go."

The vitals report is good, but Colston remains asleep during it, and the nurse informs Kayra that his doctor will arrive in an hour. She nods, and the nurse leaves. About fifteen minutes, later he starts crying in his sleep. Kayra, lying beside him, finds this to be the most unsettling thing she has ever witnessed. He wakes up screaming, pleading, thrashing in panic, or simply sweating cold. He has never just cried without any other reaction.

She props herself up on her elbow, caressing his cheek. "Colston, come back to me."

His eyes snap open, revealing their faded color. He focuses on Kayra. "It's all closing in on me. I don't think I'm strong enough," Colston says, feeling both annoyed with himself and resigned to his inevitable fate.

"No, stop that talk. Don't let the detective's words bring you down or let the maniac's subtle threats consume your mind. You will prevail," Kayra says, watching the color gradually return to his eyes.

"I need to sing," Colston says, unsure where the urge is coming from but feeling it deep within.

"Sing, baby," Kayra encourages.

"I have no idea what to sing," he replies, his mind blank for lyrics.

"Don't think, just sing," Kayra urges.

He nods and allows the words to flow from wherever the desire has come.

The song that is calling for him to sing is *Fight Song* by Rachel Platten. Its lyrics resonate with the need to heal the damage caused by the detective. Like the fire threatening to consume him, there is another fire, one of fearlessness and relentless passion. Small yet burning brightly, it remains untouched by the phantom's desires. As the song concludes, that fire begins to lose its grip and fades into the cold. Colston now understands that he can only rekindle that fire when he manages this fearful chill.

Jordan and Melody arrive halfway through. Jordan can't believe it; he is hearing Colston sing without the struggle and burden of his past. Kayra hears it too and embraces him tightly.

Colston, holding Kayra and looking at Jordan and Melody, sees his support system, small yet steadfast.

"That was beautiful, Colston," Melody says.

Jordan nods and approaches the bed. "How are you, bud?"

"I am scared," Colston replies.

Melody moves closer; it's vital for Colston to feel in control of his mind in this moment. "I know you've been through a lot, but I need you to tell me what's going on. What's making you scared?"

Colston looks at Jordan, then down at Kayra. "You guys might want to leave," he says, though he really doesn't want them to go. Given what has been shared and seen, this might be too much.

Jordan shares a look with Kayra, then reaches out to take her hand while gripping Colston's with the other. "From here on out we are in this together. Truths are craving to be shared, and we will endure them together," Jordan says.

Kayra nods and gently rests her chin on his chest.

Colston sighs, doing his best to keep his voice steady. "I am desperately trying to find the key to unlock..." He pauses, looking into their expectant eyes. Shame wells up as he chooses to lie. "To unlock that door to freedom. I find myself dragging what I call my 'moribund self' toward the cage door, a door that never seems to get any closer. I am surviving on the little hope that remains, which is quickly dimming. Now there is something new that is equally terrifying. My 'enduring self' is in the bathroom, facing torment, bound, and freezing. Ahead of me moving ever closer is the fire. Yet I make no move to escape." Colston finishes with a strangled breath.

Melody processes what has just been shared. "Okay, which part of yourself do you most often see through the eyes of?"

Colston takes a deep breath. "Mainly I am seeing through the eyes of my enduring self, trying to numb myself to what is happening and focusing on pushing forward as best I can. I am constantly trying to break open that cage. After a nightmare or when I feel beaten down by shame and guilt, I'm locked in my moribund self, losing hope quickly," he says.

"When do you feel the cold and have trouble speaking clearly?"

"It is both as the cold is present in both states. I thought going to the house would help me unlock that cage."

"You were tired of feeling trapped and incomplete," Melody recalled from the session with Todd. "This is something Todd doesn't even know, does he?"

Colston nods, ashamed, both for not telling and for what occupied his mind after his second escape attempt along with what he has led them all to believe.

Jordan responded not negatively but with concern. He had been worried about Colston not sharing everything even with his therapist, who is trained to help.

"Cole, getting help means being open," Jordan says.

The look of hurt on Colston's face is immediate. "I just--couldn't."

Melody speaks gently, "I understand why you might not have shared that with Todd. However, I would like you to reconsider and talk to me. I promise I won't leave you in the dark."

"I want to be there too," Kayra says promptly.

Colston looks at her with pleading eyes.

She caresses his cheek. "Honey, I want to help you. It's only fair that I share what happened the night of my bachelorette party."

"Please, Kayra, I wish you wouldn't hear this," he cries, staring at Jordan. "Neither of you!"

"I can say the same to you, but I want to. No matter what was said, thought, or done, nothing will change my perspective of you." Kayra states.

Colston gazes into her unwavering eyes. He drops his gaze and then looks up at Jordan, who nods in support.

There is a knock on the door, and when it opens, a nurse and Colston's doctor enter. "Sorry to intrude, but we are here to remove the IV port and conduct a final assessment." The doctor scans the others in the room.

"Please allow them to stay," Colston says, ashamed of how pleading his voice sounds. He cannot endure another blame attack alone; he just wants to go home and distract himself as much as possible, hoping to find a way to be ready.

Melody and Jordan move to the other side of the bed. The nurse removes the IV port in seconds and then leaves the room.

The doctor sighs but continues, "The contusion on your chest is a result of the impact you sustained while sleeping. While it may not be your main concern, what you should avoid is stress on your heart. The impacts don't help, but your anxiety and mental strain are significant factors. You are not in immediate danger yet, but you're teetering on the edge of heart failure." He pauses to read over his notes.

Kayra clings to Colston, her eyes wide with overwhelming worry and sadness. Jordan places a comforting hand on both Colston's and Kayra's shoulders. Colston waits for the other shoe to drop; the risk of heart failure is worrisome, but it's not his primary concern. He fears being buried alive by people who believe he is to blame. There's only so much his small support system can do before they'll suffocate alongside him.

"Mr. Ulric sent me an email before he left town. Don't worry; he does this for all his clients. He mentioned that if you end up in the hospital due to shortness of breath, dizziness, or chest pain, I should consider prescribing Selesol, a beta-blocker that addresses various heart and blood pressure issues. My notes indicate I prescribed it to you four years ago." He looks at Colston with an accusatory expression. "Why aren't you taking it?"

"I----refuse--to--rely--on drugs---to---get----me---through." Colston replies, lying back to regain control. The cold threatens to strip him of his voice again.

"Colston, your mental strain is significant, and it is negatively affecting your body. Taking the medication will help calm your mind and manage your anxiety, allowing you to work through what happened to you."

"Work th---through, no." He takes a deep breath, witnessing the doctor scowling at him. "I wish--to be believed. I want to--know---who---he is---and see him---brought to----justice."

"Babe, please," Kayra pleads, feeling the growing cold beneath the gown. "Doc, Melody, come feel the cold."

"A classic release for trauma." The doctor says.

Melody didn't need to touch Colston to sense the cold radiating off him. "Doctor?" she begins, pulling back her hand and rubbing it absently to warm it.

"Andrews. And you are?"

"I am Melody Dakota, the therapist overseeing Todd's clients while he is out of town. I will also be taking over Colston's care once Todd returns."

Doctor Andrews scrutinizes her. "Todd did mention he was bringing in a temp, but I assumed it would be a seasoned professional, not a student."

Melody fights the urge to retaliate; this is a tactic known as defenestration aimed at prompting her to assert her importance while sidelining Colston in a power struggle.

"This isn't about me; it's about Colston. The cold radiating from him is a physical manifestation of the place from which he can't escape. People who could make a difference are keeping him there, blaming him. Doctor, are you aware of what Colston does for a living?"

"He's a content creator online." The doctor can't hide the slight curl of his upper lip.

Melody notes this as another reason she'll never live here, then corrects him: "He is a singer and quite successful at that, before and after the kidnapping. There was no need for the 'stunt'. Let me ask you another question: Were you there the day Colston was rescued?"

"I was on call that day; I wasn't his PCP yet. Once Todd took him as a client, I added him to my patient list, as I do with most of his clients," Doctor Andrews replies directly, his tone dripping with arrogance.

Melody tries to maintain her composure. "So the condition he was in was near death. Do you honestly believe that if he had any control over what happened, he would have allowed it?" She pauses, noting his growing discomfort, and presses on before he can respond. "And based on what everyone else thinks, that Colston is behind this or faking it, you just told him he could die of heart failure. Do you really think he would continue such a charade given his success?" The tension in the room thickens.

Doctor Andrews glances at everyone in turn before his glare returns to Colston. He shakes his head, stands up, and says, "Here are your discharge papers, and I'm dropping you as a patient due to your refusal to listen and follow advice." He tosses the papers on the bed and leaves.

Silence falls over the room after the door closes.

Finally, Colston finds his voice, which is filled with sadness. "Is it too much to ask for a little compassion? I don't want this to kill me."

"Colston, I am so sorry." Melody says, moving to the other side of the bed.

Colston shrugs, tears in his eyes. "You laid it out crystal clear. What can I do except wait for him to show up?" He shivers, feeling unprepared to avoid being retaken, let alone to stay alive.

"All is not lost, I promise." She looks at the three of them. They all appear drained and hopeless, crushed by the weight of the world. "Jordan, could you please take a seat? I want to do something with the three of you that may help rebalance yourselves."

Jordan moves and sits on the edge of the bed, feeling an instant relief behind his eyes.

"This is a method to visually rebalance yourself; I use it all the time. I want you to close your eyes. Kayra and Jordan, go ahead and focus on your own issues; I will focus on Colston's." Melody watches them nod and close their eyes. "This isn't about escaping the madness temporarily. You are standing on a platform in the middle, maintaining balance. The four points represent mental, physical, emotional, and spiritual or social pillars of life, so to speak. Colston, your trauma has raised the corner representing your mental stability, upsetting the balance and causing the other three pillars to dip down as you focus on the elevated side. You are in a state of panic, fearing you might fall. There are external aids like loved ones and medication if needed, but even those have limits; loved ones have their own balances to maintain. In Kayra's case, her trauma clashed with yours, triggering her depersonalization episode and aggravating some feelings, which then turned into aggression directed at you. Jordan, please correct me if I'm wrong: you were injured while defending Colston?" She asks, taking a shot in the dark. She had brief knowledge of Kayra but no understanding of how or why Jordan was injured, assuming it was related to Colston.

Jordan nods.

"So something caused you physical harm. Now the two of you can't help Colston without risking your own safety. There is divine aid, but even that diminishes over time. What you need to find is a self-reliant balance, your own source of energy to create a protective shield. This will allow you to maintain balance even in chaotic times, giving you the space to reflect and make the necessary changes to restore equilibrium. I have some homework for the three of you this weekend. Colston, on Monday, I want you to share the part of your kidnapping that you have yet to express. I believe this will aid you in the way you hope it will. I want you all to have a normal weekend, hang out, relax, BBQ, play games, and do the usual things you do when friends are in town. Jordan, listen to your body; rest when you need to. This isn't about making you forget; it's a chance for mental and emotional relief. Then on Monday, we'll address it more directly."

The three open their eyes and look at one another, feeling the weight of everything.

"I am eager to give it the old college try," Jordan says.

"You never went to college." Colston playfully retorts.

Caught off guard by Colston's response, Jordan replies, "Hence the willingness." He chuckles and pats Colston's leg. "Let's get you out of here."

With assistance, Colston manages to get up and walk to the bathroom to change out of his wet gown into a dry one. He will have to wait until he gets home to put on fresh clothes. When he comes out, he feels both better and unbearably heavy. The burden of sharing his experience weighs him down, but he hopes that having Kayra and Jordan there will help and that it won't be too much for them.

"I'll text tomorrow with the time for Monday," Melody says.

"Thank you," Colston replies.

Chapter Thirteen: Reminiscing

Once home, they all plop down on the couches and chairs in the living room, mentally exhausted. Jordan is in significant pain and senses it may worsen as the day progresses. He knows he should rest, but for now, he opts for painkillers. "Kayra, where's the acetaminophen?" he asks.

"In the kitchen, in the cabinet above the coffee maker," Kayra replies.

"Okay," he says, getting up and heading for the kitchen.

Colston soon stands needing to change and says, "I'm going to grill up some burgers." He walks over to Kayra and kisses her passionately. "I love you."

"I love you, my Colston."

With a smile, Colston leaves the living room.

"Jordan, you hungry for some burgs?" Colston asks while walking in the kitchen.

Jordan has just swallowed two pills. "Dude, burgs would be great."

Colston pats him on the back and goes to the freezer. He pulls out a pack of six lean hamburgers. He puts the pack in hot water to defrost.

"Hey, while we wait for food, wanna play a game of Clue?" Colston asks, taking Melody's advice to heart.

Jordan turns with a childish grin,

saying, "Yes! It has been since never!"

"Ka! Wait! Have you played Clue?"

"Cole?" Kayra calls from the living room.

Colston glances at Jordan, who looks like a deer in headlights. Colston smirks, "You haven't?"

"Cole?" Kayra asks, coming into the kitchen with a concerned expression.

"The game was considered a bad influence," Jordan replies.

"What game?" Kayra asks.

"Clue. Jordan has never played."

"What? Wow! Are we going to play?"

"Yes," Colston says.

Six hours pass quickly along with three games of Clue. Now they sit in the backyard gazing at the stars. Jordan chuckles, "What a game!" He adopts a regal tone as he adds, "I must say, my good sir and lady, I see no harm in this game."

Colston laughs, "Too true; tis a game of deduction." Colston rubs a bit of his mustache between his thumb and index finger, "and learning the skill of reading thy very friends. To seek out the liars among us." He casts a playful, scrutinizing look at Kayra, then at Jordan.

Kayra rises from her chair and stands before her husband. "My kind gentleman, I dare ask thou to a dance beneath these beautiful stars."

Colston smiles and says as he stands. "We dance with no music to guide our steps." He takes her hand.

"Trust," she says, grabbing his other

hand and placing it over her heart, then laying her hand on his. "May the beats of our hearts be the rhythm that our feet carry us along to."

Colston moves the hand holding her hand down to her waist, allowing that arm to rest on his shoulder, gazing into her twinkling eyes. They begin a slow ballroom dance around the yard. Jordan lets them enjoy the beats of their hearts for a moment before joining in singing *Forever and For Always* by Shania Twain, the song he sang at their wedding.

Tears well up in Kayra's eyes as she leans against Colston's chest. He kisses her head and rests his cheek on it, feeling her sobbing. "Are you okay?" he whispers.

She shakes her head against his chest.

Colston stops dancing. "Love, I am right here." Kayra looks at him, and he cradles her face, wiping away her tears. "Come back to me." He uses her own trick against her. Her eyes sparkle in the starlight. "Be with me here under the stars."

His bright brown eyes draw her out of her worry. He is right, and he's here, not lost. It's painful because she knows it's not going to last. But for now, she is savoring this moment.

Kayra nods and smiles. He then turns, extending her hand to Jordan.

Jordan takes her hand, and Colston sings *You'll Be In My Heart* from Tarzan.

Jordan tries to follow the example and simply enjoy the moment. He can see that Kayra is struggling with this task. They dance to Colston's voice, keeping their minds as present as possible, ignoring the dark, looming cloud overhead.

When the song ends, Colston walks to them and embraces them. After that, they head inside to prepare for bed. Tired as he is, Colston hesitates about sleep. He feels out of control while dreaming and prays to be spared from all nightmares. He longs to hold onto this respite for as long as possible.

It is 4:15 AM, and Jordan awakens to the sensation of someone in the room. He dares not move, and after about five minutes, the feeling of being watched has not faded. Swallowing his fear, he turns to confront whoever it is. Slowly, he pivots; his mind races as he comes face to face with the masked figure of the phantom, a gun aimed just inches from his face, a finger pressed to his lips. However, that image quickly dissolves as he fully faces the darkened room and realizes it is empty. Yet his gaze falls on a shadowy corner, and his breath trembles with fear. Suddenly, a hand emerges from the darkness, blue and trembling. Jordan watches completely terrified. Colston steps into the light, a wound in his chest with crimson spreading. Jordan's heart sinks as he gazes into Colston's face, wet with tears and blood oozing from between his lips. Colston's other hand slowly reaches for his chest. "Jordan," he breathes. Jordan watches helplessly as his friend's eyes roll back into his head and he collapses forward. Jordan cries out his name.

Jordan wakes up screaming and looks at

the corner again. The frightening effects of the dream dissipate when Kayra flips on the light.

"Jordan! What is it?" Kayra asks, panicked, dropping beside the bed.

Jordan just stares at Colston, who is shirtless and free of a chest wound, only showing a bruise above his heart. Terror still grips him tightly; his eyes ache.

Kayra caresses his face and gently says, "JD, it was just a nightmare."

"Colston was in the corner, bleeding from a chest wound!" Jordan exclaims, looking at Kayra.

Colston walks over and sits on the bed. "It was a dream, buddy," he reassures him.

Jordan murmurs, "Sorry."

"Don't be, JD. It happens." Kayra replies.

Colston pats him on the back. "You going to be okay?"

Jordan looks at Colston and says seriously, "I won't be okay until that man is behind bars."

"Same here."

Colston follows Kayra out, bidding Jordan goodnight before turning off the lights.

"How have you done this for so long?" Jordan asks, still seeing the image of Colston with a wound to his chest. He then thinks of Kayra when she first saw him in that van; that had been real. This had been a dream, his mind playing on his fears, yet it remains so vivid.

Colston looks over his shoulder and sighs. "I am beat down by it every day. The shame, the fear, and worst of all, the cold. How have I lasted this long? I have Kayra, you, and music. Goodnight, Jordan." He turns out the lights and steps into the hallway.

A rush of cold hits his right side, and he grunts as it bites into his bare skin. On his left side, he is assaulted by blazing heat, causing him to gasp in panic as he rubs his seared skin.

"Colston?" Kayra's concerned voice breaks the illusion. As the sensations fade, he hears in his mind, *"Freeze to death or burn; within his grasp, you'll remain until blood is spilled."*

He feels the wobble of the platform beneath him, hearing the splintering wood of the braces. He tries to find his balance to stop the cracking, but he has no support for himself. Grasping in the dark, two strong forces pull at him, threatening to make him fall.

He feels Kayra's hands wrap around him, bringing him back to himself. "I am here," he says, twisting his face in pain. "No, it was far away; I want that feeling of normalcy back." He buries his face against her shoulder, shuddering. "I just want this to be over." He senses the cold seeping in.

"I know, hon, but maybe by keeping it so prominent, you'll grow numb to it and be able to better control the memories and their effects on you." Her words are hopeful.

Colston can't help but smile at this. "Thank you." He looks up, takes her hand, and leads her to the bedroom.

Jordan wakes up around eight but can't fully open his eyes. The bridge of his nose throbs; he moves slowly to get up; he needs to go to the bathroom.

As he steps into the hallway, Kayra just opens her bedroom door. "Jordan?" she whispers, quickly closing the door to let Colston rest.

Jordan just waves, not looking up, and continues to the bathroom.

Kayra watches him carefully make his way. She heads to the kitchen, needing a drink. Her mind is filled with worry and exhaustion. Last night was great; she hardly noticed the struggle in his eyes.

Today might be different, which is exhausting. Seeing him still asleep at this hour is reassuring. She sips some cold water, feeling lost about the future. And Monday... what will that bring?

"Kayra?"

She turns to see Jordan making his way toward her, his eyes squinting against the light, revealing deep bruising.

"JD, what are you doing? You need to be lying down."

"I will with an ice pack and painkillers, but I need to ask something."

"Sure, what is it?"

Jordan sits up at the island, trying to formulate the question. "Should I join a dating app?"

Kayra is taken aback by this question and sees genuine vulnerability on his face. "JD," she replies calmly and compassionately, "that is completely up to you."

Jordan's head hangs low, feeling both grateful and lost by Kayra's response. He is thankful she didn't push him, but now he feels lost since the choice is his to make. He rubs his hands together nervously. With this new avenue opened, he shyly makes eye contact. Kayra, with her tired yet gentle and loving eyes, easily coaxes out what he has held onto for three years. "Kayra," he swallows hard, "I am gay." The relief of finally voicing it to someone other than himself triggers a wave of emotions, and he sobs.

"Jordan," Kayra says, starting to move around the island to embrace him.

Colston, emerging from the hall, overhears Jordan. The moment he hears the sobs, he wraps Jordan in a hug from behind.

"Cole?" Jordan asks, his voice full of surprise and fearful worry.

Kayra rounds the island, and Colston lifts his left arm to let Kayra embrace him too.

Jordan enjoys the hug, realizing he has nothing to fear.

Colston moves beside Jordan. "JD, you going to be okay?" he asks, smiling broadly, a tear of pride trickling down his cheek.

"Very," Jordan sniffs. "I was hoping a chance would come up to share... because I knew that if you two were okay with it, then saying it aloud to everyone else would be easy. I've always been afraid to share this, worried it wouldn't be well received due to stress and everything else."

"You chose the best time to share JD. But

honestly, no matter when you decided to speak up, we would have stood by you and celebrated the true you," Kayra says, giving him a squeeze before releasing him. "How about some French toast?"

"Hell, yeah, and with a side of painkillers," Jordan replies.

Colston chuckles and moves to make coffee. He opens the cabinet above the coffee maker and grabs the bottle of Duramide. "JD here," he says, tossing the bottle over his shoulder.

Even with his eyes slightly blurry, his reflexes are quick and steady. He catches the bottle in his left hand, upright and off-center.

"Christ! Use the Force, JD!" Colston says in his best Darth Vader voice.

Kayra lets out a laugh. "Oh, that's very good."

Colston smiles, pleased with himself, as Kayra slides a glass of water across the island toward Jordan. The glass catches on a rough patch in the granite and topples over, spilling water across the island and into Jordan's lap.

"Aahh!" Jordan cries out of surprise as cold water soaks him.

"Shit, I am so sorry," Kayra says, rushing to grab rags.

"I know I need a shower, but Kayra, there are subtler ways," Jordan chuckles as he stands up.

Colston grabs paper towels to start wiping down the countertop.

Kayra tosses a rag to Jordan as she comes

around the island. "I didn't do it on purpose," she says, embarrassed.

Jordan moves to hug her but sees she isn't moving; water is still dripping, and she's staring at the floor. "Kay?" He barely touches her shoulder when she starts sobbing.

"Kayra?" Colston asks, abandoning his task to go to her. He tries to touch her, but she pushes him away and kneels on the wet floor. Colston and Jordan share a look of utter confusion.

They both join her on the floor. Safe from the cascade of water beneath the overhang lies the blood-smeared note. Kayra feels overwhelming guilt and anger. *"Why couldn't this have been drowned?"* she cries in her mind.

"Kayra!" Colston raises his voice to get her attention. When her eyes meet his, they shine with tears of remorse. "No, love. You have done nothing wrong."

"But the note, why is it untouched by the water? Is it a sign?" she pleads.

"A sign of what, sweetheart?" He asks gently, pushing her hair back behind her left ear.

She takes his hand in hers and whispers, "That it will happen again."

"It won't, I promise. Because you are here with me, not lost in the mind. We need to celebrate: Jordan coming out of the closet and you, for publishing a collection of poems dedicated to your father's memory."

Her gaze falls to his bare chest, the scar and bruise stark reminders of what she has done, and still he loves her.

Colston lifts her chin with his finger so she can look him in the eyes. "I'll go put on a shirt."

Kayra shakes her head and gently runs her fingertips over his chest while formulating her response. "Trauma upon the skin, a mirror reflecting shadows--things that linger beyond my control. Hands tremble; they are both sculptor and destroyer, etching lines of doubt across a fragile canvas. Heart cowers, a timid bird in the storms brewed by restless thought, yearning for resilience in every pulse. Once tenderly cradled, now fractured light, my love's heartbeat threatens to wane, but beneath it all is the heart raw yet steadfast, never shaken out of love with me. Oh Colston, may you stand unwavering! In your calm presence, I find silence, not absence. A strength unruffled like dawn breaking over storm-tossed seas. Here lies our truth: pain marks us with echoes that quiver on skin while spirit whispers softly. We endure; it's in this endurance we find couth." Kayra finishes; she opens her eyes to meet Colston's rich brown gaze shining back at her.

Jordan is astonished by Kayra's talent. He watches as Colston embraces her. "Kay, that was beautiful and so impactful. And how have I known you for so long without realizing your incredible poetry riffing skills?" He notices Kayra visibly retreating against Colston. "I'm sorry."

Colston, still holding his wife, looks at Jordan smiling to ease his worry. "You have nothing to apologize for. I believe this is a moment of emotional release expressed through her remarkable gift with words."

Kayra lifts her head from Colston's chest and kisses him. She then turns to face Jordan. "I usually recite poetry in front of others without issue, even my own. I often invite Colston to riff with me as I process my emotions. This was not just about releasing feelings; it was also a moment where I realized my husband's love will never waver. In that moment, I got lost in the words and forgot you were here." She smiles softly.

"Kayra is very modest about her creative abilities. I only discovered her impressive talent when she shared a poem with me three months into our friendship, asking me out, and further capturing my heart. I was self-conscious, but that always shed once I started singing."

"Babe," Kayra's heart races at the mention of his poem. She blushes and places her fingers on his lips.

Colston smiles apologetically and whispers, "Sorry, love."

"A poet winning over a singer's heart, how perfect is that?" Jordan muses. "Why didn't you mention the book last night?"

"This is one reason Colston and I work so well together. While I struggle to share my passions and accomplishments, he does not."

"And she constantly reminds me that the ideal body varies for everyone. I wanted to mention her book yesterday, but with everything, I didn't want to add to her anxiety."

"Honestly, if you've landed such a great guy and now have a collection of poems, you should flaunt your talent," Jordan says.

Kayra lightly chuckles. "No, stop it. I could never do what you two do." She takes Colston's hand. "I'm content supporting from the background."

"I will always be in awe of how my voice managed to enchant someone like you. I just got lucky," Colston smiles.

A loud rumble from Jordan's stomach suddenly breaks the moment, waking them to the reality that they are all kneeling in water. Jordan chuckles and pats his stomach. "Way to ruin the moment."

Colston stands and pulls both Kayra and Jordan to their feet, ignoring the tenderness in his chest. "I have a proposal. I don't know if you guys would be on board with this. The news is saying that lockdowns are coming soon. In our area, there's no mandatory order to stay indoors, just a strong recommendation. I want to get out of the house for at least today."

Kayra just nods, squeezing his hand and trying to embrace ignorance, hoping that she is not going to regret this plan.

"Jordan, don't feel pressured to join us; you really should be resting," Colston says.

Jordan looks at Colston and smiles. "I should be resting, but I want to be out with you two celebrating some great accomplishments. After I clean up, I'll lie down with an ice pack and take some painkillers while you guys get ready."

"If the pain gets to be too much, I want

you to let us know," Colston replies, releasing Kayra's hand to dry off the counter.

Jordan stands hesitantly, looking like he needs to ask something.

"JD, what is it?" Kayra asks.

His voice is timid. "Are you guys still okay with me?"

Kayra steps through the water and embraces him. "Yes, nothing will change. You are our brother."

"Jordan, you are safe and accepted a hundred times over with us. If you ever need someone to be with you as you start opening up more, we'll be right there," Colston adds.

With tears of happiness, Jordan heads to the shower, leaving Colston and Kayra to clean the kitchen.

Once they finish, Colston returns to making coffee.

"Should I still make French toast?" Kayra asks.

"I don't see any harm in it. You heard Jordan's belly; maybe he can relax and eat while we get ready."

"Could you grab me a bowl for the eggs?" Kayra asks as she gathers the eggs and bread from the fridge.

Colston, waiting for the coffee to brew, crouches down and opens the lower cabinet. "What size bowl?"

"Um..." Kayra considers. "How hungry are you, love?"

Colston smirks, turning to his left to look up at her. "Are we low on eggs or bread?"

"Cole," Kayra says, meeting his gaze. "We're fine on both. You and Jordan have about the same appetite, so I use you to gauge."

Colston thinks about his hunger level; honestly, he hasn't had much of an appetite for the past three and a half weeks. "I'm not all that hungry."

Kayra drops down beside him. "Honey, it's not the time to starve yourself. I am proud that you've maintained a weight of 220 for the last six years. We need to overcome this mental battle. You under-eating worries me."

Colston smiles; he has always struggled with his weight, but weight loss is far from his mind right now. "I know, and we will. Thank you for the reassurance."

Kayra kisses him on the cheek and whispers, "The medium gray bowl." She stands up, and Colston rummages for the bowl.

He pulls it out and hands it to Kayra, who promptly takes it and begins cracking eggs into it. "You want the serving platter too?" he asks.

"Feeling fancy today?"

Colston shrugs. "An air of class, I suppose, with all the outpouring of stuff this morning."

"Yeah, go ahead and bring it out."

Colston shuts the cabinet, spins on the balls of his feet to face the cabinets beneath the island, and hops twice over to the island. Hearing Kayra quietly giggling makes him smile and his heart swell. He opens the large cabinet, grabs the metal oval serving platter, and effortlessly spins it between his palms as he fully stands back up.

Kayra looks at him smiling and is about to lay out the first four slices of bread on the griddle. Colston sets the platter on the other side of the griddle and wipes it down. Just then, the coffee pot beeps. Colston is to the left of Kayra. He steps back and gracefully spins to be back-to-back with her, bending slightly so she can rest her head on his shoulder while he leans on hers for a kiss before spinning away to face the coffee pot.

"Want a cup, love?" Colston asks.

"Please," Kayra says, longing to abandon her post and jump into his arms. This was her Colston, the boy she had fallen in love with. Tears begin to flow, but she dares not speak, fearing it might throw Colston off balance.

"Hon?" Colston asks gently, touching her hand as he sets down the cup of coffee with his other hand.

"What?" She asks, waking up to the realization that the bread is burning.

"Babe," he says, concerned, running his fingers up her arm. "What is it?"

She flips the bread slightly darker than she prefers and turns to face him, tears on full display. "It's you, my Colston."

Colston pulls her close. "He is achievable, very hard but over time." He pauses, careful not to disrupt the balance he has achieved.

He lets her go. "I'll be right back," he says, heading toward the bedroom. He shuts the door before collapsing to his knees, trembling; his breathing is harsh and cold, causing his lungs to seize. The phantom's laughter echoes in his mind. *"STOP! Leave me be!"* he screams internally, forcing focus on Kayra and her published collection of poems. And on Jordan, coming out as gay, needing Colston to show his support.

As everything fades and the platform stabilizes, he hears the voice from last night: *"Distractions are only as strong as you are. Overcome or surrender to the path you were led down."*

He remains on the ground for a moment longer, collecting himself. He fights against the meaning of those words alongside the remnants of his nightmare, knowing that suggesting they go out could lead to trouble. He decides to pray for a little extra strength before leaving the house.

Once he manages to stand, he goes to the bathroom to ensure that his struggle isn't visible on his face. He looks drained and drops his head in disappointment. But then he hears something; curious and slightly worried, he leaves the bathroom and opens the door to his room.

Following the sound to the guest bathroom, he gently knocks on the door with his knuckle. "JD?"

Colston hears Jordan cough and sniffle before responding in the most forced calm voice he's ever heard from him. "Cole, I'm almost done."

"JD," Colston says softly. "Are you truly okay?" He then feels embarrassed for intruding on Jordan's private moment. "I'm sorry, bud. I didn't mean to intrude."

Colston starts to continue toward the kitchen. When Jordan opens the door, his wet hair clings to his bare chest, and his eyes are red and puffy. "Jordan?" Colston's tone is sad and worried.

"What a mess I've created," Jordan says, his head throbbing. The pain fails to equate to what he might lose. "I wish I could reverse time and never have told you and Kayra."

Colston is shocked. "We aren't going to tell anyone without your blessing first. What--what are you afraid of?"

Jordan gazes at him directly. "I can only handle losing one major component from my life at one time." He drops his head.

Colston quickly understands. "Please correct me if I'm wrong. The internet can be a savage place, especially for those who choose a different path."

"It's a double-edged sword. I could stay in the closet to appease the masses, but that would mean not living my authentic self. Being true to oneself online is crucial; however, it exposes you to personal attacks and hate that can make you question your identity. On the other side of that sharp edge, though, is validation and acceptance, a show of courage in a cruel world. Colston, so many people look up to us. I hate feeling like I'm letting them down by being honest about my truth." Jordan speaks with a voice full of doubt yet subtle confidence.

Colston puts his hands on his shoulders. "I understand the worry of upsetting the flow of subscribers, as they are necessary for survival. You're giving them your voice and nothing more. If they don't like who you are, that's on them, not you. You'll attract others who share your path and inspire them to live authentically, promoting happier and healthier lives." He pulls Jordan into a hug and whispers, "You're not going to lose your channel."

Jordan hugs him back, "Honestly, I'd lose my channel a thousand times over rather than lose you."

Colston fights internally as he breaks the hug and says with a smile, "Breakfast is ready. You can eat and relax while Kayra and I get ready." He pats Jordan on the shoulder and heads toward the kitchen.

"Everything alright?" Kayra asks when Colston emerges from the hall. She has arranged a platter in the center of the island, complete with butter, syrup, and utensils.

"He just needed some reassurance," Colston replies with a smile, feeling his stomach churn at the aroma of the food, which soon rumbles with hunger. "You alright?" he asks, noticing Kayra staring off with a gentle expression.

Her gaze shifts to him, but her eyes remain distant. "I'm fine. Let's go get ready."

"Hold on," Colston says as he heads to the freezer to grab an ice pack and a towel from the drawer. He wraps the towel around the ice pack and sets it beside the platter and a bottle of pills. Kayra notices what Colston is doing and decides to redeem herself by setting a glass of water down.

Jordan smiles at their care. "Thank you; I'll be good in an hour to an hour and a half." He stands with his hair wrapped in a towel.

Colston nods with a smile, and then he and Kayra head to the bedroom to get ready for the day.

Colston notices Kayra wearing a blushing smile. "What is it?" he asks, feeling giddy with delight.

"Jordan just got me thinking," Kayra replies as she goes to sit down on the bed. When Colston grabs her, mid-sit, by her waist, gently drawing her to his body and spinning her. "Yeah?" he asks with a smile.

Kayra giggles and wraps her arms around his neck, dancing with him. "Why haven't we shared our story?" She asks, looking deep into his eyes.

"I don't know, but I think it's a silent agreement that our love story is just for us," Colston responds. "I prefer to keep it between us, but if you ever want to share it, I'm on board."

"Okay, I'm on the fence right now, but I'm reminiscing," she smiles. Locking her hands behind his head, she meets his lips in a passionate kiss.

Just then, Colston's phone rings, but he makes no move to answer. Instead, he deepens the kiss.

After several moments, Colston moves to the dresser to get his clothes for the day before heading to the shower.

Kayra waits for him to start the shower

before picking out her clothes. Once she has her outfit laid out on the bed, she checks the voicemail left for Colston.

"Hi, Mr. Driscoll, this is Melody. I have you set up for an appointment for Monday at eleven. Please call if that time doesn't work."

She deletes the message. She wants her Colston for as long as possible. She reflects on their story beyond the engagement and the video they made for Colston's channel. The magic between them remains untold, their love unmistakable. How could stress have driven her to nearly kill him? That will always be a blemish, a sign of weakness, one she will spend her life trying to conceal.

"Babe! Your turn for the shower!" Colston calls.

Kayra gets up and heads for the bathroom.

"Was that call of any importance?" he asks, grooming his beard.

"I will tell you later," she replies.

"Alright," Colston says; he trusts her.

The worry is evident in her voice. He doesn't question it; he just smiles. "Do you want to go to the mall?" he asks, smacking his razor in the sink.

"Really, are you sure?" Kayra asks anxiously, "I know you don't want to be cooped up, but love..."

Colston gently embraces her. "I'll be fine; we'll be fine," he whispers. "I just can't be here."

"Could we consider the park too?" Kayra suggests rubbing his back.

"Of course. I'll let you get ready." Colston pecks her cheek and then leaves the bathroom.

As soon as he hears the shower turn on, he drops to his knees, trembling as he fights the cold. "Please God!" he prays, eyes shut tight. "Just for today, grant me this respite. In your holy name I pray."

Colston feels relief as a golden hand stabilizes him, allowing him to shield himself from the heat of insanity and the cold of his confinement.

He stands and leaves the room.

He hears Jordan snoring on the couch. Colston quietly gets himself a single slice of French toast.

A loud snort is followed by a cough. "Cole?" Jordan's voice is strained.

"Yes, sorry if I woke you," Colston replies softly.

Jordan carefully sits up, swinging his legs off the couch. "It's okay; I didn't mean to fall asleep."

"Oh, man, don't apologize for that." Colston says. He finishes applying syrup and walks into the living room.

Jordan holds the ice pack in his hands; the coolness has eased the pounding in his head. He looks up as Colston sits next to him and says heavily, "I'm so sorry."

"Cole, don't! I told you not to worry about this, please," Jordan says, placing his hand on Colston's shoulder.

Colston cuts off a bite and forks it into his mouth, nodding.

Jordan stares at him and then says

dejectedly, "With the threat of the approaching lockdowns, I am going to head out this week."

"That's okay; I... We thank you for being here." Colston replies in between bites.

Jordan nods, infusing hope into his words. "I actually feel better about leaving this time, even with Monday. Right now, this can and will be you indefinitely. I promise."

These words strike Colston, but not in a harmful way. They bolster his spirit, strengthening his defenses, and alleviating some of the weight on his shoulders. Tears fall, and Jordan immediately feels bad.

"Colston? I am sorry, I just..." He trails off, staring in concern.

"Don't be; I... needed to hear that." Colston sets his plate with a half-eaten piece of toast down on the coffee table and hugs Jordan. "To stay like this takes a lot, and I'm just riding it while my strength lasts."

"I don't like hearing that," Kayra says, as she walks in.

Colston and Jordan break the embrace.

"I'm sorry, but it's the truth. Please, for today, avoid talking about what will happen on Monday," Colston pleads. "We all need some respite to help us relax and clear our minds for what's next."

Kayra sits on the coffee table and places a hand on Colston. "Then let's change the subject." She smiles and hands a piece of paper to Jordan.

"Is this the poem?" Jordan asks.

"Yes, my poem to my songbird," Kayra

replies.

Jordan looks at her, saying apologetically, "I can't; it's a private matter." He is curious, though.

"Colston and I talked about it; he's on board if I choose to share," she smiles and nods at him to read it.

In a world where time rushes on,
There's a melody so pure, my heart it won.
For there exists a songbird named Colston; fair,
Whose voice slows time, making me gasp for air.

When his lips part and the music begins to flow,
A symphony of love from within does grow.
His gentle touch upon the strings strummed,
Resonates with mine and leaves me stunned.

Oh, sweet Colston, with your melodic might,
You entrance my soul through the dark of night.
Your voice transcends all earthly bounds,
And in its embrace, true solace is found.

Every note you sing becomes an invitation rare,
Drawing me closer into your ethereal lair.
My heart beats in time to each delicate sound,
Longing to be near you when love is finally

found.

In those stolen moments when our eyes meet at last,

The world holds its breath; oh, how time goes vast!

Imagining our souls dancing to lyrics unsaid;

Oh Colston! How I long for these dreams to thread!

Though captured am I by his musical allure,

The distance between us leaves questions that endure.

Will our melodies intertwine and be as one?

Jordan smiles and hands it back to Kayra, saying breathlessly, "Beautiful! That is beyond wonderful."

"It is; she took the initiative to advance our relationship because I think she sensed that if it was left to me, it would never happen." He smiles shyly at Kayra.

She rubs his hand reassuringly. "I wanted to show that I wish to be more than friends in a way that would stand out to him," Kayra says.

"Thank you for sharing. Come on, let's get out of here." Jordan replies.

The mall is sparsely populated, with most causing scenes complaining about masks or discussing fake news. It's Saturday, yet many shops are closed, highlighting the fear and seriousness of the virus even in rural Idaho. Before they leave, Kayra, feeling nostalgic, wants to visit the third-floor balcony. In front of The Common Book and off to the side are the restrooms. It was from this balcony about eleven years ago that she stood looking down at the concourse where she first saw and heard Colston sing.

They stand in the unusual silence of the mall with Kayra rubbing Colston's hand as they lazily lean over the railing. Jordan stands on the other side of him.

"Man, I've never felt so depressed to be at a mall," Jordan says.

Colston then gets an idea; he asks Kayra and Jordan to stay there. He takes Jordan's comment to heart and wants to join in Kayra's reminiscing. On his way down to the concourse, he searches for a song; he can't remember the one he sang that day, but he wants to find one that will resonate with everyone during this difficult time.

The song that stands out to him is Andy Grammer's *Don't Give Up On Me*. After queuing it up on his phone, he looks at all the faces around him. Their eyes show one of two emotions: worry or anger.

He hopes to transform those expressions into relief or happiness. Standing in the center, he glances up at Kayra, and Jordan, smiles and hits play on his phone. He projects his voice, ignoring the burn and the twinges of fear of punishment, allowing his emotions to lead. People stop and begin to clap, sensing fear and hopelessness fade from the area. During the chorus, he sees people dancing and snapping along. He does his best to keep his new surge of happiness from overwhelming him, causing him to break with tears.

When he finishes the song, applause erupts, and he notices several phones recording the moment. He bows and waves, then makes his way back to Kayra and Jordan.

His heart leaps with joy as he sees the light return to people's eyes. Rejoining Kayra and Jordan on the balcony, both grip his hands. Together, they leave for the park.

On their way to the park, they grab some food. Sitting on a small grassy mound, they eat and enjoy the sound of the breeze rustling through the leaves and the chirping of birds.

The park is empty, and they are far enough away from the road for their serene outing to remain undisturbed. They end up lying on the mound for hours, gazing at the cloudless sky. This entire week had been overcast. The trio relishes in their respite; it seems the sky shares their sentiment, letting the calmness of the blue and the warmth of the sun bless their day.

As the sun begins to set, Colston feels his strength waning; his extra support has faded, and he must focus on maintaining his balance.

"Guys, it's time to go," Colston says.

Kayra sits up. "You okay, babe?"

Colston rolls his head to look at her. "Honestly, the moment of quiet is fading."

Jordan sits up and says, "What you did was amazing. Please don't be hard on yourself for not being able to stay in this moment. You'll experience more and for longer periods."

Kayra nods in agreement, standing up and pulling Colston to his feet, then Jordan.

"We're here for you, so lean on us during the next step," Kayra says.

When they return home, Jordan follows through on his plan to go to bed after making a sandwich and taking painkillers.

As he bids goodnight to Kayra and Colston at 7:40, Kayra says, "Goodnight, JD."

"Cya tomorrow." Colston replies, "And JD, we are so happy for you and will be with you every step of your journey."

"Thank you, I love you guys." Jordan responds.

"We love you too," Kayra says.

Colston and Kayra remain in the kitchen, both tired but hesitant to go to bed.

"I'm sorry; I wanted to have a weekend free of the crushing memories," Colston says.

"Shhh," Kayra replies, wrapping him in her arms. "We'll figure it out."

Kayra walks with him to the bedroom. "Honey, this is the scariest time," she admits.

"Me too, but I hope God will protect me from what harms me for another night," he says.

Chapter Fourteen: Surprise Party

Colston wakes up at five after a night free of dreams that has left him balanced. He desires to hatch his scheme. His first step is to get out of bed without waking Kayra.

He slides out of bed, and on his way out of the room, he blindly grabs a shirt. Once in the dark hall, he puts on the shirt and gently knocks on the guest bedroom door.

"Kayra?"

Colston hears Jordan whisper. Colston opens the door to peek in and whispers, "No, bud."

"You okay?" Jordan asks, matching Colston's tone, and is able to see with his phone's flashlight.

"Do you mind if I come in?" he asks.

"Come in; what is on your mind?" Jordan asks, slowly sitting up. Assessing himself, his head and eyes are not throbbing, and the pain is very mild.

Colston steps in and closes the door behind him. He thinks about flipping on the light but changes his mind for the sake of Jordan's injury, "I want to do something for Kayra to celebrate her book." He says, sitting on the bed. The light from Jordan's phone shone up between them. He feels the threat of a flashback and immediately drops his hand on the phone, blocking the light. "Jordan, it is you with me, right?" Colston's voice has a quiver to it.

Jordan is momentarily confused by this change. "Yes, Cole. It is me. Are you okay?" He asks, resting a hand on his shoulder.

"Just rebalancing; hold on." Colston says, taking breaths, focusing on Kayra. A shield generates around Colston's platform, and he pushes the threat away. "I would love to be able to celebrate you too." He says, uncovering the light and seeing Jordan's face drain in worry and panic. Colston smiles and pats his shoulder, "I'm not going to out you like that, JD. I just want to show you that we are happy for you."

Jordan smiles and hugs Colston. "This is all I need. Alright, now for Kayra, what do you have in mind?"

"I know it might be short notice for most, but I want to throw a party for her." Colston explains, "A cake, catering, and guests."

Jordan stands up and stretches, saying, in a yawn, "Then let's go."

Together, they leave the house; Colston contemplates leaving a note. He decides against it and is just ready to answer his phone. He hopes that she won't be too worried, seeing that both of them are gone.

Before he gets into the truck. Colston snaps a picture of the cover of her book.

"I hate to leave like this." Colston says, climbing into the truck.

"I know," he says, glancing toward the house, "but we are together and will answer her call the moment it comes through." Jordan reassures him.

Colston nods, "Can you look up the directions to Cut Of The Cake?"

Jordan types the name into his phone, "2681 Prospect Ave.; it also seems that they open at five thirty." Jordan says.

"Perfect," Colston says.

He starts the truck and pulls onto the road. Jordan turns on the radio at a low volume.

"Who is going to be catering?" Jordan asks.

"To be honest, I don't know who will be able to do it on such short notice, on top of what is going on." Colston sounds a little disheartened.

"We'll make it work, okay? Kayra will be surprised."

Colston smiles, and he cruises along the quiet streets.

Cut Of The Cake is a Ma & Pop bakery with a rating of five stars and is highly recommended as opposed to the other three bakeries in town. Colston loves to help out local shops when he can. He pulls off the road and onto the private drive; the main private house is set on the back of a two-acre lot. The shop is a small, quick setup home painted to look like a chocolate cake, and a tall door is painted to look like the inside of the cake.

"How cute?" Colston comments as he pulls off the drive and into a gravel parking lot.

"Yes," Jordan agrees, opening his door.

Colston shuts off the truck and opens his door to the crisp morning air. The robins sing the Dawn Chorus, which echoes effortlessly through the trees.

Jordan whistles along with the birds. Colston moves to the hood and rests his arms for a moment. Relishing this moment of calm, Jordan has an arm resting on the hood as he ends his contribution to the chorus.

Colston moves around the truck. "That was nice," he says, smiling at Jordan as he moves toward the door of the shop.

Jordan follows with a grin.

The soft jingle that announces their entry fills the small space. The smell is absolutely divine and wafts around them, instantly making their mouths water.

"I'll be out there in a moment." A frail-sounding female voice calls from somewhere beyond the display counter.

"It's okay, no rush." Colston calls kindly.

He takes in the small shop, brightly lit and decorated in blue and pink stripes. He approaches the array of beautifully decorated cakes and cupcakes.

"Welcome, sirs," A small older woman greets them with a warm smile, "I am Glenna Proctor; what might I get started for you?"

"Hi, Mrs. Proctor, I am hoping to order a chocolate caramel sheet cake with an edible photo. If at all possible, to have it today?" Colston asks.

Glenna walks over to an empty order board, asking, "Mr. Driscoll, do you have a copy of the photo?" She marks something on the board.

Colston is not at all surprised that she knows who he is. He replies, "I do. I have the picture on my phone, though."

"That is okay; you'll just have to email it to CutOfTheCake@flexmail."

"Alright," Colston says, getting on his phone to send the photo. When the soft jingle sounds, he moves aside from the front of the counter, not looking up from his phone.

"Colston?"

Colston, engrossed by his task, is startled when another voice speaks his name. He looks up from his phone and turns to see who called him.

"Oliver." Colston says happily.

Oliver is shaking hands with Jordan.

"So happy to see you on your feet, both of you." Oliver comments.

"Thanks. You here getting goods for the station?" Colston asks.

Glenna lets out a light chuckle, "Exactly what he used to do. Now the poor man works for me."

"What?" Colston asks, "How?"

Oliver just looks at him, "I was operating outside of my jurisdiction and supposedly questioned a ruling set by superior authority." Oliver says it directly with a shake of his head, "I honestly think that they were getting nervous about someone snooping around your case."

"I am so sorry." Colston apologizes.

Oliver shrugs. "I am sorry that I couldn't help you."

"This is who you threw away your career for?" Glenna questions.

Colston doesn't turn, and Oliver defends himself. "It is injustice! I thought it was bad in the big city, but it is worse here," he declares.

Jordan, with eyes wide as he watches Colston intently, who is doing his utmost to avoid shutting down.

"I am sorry," Oliver says quietly, glancing at both Glenna and Colston.

Glenna shakes her head lightly and then turns her attention to Colston. "Mr. Driscoll, please disregard my outburst. It is nothing against you; Oliver has a family to care for," she apologizes.

"Mom, please," Oliver says, "I promised that I would take good care of your daughter and grandchildren."

Colston turns toward the woman and says, "There is no need for formalities; it's just Colston. I sent the photo." He then turns to Oliver and asks, "What are the odds of us meeting here, in your family's establishment?"

Oliver looks at him with a sorrowful shrug. Colston simply offers him a reassuring smile.

"Colston, the cake will cost one hundred dollars, and there is an additional fee of eighty dollars for same-day pickup. I can have it ready by five. Is that okay?"

"Mom, give him a break. You're not under any strain from his order." Oliver says.

The death glare is momentarily directed at Colston before shifting to its intended target. It sends Colston's mind into a whirl, and he counters the threat by following Glenna's glare to Oliver. *"Observe, Colston; this is a normal public dispute. There is nothing threatening here."*

"True as this is, and I respect his position of fame, I am also trying to make a living here, and times are bound to get tough," Glenna states.

Oliver is about to continue when Colston interjects, "Oliver, I appreciate what you are trying to do. I am just another customer and am more than willing to pay for my goods. That being said, Mrs. Proctor, and I mean no disrespect, but would you accept a thousand-dollar tip?"

Glenna meets his gaze and says, "I take great pride in my ability to keep running on my own. That being said, my employees, however, need to be paid. Please don't take offense if I redirect your generous tip to Oliver." She smiles and adds, "Additionally, for cakes, I require that they be picked up by you or someone you have approved."

"Jordan Youngblood," he points to Jordan, who smiles and nods, "or my dad, Elliot Driscoll," Colston says warmly before turning to face Oliver.

He stands, stunned and guilty, shaking his head.

Before Colston can say anything, Glenna interjects, stepping out from behind the counter to approach her son-in-law.

"Ollie, please don't be stubborn. That's my daughter's role. With business being slow, I can't provide you with the amount needed to manage your household."

Oliver bows his head, and when he looks up to ask a question, he glances between Jordan and Colston. "Are you guys in a rush?"

Jordan and Colston exchange a glance. "I am following your lead," Jordan says with a joyful smile.

Colston peeks at his phone: 6:28 AM. It is still too early to start reaching out to anyone.

"We have a bit," Colston says.

Oliver smiles, "Amber will arrive at seven. Could you both be here to surprise her?"

Colston and Jordan are smiling.

"Please, take a seat," Glenna announces cheerfully. "Would you gentlemen like to try my cinnamon rolls? They are fresh out of the oven."

"That'd be swell," Jordan says.

They sit at a table. Oliver shyly accepts the money from Colston. "So, what is the cake for?" he asks as he pockets the cash.

"Stop interrogating my customers," Glenna says playfully as she brings out two large, steaming cinnamon rolls.

She places them in front of Colston and Jordan, along with forks and napkins. She glances over at Oliver and says, "Not until you're off the clock."

Oliver frowns, "Fine. But I want to see Amber's reaction."

"Fine, just don't take advantage of Colston's generosity."

As they converse, Jordan and Colston take their first bites. The flavor is rich and not overly sweet, complemented by the fluffiest dough.

"Mrs. Proctor, this is absolutely divine," Jordan comments.

"Glenna. And thank you."

"I feel bad for not bringing Kayra," Colston says.

"Then it wouldn't be much of a surprise," Jordan says.

Colston smiles and nods in agreement, saying, "True." He then turns to Glenna and asks, "Could I get one to go?"

"Are you planning to go straight home?" Glenna asks.

Colston gazes at her, perplexed.

"I have a rule for my cinnamon rolls and scones: they are best when fresh. So, I'll ask again: are you planning to go straight home?"

"We are not," Colston says.

Glenna smiles and says, "Then your home will be Oliver's first stop."

Colston returns the smile, "Thank you."

She gently pats him on the shoulder before heading back to the kitchen.

They continue to eat in silence while Oliver sits at another table, reading the newspaper.

"Oh, Oliver, my daughter wanted me to tell you that she is tired of being cooped up in the house," Glenna calls out from the kitchen.

Oliver shakes his head and stands up, intending to speak with her privately.

That is when the gentle jingle resonates, swiftly followed by a gasp.

Colston observes the expression of happiness on Jordan's face.

"Dad?" The girl's voice trembles with overwhelming excitement.

Colston watches as Oliver turns to face his daughter. Colston turns in his seat and offers a warm smile toward the teen.

The teenager's smile widens to such an extent that it becomes unsettling.

"Morning," Jordan says.

A soft sound escapes her lips.

"They aren't going to bite," Oliver encourages.

Colston rises to his feet and says kindly, "You must be Amber."

At that moment, the teenager collapses in tears. Oliver rushes to her side, while Colston remains where he is, and Jordan stands beside him, both displaying concern in their eyes.

Oliver looks at them apologetically as his daughter sobs into his chest.

Jordan is about seven feet away and crouches low. "Are you okay?" he asks gently.

Amber shifts slightly to look at Jordan, "I've never been better. Just taken aback to have my two favorite singers here." She wipes her cheeks dry before standing up.

Oliver follows her and kisses her on the head. "Dad, stop!"

Colston chuckles at this and offers his hand to Jordan. Jordan takes it and is pulled up, his knees popping in the process.

"Ow! You alright?" Colston asks.

"Oh, yeah," Jordan says.

Colston takes a step toward the girl, who appears timid now that Oliver has walked away.

He extends a hand, but the girl embraces him instead. Colston immediately reciprocates the gesture. Amber cries on his shoulder, and Colston allows the hug to linger for a few seconds before gently pulling away, smiling at the embarrassed teen.

"Sorry," she says, "I was just worried that I might wake up." Then she looks at Jordan with a questioning expression.

Jordan moves in to give a hug. At that moment, Colston's phone rings, and he answers it immediately.

"Colston?!" Kayra's voice comes over the line, filled with panic.

"Babe, It's okay; I'm fine. Jordan and I just couldn't sleep, so we decided to go for a drive."

Colston hears a sigh of relief.

"Love, we will be back soon. All I ask is that you don't make any plans," he says.

"Ohh?" Kayra questions.

Colston turns and makes eye contact with Oliver. "Also, there will be a delivery for you in about..." Oliver flashes both of his hands open. "Ten minutes, with breakfast."

"Okay, I love you," Kayra says.

"I love you too." Colston hangs up and looks at Amber. "I apologize, but I had to take that," he says, sliding his phone into his pocket.

Amber simply smiles and says, "It's fine."

"Alright, Amber, say your goodbyes. You have deliveries to make," Glenna says, kindly but firmly.

"Dad, can you take a picture?" Amber asks, pulling her phone out of her pocket.

"Yeah," Oliver replies.

Amber positions herself between Colston and Jordan.

"Say, sing!"

"Sing!" they say.

The picture is snapped, and there is another round of hugs before Amber and Oliver head out for their deliveries.

"Glenna, may I ask you a question?" Colston asks.

"I'll do my best to answer," she offers sweetly.

"Do you know of a place that is open today and offers same-day catering? Also, who provides lobster tails?"

Glenna thinks for a moment and says, "Catering? I'm not sure. But The Grill Spot is open today."

"Much appreciated, and thank you for the cake if I don't come to pick it up."

"Thank you for your business," Glenna says.

It is 7:15 when Jordan and Colston leave the shop.

Jordan wants to comment on Colston's stability; throughout his time in the shop, he was waiting for signs to appear. However, making a comment would draw attention to it.

As Colston climbs into the truck, "Jordan, please stop looking at me like that." Colston says, aware of Jordan's constant vigilant eye. Very appreciative, but it is becoming tiresome; he is in control and is enjoying this moment of peace.

Jordan stares at him, then lowers his gaze. "Sorry," Jordan whispers.

Colston sighs and starts the truck. "There's a part of me that wishes I never decided to tell you or Kayra."

"Cole,"

"The encounters with Amber and Jake serve as a hard reminder of why I have kept this to myself. When I look into their eyes, I don't see the same worry that I see in yours and Kayra's." Colston admits.

"How can we not?" Jordan asks softly.

"I don't know."

"I'll do my best not to worry," Jordan says.

"As I try to find ways to keep myself stable," Colston says, looking at Jordan, who is about to argue against that statement. However, he replays it in his head, realizing that these are nearly impossible tasks for both of them.

"Trying is all we can do," Colston says, shivering slightly. "Let's get this party planned." He forces a smile.

Colston's phone rings. He pulls it from his pocket and hands it to Jordan as he begins to drive.

"Kayra, you are on speaker," Jordan announces.

"That cinnamon roll was phenomenal!"

Colston and Jordan share a smile.

"Oh, we know. Glenna was very clear about how her cinnamon rolls were meant to be enjoyed," Jordan says.

"You guys on your way back?" Kayra asks.

"In about an hour, we are working on reworking lyrics for the concert," Colston says, winking at Jordan.

"Alright, just be careful," Kayra says.
"We will see you in a bit," Colston says.
"Okay,"

Colston has arranged catering from The Grill Spot, which was more than happy to take on the job. He reaches out to Kayra's mom to extend an invitation and to request her to ask Kayra for the names of her friends. So Colston can build a guest list.

It is 8:15, and Colston has scheduled the party to start at one o'clock. Jordan suggests that they drive back to Glenna's shop and invite Oliver and his wife.

Colston thinks about it for a moment. "They are merely strangers." Colston says.

"Colston, wake up; listen to yourself," Jordan says. "You and I, you and Kayra, we were all merely strangers. But Colston, Oliver is aware. Having someone on your side who isn't your parents won't hurt." Jordan watches Colston as he speaks.

Colston is aware of the attention focused on him. He wants to celebrate Kayra today, and he is doing his best to bury his inner turmoil; unfortunately, this requires a significant amount of effort from him.

"Al----right." The cold seeps in, and Colston pounds the steering wheel with his palm in frustration, doing his best to distance himself from it.

Jordan hates watching this. "Cole, I am here. What is going on?"

Colston pulls over to the side of the road and takes a few chest heaving breaths. "Can--you drive?" Colston asks, struggling to regain control as the phantom's laughter echoes in his mind.

"Of course," Jordan says, then gets out.

Colston gets out on very unsteady legs but declines help, silently praying to God for a bit more strength. Once they switch seats, he settles back and once again focuses on surprising Kayra, just as he did during their engagement. The torment he felt then had been unable to break the surface. He hopes to replicate that moment.

"Let's go see if Oliver and his wife want to join us. Then, let's stop by Theo's Odes," Colston says.

Jordan drives them back home around 9:30, with a total of eleven guests confirming their attendance. Colston is beaming; he had initially thought it would only be the three of them and their parents.

When they arrive, Kayra greets them outside. She gives Colston a hug and kiss before hugging Jordan. "You guys get stuff worked out?" she asks.

"For the most part," Jordan says. "There's just some vocal confusion that we need to hash out in the studio."

Kayra raises an eyebrow at this, but Colston steps in to salvage the situation. "It happens from time to time; it'll work out in the end," he says, smiling reassuringly as he leads them inside.

Colston is uncertain about his next steps. Should he wait for people to show up, or should he find a way to lure Kayra away?

Thankfully, her mother lured her out of

the house under the pretense of needing help with something at her place. Allowing the guys and Colston's parents to prepare the house.

Colston is not under stress; he moves through the house with ease and calm, in contrast to his mom. Both he and his dad simply allow her to be.

"Son, are you worried about snoopers?" Patricia calls from the hallway, standing outside Colston's studio.

Colston and his dad are in the back of the house, preparing the sitting room. They exchange a glance as Colston approaches the doorway. "We are all adults; however, my studio will be locked anyway!"

"Alright,"

The doorbell chimes.

"Got it!" Jordan announces from the living room, where he has been resting for a while, allowing the painkillers to take effect.

He opens the door to Oliver and his wife, and behind them stands another woman. "Welcome! Come on in," Jordan warmly invites them. He then calls out to Colston, "Yo, Cole, the guests are starting to arrive!"

Colston leaves his dad in the sitting room. Once out of sight of anyone, he lifts his hand to his chest, and his body trembles.

In his mind, the platform wobbles as he screams and begs for it to stabilize. The fire is closing in, and he is too weak to move.

He manages to remain upright as the voices of his guests reach him.

"Please, God," he prays. *"Where is my key?"*

He could pray for the strength to prevent his inner turmoil from ruining Kayra's special day. To gain that consistent strength, he must unlock that cell.

He is managing everything with the help of controlled breathing. Afterward, he goes out to greet people.

The vehicles are parked in a free parking area at the end of the street. The food, steak, lobster tail, mashed potatoes, and salad, occupies most of the kitchen. The house smells incredible; however, it unfortunately makes Colston feel dizzy.

Colston's phone rings, and he signals for everyone to be quiet.

"Hello, love," Colston replies cheerfully.

"Hi, sorry it took so long. We are on our way," she says, a clear smile on her lips.

"Alright, Jordan and I might be singing, but we're not recording," Colston says.

She whispers, "I just want to be in your arms today."

This worries Colston a bit, but he doesn't let it show to those around him. "Of course, honey. See you soon; I love you."

"Love you too."

Colston hangs up. "We have about fifteen minutes." He announces.

The random conversations swirl around Colston, but they merely serve as background noise, overshadowed by the anguished tone that accompanied his wife's simple request.

"Hey, son." His dad interrupts his

troubling thoughts.

He smiles, "Yes," wrapping an arm around his dad's shoulders.

He pats Colston's chest, prompting a grimace from Colston. However, his dad remains oblivious to his son's discomfort as he continues, "I need you to back me up here."

Colston's mom glares at Elliot, "Don't you dare bring our boy into this." She is controlling her voice, and she vigorously points at Elliot.

"Mom, Dad, please," Colston says gently but firmly. He is trying to gauge whether this is a joke, as it is unusual for them to bring an argument to his home.

That appears to break their deep disagreement; they also seem confused.

"You okay, son?" Elliot asks.

Patricia cradles Colston's face and says, "You look exhausted and slightly feverish." Then she adds her hand to his chest.

Colston gazes into the expectant eyes of his parents, overwhelmed by a profound sense of confusion.

As the sound begins to fade, Jordan's voice pulls him back from the brink, "Colston! Kayra's here!"

"Kayra," he whispers, pulling away from his parents. "Alright, everyone," Colston says as he joins Jordan near the door, holding one of Kayra's books.

Colston beams as he waits for the door to open, making a conscious effort to be fully present.

Kayra steps out of the car, weighed down by anxiety.

"Kayra?" her mom calls out after her.

"Thanks, Mom," she says while walking backward toward the door. She watches her mom step out of the car. "I'm fine, I promise." She struggles to hold back her tears.

That looming heaviness appears to have intensified within her soul, fostering a sense of finality that threatens to engulf her. Being apart from Colston today makes her feel an urge to cry.

She opens the front door.

"SURPRISE!" This chorus halts her at the threshold.

Immediately, she is filled with immense joy as she sees Colston beaming while holding one of her books. However, she is also overcome with great trepidation.

Colston notices her apprehension and rushes to her side. The embrace is tight and filled with fear.

"Ka, I'm sorry. I should have said something," he whispers.

"No, no, thank you; just don't leave my side for a bit," she whispers tearfully.

"I promise," he says, tears welling in his eyes.

She then turns to face everyone, savoring her moment hand in hand with her husband.

Food was enjoyed, and laughter could be heard among the guests. However, an overall sense of gloom lingered in the house, stemming from the interaction at the door. This created the impression that all was not well between the hosting couple.

"Cole?" Jordan taps his shoulder.

He and Kayra are conversing with Oliver's wife, Nora, and one of Kayra's friends from an online poetry group, Layla Mcrae.

"Yes?" Colston asks, glancing over his shoulder.

"It is nearly time to get the cake. I think it would be good for you and Kayra to get some fresh air," Jordan suggests, whispering.

Jordan has been careful while watching Colston to avoid alerting him. He has noticed a change in Colston's posture, which has become increasingly slouched as his strength diminishes; he has also not seen him eat anything. Earlier, Colston's dad approached him with this question. "Hey, is there something going on between Colston and Kayra?"

The truth was quite the opposite. To answer the question, Jordan said, "I have been here for a week, and they are perfectly fine." He then excused himself before Colston's dad could start probing further.

Colston lacks the strength to deny the truth that he and Kayra need fresh air.

"Sorry to interrupt," Colston says, "but I need to go pick up the cake." He leans in and kisses the side of Kayra's head.

"I should go with you," Kayra says.

"I'm sure he can manage. And perhaps the cake will arrive here in one piece," Layla says with a smirk.

If music had been playing, it would have stopped, while all the guests who heard the comment are now observing the situation.

However, the awareness of the lingering gloom in the house is overshadowed by the joy of Kayra's accomplishment. There is an etiquette to such occasions: enjoy yourself, avoid addressing the elephant in the room, and refrain from making any questionable jokes toward the hosts.

Colston, who is well-established in the online world, is accustomed to comments like these. However, Kayra is very protective against such remarks, and unlike the last time, she is ready to defend him.

Jordan, Oliver, Elliot, and Theodore are close enough to hear the comment. Jordan and Elliot are prepared to step up in defense, but Kayra beats them to it. She knows that the remark affected her more than it did Colston, and in her current state, laughing it off is not an option. "Layla, I'm grateful that you could attend this surprise party, but I don't appreciate you turning my husband into a punching bag with your sly comments. I would prefer it if you left my home," Kayra says calmly.

The change in expression on Layla's face is amusing, shifting from self-satisfaction to complete shock.

Nora interjects, "I have taught my children that comments like that should only be made in the presence of family or close friends."

"Nora," Oliver whispers from the right side of Colston.

Theodore interjects, "Your lady is correct; we are all adults here. Feel free to make sexual jokes, slapstick humor, and the like. We do not need to resort to jokes that target individuals. Such behavior is juvenile."

Layla quietly slips away as everyone else agrees. Kayra wraps her arms around Colston, who lifts her into his embrace.

"Could I have everyone's attention, please?" Colston calls out.

A small, nervous squeal escapes from Kayra as she buries her face in his neck.

"I want to thank all of you for attending on such short notice. I wanted to celebrate my wife's accomplishments because she supports all of mine. I need to retrieve one last item for us to enjoy, and I will be taking the guest of honor with me. I hope you all enjoy yourselves and linger for a while longer. I know it is a Sunday evening."

A male clears his throat and says, "Colston, Kayra, I can't speak for everyone, but for me, gatherings like this are enjoyable. It's a relaxed way to come together and celebrate someone's achievements, a welcome break from the state of the world."

Colston simply nods to the man, "Kayra and I shall be back." He smiles and looks back at Jordan. "Could you entertain?"

Jordan pats his back and slowly pets Kayra's head.

"Sorry about this, Jordan." Kayra whispers.

"You are fine, Kayra. I'll take care of everyone; you guys go."

"Thanks, brother," Colston says, then walks out carrying Kayra.

Colston reaches the truck and gently sets Kayra down. "Babe, are you alright?"

Kayra gazes into his eyes and says, "I am so grateful for you. I worry about you, and not having you by my side this morning really affected me."

"I'm sorry; I didn't want to wake you and spoil the surprise. I also didn't want to leave a note," Colston says as he opens the door for her.

Kayra gets in. "I can't believe you did all this for me!"

Colston smiles and says, "I wanted to do so much more."

Colston shuts the door and begins to walk around the back end of the truck. Suddenly, he collapses to one knee; his vision blurs, and his body trembles.

"Colston!" Elliot calls from the front door.

Kayra looks at Elliot as he runs out of the house. She opens the door. "What?"

"He collapsed!"

"Son!" Elliot drops down beside him. "What is wrong?"

Colston simply shakes his head and replies, "Nothing, Dad, just tired."

"You are on your knees, trembling. What is wrong?"

Colston looks up at his dad, ready to reveal the truth. However, at the last moment, he decides against it, "Sleep has been hard to come by, and I've been up since five."

"Are you sure, son?"

"Yeah, once everyone leaves, I'll crash,"

Colston says.

"Babe, I'll drive," Kayra says.

Colston stands up with assistance from his dad and backtracks to the passenger side.

Kayra jumps into the driver's seat while Elliot helps Colston get into the truck. He pats the inside of the door and says, "Be safe," before walking back to the house.

Kayra pulls onto the road and asks, her voice filled with concern, "Hon, what is going on?"

Colston says, struggling, "Just----focus----on you, please?"

Kayra grips his hand. "Colston, you are being crushed. I appreciate that you are enduring this for me, but, sweetheart, please stop burying it. If you need to isolate yourself, please, babe, do it," she says, tears welling in her eyes.

"But... the party and you?" Colston asks.

"Hon, you have done wonderfully. I need you to be okay."

"It hurts------so----bad." Colston sobs, "holding----the----burning----poison. Babe, how------can I--------get----rid of------it?"

Kayra is lost as to what to say to ease his pain. She wonders if her request for him to let her in has made it impossible for him to hide it.

Colston leans his head back against the seat, his head pounding. He tries to compose himself, but his stomach growls loudly. He groans, realizing that he hasn't eaten since the cinnamon roll he had early this morning, which was around 6:30 AM.

"Have you not eaten today?" Kayra asks,

her voice tinged with panic.

"I did this----morning," he says, still trying to hold things down. "Babe, I'm sorry, but tonight------I'm going----to be a------mess." He squeezes her hand.

"You won't be alone."

When Kayra sees the cake, they are at home, and it is now taking the place of all the food warmers on the island.

"It's beautiful!" she exclaims.

Colston beams, "I know; I kinda don't want to cut into it."

"Cakes are meant to be eaten," someone remarks, eliciting several chuckles in response.

"So you'd be correct," Colston says, cutting into it.

He serves his wife first, then dishes up the rest. However, the hollowness in his stomach prevents him from serving himself, and a memory threatens to overwhelm him, placing him in an even more uncomfortable situation. He quickly excuses himself and retreats to his bedroom. Once there, he collapses onto the bed.

Landing haphazardly on the edge of the tub, his captor held the tray with the uneaten piece of cake. He spoke levelly, attempting to conceal his hurt. "You know, Colston, if too many things given in kind are rejected, don't expect anything in kind when you actually deserve them."

Colston had maneuvered himself off the edge of the tub and onto the floor as he hissed, "Things given in kind between friends are always welcomed. Things given in kind to smooth over a difficult situation are not welcomed!"

His head was wrenched to the right as the tray struck the side of his head. When he regained his bearings, Colston discovered that he was alone.

Coming back to consciousness, he hears a ringing in his right ear and feels nauseous. He manages to slide his head over the edge of the bed just in time to vomit bile.

He hears the door close, and a hand rests on his shoulder.

Colston looks through teary eyes. "Mom?" he asks weakly.

The hand rubs his back as Patricia kneels down, her eyes filled with concern. "Baby boy," she coos, running her fingers through his damp hair.

"Is everything fine out there?" he asks, struggling to suppress the urge to dry heave.

"Yes, you did a fantastic job putting this together. But you are not fine," she says, offering a sad smile.

"I am; I have just come down with something," he lies.

"No, Colston." Her voice takes on an edge that alerts Colston to impending danger. "You are coming home for good!"

Colston attempts to move quickly but ends up vomiting again, this time onto the sheets. His body experiences alternating hot and cold flashes, and the world spins so rapidly that closing his eyes does not alleviate the sensation.

"Honey, she is trying to kill you. However, someone cares enough to reach out to me."

"Stop--" His words are interrupted by her

hand pressing against his mouth.

He shakes it off and tries to slide off the other side of the bed.

Patricia erupts in anger, slapping Colston across the face multiple times. She growls, leaning in close to his ear before holding her phone in front of his blurred vision.

The still image from the video captures Kayra's bachelorette party. It is zoomed in from the left side, through the people who were piled on his limbs. Kayra is positioned above him, holding a kitchen knife just a few inches from his chest.

Colston smacks the phone out of his mom's hand and onto the floor. "I don't know------who------sent that------but--------she------was--------being--------forced."

Patricia's eyes narrow. "She should be in jail for attempting to stab you in the heart."

Colston rolls his head to call for help. Patricia circumvents this by slamming her hand under his chin, forcing it closed. "Cole, I am your mom, and I know how to help you."

Colston, fed up with the physical abuse, grabs her wrist and pulls it away from his chin. Unable to suppress the urge to vomit, he rolls his head to the right. When her other hand grabs his chin and forces his head back, bile erupts, splattering across his face. He is in danger of choking on his own vomit. To save himself, he places his hands on his mom's upper arm and shoves. She releases him momentarily, allowing him to roll onto his side and cough out the vomit that threatens to suffocate him.

"Call for help, and I'll kill her!"

Colston's world snaps to attention as he rolls off the bed. "You did not just threaten death on my wife!"

Patricia quickly realizes her mistake and desperately tries to rectify it. "No, honey, I would never. But you are not safe with her."

"How about what you just did? Trying to make me choke on my own vomit?" he says as his world begins to spin again. He takes a few unsteady steps toward the door, still aware that there are people in the house.

Patricia swiftly reaches the door ahead of him and locks it.

"Mom----I------don't------belong----to------you!" He collapses to the floor, his heart hammering in his chest. "DAD!"

Patricia growls and joins him on the floor, exclaiming, "Damn, daddy's boy!" She then proceeds to slap him a few more times.

"Colston! Unlock the door, please!" Elliot calls through the door.

Patricia retreats to the bathroom.

Colston can hardly breathe. "Dad!" His voice is airy. "Please," he is trying to calm himself down so he doesn't fall unconscious or, worse, have a heart attack.

The door is forced open, and Elliot stumbles inside, followed closely by Kayra and Jordan.

"Colston!" Elliot drops to the ground and wraps him in a hug. "What the hell?"

"Mom----in----the------bathroom--------

she----slapped----me----and--threatened------Kayra." Colston's body began to tremble with fear of not being believed again.

Elliot helps Colston into a seated position against the bed. "I'm sorry; I didn't think she would try anything," he says, gently rubbing the visible red marks on his son's cheeks.

"Nor----did----I," Colston swallows hard and attempts to compose himself. "On her phone." He points toward the phone on the floor.

Jordan moves to pick it up just as the bathroom door swings open.

"Oh, Jordan, that would be mine. Colston knocked it from my hand when he was having one of his fits," she says in a friendly tone as she reaches to take her phone from Jordan.

Jordan takes a step back and says, "Your adult son doesn't throw fits. He was likely trying to defend himself."

The calm expression on her face vanished, startling Jordan. "I am his mother, and how dare you accuse me of harming my son?

"Yes!" Elliot exclaims as he stands and moves in front of Jordan, who immediately drops down beside Colston. "There are clear signs that you slapped our son. You promised me that you were better." Desperation is evident in his final words.

"MY SON!" Patricia screeches, staring directly into Elliot's shocked face. "Colston is not your son!"

Patricia seizes the moment to position herself next to Colston, practically shoving Jordan aside to achieve this. Jordan is taken aback by her behavior that he has no reaction. Colston wears a similar expression to his father, "Dad?" His voice trembles with uncertainty.

Patricia rolls her eyes and attempts to caress his red cheek.

He jerks away at the memory of the phantom doing the same thing and screams, "Don't touch me! I want you to leave!"

Patricia's hands encircle Colston's throat, forcing his head back against the bed. "Don't move! Anyone!" she commands.

"Mom," Colston begins.

Patricia presses her thumbs firmly against his neck. Colston is not entirely deprived of breath and tries not to panic.

"Stop!" Kayra exclaims.

"Oh, stop it. My son is merely your cash cow. You never loved him!"

Oliver rushes in and puts Patricia in a headlock. She immediately releases Colston and begins screaming for Elliot.

"Just take her outside," Elliot says, defeated. He kneels at Colston's feet.

Colston's world continues to spin, and the threat of fainting looms over him. He grips the hands of Jordan and Kayra tightly. "Dad," his voice is a bit rough. "That is not true, right?" Colston asks, fully aware that if it is true, he will always consider Elliot as dad.

He moves forward, crouching over Colston, who leans in, allowing Elliot to cradle him. "You are one hundred percent my son. She is just playing a sick game."

Colston feels Jordan and Kayra release

his hands. He fully embraces his dad, breaking into sobs against his dad's shoulder, "Dad, I don't want her anywhere near us," he says. In the strong, protective arms of his dad, Colston feels secure enough to relax. With all the stress mounting within him, he goes limp.

"SON!" Elliot exclaims, panic rising in his voice as he gently maneuvers Colston back against the bed. Jordan moves aside to give Elliot space. "Cole? Come on, son," he urges. Elliot positions himself beside Colston and locks eyes with Kayra.

She has tears in her eyes. "Just hold him, please." Elliot looks at her in confusion. She recalled the moment after the wedding when she had hugged her father. Despite the horror that had preceded the joyous event, of which he was unaware, Kayra had felt safe and ultimately fainted. Savion had held her until she woke up thirty minutes later. "He's safe; let him sleep."

Elliot allows himself to release the panic and settle into a comfortable position to hold his son. Tears fall, and he whispers, "I thought I'd never be able to hold my boy like this again."

Kayra pats him on the shoulder and says, "Jordan and I will take care of everything else. You just need to be here." She lifts Colston's hand and kisses it before leaving the room with Jordan.

Chapter Fifteen: Freeze or Burn!

Patricia had made a tremendous commotion as Oliver dragged her out of the house. He warned her to keep her distance or he would call the police. At that point, she left.

"Oliver, thank you," Kayra says as she reenters the front area of the house. She stands before the guests, feeling both grateful and apologetic. "I want to thank you for coming, and I am sorry for the disturbance."

"Are you okay? Is your husband alright?" Asher Harrison asks.

Kayra fights back tears, saying, "We are fine; it's just bad timing for everything."

Jordan, after receiving one final round of collective congratulations, urges her to return to Colston. He and Oliver will take care of everyone.

"Dad?" Colston wakes up after about fifteen minutes, feeling groggy and sore.

"Shhh, I am here," Elliot says, trying his hardest not to alert Colston to the cold now radiating from him.

"Be straight with me," Colston says as steadily as he can. "It won't change anything, but I just want to know: you are truly my dad and not just saying that, right?" He exhales deeply.

"Do I need to get you some help?" Elliot

asks.

Colston folds into his dad's chest and pleads, "No. Please answer----the----question."

Elliot continues to hold him. "Colston Zamir Driscoll, my DNA is a part of you, I swear to you."

Colston looks his dad in the eyes and asks, "Then why did she do that? She clearly knows that I am a daddy's boy, but it shouldn't matter since I am an adult." He then moves to sit beside his dad.

Elliot shakes his head. "I don't know," he admits, sounding exhausted. "It's either that she wants you back in the house or she wants another child. I won't allow either option. She was getting help and claimed she was improving." Tears fell. "The moment she wrapped her hands around your neck, I should have pulled her away. I was just so stunned by it."

"We all were," Colston states.

The door opens, and Kayra enters. "Colston." She shuts the door behind her before collapsing onto the floor beside him.

Colston holds her close as she rests against his chest. "I want this madness to end!" she cries, looking up into his pain-filled yet calm eyes. "Why, Colston? Why are you so calm when the world is trying to kill you?" She clutches a fistful of his shirt, her eyes pleading.

"I just have to be," he replies. He then feels the monster stir within him; however, that monster has now become easy for him to overpower, requiring little to no effort. It is the only thing he has power over. "When I reveal what I have kept so close, you'll understand more. But you put it perfectly: we become angry at the world, taking out what is hurting out on it. Once we are spent, we can begin the grueling task of rebuilding, only to be destroyed again when a new problem appears.

"The Vicious Cycle."

Colston looks up and sees Jordan standing in the doorway. "Yes, if I can remain calm in the face of adversity, the victory won't be tainted."

"But you can still defend yourself," Elliot interjects, noticing Jordan's indecision about whether to stay or leave.

"I defend myself in my own way," Colston says.

"Jordan, come here, son," Elliot says, extending his left arm.

Jordan's heart leaps at the word 'son,' but he remains where he is. It is a family moment, and he does not want to intrude. "I am fine right here, sir."

Elliot looks offended. "JD, you come over here. You are just as much my second son as you are a brother to Colston and Kayra."

Jordan begins to tear up, realizing that this may be the last time he hears another man call him 'son' out of genuine care. He shifts and sits under the arm of his best friend's dad.

"Cole," Elliot begins, momentarily at a loss for words. After a brief pause to collect his thoughts, he continues, "I realize that I've been excluded from a lot due to Patricia's behavior. I sensed that something was off today, well, to be honest, this entire week. You usually check in with me regularly, and seeing you today, I noticed the weight you're carrying."

Colston lowers his head; *I can no longer conceal it. Gradually, I will lose the remnants of myself that I have left.* He releases a sob, saying, "I am sorry." He must wonder if he is too far gone, as the grip of the nightmare has a steel hold on his soul. As futile as it may seem to continue fighting, he must do so for all those who care.

"Son?" Elliot asks.

"Dad, this week has been tough," Kayra says. "Jordan and I have become privy to just how significant this struggle has been for him. We are helping him to overcome it, but as you can see, it takes a great deal of energy from him."

Elliot looks at Kayra with concern. "I thought he was getting help."

"I thought so too; Todd seems to be siding with the police," Colston says, his voice wavering.

The look of shock that spreads across Elliot's face reveals that he has not been exposed to the corrupt system. "What? How? Son, let me help," he says.

Colston simply looks at him and shakes his head. "I barely have the strength to fight against the trauma. It would be suicidal to fight against the system. They are convinced that I was behind the kidnapping and that the trauma is merely an act. Before he left town, Todd warned not only the police but also the healthcare system that I might act out," Colston says. He feels himself growing lighter, as if his mind is experiencing a delayed reaction to what his mother did. An overwhelming sense of dread threatens to overtake him. He thinks of the empty stage, desperately wanting to maintain control. He cries; is control beyond his reach at this point? The seats are engulfed in flames, threatening the stage, his safe space. A voice at the edge of his hearing screams, "BURN OR FREEZE!"

Both Elliot and Kayra sense the panic coursing through Colston. Kayra quickly begins to rub his face and then reminds him of his happy place.

"It's on fire!" Colston exclaims, writhing in pain.

Elliot holds his son tightly, filled with fear, while attempting to offer him comfort. His son's eyes are closed, and he is crying, beads of sweat glistening on his brow. "What is happening to him?" He asks with tears of his own.

Jordan responds while Kayra is trying to coax Colston back, "He's having a flashback."

Colston can hear their voices around him as he searches for the door. The thick smoke blinds him and threatens to suffocate him. He begins to cough. Elliot quickly reacts to the sound of Colston's cough, effortlessly shifting him onto his side on the floor and bracing his arm across his chest.

Kayra is now lying flat on the floor, hoping for his eyes to open. "COLSTON!" she screams, watching him gasp for breath.

Colston lies on the stage floor, his shirt pulled over his nose. Tears well in his eyes as he crawls, hearing his wife's voice scream from within the inferno, "COLSTON!" This causes him to repeat, "It is not real! This place can't hurt me!" He feels himself cracking under it all. Turning his head toward Kayra's voice, he is about to call out when a pair of hands emerges from the smoke. They scoop him up by the throat and slam him onto his back. The hands, solid up to the mid-forearms, are connected to a wispy black form, while the eyes are black orbs flickering with the hellfire of insanity. The grip around his throat pulses with a frigid cold that encases Colston. His mind goes blank as the cold travels down, freezing his blood flow and causing his heart to stop. The wispy form leans in close and whispers, "*My dearest Colston, I only wanted to help you, to make you better. It is you who is tormenting yourself. Let go and realize this is the only way forward. My role is to help you, and your role is to sing!*" Then, it disappears, allowing the intense heat to warm Colston's body.

Elliot has been performing CPR on Colston for the past ten minutes when he suddenly takes a sharp intake of breath.

"Son!?" Elliot cries, pressing his hands against Colston's chest, feeling the rapid heartbeat.

Colston awakens in excruciating pain and sees the concerned, tear-streaked faces of Kayra, Jordan, and his dad gazing down at him. A wave of panic washes over him. "What happened?" he croaks, his voice raspy. He feels a tickle in his throat but manages to suppress the urge to cough.

"You stopped breathing," Kayra says, placing her hand on Elliot's.

"You still aren't fully here, are you, Colston?" Jordan's words came at Colston like a knife, clean and sharp.

He looks at Jordan, whose eyes are fixed intently on him. Though his gaze lacks weight or judgment, it is filled solely with care and love. Colston breaks down, saying, "Please, I can't fight it anymore. I'd rather freeze than burn."

"Then talk; don't be in there alone. Consider it practice for tomorrow."

Colston observes a look of confusion break over his dad's face; however, Elliot remains silent, regarding him with love despite his own bewilderment.

"Kayra, I will share if you share what is hurting you." He reaches for her hand and gently holds it. "Please, love."

She moves her other hand from his chest to his face, gently wiping away his tears with her thumb. Nodding, she fights back her own tears. He takes a deep breath and addresses his dad, "There isn't any violence, but there is aggression. If--I--can----keep----it----together to share--what--was----running--through--my mind, it might--get-hard-to-listen." Colston warns his dad because this will be the first time he's hearing any details about what happened.

"I can handle it, son."

Colston surrenders to the struggle...

Colston woke up coughing, his body drenched in beads of cold sweat. His thrashing had pinned his head and neck into the corner. The blankets lay across the lower half of his body, while his bound wrists rested at his side. He couldn't tell if the wetness on them was blood or sweat. He needed to regain control of his breathing. It was just a dream, he reassured himself. He kept his eyes closed against the harsh light from the flashlight his captor had left behind, intended to help him adjust to the brightness because he sings tomorrow. Even through his closed eyelids, the light probed at his hectic mind. He shifted to lie flat on his back, his face contorted in silent agony. His head vibrated, but he blindly and painfully pulled the blankets back up to his face to block out the light and retain warmth.

The cold and the fear of death, though they would be a relief, made it nearly impossible for him to return to sleep. His sick body craved rest; lying beneath blankets on the frigid floor, he struggled to concentrate on his physical needs. Instead, he focused on his breathing and staying warm, calming himself with thoughts of Kayra until he drifted in and out of sleep or unconsciousness. At that point, Colston could no longer discern the difference.

The sound of the generator whirring to life jolted Colston into full awareness. He was alive, a plain stroke of luck. He heard a series of sneezes coming from somewhere beyond the door. That man was sick too; perhaps this would lead him to ease up on the harsh treatment. Nevertheless, Colston could not depend on that for his chance to escape. It would ultimately come down to his performance, the only aspect over which he had complete control, and he was determined to make the last within this man's grasp.

The generator fell silent, and he listened intently to the

footsteps. Hiding under the blanket like a child trying to convince his parents that he was not in bed, he felt a creeping sense of dread. The wood creaked, echoing in the cold stillness... then nothing. Colston's heart was heavy with fear and sadness. What had happened? What was coming? He wanted to call out, seeking the comfort of the man who was his key to survival, yet a small part of him hoped that the door would remain closed. He heard the click of the lock, and he could have sworn his heart stopped.

"Colston?" The voice was raspy.

Colston decided not to respond, both in defiance and practicality. His voice was not being properly cared for, so he needed to conserve what remained for tomorrow. Additionally, he was reclaiming control.

The door swung open, and the blanket rippled slightly from the rush of air that entered the room. He was grateful for the blanket covering his face, shielding his eyes from the harsh sunlight filtering in. Although he wanted to maintain his streak of defiance, he needed to be mindful about testing the man's patience and how much more he could endure before he could escape this nightmare. He allowed his bound hands to relax slightly, wincing at the burning sensation in his wrists. The blanket slipped from his face, settling around his neck and allowing the cool air to soothe his feverish skin, which intensified the throbbing in his head and sent a pins-and-needles sensation throughout his body. He kept his eyes closed against the light.

"You will answer me when I call." The man's voice grew nearer.

Colston opened his eyes and looked up. His gaze met a pair of emotionless voids.

"You--wish me--to sing tomo-rrow, then I--need to save---my voice." Colston croaked.

Colston saw it again, a pause; however, his captor

seemed prepared this time. The tray and mug were set down on the floor, and moving with purpose, he stepped above Colston. He reached down and scooped his fingers deep, so he got the vest, pulling up the blankets. He folded his hands back toward his chest. Colston felt his back lift off the floor; the closer his face got to the man's, the more the insanity intensified.

The man leaned close to Colston's left ear. "You will make some sort of sound in response to my calls. Make me have to repeat myself; I won't hold back." He dragged Colston and propped him up in the corner.

Colston understood the weight of the words. He also recognized that what he kept witnessing was not merely the man's wrestling with what was right or wrong, but it was simply him losing control.

Colston was so numb to pain that he barely reacted to the movement when he was handed the tray of food and a warm mug of honey tea. His captor abruptly and swiftly exited the room, triggering a faint alarm in his mind as Colston let the lukewarm tea, thick with honey, soothe his sore throat.

He rushes back, exclaiming, "Take these," as he drops four white pills onto the tray.

Colston looked up, and he watched the calmness transform into a snarl as the man crouched down to his level.

"You are sick." His hands were on Colston's face so quickly that he just sat there, too weak to fend them off. The hands cupping Colston's face were firm. "You, my precious, have no one to blame but yourself. I didn't plan on caring for a man-baby. But. Here. I. Freaking. AM!" Nails dug into his skin as their foreheads pressed together. "Take the damn meds, or I will force them down your throat! Take heed that I am allowing you to do it."

He released Colston's face, and Colston merely looked

down at the mug in his hands. It was empty of liquid, with only a thin layer of honey coating the bottom. Colston listened as his captor stood there in a huff.

"You have food. You have ten minutes. If I come back and the pills are not gone, I will force-feed them to you."

Colston looked up just as the door slammed shut. Although he was reluctant to accept any form of medication from the man who had placed a chloroform-soaked rag over his face, he knew that any assistance in alleviating his worsening symptoms would be a blessing. He used the buttered bread to swallow the pills, then turned his attention to the cold chicken breast. Halfway through his meal, the man returned, this time armed with a flashlight that had fresh batteries.

"Are you a good boy?" he cooed.

Colston kept his head down and his eyes closed as he slowly nodded.

As his feverish mind transported him back to his twelve-year-old bedroom, he was suffering from pneumonia. Curled up in a ball in the center of his bed, his eyes were red from crying as he struggled with the blanket. When it covered him, the heat was unbearable, but without it, he shivered uncontrollably. He pleaded with his mom for some medicine. She would enter the room with a cold rag and place it on his forehead, saying, "Baby boy, trust me, I am helping you fight this naturally."

"I want Dad," he cried, sending himself into a coughing fit. His ribs and head ached with every cough.

"You don't want to risk getting him sick; we could end up homeless," she cooed.

Colston was fed up and scared at that moment when he heard the front door open later that night. He screamed for his dad...

Back in the bathroom, he wished he could call for his

dad.

"That wasn't so hard, was it? Soon, some relief will come because you accepted help. If you accept my help, you can have a comfortable bed," he purred.

Colston looked up, narrowing his eyes to see beyond the light. His head disapproved of this action. He contemplated speaking to challenge the situation but instead settled on saying, "I just--want to go--home."

The horrid excuse for a human extended his arms out to his sides and laughed, continuing to chuckle as he spun around and exited the room.

Colston stared at the door, listening as laughter faded into a small coughing fit. He neither smiled nor wished ill intent brought by the coughing; the hollowness within him was too profound. No matter how much he tried to ignore it, the emptiness only grew, becoming all-consuming. On the eve of a performance, one for which he had no idea what he would be singing, even the thought of practicing felt more like a chore than a joy. He could kill that man for that reason alone. Sure, the kidnapping and torture were ample cause for overwhelming anger, but for Colston, it was his passion for singing that truly mattered; he had built a career out of something he deeply loved. He had a feeling, no, he knew, that he wouldn't simply be able to walk out of here. He needed to outlast his captor... somehow.

The pills were taking effect, or perhaps he had simply grown accustomed to the pain, as the throbbing in his head had subsided. His throat remained a nuisance, but it could have been worse.

"I am still alive, my heart is beating, and my mind is producing thoughts. Breathe; I am singing tomorrow. Oh, this puppet will sing!" This little proclamation made him smile.

Colston drifted through the remainder of the day,

remaining sufficiently aware around mealtimes to respond appropriately. Lunch consisted of two mugs of tea and two additional pills. During the intervals, he conserved his energy. He was playing the quiet game, reserving his grudge-bearing assault for the upcoming performance. It would ultimately depend on his ability to blindside his captor. Colston needed to bear all he had left tomorrow. This manipulation of Colston's Creepy Covers was designed to shape him into what the man desired, which was merely for him to hold on to Colston. Thus, cycling back to Creepy Covers is a continued way to keep Colston's voice and presence fresh online. This indicated that his captor did not intend for long-term imprisonment; Colston's death was being delayed for the sake of entertainment until he lost his authenticity, at which point his captor would be satisfied. He was just the pawn at the same time the main character, having all the control while having none.

After that, he feels both better and worse at the same time. There is something cathartic about expressing his feelings aloud. However, witnessing the horror, sadness, and sympathy in the eyes of his loved ones is painful. Yes, he is still present, but the thoughts that consumed him during that time are embarrassing now.

"Son, I am sorry. I know there was no way for me to help you then, but when you were twelve, you were sick for six days before you finally screamed for me. When I gathered you up in my arms, I realized that your mom had been lying to me about your care." He drops his head and starts to move away. Colston stops him by rolling toward and placing a hand on his shoulder. "Please, let go; I caused you so much harm by staying with her."

"She was your wife and my mother; it's okay," Colston says, sitting up with a little help from Kayra. "I still love you."

Elliot looks back at him and whispers tearfully, "How? How can you, when I have put you at risk for your entire life?"

Kayra's heart stirs with pain as she shares that sentiment. "Because your boy understands that humans make mistakes and that love is a difficult emotion to abandon," Kayra says.

Colston takes her hand, resting his arm over hers, and brings their joined hands to his chest. Kayra leans against his shoulder and says, "In all honesty, Cole, if you were any other guy, the wedding would never have happened. However, after I tell you what I need to say, if you feel you need a break, I will understand."

He turns to meet her gaze and says, "Never. We'll get through this together."

"How is it that we, when taught to tell the truth, can be so destructive?" Jordan asks. "Or at least, that is what our minds do: they prepare us for the worst-case scenario so that people's reactions, if negative, have a lesser impact. Or like this, apologizing even before speaking the truth." Jordan turns to look Elliot in the face. "Elliot, in light of the truths being shared and the tender expressions of care and affection you've shown me, I feel guilty for not revealing my truth." He pauses, gazing into Elliot's gentle yet strong features. "I am gay," he says, watching as Elliot's expression hardens. Jordan's heart sinks, but he reminds himself that he doesn't need everyone to accept him. After all, Elliot is not his father.

Elliot says nothing to ease the pained expression on Jordan's face and pulls him into a comforting embrace, resting one hand on the back of Jordan's head. He glances at his own son and daughter-in-law, who are smiling warmly. Once Jordan reciprocates the hug, Elliot speaks gently. "What hurts is that you believe your family won't love you unconditionally. Whether you identify as gay, bisexual, transgender, or anything else, you are my son. Though you come from a different bloodline, you are no less important than Kayra, who married into our family. You have shown love and care toward Colston and Kayra, and you have treated me with respect. That is all I could ever ask for." The embrace tightens.

As Jordan pulls away, tears in his eyes, he says, "We should be able to believe that we can be our authentic selves without fear of judgment or abandonment within the family circle."

Elliot nods, "Like with Colston's warning, that was appreciated. I am his father and meant to protect him. Seeing him after his rescue filled me with overwhelming guilt."

Kayra gently places her hand on his arm. "If you wish to hear what happened the night before the wedding, it is a violent story. I haven't heard Colston's full account of that night, just as he hasn't heard mine, except for what we experienced together."

Colston nods, "And Jordan doesn't even realize that his timely arrival legitimately saved me from a slow and painful death."

Kayra immediately leans into him as he rubs her back with his right hand. Unable to contain her emotions any longer, she cries into his chest, "They used you to make me lie!"

Chapter Sixteen: The Rite of Cherish Severance

Colston looks at her fearfully and asks, "Who made you lie?"

She leans against him, feeling a headache beginning to form. She had hoped that this would never come to light. This one betrayal, against the truth, against Colston, and worst of all, against herself, was overwhelming. "The entire system was complicit in the effort to keep you away from the trial."

Colston lowers his head, feeling demoralized and infuriated by being treated like an unruly child. "So, what did they make you say happened? Because I am pretty sure that the video Mom tried to show me is the moment you were forced to kill me."

The other three speak simultaneously, with Kayra exclaiming in shock, "What! There is proof!"

Jordan exclaims, "The hell?!"

Elliot exclaims, "What the hell?"

At that moment, Jordan pulls Patricia's phone from his pocket, then stops and looks up. "This isn't like recounting in words," he says.

Colston nods. "If this is the moment I believe it to be, it's going to be chilling."

Jordan extends the phone to Elliot, who promptly pushes it back, saying, "No, I... don't want to know why it's on her phone."

"She just said that it was someone who

cared enough to reach out to her, which shows that Kayra is trying to kill me," Colston says, feeling Kayra shudder against him.

"There is no code to access the phone," Jordan reports.

"First, Kayra, I followed the case like everyone else in this town. I didn't know you were the hidden survivor. I mean, there was no way I could have guessed, but it was reported that you were forced to stab your brother during that ritual, after which he fell into a coma and died weeks later. But you are an only child, right? Why the hell exclude Colston, the true victim, from seeking justice?"

"They were concerned that I would shift the focus of the trial to my kidnapping," Colston says.

"Additionally, Jordan, the true hero of that night, was excluded and replaced by a fictitious friend of mine, with whom I was no longer in contact by the time of the trial, and whom they were unable to locate," Kayra explains.

"How in the hell did they get away with that?" Elliot asks, holding Jordan close.

"I don't know about everyone else, but I was promised that if I refused, Abigail would go free, and Colston would undoubtedly be killed," Kayra says.

"I'm sure it would be best for them if I died," Colston says.

"No, your survival amidst all of this is proof that they are wrong, and they are likely terrified of everything that may come to light," Jordan says.

Elliot sighs as he catches a glimpse of the phone in Jordan's hand, noticing the still image displayed on the screen. He shifts his gaze away and asks, "Jordan, are there any other messages before the video?"

Jordan attempts to scroll up. "No, it is only the video, and the number is restricted," he says.

"Don't play the video yet," Elliot says. "I want to hear the full story."

"Dad, brace yourself," Colston warns.

Elliot tightens his grip on Jordan. "What real hell happened that night?"

Kayra begins...

It was the night before the wedding. Jordan was in charge of Colston's bachelor party, while Abigail had gained the right and trust to host Kayra's bachelorette party.

Kayra parted from Colston's side at one o'clock that afternoon. Abigail wanted her to enjoy her last day as a single woman. In response, Kayra always corrected her, saying, "Abby, I am beyond excited to become Colston's wife."

"This is what they all say, but I have been proven wrong before, which is very rare." The way she expressed this was consistently sly and suggestive, leaving Kayra feeling uncomfortable.

She allowed Abigail to honk because she didn't want to leave Colston.

He kissed her forehead and said, "My love, tomorrow we will be married. Enjoy tonight. Jordan, Decklin, Adam, Grayson, and I are just going out for drinks and karaoke. If you need to call just to hear my voice, that's perfectly fine."

"Really?"

"Yup, go have fun, and I'll see you tomorrow."

They shared a passionate kiss, and then Kayra departed.

"Come on, girly!" Abigail shouted as soon as she exited the house.

The feeling of absolute bliss guided her steps, knowing that the next time she entered the house, she would be Mrs. Driscoll. However, this joy was nearly overshadowed by a lingering fear, a fear that intensified in the presence of Abigail. Her heart ached for Colston even more. Her heart sank when she noticed that James was in the back seat. The sight of him nearly brought her to tears, and to make matters worse, she had to sit in the back with him because the front seat was cluttered with stuff for the party. A slight, knowing smirk played on Abigail's lips as she silently directed her to the back.

Kayra could hear Colston's voice gently encouraging her to enjoy herself, but she also didn't want to disrupt his evening.

"Good afternoon, Kay!" James greeted her in a smooth, rich voice. He then presented her with a rose. "A rose for the pretty lady."

"Much appreciated, but you are much too forward. My groom might be looking." She lied about the last part; she knew full well that Colston didn't peep, but James didn't. She simply didn't want to accept the rose.

"He almost didn't let you come, didn't he?" Abigail asked as she pulled away from the curb.

"Actually, it was me who didn't want to leave." Kayra said, in complete honesty.

Kayra, hoping for a witty comeback, was met with narrowed eyes looking back at her from the rearview mirror. "Oh, Kayra, you'll have your entire married life. My parties are the ones you want to attend, trust me," she said, her voice smooth. "We will go to the house at seven to get the party started. You are being treated today."

It was a complete spa day, with freshly manicured nails and

a stylish haircut featuring blonde highlights.

At one point, James finally left them alone, and Kayra promptly said, "Abbs, I am very uncomfortable with James. I am to be married tomorrow, and he's treating this like a first date."

"Chill, Kay, he is smitten, and that is true. He enjoys the challenge. You should play hard to get, you know. Just throwing him a bone once in a while won't hurt. Sure, you are committed to Colston, but the game never stops. He plays the game too."

Kayra fell into silence, her mind swirling with doubt and uncertainty. Was she right? Does Colston truly play? Is he fully committed? Should she leave the exit door ajar?

Throughout the remainder of the outing, she silently cried while maintaining a smile. Each time her hand brushed against James, she felt a wave of nausea. For him, every touch seemed like an invitation.

Abigail was viewing with immense satisfaction.

Kayra desperately wanted to call Colston, but she gritted her teeth and promised herself that after the wedding, she would no longer be friends with Abigail.

When they arrived at the house, Kayra felt overwhelmed by the large number of people. Abigail guided her through the crowd toward a side room near the stairs. Once inside the small bedroom, Kayra noticed a thin red shirt laid out on the bed, emblazoned with the words 'Bride to Be' in gold lettering running the full length of the shirt.

Abigail spun her around by the shoulders, bringing them face to face. Kayra said, "I don't think this is a good idea."

"Nonsense! Kayra, relax. I promised Colston that you would be safe and comfortable. You are the safest among all these people here to celebrate you! You may feel out of your element, but I assure you that once you relax, you'll be able to enjoy yourself." Her eyes sparkled with sincerity that Kayra found difficult to see through. "Now, get changed so the party can begin." Abigail ran her hands down Kayra's arms to her hands and attempted to 'accidentally' slide Kayra's engagement ring off.

Kayra balled up her fist. "Abbs?"

"Sorry, get changed," Abigail said as she left the room.

Kayra stood staring at the clothes laid out for her. The words, 'Bride to Be' caused tears to run. Is she too loyal to let her hair down? If he gets wind of this, will it be the end for them?

Her phone chimed as a text message came through. She checked to see who it was from and smiled upon seeing that the message was from 'Husband'; for the past two years, she had saved Colston's name as husband in her phone. She opened the message, "My beautiful wife, I hope you are enjoying yourself. The guys and I are about to head out to the bar. I love you and can't wait to see you tomorrow."

Paralyzing were those words; she had been doubting Colston. There was a knock on the door. "Kay?" The voice belonged to Sadie.

"I am not ready," she said tearfully as she pocketed her phone and the door opened.

"Kay?" Sadie asked, shutting the door and gently rubbing Kayra's shoulders. "If you have doubts, listen to them. The time you spend doting on a single person is time wasted, making you question everything. Get dressed; we are waiting for you."

The door opened and closed once more. She was alone and had changed into the shirt and short shorts. As the next few hours passed in a trance-like state, James was always present.

All sense of time was lost to Kayra, and everything swirled before her eyes. Then suddenly, the snap of fingers pierced through the chaos. Abigail stood in plain view, declaring, "It is time! Kayra, you and James go upstairs. Enjoy an honest, beautiful man and discover what you are willingly throwing away."

"NO!" Kayra screamed. "I was trying to have fun, but I am dedicated to my husband!" She yanked her arm free from James.

"No doubt Colston is getting some right now, though he would have to beg for it."

Kayra let out a frustrated scream, "I will never understand you! I want to leave!"

Kayra was then restrained by a strong man, who pressed a hand against her mouth and wrapped an arm around her waist, hauling her upstairs. Once they reached a room, before the man released her, Abigail injected her with a substance.

Kayra, in tears, felt heavy, and when Abigail gently touched her face, it produced a small electric shock.

"Kayra?" Her voice echoes, resonating deeply in Kayra's mind. "Relax, James will be here in a moment."

The moment Kayra found herself alone, her hands numb, she took out her phone and dialed Colston...

Colston's party was a light, drunken night of karaoke. It was simply a celebration of the upcoming union, not the end of bachelorhood, as many might suggest.

Colston, unfortunately, had to cut the night short as he wasn't feeling well. A headache and a slight stomach bug had struck him the night before and lingered throughout the day. He kept this from Kayra because he wanted her to enjoy her evening without worrying about him.

Jordan and the other three groomsmen were encouraged to stay and enjoy themselves while he opted for a taxi ride home. However, he quickly regretted this decision; the ride was not smooth, and the music was excessively loud.

Once out, he vomited in his front yard, feeling slightly better afterward. As he entered the quiet house, he realized it would be the first time in five years that he would be going to bed alone. He kicked off his shoes at the front door and removed his shirt while walking to the bedroom. After brushing his teeth, he collapsed onto the bed at around 10:40.

Hours later, he was awakened by Kayra's ringtone. He scrambled to answer the call, a smile on his lips and joy in his heart. "Babe?" he said, his voice still groggy.

Kayra must have been getting ready for bed and wanted to hear his voice. However, the voice that Colston heard was far from happy and joyful. *"Cole? I need you to come get me! Please!"* Her voice was a whisper, trembling with fear.

The overwhelming sleepiness and lingering sickness were instantly replaced by panic. The joy in his heart drained and was replaced by fear, and his smile morphed into a snarl.

"Are you at Abigail's?" he asked, springing out of bed.

"Yes--"

"What the hell are you doing on the phone? Get in bed!" a voice bellowed.

Colston listened helplessly as his wife begged and cried. The man growled, and Kayra's terrified scream was abruptly silenced when the line disconnected. Colston stood in the dark hallway, his entire body trembling as he fumbled to put on his shirt. With his shirt half on, he swung open the door to the guest room. "Jordan?" To Colston's despair, the bed was empty. He managed to get his left arm into the shirt and pulled it down over his chest. Her scream echoed within the walls of his mind. "Kayra!" he cried out, forcing on his shoes as he dialed Jordan...

Kayra's phone was forcibly taken from her hand by James. He examined the phone and called out. "Abigail, she made the call! He is on his way!"

Abigail entered the room with the broadest smile on her face as she approached Kayra, who was trembling in the corner.

Abigail effortlessly lifted Kayra off the floor and helped her sit on the bed. "The next step will be hard. You are going to free yourself from the abuse that Colston will begin to inflict on you in a few months. He will become insecure, and you will become a prisoner. For now, stay here with James while we prepare everything. James, please behave yourself."

"Promise."

It was nearly two in the morning on what was meant to be the happiest day of his life; instead, Colston found himself sprinting out of his front door, his heart racing with fear as he rushed to save his wife. After two rings, Jordan picked up, and Colston could hear the thumping of music and the chaotic chatter in the background. *"Bud, what is it?"* Jordan's voice sounded carefree.

Colston was climbing into his truck. "Jordan! Kayra's in trouble!"

"What?" The tone had shifted, and he appeared to be in motion. *"Hold on, Cole."* Colston heard the music fade, followed by the sound of a heavy door opening and closing. *"What do you mean she's in trouble?"*

"I mean," he said, trying not to yell as he started the truck, "she called me to come get her. She was begging and crying because there was a man in the room with her!" He shifted the truck into gear and drove onto the road. "I need you to stay on the phone with me. I'm heading to Abigail's now."

"You got it. Do you need us to call a taxi? We can be there to help," Jordan asked.

"I don't know, man. I don't know what I'm walking into. I just need to know that Kayra is safe." He began pounding the steering wheel; tears of frustration fell. "JD, I knew it! I sensed something was wrong, but Kayra seemed so happy. I let her down."

"Hey, stop that. You haven't let her down. You were simply respecting her wishes and not allowing your grievances with

Abigail to interfere." Jordan then became extremely serious. *"Do you think you're walking into danger?"*

Colston could not feign ignorance regarding this matter. "I believe that I might be."

Jordan sighed, realizing that there was no stopping him since Kayra might be in trouble. *"How far away are you?"*

"Five minutes," Colston said. "The roads are barren."

"Listen to me: when you get there, put your phone in your pocket on speaker. So we can hear what is happening. If it sounds like you are in trouble, we will call for help," Jordan instructed.

"Alright," Colston said as he pulled onto the street, his heart pounding. "They better not have hurt her."

"You aren't there to fight; you are there for Kayra," Jordan said, aware that he was preaching to the choir.

"I'm here; you're going into my pocket."

There was a line of cars parked along the sidewalk in both directions, forcing Colston to park four houses down from Abigail's two-story home. He found this situation suspicious; Abigail had gone to great lengths to secure the right to host Kayra's party, and he regretted not confronting her about it. Her house was the only one on that stretch of street with lights illuminating nearly every room, and even from his vantage point, he could hear the music blaring. "Jordan, get down here ASAP," he said aloud, starting to jog up the sidewalk. He had been cane-free for a month, and running on his ankle might pose some challenges, but he couldn't care less at that moment. The loud, deep bass of the music reverberated in his chest, and he wondered where the police were in response to the disturbing the peace calls. He was two houses away when a group of about ten people on the front lawn, being rambunctious, noticed his approach.

"Yo! You are not welcome here!" a voice shouted.

"Yeah, fatty, get lost!" Another shouted.

Colston, unfazed by the comments, continued toward the front door. He had half expected them to try to stop him from entering, but they merely watched him run by laughing. Colston had only a moment to realize that he was running straight into a trap when he burst through the doorway and shouted over the music, "KAYRA!"

Everyone turned to look at him. The lights went out, and Colston was struck unexpectedly on his right side by a blunt object. He let out a cry of pain and struggled against the many hands trying to restrain him. "GET OFF!" he roared.

He received a solid blow to the chest and right leg. Colston collapsed; for a moment, he felt his heart flip-flop in his chest, and a heaviness settled in his neck. He hit the floor, struggling to breathe. As he felt ropes being tied around him, *NO! NO!* his mind screamed. He was being moved, unable to see, and barely able to speak. When he finally stilled, he found himself sitting up in a chair.

A light illuminated the area in front of him, revealing Abigail, Lucy, and Sadie. Lucy and Sadie were dressed in revealing outfits, black with red accents, while Abigail wore a similar style, featuring red with black accents.

"YOU BETRAYED US!" Colston yelled.

Abigail smirked, "No, you betrayed yourself. And you knew that, didn't you?"

Colston simply stared at her. "Just let me leave with my wife, and our lives will never have to cross again."

"That is not how this works. People with looks like yours are a disgrace, and your fame is equally disgraceful to those who possess beauty. Kayra belongs in this world, and you are holding her back!"

Colston felt as if he were going crazy listening to this delusion. "You are crazier than I thought; looks eventually fade with age. The look of you has already diminished because of your attitude.

Abigail took a very aggressive step forward toward him, but Lucy and Sadie stopped her before she could take another.

Lucy glared at Colston, saying, "The influence she has is immense."

Abigail turned and slapped her; Lucy merely bowed her head. When Abigail looked back at him, he felt an urge to recoil. There was a frenzied danger in her eyes, and a wide smile slowly spread across her lips. "Bring down the bride, for her groom awaits!"

Colston could hear shuffling to his right but could not see anything. He was furious that this was even happening; he could easily free himself from the ropes that were loosely tied around his chest and arms.

A tall man in boxers entered the illuminated area, with Kayra trailing behind him. One of the man's hands was tightly gripping both of Kayra's wrists. She looked drugged, but her eyes sparkled with fear as she looked up at him.

"Kayra?" His voice was low and filled with concern.

"Colston," her voice was barely audible.

The man yanked on her wrists, causing her to whimper. Colston lunged forward, tugging at the loosely tied ropes. He tackled the man, sending him crashing into Abigail.

Colston shouted over Abigail's screams, urging Kayra to run.

Kayra struggled to move forward, hindered by the crowd of people blocking the way to the door and the numbness that enveloped her. Colston fought against the numerous hands reaching out to seize him. Frustrated, Kayra gave up on running and draped herself over Colston's back. "Abigail, stop this! Let me leave with my husband!" trying to sound resolute.

Abigail laughed, "I am Abigail Sunderland, and I never admit defeat!" She snapped her fingers.

Kayra was forcibly separated from Colston, and before he could react to assist her, he was struck across the face. The blow instantly dazed him, and he found himself rolled onto his back. However, a sharp whiff of smelling salts quickly brought his body and mind back to alertness. He attempted to move, but several people extended and then piled onto his limbs.

"Stop this! Let us go!" he insisted.

Abigail looked down at him. "No, this will be a lesson, a clear declaration that these two worlds cannot mix."

"Abigail, please, I made a mistake!" Kayra pleaded.

She turned on Kayra and asked. "Yes? And..."

Colston lifted his head and met Kayra's gaze. She held his stare in silence for an extended moment, prompting Abigail to kick Colston's hip and shriek, "AND...?"

Kayra watched her husband writhe in silence; tears fell. She then turned to Abigail, who was seething with anger. "I have no idea who you are or what kind of cult you want to run, but I want nothing to do with you! Let Colston and me go!"

Abigail sneered, "A cult, you say? It's time for the rite to be performed!" She snapped her fingers once more.

The people who were piled on Colston's limbs tore his shirt from his body as a knife was placed in Kayra's hand. A man stood behind her, gripping his hand firmly around hers. "NO, NO!" Kayra screamed as she was forced toward Colston.

He struggled, but to no avail.

"Kayra, one simply does not leave my world. Since Colston is the one preventing you from fully embracing it, you must free yourself of him."

Kayra was compelled to kneel on Colston's stomach.

"I am sorry, my love," Kayra cried, fighting with all her might.

"Abigail!" Colston shouted as loudly as he could. "This will not free her!"

Abigail snapped her fingers, halting the knife high above Colston's chest. She glanced down at him, then gently rubbed Kayra's quivering chin. "Explain yourself, you fugly excuse of a man!"

Kayra let out a scream, "What kind of monster are you?" She was locked in place by the strong man behind her.

Colston sensed that she was about to strike Kayra, so he quickly diverted her attention to himself. "Kayra is, and will never be, part of your world. If you believe that making her kill me will free her, then you do not understand true love and will never feel its touch! Kayra will resent you, hate you, and do everything in her power to escape you!" Colston saw her face contorting in fearful understanding as he glanced at Kayra's tearful expression. "You had a good friend in Kayra; after I am gone, you will have lost her too."

"YOU THINK YOU'RE HIGH AND MIGHTY!" she screamed at him. "Do it, or I'm going to smash his face in!"

"No! Colston!" Kayra cried as the hand guided hers downward.

Colston looked her in the eyes and said, "It is not your fault. I love you."

Kayra's body trembled as she struggled, but the tip made contact with Colston's skin. When it penetrated, it began to slide into his--

"Christ! Stop!" Elliot shouts as he rises to his feet.

"Dad? I'm sorry," Colston says, extremely startled. He slowly gets to his feet to comfort his dad, and when his dad spins around, he grabs Colston and pulls him into a tight hug.

"No, son, I'm sorry. Kayra..." He glances over Colston's shoulder.

There is tension as Elliot searches for

words; Colston immediately interjects to defend, "Dad, Kayra was fighting with all her might."

Elliot releases the hug and holds Colston at arm's length; his face twists in pain and fear, his eyes fixed on Colston's chest.

Colston grabs the collar of his shirt and pulls it down, revealing the scar on his bruised chest.

Elliot pulls him back into his arms and shakily whispers, "How are you not dead?"

"Jordan," Kayra replies to the whisper. "He got the police there just in the nick of time."

Elliot holds Colston at arm's length again. "If that video didn't exist, though I never want to watch it, I would not have believed what you just shared. The reason being is that very day you two got married. Married! And we had no idea of the trauma you all carried." He pulls Colston into another hug. "Jordan, please tell me, how did you get the police there?"

"Dad, are you sure?" Kayra asks gently as she watches Colston protectively.

He nods affirmatively against his son's shoulder.

Jordan looks at Kayra before he begans, "I heard Colston roar, 'GET OFF!' followed by a breathless grunt, and that was when the phone cut off. I immediately called the police. Not leaving anything to chance, Decklin was still trying to get a taxi. The back-and-forth with the police was maddening; they had prior knowledge of a bachelorette party, and with Ms. Sunderland as the hostess, they were aware it was going to be loud. They told me to just go sleep in the basement. I was infuriated and extremely worried for Colston because I knew that what I heard indicated he was in trouble. 'I am calling because there might be an issue at the house; the bride had called the groom asking him to come get her. I heard him yell for someone to get off, followed by a breathless grunt, and then the phone cut off.' The dispatcher laughed before replying, 'Well, he is breaching a long-standing tradition of these types of parties, and perhaps it was a ruse set up by the bride. Honestly, that dumbshit deserves what he gets, and how embarrassing to be at the hands of females'. I was dumbstruck by the way this was handled. So, I pulled the fame card. At that moment, the taxi was about to pull up. 'You have five minutes to send units down there, or you will most likely have three or four dead people on your hands, and two of them are well-known online to over 7 million people.' I hung up at that point, fed up with the bullshit and prepared to do some damage if Colston and Kayra were hurt, willing to go down swinging. We arrived at the house just as the police did. At that moment, Colston and Kayra began to scream."

Colston feels his dad's fingers gripping the fabric of his shirt as he sobs. His heart aches for him, and he is grateful for his decision not to reveal more about what transpired during his kidnapping. "Dad?" His voice is soft.

"No, Cole!" Again, Colston is held at

arm's length, tears streaming down his dad's face. "How the hell are you still so gentle? You were..." His eyes flash with horror. "Son, if you were willing to share that collective experience with me, I can't imagine what you will reveal tomorrow. I received a glimpse, and that is all I ever want; I will never forget walking into that hospital room after they recovered you. I thought I was going to watch you slip away." He turns to Kayra. "I cannot begin to fathom your fear. The fact that you are still by my son's side and love him as you did before everything means the world to me. And Jordan, you saved my son's life, and you have always been there for him. I will never be able to thank you enough. Now, my kids, I need to sleep."

Jordan and Kayra stand up, and along with Colston, they embrace Elliot. Afterward, they leave the bedroom: Jordan heads to his room, Kayra goes to the kitchen to get a drink, and Colston and Elliot proceed to the living room, where they move the coffee table and pull out the hide-a-bed.

Kayra and Colston lay in bed. "Colston, I feel one hundred percent lighter now that I've shared that with you."

Colston holds her close. "I am sorry you had to endure that. I should have been more vocal," he says, feeling the cold beginning to take hold. He fights to remain present with Kayra.

Kayra rubs his cheeks and kisses his nose. "We are here, in each other's arms."

"I am scared for tomorrow," he says.

"You won't be alone; let's sleep, babe."

Colston was awoken early on the day of their wedding by Kayra sobbing against his chest. "Kayra?" he asked, wrapping her tightly in his arms.

Her fingers ran over the patched wound. "It happened!" she said. "Yet, you hold me like it didn't."

That took Colston by surprise. "Hon, because I was watching you fight to save me. You had no control."

"I wish I did enough to see Abigail for who she really was."

"And I wish I would have told you my honest thoughts about her." Colston admitted stroking her hair.

There was a knock on the front door, quickly followed by Jordan exiting the guest bedroom to take care of who was at the front door. He seemed to have greeted someone and let them into the house.

Kayra and Colston made no effort to get up. He was staring at the ceiling, Kayra clinging to him. He was contemplating his next statement, thinking it for the best in light of what happened. It was with a heavy heart he said, "Should we postpone the wedding for a week or two?"

Kayra was dreading this but knew it was coming. She knew that his view toward her had changed. She can't see past what she did, and she didn't expect Colston to. Kayra looked at him with painful tears. "Colston, please don't play coy with me. Honestly, is this the end of us?"

The look of worry that spread across his face as he got up on his elbows, ignoring the twinges of pain, "Jesus, honey, I merely suggested it to give us time to heal and rest. Why? Are you scared because of it?" He asked, looking her in the eyes.

"I know we were in the same place, and you experienced the same horror I did. You were seconds from a slow, painful death at my hand."

Colston moved to sit up and took her hands in his, "Love, it wasn't you. You weren't drunk, high, or having a mental breakdown because of stress. Someone physical was guiding your hand; you were overpowered, but I saw and felt the fight. I will never forget that. Kayra," he made sure the ring was visible. "I am steadfast in my dedication to you and nothing. I mean, nothing will change that." Colston leaned in and kissed her, which she immediately deepened.

"Do I hear the bells of marriage?" Colston asked between kisses.

Kayra caught his eyes and cradled his face as he smiled at her eyes filled with love. In her mind, she was repeating, *I willingly did not brandish the knife; escaped the nightmare did we; now I become his wife. If he'll take me, I will take the hand of he. My Colston, I love thee till the last breath.*

Chapter Seventeen: Last Chance

On Monday, March 9, 2020, Kayra wakes up at eight-thirty after a restless night of sleep, having stirred every half hour to ensure that Colston was still breathing. The haunting events of the previous evening replay in her mind, and as she quietly prepares for the day, she feels a heavy weight of worry pressing down on her. It is almost worse than waking up alone. She glances at her dear husband, who is sleeping soundly. The remnants of the night linger on his brow in dried streaks of sweat, but now his face appears relaxed and peaceful, hopefully far removed from his pain. *"What is today going to do to you?"* she wonders.

Yesterday, he fought valiantly to create a day dedicated to her. She gently caresses his cheek.

He groans and turns away, pulling the blanket up to his shoulders.

She smiles sadly. "Babe," she begins softly, "we are seeing Melody at eleven."

Colston hears this as he clings to sleep; he just wants to cry. He believed he was prepared to share the most difficult and vulnerable moments of those ten days when his spirit was shattered, and the overwhelming darkness made him feel that escape was impossible, let alone survival.

"Kayra," he says, his eyes still closed.

"Are you sure you want to be there? Because I want to take back my word about today," he adds tearfully.

Kayra lies against his back, rubbing his arm. "Honey, please, you need to get it out. What are you afraid I'll hear?" Her voice is gentle.

He rolls to face her and opens his red-rimmed eyes. "I fought so hard to get away, but he always had the upper hand." He holds her hands in his, trembling. "He beat me down so far. I don't know how I even survived." He hides his face in shame.

Kayra's heart skips a beat. She lifts his chin, but he avoids eye contact. "Look at me."

His eyes shift to meet hers. "You are still here; your heart still beats. I will not think any differently of you. That monster tried to kill you by stealing your sense of self. Perhaps after sharing such a heavy memory, that sense of self will return, granting you full control over the impact these nightmares have." She was explaining exactly how she felt last night.

There is a hint of a twinkle in his eye, and Colston finds himself readily agreeing with her words. She spoke directly to his heart, and with her eyes glinting with relief, he hopes it will be that easy for him.

He kisses her and then gets out of bed.

"I am going to wake up Jordan," she says, getting out of bed. "You are not alone."

"I know." His voice is barely audible, and his chin quivers. "I--am--so--scared."

She moves around the bed to him and grips his hands tightly. "Please, just don't be there," he pleads.

Her heart sinks as she gazes into his eyes. "I want to help you, and I want you to know that you can trust me not to turn my back on you." She leans in and kisses him before heading out of the room.

Colston stands there, watching her walk away. Tears stream down his face, and he makes no effort to stop them. His heart pounds in his chest as he attempts to calm himself by taking deep, controlled breaths.

Kayra knocks on the guest bedroom door and softly calls out, "Jordan, we are leaving in an hour and a half."

"Come in," Jordan says groggily.

Kayra opens the door. Jordan, still lying down, asks, "How is he doing?"

"He's scared," Kayra says. "He doesn't want me to be there."

Jordan stares, contemplating whether this is a good idea. "What are we in for?"

"He was ready to die," Kayra shudders. "We are about to hear a very vulnerable moment," she adds.

"Kay, is this a good idea?" He asks flatly.

Kayra bows her head. "I have to believe that it is. Something is going to give soon, and I'd rather not see him crumble under the weight."

"He's actively being hunted, and we have all been careless!" Jordan exclaims, sitting up despite the head rush. "We, you and I, need to be on high alert, acting as his physical shields."

"I was considering taking him away from this town for a weekend. I understand that, in the grand scheme of things, it may not mean much. But I simply want to spend time with my husband. I caught a glimpse of that over the weekend, even though I could see the toll it was taking on him." Kayra realizes how inconsiderate that sounds; she rushes over and embraces Jordan. "I--I..."

Jordan rubs her back and says, "I understand what you mean; it does seem so bad. We just want him to get better because we are doing better ourselves. The glimpses we catch of his potential make us crave more, and that's when we become just as negligent as the police. We see his capabilities, and we grow weary of his struggles. But Colston is reaching his limit; we both know this. Can we agree that today will be the last time we push him to open up?" Jordan immediately feels a pang of guilt, knowing that he is about to share his worst moment, which might ultimately make it easier for him to share everything else.

Kayra breaks the hug and says, "I am going back to Colston."

Colston is nervously buttoning up his shirt while staring at himself in the mirror. The prospect of sharing his thoughts is far more enticing, albeit frightening, than the fear of a negative reception. He is still recounting a traumatic experience, even as his anxiety should be directed toward the fact that the phantom is preparing for a second encounter, while he remains hopelessly ensnared in the first.

"Cole, what would you like for breakfast?" Kayra's voice is soft and soothing.

Still, the thought of food is nauseating; however, he does need to eat something.

"Eat; you'll need to maintain your strength."

The voice of the phantom echoes menacingly in his head. He shivers, closes his eyes, and presses his palms firmly against the dresser. "Maybe just an egg," Colston says in a raspy voice, his expression one of repulsion.

"An egg? Colston, you haven't eaten anything in the last twenty-four hours," Kayra says.

Colston looks at her squarely. "Nothing sounds appealing." He sounds so disheartened and uncertain.

Kayra rushes to him and cradles his face in her hands. "Please, this is weakening you. This is what he wants. Don't give up; you've been doing great. I will not let go, and I need you not to let go either."

"I'm trying," he says tearfully.

This is breaking Kayra's heart. She embraces him and whispers, "How can I help you?"

"You're doing it," he breathes into her neck. "Don't let me go."

"I promise."

Hand in hand, they leave the room and

hear the shower running. They then proceed to the kitchen to wait for Jordan.

They can hear Elliot's loud snoring from the front room and do their best to remain quiet.

As Jordan gets dressed, he feels uncertain about how to act. He knows that Colston is scared and doesn't want anyone to hear about this moment. Tears well up in his eyes as he asks his reflection, "Am I ready to hear this?" He genuinely doesn't know. Nevertheless, he wants to show support and reassure Colston that he is no longer trapped in that situation. However, he instinctively understands the shame of being beaten by another adult and feeling defenseless against it. He hopes this doesn't push Colston to the brink; that man can't endure another disappointment.

He takes a moment to gather himself before opening the door, stepping out of the bathroom, and walking into the kitchen. The air is heavy with fear. No words are spoken; only hands are clenched tightly, and faces are streaked with tears.

How they would give all the money they had to reclaim the weekend. The hopelessness in Colston's eyes represents a stark contrast to the joy he exhibited on Saturday and even Sunday.

"Let's----go." Colston urges, taking the lead; if he doesn't, he knows he'll buckle under the pressure.

They enter the suite at 10:56, and Melody

opens the office door, inviting them in.

Colston walks as if he is burdened by a ball and chain. Jordan and Kayra sit on either side of him, and he is grateful for their presence, as it alleviates the feeling of being scrutinized by too many eyes.

"Colston, whenever you are ready," Melody says, sensing the tension and fear. She doesn't want to give him the opportunity to deflect.

He tries to avoid hyperventilating. His left hand is intertwined with Kayra's.

He allows the memory to fully come alive: "This was following the singing of 'Ineffective...'"

Singing had never caused him such pain as it did after what Colston had just done. His heart ached, and his voice trembled with sorrow; he was genuinely uncertain if he could endure that again. Pouring one's heart into a song was one thing, but he was battling a madness that could never be appeased.

Ineffective by Life Surge, an alternative rock band, was an anthem celebrating the journey of self-discovery amidst the chaos of the world. However, Colston felt so defeated that the lyrics seemed to be in a foreign language. The power of sung words had always lifted his spirit, which is why he sings. Yet, when he performed under pressure, he found himself bludgeoned in the middle of the song, causing him to tighten up. Thus, chasing the emotions away from the lyrics, rendering every word that escaped his lips tainted. His voice was being puppeteered, his emotions were being erased from his voice, and his heart lost its joy.

In the cold darkness of the bathroom, Colston dropped to his knees. His mind was blank with terror, and tears streamed down his cheeks as he stared into the abyss. His joyless heart continued to beat in his chest. He began to pray, surrendering himself into God's hands. His faith was not yet extinguished; he understood that if he were to survive this ordeal, he needed assistance.

Silence enveloped him as he concluded his prayer. Leaning against the wall, he felt the cold seep in, and his eyes fluttered shut. He hoped they would open once more.

His eyes fluttered open, and his chest tightened at the sound of wood creaking. His stomach growled painfully. "How long was I asleep?" he wondered to himself.

The door swung open, allowing the light of a new dawn to pour in, while a rush of cold air enveloped Colston. He shut his eyes and turned his head away, as the chill momentarily took his breath away.

"I would have fed you last night," his captor began. Colston heard a snapping sound near his head. He opened his eyes and saw the man standing over him. "You will look at me when I am talking to you," his captor commanded, his voice sharp.

He set the tray down beside Colston, then stepped back and crouched in the doorway.

Colston nodded and reached for the tray, which held a microwave breakfast. The aroma of the meal made his body instinctively want to reject it, but just as his wrists were numb from the tape, he chose to ignore his discomfort and eat, knowing he didn't know when he would have the opportunity to do so again.

"As I was saying, Colston, I would have fed you last night. However, your attitude indicated that you needed some time to reflect. I'll have dinner for you tonight; I have other matters to attend to."

He picked up the nearly empty tray and left behind a jug of water. Standing there, he looked at Colston with disappointment. Then he said gently, "Manners, Colston. Say, 'Thank you.'"

"Thank you," Colston replied softly, despising himself for yielding so easily.

His captor nodded and departed, leaving Colston confined in the darkness.

He slid down the wall until he could rest his head on the edge of the tub. For a brief moment, hatred enveloped his heart, temporarily displacing the terror. Being treated like a child throwing a tantrum was demoralizing. As he started watching the dark patterns swirling in his increasingly blurred vision, he questioned why the feeling of hatred, which seemed justified in his situation, could not endure. He pondered this for a while...

Colston concluded that he had no time for such a draining emotion. Hatred would only cause him to miss his chance for escape due to a desire for revenge. He trusted God to provide him with the strength and clarity needed to get through this. For Colston, it would be a profound victory to not be led astray by hatred. This man could believe whatever he wished and do whatever he deemed necessary to compel Colston to fulfill whatever it was he thought he needed.

Colston felt the overwhelming urge to sleep, curling up as best he could. He kept the fading warmth close and allowed himself to drift off.

"Wake up!" His captor's voice was aggressive as a heavy blanket was thrown over him.

Colston, groggy and disoriented, attempted to wrap himself as much as possible in the blanket when a food tray was slid across the grimy floor toward him. For the first time in days, he began to feel a hint of warmth on his torso and legs. He reached for the tray, craving something hot to eat.

"Your fans preferred your method after I struck you." The soft voice caused Colston to freeze, feeling like a mouse before a snake.

Colston had taken only a few bites of the warm meal when his appetite vanished.

"You need to eat; you need your strength." The quiet voice spoke, but Colston sensed an almost twisted pleasure emanating from his captor. He glanced up and locked eyes with him. His captor's gaze narrowed at Colston's frightened expression. "You need to listen to me, Colston. You must stop lying to yourself. You're going to plateau if you aren't willing to adapt to suit your audience. Otherwise, you'll be wasting your 'god-given' talent. Embrace this change." The quiet voice metaphorically stabbed multiple daggers into Colston before he turned around aggressively, slamming the door behind him.

Unable to consume any more food, the blow to his self-esteem made him long to curl up in the growing warmth beneath the blanket. Colston drifted into a sorrowful slumber.

A dream unfolded in the form of a silent cinematic film. The scene began with him running through the forest, his hands still bound. He ran swiftly, filled with panic, and soon faded into the distance. The view then zoomed back to the house, focusing on the bathroom door, which was not secured by a deadbolt.

He jolted awake. God had finally provided him with an answer: "I must escape now."

He forced his aching body to its feet; the cold gripped him the moment the blanket slipped away. He resisted the urge to grab the blanket and instead crept forward. His hands extended before him to locate the door. Numb fingertips brushed against the surface, sending an unpleasant tingling sensation up his arms. He bit his lower lip and searched for the doorknob, being careful not to jostle it. Grasping the knob with both hands, he turned it slowly. He pulled the door open slightly before it caught on something.

He took a deep breath to steady himself, his heart racing with every movement he made from his spot on the floor. Was he strong enough? He shook his head; it was far too late for that; it was now or never. He yanked on the door with all his might. The wood splintered under his strength, having rotted away from years of neglect. Colston hurled a piece of the door behind him and dashed outside. Leaping over the section of floor that creaked, he shouldered his way through the front door. His panicked mind prevented him from attempting to sneak out stealthily. Stumbling into the new dawn, which offered him guidance, he felt it beckoning him toward the forest. He spotted the van once more but chose to ignore it.

"Colston! YOU CAN'T GET AWAY!"

Colston sprinted into the forest, panic setting in.

"YOU'RE GOING TO REGRET THIS WHEN I CATCH YOU!"

A cold wind enveloped him, its bitter bite nearly halting his progress. No, please! he silently pleaded, pushing forward fiercely. He couldn't give up now that he was free and had been shown the way. For the moment, he navigated the uneven terrain with relative ease. He didn't hear his captor behind him, a concern he couldn't afford to entertain. Despite the burning in his lungs, he maintained his pace. Tears blurred his vision from the frigid air, and with every step, his legs threatened to give out.

Colston focused on his breathing. He inhaled slowly through his nose... one... two... three... and exhaled slowly... one... two... three... again. As he controlled his breath, he listened intently for any sounds of his captor behind him while carefully watching where he placed his feet. The last thing he needed was to twist an ankle on his way to freedom. As he fell into this trance-like state of running, he continuously scanned his surroundings. He felt himself distancing from the bizarre and maddening situation around him; everything seemed the same, and he questioned whether he was running toward something or away from something? His mind was frozen, unable to articulate what he felt. It was a sensation, an endless cycle of running, devoid of light and any sense of relief.

The woods were preparing for winter, with most of the leaves already on the ground. Something dark emerged from the treeline, capturing his attention and bringing his wandering mind back to the present. Colston pressed on, knowing that if he saw it, then his kidnapper had seen it too. He had to reach it first.

What first began to manifest between the trees was a road, a paved road. Colston's heart raced with a mix of joy and fear. If he could reach it, he might flag down a car and get help. As he approached the treeline, the blacktop road started to ascend into the sky, transforming into a cliffside. Colston's heart sank, and his first misstep occurred, causing him to stagger diagonally to the left. As he emerged from the trees, a strong gust of wind greeted him from the right, instantly cooling the sweat on his bare skin. The road was, in fact, a cliff that towered seventy-five feet above him, imprisoning him in the forest. He was still several feet away from the cliffside, on the threshold of its rocky terrain, when he halted his advance. His legs trembled beneath him, and his chest heaved as defeat engulfed him.

"Colston! THIS IS A SIGN! LISTEN TO IT!"

The voice was closer than Colston had anticipated, startling him into action. His heart pounding in fear, he scrambled to the left. With no direction and his hope fading, he began to cry tears of failure as the rhythmic thudding of fast-approaching footsteps grew louder, closing in from an angled pursuit.

"Colston!" The snarl came from his right.

Colston charged straight ahead, giving it everything he had. If the man made even one mistake while Colston made none, he could still escape. He heard a guttural cry as the man lunged at him, fingers clawing at his arm and elbow. Colston twisted slightly with a cry of hope, trying to regain his balance, but he was sent crashing to the ground, his right arm absorbing the brunt of the impact. Adrenaline dulled the pain as his mind screamed, 'RUN!' Colston used his bound wrists and forearms to push himself up, his legs pumping and his feet scraping across the frozen soil. The moment he was upright, he began to run. A rush of cold air swept up his bare back, cooling the sweat as the back of his vest was tugged.

"STOP FIGHTING!" The words reverberated through Colston's very core.

"NO!"

Colston countered the backward pull by driving his body forward. He quickly realized that he was accomplishing nothing, merely wasting energy he could not afford to lose. He twisted to the right, extending his clenched fists, and pushed against the man's chest. However, the man stepped forward, absorbing the full impact of the blow, and enveloped Colston in a tight embrace. The collision of their bodies caused them to tumble to the ground. Colston felt nails digging into his back as they walked to the center of his back, threatening to interlock. He gazed into dark, vacant eyes and a face contorted in a permanent snarl.

"Last chance." The cold, breathless voice echoed through the air.

Colston responded in one fluid motion. He drew his right knee up toward the vulnerable spot while simultaneously driving his fists into the chin of his captor. The strikes connected, though not with the force he had hoped for; nevertheless, it was not a waste of energy. Hearing the painful grunt and feeling the arms loosen, Colston was able to roll free and rise to his feet. Before proceeding, he glanced around.

Should he continue on the path he had been following or take an alternate route? Something urged him to choose the latter, but that would require him to navigate around his captor, who was currently curled up in a ball. He wanted to avoid any possibility of a surprise attack. Ultimately, he decided to stick with the route he had taken before the confrontation. In the distance, he noticed something and squinted to discern what it was. It turned out to be a decrepit wooden fence. A fence indicated a property line, which meant people.

It took all of Colston's willpower to get his weary body moving. A gust of wind struck him in the face. He raised his wrists as if to block a punch, his head pounding with each step. Breathing in the bitterly cold air was extremely uncomfortable, and he stumbled frequently. As he jogged, he tugged and twisted at the tape binding his wrists. By the time he reached the fence, he had failed to break free. He paused to peer through the trees, knowing it was a slim chance but hoping to catch a glimpse of any sign of life. When nothing caught his eye, he continued along the narrow path.

He trudged onward, the sun obscured by clouds. Exhaustion enveloped him, and his mind felt vacant. He failed to notice the hole dug by a creature, and his left foot slipped in, causing him to tumble. "No, no, please!" he pleaded silently. Colston gradually rolled onto his side, extracting his left leg, and cautiously moved his ankle. The pain was nearly unbearable. He looked up, took a deep breath, and stood. He limped forward, aware that he had to keep moving.

Colston pulled against the tape once more, steadying

himself against the tree. He gritted his teeth, certain that the skin beneath was rubbed raw. He fell to his right knee to prevent himself from collapsing entirely out of sheer exhaustion. His right shoulder and arm scraped against the tree, releasing a sharp puff of breath. How he longed to simply lie down in the dirt. But he didn't have time to be still! He prayed for the strength to continue and for temporary healing so he could escape. He regained his footing and prepared to push forward.

A sudden impact slammed across his mid-back, forcing the air from his lungs as he fell forward. His chest hit the ground, and his head bounced off his left inner bicep. Struggling to catch his breath, he slowly rolled onto his right side and drew his legs in. A sharp kick to his tailbone caused him to arch his back in agony. He attempted to yell out in pain, but all that escaped him was a gasp for air.

His pounding head, tears streaming down his face, and difficulty breathing made sound nearly impossible to track. A ringing noise intensified in Colston's ears, and as his captor began to shout, Colston struggled to comprehend the words. He attempted to crawl away on his side but then felt a sudden weight pressing down just above his hip. His right arm and back became punching bags for the man's blows.

"DAMMIT, LEAVE ME ALONE!" Colston yelled, attempting to throw his captor off him.

The captor slammed his forearm against Colston's temple, causing the back of his head to bounce off the frozen ground. Colston was instantly dazed and ceased to fight back. He felt one hand gently caressing his cheek while the other softly yet forcefully turned his chin, bringing him face-to-face with the insanity that was uncomfortably close, even through his double vision.

"I am meant to save you! Never meant to harm you! But you are torturing me, my Colston. If only you just listened and tried." The tone conveyed love, yet it was laced with an underlying desire to prove something, something that was beyond Colston's ability to identify in his current predicament.

The feeling of loathsomeness was replaced by a sense of calm. The fear inside his heart was escaping; he understood that there was a strong possibility he would die right here. He was not about to fade quietly into the darkness. He constructed a statement within his numb mind and fading awareness. This statement needed to convey two things: first, that this man would never achieve what he desired, and second, that he wanted to feel a sense of satisfaction if this would be the last thing he ever spoke on earth.

"Whatever plan you envisioned was never going to materialize because I never wanted you."

The eyes locked in intense anger as Colston numbly felt a hand wrap around his throat. He could only hope that the next part would be over quickly.

"HOW DARE YOU!!!"

Each word was emphasized with solid hits to Colston's numb body. Then, with the slightest pressure applied to his throat, Colston, overwhelmed by weariness and hopelessness, was engulfed in nothing more than a painless darkness.

Chapter Eighteen: Locking the Cage

Colston drifted gently on waves of cold comfort, with occasional sharp jolts of painful reality serving as reminders that he was still very much alive. However, with every receding wave of pain, a distant concern took its place. How could he remain so calm about his potential death? He had no idea where he was, nor did anyone else, and they were unaware that he had truly been kidnapped. He didn't want to leave Kayra behind, wondering, 'What if' for the rest of her life. There must be a reason why he was still thinking and still breathing.

In a moment of intense pain, he could hear a faint sound of hammering. This, of course, contrasted sharply with the persistent thudding that Colston was currently experiencing. For a brief time, he was allowed to retreat into the cold confines of darkness. His consciousness lingered, waiting to be encased in the sensation of nothingness. Here, nothing could touch him. His mind was clear, calm, and safe in the darkness.

It felt foreign for silence to persist for Colston, the music man he was, to experience such silence, as there always had been a tune in his head. He remained tranquil, aware that all he needed to do was let go. Yet, he wasn't ready to release his hold, though he couldn't recall the reason for his reluctance. A faint memory of an all-encompassing love lingered just beyond his reach, teasing the edges of his mind. He attempted to concentrate on it, hoping to bring it into focus, but it faded into the deepening darkness.

Is this death? A dream? No! Is this it? Am I dying? No,

please, I need--I WANT more time! I have so much more to give, to see, to do! I'm young. Please, God, grant me a second chance! I don't want to die here, cold, alone, and imprisoned by a madman! And my voice, this talent that You bestowed upon me, wasted! I just wanted to warm people's hearts and bring them together. This wretched bastard has taken his liberties too far! Please, God, I beg You. Let me live!

"Colston, calm thy mind." Colston surrendered completely to the familiar, loving, and authoritative voice that resonated within him. He felt himself being lifted and gently embraced, enveloped by a profound sense of love and safety.

"Colston, my son, your time upon the earth is not yet complete. This is merely a deep and restful sleep I have placed you in to heal. When you awaken, you will find yourself in a world where hardships and dangers still exist. You will possess the strength to persevere. Do not forsake the gifts I have bestowed upon you. Now, rest."

Colston heard these words as he leaned against a solitary tree. Golden rays from the rising sun illuminated his upturned, tear-streaked face. He gazed over the expansive, pristine valley from his perch on a green hilltop. The words seemed to ride on the wind; upon hearing them, his heart swelled with warmth, his body felt stronger, and his mind sharpened. In his hand rested a writing pad and a pencil. However, as he looked at the words, they appeared blurry to him. *Not yet.* He set the pad aside and stood up.

"Let the danger come! I will prevail, even if it seems grim."

He stepped away from the tree and descended into the valley. The clouds overhead darkened, and the grass beneath him turned brown and withered with each step. The sun's rays had vanished, replaced by a biting cold. Despite the growing fear in his soul, Colston knew he had to fight to return to his loved ones and pursue his passions. He refused to allow this man to taint his gift and joy in life due to a twisted belief. Colston collapsed at the bottom of the hill, every ounce of energy sapped from his body. However, his courage remained steadfast. He rolled onto his back, gazing up at the ominous sky, and there he drifted among the desolate fog. Whispers swirled around him during his time in the fog.

Broken the music player. My Colston, buried, lost beneath the weight of life. Why must it be deaf? Why does it skip? Every note and rests are so important. I can help!

These whispers gradually urged him to detach himself, and he drifted deeper into the fog, oblivious to everything around him. He floated, unaware of time or anything else for that matter, until a slow but tightening grip on his left leg began to slow him down. The pressure on his leg annoyed him, as Colston longed to remain lost in the fog of oblivion. The grip tightened, pinching him, and he sensed a gradual return to his body.

The aches and stiffness coursing through Colston's body reminded him that he was, indeed, alive. His mind spun through the heaviness of the mental fog, making it difficult to focus. The faint taste of vomit lingered in his mouth, and the familiar chill of cold porcelain rested beside his head. What had he been celebrating last night to end up like this? He attempted to open his eyes, but his eyelids remained shut in protest. When he tried to lift his hand to rub his face, an intense burning sensation shot through his wrists... And! Are they bound together? What had transpired the previous night? He felt the heft of a blanket as it was pulled up with his hands. Desperately, he tried to recall the events that led him here. The uncertainty was terrifying; was Kayra in danger? With that thought, he gingerly worked his arms free from the blanket to rub his eyes, causing it to slip from his shoulders. The bitter cold air quickly sapped away what little warmth he had left. Colston painfully unlaced his fingers, and just as they neared his eyes, he heard the creak of wood.

Colston's chest tightened with an overwhelming fear, an intense sensation that his body recognized, even if his mind did not at first. He quickly rubbed his eyes, forcing them open into a squint. The fog in his mind was stripped away as he heard hollow, faint footsteps approaching. He held his breath, his head pounding with pain, and waited in the darkness that enveloped him. His mouth felt as if it were filled with cotton, and his stomach contracted violently from hunger. How long had he been unconscious?

He slowly turned his gaze to the right; the throbbing in his head made it difficult to concentrate. His eyes faintly discerned the familiar contours of his prison. Colston was in the bathroom again. Involuntary tears streamed, stinging his skin as he attempted to locate any signs of a food tray or a water jug. Either none were present, or the pain in his head made it so he could not see any.

The cold darkness of the four walls held him captive. He had failed to escape and barely survived the fight in the forest. Still, he had to rely on the vile excuse for a man for his survival. He longed to curl up into a ball, but he was unable to do even that on his own. Shame welled up inside him, adding to the weight of the mental anguish that came with knowing he was helpless. Colston was ensnared by his own weakness, and to see the light of day unbound, he had to play into the man's hands, at least for a little bit. A shiver of disgust coursed through him, but he did what he could to survive.

He closed his eyes and visualized himself standing in front of an open cell. This action stemmed from a deep-seated desperation to protect himself. His compassion, kindness, and hope were at the core of his being. The

World's Song would calm the beasts, and these were his contributions to that melody. A ball of shimmering golden light floated from his chest and glided into the cell. Colston shut and locked the door, bowing his head in sorrow. This left him feeling empty, worse than any physical pain. Colston's heart beat in a cavity devoid of warmth. He gripped the bars, trembling, and with his forehead resting against them, regret washed over him. Colston had finally run out of tears to shed. He was broken and beaten into submission. His choice was made, and outside the hollowness, back in the realm of pain, where survival was uncertain, he opened his mouth. The dryness and stiffness of his tongue rendered him voiceless. With great effort, he moved his tongue in hopes of generating moisture. He wet his gums, forcefully swallowing and coughing to get things working smoothly again. He drew in a breath, looked down at his feet, and released a hoarse call in a voice that felt worn and forgotten.

"Hey!"

The sound of the deadbolt unlocking pierced the cold stillness, deepening Colston's sense of hopelessness as the door swung open. A rush of fresh, frigid air rolled over Colston's blanketed body and caressed his face. He briefly glanced at the silhouetted figure of his captor in the dim light before closing his eyes. He heard his name spoken softly, infused with a mix of relief and fear.

Did he think I was dead? How long had I been unconscious? It must have been over a day, considering how dry his mouth was and how hungry he felt.

"Yes, Colston?" The man spoke as a father would to a disobedient child, urging them to acknowledge their mistakes and apologize. The relief and fear that had been palpable just moments before were now absent.

"May I...have some...food and...water...please?" Colston asked weakly, demonstrating to the man that he posed no threat.

The man turned and left without saying a word. Colston heard the generator whir to life and glanced toward the door. The new plywood door had been left ajar. Colston loathed the open door, which taunted his helplessness; more importantly, he wished for it to be closed, as whatever warmth had been in the room was now gone. The man must have fixed the door while Colston lay on the cold floor, teetering between life and death, yet he did nothing to help him. Colston lacked the strength to wrestle the blanket back over his shoulders, allowing the cold to settle into his chest cavity, a horrific reminder that his life had been beyond his control since the beginning of this ordeal. He heard the generator shut off, followed by slow, hollow footsteps, accompanied by the mouthwatering aroma of warm food.

"Colston, you must pace yourself. You don't want to throw it up, as this is all you'll have for the next few hours." The man ridiculed him as he entered the room.

Colston's eyes were fixed on the tray of steaming food, and he found himself constantly swallowing the accumulating saliva. Not only was it food, but it was warm food. He could already feel its heat warming him. However, the saliva had built up too much for him to swallow, and he began to choke. He attempted to roll onto his right side, and thankfully, his body complied. Using his bound wrists, he propped himself up to avoid rolling completely onto his stomach. He tried to clear his airway, but gasping for air only caused more saliva to slip down into his windpipe. His eyes watered as he struggled to breathe properly during the coughing fit. His head throbbed, but finally, the coughing subsided.

Sometime during the coughing fit, the man had shifted and now stood over Colston, with a foot on either side of him. A heavy hand pressed into his shoulder, while the man's chest seemed to bear down on him. Lips brushed against his ears as the man's ragged breathing made it clear that he was angry.

"Are you done? I'm trying to help you, and yet you're so worked up over some food that you choked on your own spit. How tragic it would be to die, choking on a filthy bathroom floor." Another hand aggressively cradled Colston's face. "I. Am. Your. Everything." The desperation Colston heard in that voice sent chills down his spine.

Quickly, he was rolled onto his back as the man's hands were shoved under Colston's arms, forcing him into a sitting position in the corner against the tub. Colston's body buzzed, and sound was muffled by his own breathing.

"Oh, shut up, you big baby." The voice was muffled and sounded distorted.

Colston could see the man moving his wrists above the blanket, but he felt none of it, only a persistent buzzing sensation.

"Colston! Breathe!"

Colston's eyes were fixed on the increasingly panicked expression on the face before him as his chest failed to draw in a breath.

The man cupped his face and began to drift away.

Seeing the fear on his face brought Colston a sense of satisfaction as he slipped further and further away. An electric jolt coursed through his body, bringing all sensation back into him.

He let out a cry, weak yet filled with pain and despair.

"Be grateful; open your eyes," the man ordered.

Colston struggled to lift his eyelids, and when he finally managed to do so, he saw the man was holding food.

"Open your mouth," he said, placing his other hand on the back of Colston's head.

Colston was hand-fed his first meal in days. His body was desperately trying to quit on him, attempting to reject the food. Twice, that buzzing sensation returned. The first time, he slipped into unconsciousness but was jolted back to awareness. The second time, having consumed a fair amount of food, he managed to resist losing consciousness.

The man looked at him with extreme disgust. "Are you going to die on me if I leave?"

Colston simply gazed at him; he felt too weak to formulate a response. Even if he could, what would it accomplish?

The man shook his head and walked away.

Colston drew his legs close to his chest and maneuvered his arms beneath the blanket, attempting to drape it over his shoulders. However, it kept slipping off, so he made sure to hold what he could against his chest. He concentrated on staying warm without moving too much, as he wanted to avoid the return of the buzzing sensation. Exhausted, he could do little more than listen intently for any footsteps signaling the man's return.

There was something lingering in the back of his mind. As much as Colston recognized that the man was utterly unhinged, he also saw him as a lonely fan. The man held steadfast in his convictions about Colston's 'fear of failing', but was that truly Colston's fear? The desperation behind the phrase 'I am your everything' left Colston with an unclear notion of how or why, but he was fairly certain it wasn't directed towards him. An insane person without a purpose is scarier than an insane person with a purpose.

Unsure of what lay ahead, Colston could only conserve his energy, wait, and listen.

The relentless cold let him know that night had fallen. The blanket offered little comfort, rendering it almost useless. Nevertheless, he struggled with it as he lay down, attempting to wrap himself in its fabric to conserve body heat. He drew his knees to his chest, his fists resting in his lap. Shivering uncontrollably, he fought to prevent the tremors from vibrating through his head.

He heard the sound of hurried footsteps. Colston wondered what this man could possibly have planned. Dinner, which had been nothing more than microwave mush, was a few hours ago. The door opened, and he was momentarily blinded by a flashlight shining in his eyes, causing him to shy away. Shadows fell over his kidnapper as the man stood over Colston before squatting down.

"H-hey." His voice trembled from the cold, and he could see the puff of steam rising from his mouth.

"Colston," the man called coaxingly, "I have another blanket for you." Colston briefly gazed into the eerily lit spheres but found it difficult to maintain that gaze. "It's your fault," the man hissed, tapping Colston's left cheek. "If you say it and truly mean it, your accommodations can change."

"S-say... what?" Anger, along with a much stronger emotion, began to stir within Colston as another blanket was tossed over him. The man stood up, visibly disgusted.

"Are you serious? Colston, it's like I care more than you do! I am all you have! What do I have to do to get it through your thick skull? Have a nice sleep!"

The man turned and stormed out, slamming the door shut and locking it behind him. Colston was grateful that he had not been subjected to the man's wrath physically. He had nothing to change for this man; defiance surged within him, whether he wanted it to or not. It was either that or succumb to the insanity, which Colston was determined not to do as long as he had breath in his lungs. He wrapped himself in the blankets and offered a prayer of gratitude and strength. After finding solace in his prayer, he fell asleep.

The door swung open with a loud bang, jolting him from a deep, dreamless sleep.

"Colston!" Fervent words were hurled at him loudly. "Breakfast, no more attitude from you. You have two days before you perform."

He moved over to Colston, set the tray down, and crouched at his feet, his eyes fixed on Colston's face. His gaze narrowed, and Colston flinched as a hand shot toward his head.

"No!" His captor growled, firmly gripping Colston by the back of his head and plastering the other to his forehead. "You have a slight fever. If you fall ill, my dearest Colston, I will also become unwell."

"Not sur-prised about the fever." Colston gazed directly into the eyes of intense heat.

The hand that had been checking his temperature suddenly struck his right cheek. Colston wanted to retaliate, but the sickness and concussion rendered him unable to do so. The man exhibited the same intensity as Colston; he could see it reflected in his eyes. Colston kept his head down, taking deep breaths to maintain his composure, and the man eventually left him alone. He needed to conserve his energy for the performance in two days.

Colston concludes the retelling of the darkest period, but he has revealed the truth. He locked the cell, not the phantom, and he has lost the keys. Kayra has been loving a stranger, while Jordan has been singing with a passionless husk. It is his fault that they are suffering. He cries in the silence that lingers, waiting and wondering. A cold swell rises within him as that buzzing sensation works its way up his body.

A voice resonates within his soul, *"Truth shared, yet one truth remains. Making the shared seem so absurd and barren when compared to this terminal truth."*

Colston's attention shifts to Kayra's hand clasped in his, and the sweat between them fades as the buzzing sensation intensifies. The world around him fades into transparency, merging with the street clock. The relentless ticking consumes Colston's thoughts, and beneath the sound, a voice speaks again. *"The truth so spoken leaves you exposed. No relief to be found; made to think it might. Yet, your path runs a different course."*

Colston feels himself falling; the world around him swirls. His back strikes the stage as the overpowering scent of smoke fills his final breath.

"FOCUS!" The voice commands Colston from his deadend state. The world shifts once more; his chest rises and falls in a gentle rhythm. An unseen force propels him into an upright position, and he finds himself leaning against the solitary tree on the hilltop.

From the pristine valley comes Jordan's voice, "He's breathing again!"

"Please, babe, come back!" Kayra's voice urges him.

Colston communicates, "I'm searching for something." From where he is, his lips remain still.

He receives a panicked response from Melody: "Colston, please, I advise you to come back. It is not worth your life."

The voice from before fills the clear sky: *"The arms of death so many times you've denied them hold you. Why? With the final turn that lingers and the pain that resides, is the final solo battle worth it all?"*

Colston's gaze remains fixed on the sky as his left hand finds the writing pad. The first sensation is warm and electric. He addresses the darkening, crackling sky, saying, "How I long to see the fire extinguished and the insanity erased, leaving me to sift through the ashes for my key. I am meant to combat the fire from its center, yet I have stood surrounded by flames without a means to fight. Now, free from one crushing truth, I am left with the final one. I am finally allowed to exploit the loophole in fate's design." He picks up the writing pad.

The world fades into darkness, leaving only a beam of white light shining down on Colston. The previously blurry words are now clear.

I do not carry a traditional sword and shield.
Against the phantom, I must wield what I know.
Appeal to the lonely fan; sing.
Appeal to the phantom; sing.
Let Me Through, Let Me Go!

Jordan sits on the floor, holding Colston's left hand, unable to hold back tears, while Kayra cradles the rest of him. What had he witnessed? Was that release strong enough to nearly kill him, or was it the overwhelming guilt and shame? When Colston had spoken, his voice was calm yet earnest. That voice emerged moments after a few chest compressions. It was an agonizing twenty minutes later when his breathing gained a more active rhythm.

"Cole?" Kayra asks, rubbing his face.

Melody leans forward. "Colston, I need you to tell me where you are right now. If you don't communicate, for your safety, I will call for an ambulance."

"I'm here; I just need a moment," Colston whispers in an airy voice. "Kayra, I'm sorry. I locked the cage, not the phantom." He opens his eyes. "I can't free myself. This is all my fault. I'm sorry."

Kayra pulls him close to her chest. "God, honey, no. You did what you had to do to avoid losing yourself." She gently rubs the side of his face and leans down to kiss him.

"Stop," he whispers before their lips meet.

Kayra whispers, "No, you are my husband, and I will always love you." Her lips meet his.

Colston cries and kisses her back, feeling relief wash over him. He understands that his truth lies in the eyes of his wife, who bravely accepts it because she wants him.

He turns to Jordan and squeezes his hand. "Sorry for lying to you, JD."

Jordan shifts closer. "Cole, there was no lie. Sure, there was a change, but it was still you. Even with the change, you remained kind, loving, and gentle, showing a fervor for life."

"I don't understand how this is happening. I feel incomplete and am beyond frustrated by it. Yet, you all seem unaffected by the fact that I returned to you broken."

Kayra reaches for Jordan's hand and places it on Colston's chest, then places her own hand on top. "You came back to us alive. We will provide you with the stability you need so you are not alone as you work to open that cage."

"Colston?" Melody asks softly.

"Yeah?" Colston makes no attempt to leave his wife's embrace.

"Did you find what you were searching for?"

"Yes, it was in the writing pad..." As the words leave his lips, a painful jolt ripples through his body. He gasps and arches his back, finding himself on an unstable platform that continues to wobble, threatening to topple. Desperately, he reaches for anything to aid with balance. Suddenly, a chain drops from above; he grips it tightly, stabilizing both himself and the platform. His right side feels as though it is buried in snow, while his left side is being scorched by an open flame. He screams, the sound echoing in the hollow space, and looks up. The chain leads to a bright light.

"Cole?" Kayra asks, her voice filled with concern.

"Yeah," this comes out extremely breathy.

"Look at me, please."

Colston does.

Kayra holds him tightly. "I am right here," she says, her eyes glinting with tears of frustration and guilt. As she eyes Melody, saying, "Wasn't this supposed to help him, to free him?" She had promised that he would feel relief after sharing his burdens.

Melody looks at her with care and honesty. "The residue will linger. Having shared and accepted that he is not going to be abandoned, along with the amount of trauma he endured, that he is finally being taken seriously. However, he still has a long road ahead of him."

"I wanted to die then and so many times afterward," Colston admits. "The pain and the fear, I wanted to let go."

Kayra squeezes his body.

"I-just----kept----breathing----as----God----was----not----ready----to take------me." Colston looks at Melody. "What----is----the----lesson----here?" Colston questions, desperate for any sort of understanding.

Melody gazes at him, sensing the desperation in his voice. She leans forward and says, "There is no lesson to be learned from this; yes, when events unfold, there is often a purpose. At least we assign one to better understand and cope with it. Colston, what you demonstrated is your relentlessness, courage, and bravery. There is no doubt in my mind that you were meant to die in that house. The lesson is not for you; rather, you are the lesson." Melody stares into his faded eyes. "In those distant, faded eyes, I see the fire."

Colston stares back, still gripping the chain tightly. He is afraid to shift fully away; what if the chain fades after a while? He will undoubtedly fall, so he must use this aid wisely, as there may not be another.

"I----need----to----go----and----

ready----my----sword----and----shield." Colston gasps and, with Kayra's help, sits up.

Jordan and Kayra exchange worried and confused glances at Colston.

"Colston, I think we should meet on Wednesday, just the two of us. I want to ensure you are okay, and afterward, I can meet with both of you."

Jordan nods.

"Thank you," Kayra says.

Jordan and Kayra must support Colston as he attempts to stand. He struggles to get his legs to hold him, feeling a weakness that he finds unsettling, one he cannot overcome.

Once inside the truck, Kayra is behind the wheel, Colston occupies the passenger seat, and Jordan is seated in the back.

"How are you feeling?" Jordan asks.

"I--don't----know. Nothing's---really----changed!" Colston says he is finding it difficult to remain optimistic.

"What about your... sword and shield?" Kayra asks, curious about what that means.

Colston takes a deep breath, gathering his thoughts within his mess, "It's out, no longer weighing me down." Tears begin to flow. "Yet, the relief I expected to feel is absent; I still feel crushed because I held on past that moment. There have been countless times when I wished to stop breathing. After all I have fought through, losing everything because of memories feels shameful. When I am lost within, engulfed in darkness, I just want it to end." Colston shakes his head, takes a shaky breath, and wipes away his tears. "I have one chance to get this right, my shield and sword. They must protect me and allow me to escape the phantom's grasp once and for all."

Chapter Nineteen: Loophole in Fate's Design

Once home, Colston still struggles to fight off the weakness in his legs. He leans his head back against the seat while Kayra and Jordan stand by, prepared to help him.

"Just..." Colston says, covering his face with his hands.

"Hey, listen, it's going to take a while," Jordan says, trying to sound hopeful.

"It's been long enough! I couldn't escape; I can't unlock the cage that I locked! I want to be done with it all," Colston says, crumbling.

Jordan grips his hand as Kayra places her hand on his chest. Her voice is strong and resolute. "Colston, you are not alone. We will not leave your side. The fact that you are still alive demonstrates your strength in enduring everything and your desire to continue living."

Jordan adds, "There is a reason for you."

Colston's hands drop away; he feels drained. He moves to get out, accepting the help.

As they enter the house, Kayra says, "Colston, you should eat and sleep."

They also discover that Elliot is not in the house.

Colston nods in agreement; sleep sounds incredibly appealing at that moment, but he knows he must take care of something first.

"Just let me go to the studio for an hour," he says, grabbing the cane for the first time in four years.

"An hour," Kayra says, kissing him.

He nods and proceeds to his studio.

Once inside, he stands with his back against the locked door. His breath comes in heavy gasps as he drops the cane and clutches the sides of his head, doubling over in a silent scream.

He waits for a voice, any voice.

"What!" he screams internally. *"No questions or feelings of regret!"* Colston stares at the floor.

His hands fall to his sides. Of course, there is no voice, for he is no longer being crushed by that memory. Now, one overwhelming sensation prevails: survival. But before he pulls up the lyrics to Let Me Through by CG5, from which he will build his sword and shield.

He settles and drafts another original song titled *The Poison Within.*

I sip from the cup of venom,

Yearning to shut my lips tight 'gainst its fiery sting.

Though I know it's deadly, a slow, silent killer,

I swallow the madness, defying death a bit longer.

Caught in the grip of poison from his lips,

No escape in sight; trapped by destiny's eclipse.

Surely there's a way to defy this

preordained end,
I refuse to accept the fate that fate intends.
Searching for a path to reclaim my own control,
Shrouded in coldness, with hope consumed by dread.
Inside, a war rages, doubts swirling like a storm,
My faith teeters on the brink, torn and worn.
Clawing at the walls of my besieged mind,
Anguish carving trails in the fabric of my sight.
Every fiber aches with relentless pain,
Panic suffocates courage, tightening its chain.
But I won't let the flames of fear engulf me,
I seek a way to break free, to set myself at liberty.
Summoning strength from the depths of my soul,
With each breath, I defy fate's relentless toll.
No longer bound by the poison's tight grip,
I rise above, reclaiming my path, never to slip.
Yet reality, cruel and unforgiving, looms near,
Dreams shattered by the harsh truth, I fear.
As my breath slows to a gentle whisper,
Pain and fear ebb; my resolve grows crisper.

To my loved ones, I apologize for my final surrender.

The poison overwhelms, too heavy a burden to bear.

Slipping beneath the surface, fate's cruel design,

Choked by the poison, life's final sign.

In a desperate cry, a silent scream,

I fought till the end, now succumbing to fate's dream.

Colston reads it repeatedly; the words are painful to digest. He has expressed his thoughts in a form that calms his mind, alleviating its worries. Should he fail in the upcoming battle, this will immortalize his struggle and acceptance. He folds it up and places it in a drawer.

With a deep breath, he gazes at Let Me Through; he had recorded this song months ago and uploaded it to his channel, but he kept it private for a reason unknown to him, and now he begins to re-lyric.

The hour crawls by for Jordan and Kayra, haunted by Colston's words that had once been his reality. The silence lingers for what feels like an eternity. After about thirty-five minutes, they hear a muffled song playing in the studio, but there is no singing.

"I hate to say this, but I have to go home tomorrow." Jordan is resolute in his decision to leave.

Kayra pats his hand and says, "I... we appreciate your presence here. It means a lot."

"I'm glad I was here to help and learn. I hope he finds relief soon." He glances toward the door, feeling a strong urge to be with him at this moment. "I want you guys to come stay with me. Take him for a getaway after he sees Melody on Wednesday. Then on Friday, I'll come down to help you pack." Jordan states this firmly, leaving no room for discussion.

Kayra smiles shyly and says, "JD, are you sure?"

Jordan moves over to the couch and hugs her. "He needs to get out of here."

"I know," she replies. "Let's discuss it together."

"It has been almost an hour," he says, locking eyes with Kayra. A sense of lingering dread hangs in the air.

Kayra can't shake the weight of her thoughts and what they might mean. What is the purpose of all this? After five years of struggle and experiencing two nightmares in a row, she requested that the door stay ajar, the public slip-ups, and the phantom not be dead, as Colston had hoped. As she watches Jordan exit the living room, she prays to God that this concludes with the phantom dead and Colston free from his suffering.

Jordan stands at the door, poised to knock, when he hears Colston singing. Although he is not singing at full volume, the raw emotions are palpable.

"Please, oh please, I'm down on my knees; let me go!

I sing my song; let it echo wide. Please, I beg on my knees, let me go!"

Jordan is struck in the chest by these lyrics. He rests his forehead against the door. As the dread deepens, he envisions Colston fighting against his captor with all his might in the woods. The odds are stacked against him. In those words, Colston is pleading for relief, for release.

He knocks on the door, "Colston, bud, it's been an hour." His voice is quiet as he calls through the door.

"Right," Colston says, followed by the sound of the door unlocking. "Come on in."

Jordan opens the door just as Colston rolls back to the desk, closes a document, and a video of himself singing. He turns to face Jordan; his eyes are red, and he wears a melancholic smile. Yet, amidst all of this, there is a certain glow about him that Jordan noticed after returning from his first session with Melody.

Colston sees Jordan's hesitation. "JD, what's on your mind?" His voice is thick with emotion. He shuts down the computer and turns to face him fully once more.

"So much," Jordan pauses as the phantom's words echo in his mind. *"Colston is mine to save, but if he resists, I'll kill him. If you want him to stay alive, I suggest you tell him to let me take him."* Jordan covers his ears and releases a whimper.

Colston stands and asks, "Jordan?" while placing a hand on his shoulder. "What is it?"

Jordan gazes into Colston's concerned eyes and says, "The words he whispered in my ear, the power he asserted, was just maddening."

Colston's eyes flash the truth. "I have a plan for surviving the meeting, but..." He trails off.

Jordan pulls him into a desperate hug, holding the other man tightly. "Promise me you won't go looking for him," he sobs.

Colston returns the hug, whispering, "I will not willingly go to my death. However, I also don't want anyone to get hurt."

The embrace lingers, as both of them understand and sorrowfully accept the moment.

"Colston, I am going to leave for home tomorrow," Jordan says, tearfully breaking the embrace.

"It means a lot that you came here. Jordan, what has just been realized? Please, I beg you, keep this from Kayra," he says, struggling with his emotions.

Jordan nods and says, "I'm glad I came. Do you think we can pull off a chill night? Also, Kayra and I have something to discuss with you."

"Of course," Colston replies effortlessly, draping an arm around Jordan's shoulders as he guides him out of the studio. "How does steak, asparagus, and mashed potatoes sound?" This time, at the mention of food, his mouth begins to water.

"My Lord, that sounds divine," Jordan says with a smile.

"Hey, babe!" Colston calls as he and Jordan enter the kitchen.

Kayra comes into the kitchen with a smile on her face. "Yes?"

"You up for more Clue?" Colston asks.

Kayra runs and leaps into his arms, and

Colston gently swings her around.

Jordan laughs joyfully while watching this. Although his heart is breaking, he remains hopeful for the best amidst all this uncertainty.

Colston prepares the meat, Jordan makes mashed potatoes from seven whole potatoes, and Kayra prepares the greens.

"So I am going to leave tomorrow to get some work done. However, I was speaking with Kayra, and I was wondering if I could come down on Friday to help you two pack. To come and stay with me for a period."

Colston understands that everything depends on his agreement with the idea. He doesn't want the showdown to take place at Jordan's. However, the desire to escape is strong, even though he knows he will be ridiculed for fleeing and admitting guilt. He must convince himself that as long as he carries the lyrics with him every time he leaves the house and, of course, continues working with Melody, he can achieve a semblance of a normal life. Perhaps distancing himself from the living memory will mark the beginning of a new chapter. "Let's do it," he says after several moments of silence.

"Really?" Kayra and Jordan say simultaneously.

Colston glances over his shoulder, laughing as Kayra and Jordan play Rock, Paper, Scissors. They both throw rocks, but after a re-roll, Jordan emerges victorious with scissors.

"Ha! Ah, victory!" Jordan exclaims

triumphantly.

Kayra smiles and bows her head. "I concede, and according to the terms, you gain a request that I cannot refuse," she recites formally.

Jordan rises from the bowl of half-mashed potatoes and glances at Kayra as he approaches Colston.

Colston is mixing seasonings in a small bowl, blissfully unaware of the antics occurring behind him.

"Hey," Kayra says with a warning tone, "I am not at liberty to speak on behalf of my husband." A slight, understanding smile graces her lips.

Colston glances over his shoulder in confusion. "What?" He notices the expression in Kayra's eyes and sees Jordan standing behind him, looking playful and bashful.

"I want to go first when we play Clue," Jordan says, suppressing the desire to kiss his friend and simply pats him on the shoulder. He then attempts to retreat back to the bowl.

Colston and Kayra share a brief, quiet exchange, just once, to get it out of the way. Kayra trusts Colston, and she nods to him in agreement.

Colston gently grabs Jordan's retreating arm. "You want to go first in a game, or is there something else you're too shy to ask for?"

Jordan's heart races as he looks at Kayra, who simply nods in encouragement. Taking a deep breath, Jordan takes the plunge and spins to be engulfed in Colston's arms as their lips meet.

Colston senses a wave of tension dissipate from Jordan's body. Eyes closed and their bodies pressed together, Colston graces Jordan with the full, true experience he desires in this once-in-a-lifetime chance.

Jordan pulls away after a few blissful moments.

Colston smiles at him and gently lets go, "Good?"

He nods, "Thank you; I am sorry."

Kayra walks behind him and gently pats his back before settling into her place in Colston's arms. "JD, it happens. You two are close. I appreciate you asking, and that was the one and only."

"Yes, once was all."

They all share a warm embrace before returning to their respective stations.

Colston drifts on the turbulent waves of succor for the entire night. He despises the unpredictable pulls within himself, standing on the platform and gripping the chain so tightly that his hand is bleeding. He hears the relentless ticking but struggles against the overwhelming urge to complete what remains unfinished. Yet, he cherishes the high moments when worry, fear, and wondering are nearly nonexistent.

The night concludes on a positive note, filled with smiles and good spirits. Colston decides to go to bed, knowing that a restful night's sleep will enable him to work effectively all day tomorrow.

The house sits still at 9:30 p.m. and

remains that way until 10:00 a.m. the following morning. The three occupants of the house are awake, having enjoyed a full night's rest. With sore necks from sleeping so soundly, they groggily make their way to the kitchen for coffee and sustenance.

Colston and Kayra walk hand in hand into the kitchen.

"Did God place us under a safety blanket?" Jordan asks, stretching gently and yawning.

"Brother, he did something," Colston says, smiling as he prepares the coffee pot.

"Bacon and eggs, guys?" Kayra asks.

"Sounds lovely," Jordan says. "I feel euphoric, but I have no idea why."

"A phenomenal night of sleep can reset the mind, or so I've read," Colston says with a broad smile.

Kayra and Colston are performing a dance around each other as they work in tandem in the kitchen. Jordan watches this with awe and amazement.

The air feels distinctly different, lighter in some way. However, none of them draw attention to it for fear of shattering it.

"JD, coffee order, please," Colston calls out.

"Splash of milk and two shots of creamer, thanks."

Colston moves with such weightlessness and steadiness that he allows it to be, neither thinking about it nor questioning it. He silently expresses his gratitude to God.

Kayra twirls around Colston, their backs

touching, and spins beneath Colston's raised arm to reach for the fridge. Just as Kayra is about to pull it open, Colston sidesteps and extends his hand, offering Jordan's coffee.

He takes the mug, captivated by the moment.

Kayra tilts her head, and Colston turns back to meet her lips with his. They share a silent chuckle, tears glistening in their eyes. They simultaneously break apart and conclude the spectacle.

"What was that?" Jordan asks.

"Our first shared home was a trailer. On mornings like this, when we both wanted to do something in the small kitchen. We began to move in a dance-like fashion, learning to read and feel each other." Kayra explains, "It's been years."

"It seems to be ingrained in us," Colston states.

"You guys are full of surprises."

"We're not," Kayra expresses, plating the food.

"I wish to find someone who enjoys life," Jordan says.

"You will, JD; I have faith in you," Colston says.

Kayra places a plate in front of Jordan.

"Thank you for breakfast and the show."

"It's nothing," Kayra says. "It's refreshing."

"We've been going mad these last couple of days; finally, the madness has been silenced," Colston says.

Jordan and Kayra watch with bated breath as Colston maintains his steady composure, his glowing presence radiating confidence. He smiles reassuringly and says, "It's okay, guys; I am in control."

The expressions on their faces reveal a profound sense of relief.

"That is great to hear," Jordan says.

These breaks have always been fleeting, but they are often spent working reasonable hours. As a result, Kayra can enjoy her husband's company at night.

Kayra takes his hands and gazes into his bright eyes. "I've missed this."

"I know," Colston whispers. "JD, when are you needed to leave?"

"Why?"

Colston shrugs, "Wanna work on a cover?"

"Sure, what song?"

"How about Right Here by Ashes Remain?"

"Let's do it."

Colston and Jordan by four have a decent rough cut for the cover, but Colston's sword and shield remain unfinished as time continues to tick away.

Kayra and Colston wish Jordan a safe drive home at six.

"Let's watch a movie," Colston suggests.

Kayra nods in agreement.

As the movie plays, Kayra rests against Colston, listening to his steady breathing as he drifts in and out of sleep. She senses his quiet calm, which dropped over him after he opened up. This tranquility is both frightening and a welcome contrast to his demeanor over the past nine days.

"Ka?" Colston asks, sounding half-asleep.

She tilts her head to look at him. His

eyes are closed. "Yes, love?"

"I'm safe here, aren't I?"

No doubt, his mind is refusing to quiet in the midst of trying to rest. Kayra places a hand on his chest; that heartbeat is both calming and strong.

"You are home and not alone. You are as safe as you can be."

"Thank you," Colston whispers, and his body fully relaxes. His arm slides off Kayra. She watches as Colston's head gently rolls to the left.

After an hour and a half, Colston awakens, feeling slightly disoriented. However, when his arm brushes against Kayra, who is resting on his chest, he smiles softly.

"Cole?" Kayra asks, sensing Colston's movement.

Colston yawns and says, "How about dinner, then bed?"

Kayra stands up and gently pulls Colston to his feet, and together they walk to the kitchen.

As Colston preps dinner, baked Tuscan chicken accompanied by leftover mashed potatoes from the night prior, Kayra sits at the island, sipping a glass of wine.

When he is startled by the simultaneous crash of a chair hitting the floor and glass shattering, Colston spins around, his eyes wide, "KAYRA!"

He takes a step, hurrying around the counter, when he hears a heavy sob, "KAYRA!"

"I AM SORRY!" Kayra screams, her body shaking.

Colston discovers Kayra curled up on the floor, surrounded by shattered glass and spilled wine. He approaches her and gently scoops her into his arms, feeling her heart racing.

She claws desperately at his shirt, shouting, "WHEN YOU DIDN'T CALL! I... SHOULD... HAVE... CALLED... FOR... HELP!" She is left gasping for breath.

Colston settles on the floor, away from the glass, "Baby, baby, shhh, it's okay." Colston is trying to suppress his trembling fear.

"IT'S... NOT!" She is very lightly hitting his chest. "I... COULD... HAVE... SAVED... YOU... FROM... THE... TORMENT!"

Colston presses her hands against his chest. "I am right here. I'm not going anywhere."

Kayra continues to sob and tremble against him. "I'm sorry," she whispers.

Colston gently cradles her face in his hands. "You have nothing to be sorry about. There was no way you could have known the truth of the situation." He wipes away her tears. "Please, love. I am here."

"Yet, I almost abandoned you!" Her face contorts with emotion as she collapses into his chest.

He wraps her tightly in his arms, his chin gently resting on the top of her head, "Shhh. Sweetheart, breathe." He is gentle with his words as he tries to guide her out of the panic attack.

She shakes her head, saying, "I don't deserve you!" Her voice is muffled against his chest. "HE hunts you and haunts you; dreams become reality, and reality becomes dreams. You still stand, shrouded in fear, yet you stand! How?!" She asks, not looking up.

"You," he begins, "with all the life I have left to live. It is made possible with you by my side." Tears begin to fall from his eyes. "I survived because thoughts of you kept me alive while in the phantom's grasp. With the new tools granted to me by Melody, I envision us reclaiming our lives."

She meets his gaze, her eyes brimming with love and trepidation. He leans in and kisses her.

At 1:25 in the morning, Colston awakens in a cold sweat. The burning sensation in his wrist subsides, along with the soreness throughout his body. His mind is filled with the contemptuous laughter of the phantom, and his body shivers as the shadow of the phantom looms too close for his comfort.

His mind flashes to the half-finished sword and shield, accompanied by the mocking voice of the phantom. *"Fighting will get you nowhere."*

He jumps out of bed and rushes to his studio, where he spends the next few hours completing the re-lyric.

The weariness and fear have set in every word written; it began to take on a life of its own; Colston hears a completely different melody, loosely using the original as a guide for direction. He hates that this is happening, placing him back in that bathroom waiting to sing the second song. Meant to be just a rework to help him fight, it turned into an anthem of desperation and fear. Tears are flowing when he puts the final period; his hands are folded with his chin resting on them.

"Have I sealed my fate?" He rests his arms on the desk and then lays his head down. "Lord, I am not ready to die." He whispers.

"Colston?" Kayra wakes up to find him missing from her side. Panic courses through her as she calls out, "Colston?" a bit louder while getting out of bed.

"In the studio," Colston calls wearily.

He had fallen asleep at his desk. "I didn't mean to scare you." He hears her rush in.

"It's fine," she breathes, kneeling next to his chair. "I didn't hear you get up last night," Kayra admits, her voice tinged with sadness.

"It's okay; I didn't want to wake you," Colston expresses, his voice striving to remain steady.

"A nightmare?" Kayra asks.

"Kinda," Colston says, struggling to find the right words to describe what it was he experienced last night, "an... overwhelming presence, a looming shadow."

Kayra looks at him directly and says, "I will be right here. I've been thinking that we need to get away for a while, just the two of us, before we go stay with Jordan."

Colston pulls her into his lap. "That does sound great," he says, wrapping his arms around her and gently resting his face against her stomach. "I want to enjoy life."

"And you will," she whispers, cradling his face and lifting it to gaze into his eyes.

His brown eyes shimmered with tears. "I am trying. Have you got an idea for our escape?"

A soft, yet disheartening smile touches her lips. "Yeah, but..." She trails off, releasing his face and averting her gaze.

Colston gently cups her face. "Kayra, where is it?"

Kayra sighs, "Due to the fear of the virus spreading, most hotels and city vacation spots are closed. However, the Highland Woodland Getaway remains open."

"That's down in southern Idaho, right?" Colston asks.

"Yes," she says, maintaining her worried expression.

Colston immediately senses her unease. He gently rubs her back and says, "We need to step away before the lockdowns actually go into effect. It may be the woods, but it's in the South, and I'll be with you. Let's take it," he says, smiling.

"Truly?" Her eyes are shining.

"Of course."

They share a lengthy, passionate kiss.

Means to an End... My dearest Colston, you are the end.
Means to an End... My dearest Colston, you are the end.
Means to an End... My dearest Colston, you are the end.
Means to an End... My dearest Colston, you are the end.
Means to an End... My dearest Colston, you are the end.
Means to an End... My dearest Colston, you are the end.
Means to an End... My dearest Colston, you are the end.
Means to an End... My dearest Colston, you are the end.
Means to an End... My dearest Colston, you are the end.
Means to an End... My dearest Colston, you are the end.
Means to an End... My dearest Colston, you are the end.
Means to an End... My dearest Colston, you are the end.
Means to an End... My dearest Colston, you are the end.
Means to an End... My dearest Colston, you are the end.
Means to an End... My dearest Colston, you are the end.
Means to an End... My dearest Colston, you are the end.
Means to an End... My dearest Colston, you are the end.
Means to an End... My dearest Colston, you are the end.
Means to an End... My dearest Colston, you are the end.
Means to an End... My dearest Colston, you are the end.
Means to an End... My dearest Colston, you are the end.
Means to an End... My dearest Colston, you are the end.
Means to an End... My dearest Colston, you are the end.
Means to an End... My dearest Colston, you are the end.
Means to an End... My dearest Colston, you are the end.
Means to an End... My dearest Colston, you are the end.
Means to an End... My dearest Colston, you are the end.
Means to an End... My dearest Colston, you are the end.

Chapter Twenty: Means to an End

Colston stands and gently places Kayra on her feet before stretching.

Kayra admires her husband. As a question forms in her mind, she does not hesitate to ask, "What if he comes for you with me by your side?"

Colston straightens and looks at her, then caresses her cheek. "Your place is behind me. I will protect you from the insanity that binds me so tightly." His voice is soft.

"Who is going to protect you?" Tears glisten in her eyes.

Colston shakes his head and holds her tight. "I'll make us breakfast," then he leads her out of the studio.

Breakfast consists of biscuits and gravy, which they enjoy in silence. Kayra washes the dishes while Colston takes a shower. His mind is unusually calm, which is both strange and somewhat scary.

While enjoying this eerie stillness, it is suddenly flooded with a memory.

After the final note, he let out a cry, not in victory or frustration, but out of sheer terror.

Colston bowed his head, feeling the weight of the performance lift from his shoulders. However, a new weight settled upon him, the weight of the unknown. Colston realized he could not endure another performance like that, and he wondered if his captor understood this. Involuntary tears streamed down his face as he was roughly handled, with not a word spoken by the man. During the brief trip to the bathroom, all of Colston's weight came down on his left ankle, causing him to crash to his knees on the dirty hardwood floor.

The nails of his captor dug into the skin of his inner bicep as he was lifted to his feet. Still, not a word was spoken. For Colston, this silence was worse than any words could be.

He turns off the water, striving to detach himself from the memory. Stepping out of the shower, he lands awkwardly on his left foot and is sent sprawling to the floor. He cries out and flinches as he momentarily feels the sharp pain in his ankle, followed by a tightening grip on his inner bicep. Accompanying this grip is a mocking, echoing laughter.

Kayra comes running when she hears him cry out and hits the floor with a thud.

"Oh God, Colston! What happened?" She asks in a panic.

The pain subsides as he is overcome with embarrassment. He allows Kayra to help him lean against the wall.

"Is it your heart?" she asks, her hand immediately resting on his chest.

"No, just a flashback," he says, effortlessly and painlessly rotating his left ankle.

"You sure?"

He nods and says, "Didn't mean to scare you."

"Stop," she says, kissing him. "It's almost time to go."

"Alright,"

After getting dressed, he enters the studio and prints two copies of the reworked song. He understands that it isn't the best, but he hopes it will come alive and carry a punch when performed. The moment he slips them into his pocket, a surge of confidence courses through him. He might be able to stand his ground... or at least he hopes so. As he notices his hands shaking, he stares at them in confusion. *Why?* This question remains unanswered.

"Ready to go!" He leaves the studio.

He drives without feeling overwhelmed by stress about going to therapy. As he pulls into the parking lot and turns off the truck, he gazes at the darkening sky and remarks, "Looks like we might get some rain."

"I hope not; I want the sun."

He leans over with a smile and kisses Kayra. "See you in an hour."

"Do you need me to come in with you?" she asks.

"I've got this one, babe," he smiles.

"I love you," Kayra says.

"I love you too," Colston says as he shuts the door and walks into the building.

He arrives at the suite, expecting to find Melody in the reception area. However, it is empty, which is not overly concerning, as she may be with another client. The reception area is significantly dimmer than usual, almost resembling the lighting that

Todd typically uses.

Not dwelling on it, he opens the door and steps into the suite. Colston instantly senses that something is amiss when the sharp scent of gunpowder assaults his nostrils. He quickly attempts to retreat from the suite.

When Todd stands up from behind the desk, aiming a gun at Colston, he says, "Make a sound, and you are dead. Step away from the door and throw your phone away." Todd looks jaded.

Colston raises his trembling right hand, releases his left hand from the door, and slowly takes two steps into the room while reaching into his pocket for his phone. For a brief moment, he considers calling for help.

"Colston!" The voice is sharp and commanding. "I won't hesitate to shoot. Now throw it away!"

"Whoa! Hey, there's no need for this," Colston says, tossing his phone aside. "Listen, I understand that you are upset with me for requesting that Melody be my therapist from now on. But," he points at the gun, "this is beyond excessive. Let's be civil about this." Colston is desperately trying to defuse the situation.

"Colston," Todd says, shaking his head, "I am afraid you are misinterpreting this situation.

Colston stares, extremely confused. "What have I done?" he asks, his voice much more tentative.

Todd's annoyance is growing. "In our lives, we are dealt a wild card, and at other times, we are merely pawns. Regardless, there is a responsibility."

Colston could not believe what he had just heard. "No," he whispers, feeling himself mentally collapse.

"Yes," Todd counters, "it is a clear sign." His voice rises as Colston struggles.

"This can't be happening again," Colston says, half to himself and half out loud. He can't allow it; if it comes down to it, he would rather die than be held captive again.

"I am somewhat vexed by your goddamn stubbornness," Todd said, the hand gripping the gun, moving back and forth at every other word. "It's a shame about Melody; she had real promise. But you put her in harm's way." A sly smile spread across his face as he delivered the final line.

Colston wants to scream, but the gun keeps him frozen in place. He needs to find a way to escape. "What is it that you want from me?"

"Just play the part you were meant to. Clearly, you must now realize that even God has forsaken you on this path." Todd vaults over the desk with lightning speed, keeping the gun trained on Colston the entire time. Colston does not dare to move.

"I was also forsaken! I love to help people, but I failed the one who needed me the most. My hateful and vengeful feelings toward my kin permitted me to create a monster!" He cries, tears streaming down his face, and the hand gripping the gun trembles. "But," a crazed smile spreads across his face.

Colston feels nothing but cold and fear.

On the platform, the chain in his hand jerks upward. As it yanks his arm up, the chain slices deeper into his already bloody hand; nevertheless, his grip remains firm. This leaves Colston trembling.

"Learning occurred, and intelligence emerged that would have otherwise been squandered! Colston, I apologize, but I couldn't allow it all to be wasted."

Colston is only vaguely aware that a door to his left, just at the edge of his vision, has begun to open slowly. The gun aimed at him, and the overwhelming sense of foreboding holds his full attention.

"What------is------this?" Colston asks in desperation.

"Ask yourself this: why, in the past five years, have you made no progress? I made it abundantly clear that I only work with a single client for a maximum of two years."

Colston feels anger surging through his fear. "Did------you------ever------intend------to------help me?" He is pleading, tears rolling down his cheeks.

"No," he replies tersely, "I was assisting someone else."

Colston senses a presence within the darkened doorway. He gathers the courage to take a full look in that direction.

"Colston, you're merely a means to an end!" Todd exclaims.

Out of the darkness emerges hands. Colston reacts by spinning away and toward the door, his hands grasping the doorknob.

"Don't!" Todd warns.

"Colston, if you leave, I will burn your

world. Your wife, your friends, your parents, and any fan who dares to speak your name."

The voice washes over him like an arctic wave, rendering him paralyzed in fearful agony. Colston's hands drop to his sides, devoid of strength. Suddenly, hands grab him by the shoulders, spinning him and throwing him to the floor. He rolls until he is against the desk. "STOP!" he screams.

He is face to face with the phantom, who has halted his advance. Colston stares at Todd, who remains motionless, resembling a mere spectator. The gun is no longer aimed at him.

"You------kept------me------trapped!" Colston slowly sits up.

"My uncle owed me," the phantom says, looking at Todd. "For a life of torment!"

Todd raises his left hand from behind his back. The phantom flinches and takes a step back, resembling a beaten animal. In response to the phantom's reaction, Colston flinches as well.

"Don't, you! The headache you've caused is unbearable, you useless sack of Dog Water!" Todd chastises.

Colston gradually rises to his feet.

"But," he says, his voice quieter and almost caring. "Boy, you did learn."

Todd turns to Colston, and the phantom does as well. Colston is fully on his feet, trembling with fear.

"Colston, there is no use fighting," Todd says. "He is the wild card, and you are the pawn. Accept it, as he has."

Colston observes the compliment wash over

the phantom, and the smile he offers Colston resembles that of a joyful youth who has finally gained the attention of an absent parent.

"You can't be freaking serious, Todd. The----both----of----you----are----crazy!"

Todd throws his head back and laughs before looking deadpan at Colston with a serious expression.

"No, I made a mistake, and he chose you. When he came to me in tears, confessing that he had let you go in a moment of weakness, I decided to help him while also teaching a lesson. The police never provided me with your file; I inquired about you two days after your escape for the sake of this useless sack of Dog Water." Todd glances at the phantom and gestures toward Colston. "He's all yours."

The phantom faces Colston. "My dearest Colston, it is great to see you," he says with a warm smile as he takes a step forward.

"Don't-come-near-me!" Colston exclaims, his heart racing with fear and betrayal. To steady himself, he reflects on the people in his life. He means something to them, and he must fight.

The phantom extends his arms to his sides and declares, "You are mine! Leave with me, or you will end up in a body bag!"

Colston steps forward and shoves the phantom back, who then grabs his wrists, their eyes locked in a daring challenge. Colston battles through the paralyzing fear that ensnares his mind, pulling himself free from his bound and frozen state and fully embracing his current self. Seizing the moment, Colston catches the phantom off guard, causing him to stumble beneath his feet and release his grip on his wrists. Taking advantage of this, Colston makes a dash for the door.

A gunshot echoes through the small room. Colston emits an anguished cry and collapses to his hands and knees, feeling a searing pain along the side of his right thigh. Tears blur his vision as he looks up and realizes he is only three feet from the door.

A hand grips his hair, wrenching his head back. His tear-filled eyes meet the voided eyes of the phantom. The phantom's lips are inches from Colston's ear, whispering menacingly, "My promise stands: you will watch the world burn around you, simply because you refuse to see what I offer. Innocent lives lost; all the torment wrought starts with you, Colston. It can end with you too."

Colston swallows hard, his throat constricting painfully as his neck is wrenched back. "Please, let me have a chance to win my freedom," he pleads.

The phantom caresses Colston's cheek and bearded chin with a glowing, satisfied smile. He whispers, sending a chill down Colston's spine, "Why would I do that when I have you now?"

A headache is starting to grow, and his thigh is throbbing and prickling. "Please," he utters weakly, "let me----try. Sing with me."

The phantom roughly releases Colston,

throwing him onto his hands and knees. He rubs his neck and shifts his weight to his left leg as he glances over his shoulder, noticing the phantom shakily gripping his own head. Colston seizes the opportunity. "Let the music end the torment; we can do it together." Revolted by his own words, he finds himself with no choice. A moment of terror flashes through his body at the realization if he hadn't completed his sword and shield this morning.

The phantom falls to his knees. "Colston," he says, his eyes bright and filled with pain. "I told you that the house and the karaoke bar were the only times I would allow your voice to affect me and let blatant disrespect slide. I gave you five years."

"No, I lay day after day, being crushed by what you did!"

The phantom emits a guttural cry and forcefully shoves Colston off his hands and knees. As Colston falls onto his back, he reaches into his pocket and pulls out the phantom's lyrics to *Let Me Through*, "HERE!" He holds it out in front of him.

The phantom brandishes a knife, swiftly reaching into the shadows of the adjacent room to retrieve a roll of duct tape. He is almost upon Colston when the paper is thrust into his face. In an attempt to swat it away, he slashes Colston's arm.

Colston cries out, but he remains resolute. Refusing to let his defenses falter, he pleads, "Please!" through gritted teeth, shaking the paper in his hand. He observes as the deadpan eyes gradually shift their focus from him to the paper, gaining a hint of color as curiosity begins to blossom.

The eyes, now displaying a faint blue hue, shift back to Colston, holding a look of annoyance. Colston maintains that gaze for a moment before returning his attention to the paper. The phantom drops the knife and seizes the paper instead. Colston sits up and adjusts his position, creating distance between himself and the phantom. Cradling his bleeding left arm and gazing at the wound on his thigh, he feels an intense tingling sensation radiating around the area. He breathes slowly and steadily to control the pain. While doing so, he glances up at Todd, who observes the scene with a bored expression.

Colston wants to lie back down and remain still. He feels shame rising in the pit of his stomach; he refuses to be a failure. If this is to be his final stand, he wants to be fighting, not cowering in fear.

"Are these your words?" the phantom asks curiously.

"Yes," Colston replies.

"You understand my role in your life. How can you fight this?" His eyes are bright, filled with hurt and confusion.

Colston scoots back against the wall, using it for support as he stands up. The phantom's eyes narrow as Colston positions himself beside the door. In a warning tone, he says, "Colston, don't play with me."

Colston shakes his head. "No games, just know." He points with his right hand. "Words can be a double-edged sword; they thrive on emotion and interpretation." He stands with the support of the wall, placing most of his weight on his left leg. His entire body vibrates with pain, and he hopes to ignore it for the performance, just as he had ignored the cold, the pain, and the fact that he was dying while he sang the second song at the house.

The phantom glances at the paper and then back at Colston, his expression a mix of utter confusion and hints of anger.

"If you expect the most from me. You must first understand the world of music from within," Colston says. "On my phone, there is a private video on my channel titled 'Let Me Through,' which you can use for practice."

The phantom's eyes narrow. "Trust your voice."

Colston took a painful breath. "You need the practice, so this sounds good for gaining understanding. I trust my voice."

The mixture of satisfaction and utter terror flashes across the phantom's face. In that moment, Colston realizes he has the high ground, a position he intends to maintain. The phantom narrows his eyes and states, "So if I somehow 'break', I let you go. And," a smirk spreads across his lips, "if I remain steadfast in my commitment to your voice?"

Colston, drawing from deep within to make his response sound sincere despite his resignation, says, "I will go with you quietly." Although he knows this to be untrue, merely uttering the words fills him with dread.

The phantom leaps to his feet and gazes at him intently. "With no chance of escape?" Colston, his heart heavy, nods and breaks eye contact. The phantom grips his chin, forcing him to meet his gaze once more, and growls, "Speak it!" Colston turns his face away, resulting in a sharp slap across his cheek.

The look of absolute distress appears in the phantom's eyes as Colston takes the hit and maintains eye contact. Colston breathes, "Yes, I will belong to you," and tears stream down his face.

The deadpan eyes return, boring into Colston as if searching for something. He silently nods, feeling content, and steps back. "Fine, I'll indulge you," he says, before going to retrieve Colston's phone from the corner.

"You have five minutes," Colston says, his discomfort palpable.

He glances at Colston, looking dumbfounded. "Just where do you get off telling me what to do?"

"Showing the same courtesy you showed me, more so." Colston says.

The phantom scowls and goes about practicing. Colston struggles to remember his lyrics amidst the buzzing in his head. He is vaguely aware of the increasing numbness spreading down his leg and into his fingers. He can see blood flowing, but he can't feel it. Well, that can't be good. Colston limps to the desk for support. Leaning heavily against it, barely hearing the phantom's practice, he closes his eyes. *Colston, don't!* That voice lingers at the edge of his hearing. Opening his eyes, which is difficult due to his exhaustion, he gathers himself, ready to pour everything into this one song. He thinks of Kayra and silently apologizes, *"I tried, my love; I am so sorry."* Then he straightens up, takes a few deep breaths, and declares as assertively as possible, "Time's up!"

The phantom stops the song and looks at Colston with distaste. "I hope you'll enjoy living with your wrists bound," the phantom says.

"Hold your breath for singing," Colston retorts.

They stand squarely, and the song starts, Let Me Go/Let Me Through.

Colston/Phantom: I want you to know the chains you've forged./I need you to grasp the power that's yours to claim.

Help I didn't ask for./Take my hand; let me guide you.

I sing for my life, though you hear it not./I poured out my love, yet you turned away.

Blinded by wrongful thoughts and misguided belief./I wept when I let go too soon.

Left on a cliff, I'd rather be dead./But I'm ready to try again.

Fighting the chains with songs./Your voice, it's like heaven's choir.

Why must you cling with your sharp claws?/Why must you deny me?

Release your grip; let me free./Lower your walls; see the truth within.

There's nothing left for us to share./Realize what you truly desire.

I'm breaking free!/I mean you no harm, just sincere admiration.

I sing my song all night; let the world hear./You sing your song for me, crystal clear.

Please, oh please, I'm down on my knees; let me go!/Please, oh please, I'm on my knees; let me through!

I sing my song; let it echo wide./You sing your song for my heart alone.

Please, I beg on my knees, let me go!/Please, I beg, on my knees, let me through!

The eyes of the phantom flicker between blue and black, each reflecting a desperate plea. The realization of the conflicting words that Colston is singing compels him to lay weak hands on Colston, attempting to silence him while still keeping pace. However, Colston easily pushes the phantom's hands away from his face. Despite the injuries to his body and the mental fatigue from the situation, he draws strength and power from reveling in his domain. He feels untouchable, granted healing as he pours his heart into his song to defeat the phantom and secure his freedom. The pleading look in the phantom's eyes seems to beg him to surrender, but Colston counters with a voice that shatters barriers, infused with raw emotion.

I don't understand why you keep trying?/I can't grasp why you resist?

To control my life, you are not deserving./Your uncertainty tortures me.

You hold no power over me!/I'm torn between love and frustration.

My talent is mine, never to be controlled!/ My dear Colston, relieve my agony!

My phantom, you will soon fade to nothing./ If only you could see the truth in my eyes!

Why must you cling with your sharp claws?/ Why must you deny me?

Release your grip; let me fly free!/Lower your walls; see the truth within!

There's nothing left for us to share!/Realize what you truly desire!

I'm breaking free!/ I mean you no harm, just sincere admiration.

I sing my song; let it ring through the night!/You sing your song, but cower without me!

Please, oh please, I'm down on my knees; set me free!/Please, oh please, I'm down on my knees; can't you see!

I sing my song, let it echo and soar!/You sing your song, but I crave so much more!

Please, I beg on my knees, let me go!/Please, I beg, on my knees, let me through!

Phantom/Colston: Let me through!/ I won't be molded. I will fight till the very end./Let me through!/I'll win; I'll beat you./Let me through!/ I'll break you. Let go, let go, let go. Let me GO!

The song concludes with both men on their knees, tears streaming down their faces. It had been an intense power struggle, with each wanting their lyrics to resonate above the clamor of the other, harmonizing at times. Had it not been a high-stakes duet, it could have been truly exceptional.

Colston collapses back onto his left elbow, resisting the urge to lie completely flat. His head is pounding, and a tingling sensation radiates through his thigh, intensifying in waves with each throb of his head. He cannot feel the fingers on his left hand, and the electric pulsing in his lower left arm is enough to make him want to pass out. His vocal cords are wrecked; he has never poured so much into a performance. An overwhelming sense of triumph has settled over Colston, preventing his heart from simply giving out. The words were his own, and he was authentically himself during the performance, singing for freedom. He still needs to escape, but he feels a sense of contentment. Despite gripping the chain that keeps him steady and the fact that the damn door to the cage remains locked tight while the fire dances ever closer, he is satisfied.

He watches the phantom struggle to hold himself together. "What have you done? I SAID, 'DON'T PLAY WITH ME'!" he weeps.

"I----sang----for my----life." Colston says weakly, his voice raspy.

The phantom shakes his head. "No! You don't understand!" he cries. "You... you." His body trembles. "I... love... you." He crawls closer to Colston.

"Look at me," Colston requests.

The phantom looks up. His eyes are bright and filled with terror. Colston's heart leaps as he comprehends what he is witnessing, but his mind cautions him.

"I...never...meant...to...hurt...you." He collapses against Colston's chest, sobbing, his fingers clutching the fabric of his shirt.

Colston is knocked fully to his back. The urge to comfort this man is present, but Colston can't bring himself to do so. What this man... both men had stolen from him is unforgivable. Yet, he had won; now he needed to find the right words to secure his escape.

"If... you... love... me," he gasps, his chest heaving. "You'll let...me...go. You can remain... in my life, as many others do." Colston coughs, tasting blood. "I share my voice so it doesn't go to waste. Please." He must pause; he is exhausted, and his voice is nearly gone.

The bright blue eyes, for the first time since the start, show Colston true understanding.

The phantom sobs into his chest, "You...can...lea--"

"ENOUGH!" Todd bellows, interrupting the phantom.

The phantom and Colston both flinch. Todd approaches them, grabbing the phantom by the hair and pulling him away from Colston.

"Stop! Please," the phantom cries, finding himself in a position similar to that of Colston a short while ago.

"You useless sack of Dog Water! You are weak; I was almost proud of you. What is conviction and the destruction of another's life when you are tripped at the finish line by compassion?" Todd screams this directly into the face of the phantom.

Colston, witnessing this disturbing scene, wastes no time in gradually shifting his position in an attempt to try to get up.

"The moment you acted on your obsession was the moment you simultaneously unleashed a new kind of hell into my life, while your intelligence and determination left me in awe!" The gun that had been waving about is now aimed at Colston, and Todd forces the phantom to look, declaring, "You have him, your prize. Finish your task!" He stomps a foot down on Colston's chest to keep him immobilized.

Colston lets out a faint cry.

"No!" the phantom screams as he breaks free from Todd, stands up, turns, and kicks the leg pinning Colston.

Todd backpedals in utter bewilderment, a feeling intensified when he finds himself staring down the barrel of a gun.

"Uncle, my conviction regarding Colston is not for you to use as a means to seek clemency. Put the fucking gun down!" The phantom commands.

The look of superciliousness drains from Todd's face, along with all color. He slowly sets the gun down. "Boy, now this--"

"No! No more." He retrieves the gun and pistol-whips Todd across the face.

Todd cowers but remains on his feet. When he looks back, his face is smeared with blood.

"Go sit in your office!" the phantom commands.

Todd follows instructions obediently. The phantom confronts Colston.

His heart sinks as the bright blue eyes that once held understanding are now lost in the dark orbs. Colston realizes that he has lost his chance to escape with his life.

Getting back on his elbow, he implores, "Please, let me go." He had to try once more.

The phantom drops beside him, his knee landing on Colston's right forearm. Colston lets out a small cry as a hand grips his throat. He struggles to remain on his elbow, causing increasing pressure to be applied against his throat.

"Colston, my dearest Colston, I cannot let you go. It would be irresponsible of me. I can see that you are drowning, and I can help you. However, your eyes have betrayed you." Colston is forced onto his back.

He lets out a strangled cough, staring into those hellfire eyes.

"Even if I took you again, your means to keep breathing and my torture prolonged. Not only did your eyes betray you, but the very words you sang!" The phantom pressed the barrel of the gun against Colston's chest.

The hand at his throat is a singular pulse away from robbing him of his ability to breathe entirely.

"I don't want to kill you!" the phantom screams.

"You don't have to do it! No one is forcing your hand!" Colston says, sensing hope returning.

"But," the phantom's voice trembles, "the suffering, the suffering of what is incomplete. I can't just let it be!"

"The suffering is not mine! It is yours and yours alone that you have imposed upon me!"

"NOO! Colston, NOO!" the phantom screams. "How could you say that? You wrote those words for me. There must be a part of you that understands me." The desperation is clear in his low voice.

"Those words, which express what is desired, should come from the person whose sentiments resonate the truest. You long for those words to emanate from a place of love, yet in reality, they arise from a place of hate!" Colston had gathered enough saliva to spit it out with the final word. "You were and are nothing but poison to me," Colston says, his voice strained and vehement.

The phantom's expression falters. "What?

The hand on Colston's throat trembles, and the barrel of the gun presses painfully into the flesh to the right of his sternum.

"From the moment you covered my mouth with that rag, everything I did was never for you; it was done in spite of you." Colston speaks, fully aware that he is pushing him to the brink. He had accepted his fate sometime ago and understood that their encounter would end in bloodshed. Nevertheless, he fights until the very end. Shifting his gaze to the left, he observes his left hand, stiff with drying blood, clenching into a fist, sending intense tingling sensations up his arm. He throws the punch, utilizing the full range of his arm and rotating his chest, striking the side of the phantom's head.

The hand holding the gun moves away from his chest, but it discharges before it is fully cleared. Colston lets out a gut-wrenching howl as an intense burning sensation radiates down the right side of his chest.

The phantom cocks the gun and places it back on Colston's chest, tears streaming down his face. The hot muzzle singes Colston's shirt and the skin beneath it.

"Please," he whispers, his voice barely audible and damaged. This plea is not directed at the phantom; rather, it is a desperate call for what is unfolding within his mind.

Colston's frozen and battered body has finally reached the door of the cage. Using the bars to hoist himself up, he begins pulling, yanking, reaching, screaming, and pleading. He desperately craves that locked warmth and hope for his final escape attempt. He needs the door to open before the gun fires again.

There are tears streaming from the phantom's dark eyes as he speaks; his voice is filled with frustration and anguish. "Poison? All I have done to help you, POISON!" he gulps. "My Colston, this is where you die!"

Colston stares, breathing pained breaths. As he has no more words for his murderer, he has taken enough. He prays for a miracle that will allow him to share his final words with Kayra.

"FIGHT! FOR THE LOVE OF GOD!" the phantom screams in his face. "Please... live!"

Colston lies there, staring blankly into those black eyes. Fighting he is, by staying silent. Claiming death as his own right, though, done by someone else's hand. His life has always been claimed by others who believed they knew what was best for him. Colston is prepared to die to break that cycle. Tears slide down his face as he offers a silent apology to those who truly deserve it.

"Fine, then that's it. All the torment ends." His voice is filled with love and compassion.

Colston sees his reflection in the darkness of the eyes. The platform pivots violently, the chain rips from his grasp, and he plummets toward the fire. A painful shockwave ripples through his body. His ears ring, and he struggles to catch his breath. The phantom caresses his cheek, and Colston reads the phantom's lips. "In the arms of eternal slumber, we are free. I will see you soon." Releasing his stranglehold on Colston's throat, the phantom stands and walks out of his sight.

Colston lies on the floor, staring up at the ceiling. His world spins as he feels his heart pounding against his chest, numb with pain, yet he cannot draw in a breath. His ultimate failure and his fear of dying alone have come to fruition. He was a fool to believe he could escape fate's preordained end.

The cage in his mind finally bursts open, launching his freezing, broken body backward. As he helplessly flies through the air, he tilts his head back to see where he is about to land, and that is when he catches a glimpse of a fire rushing toward him. At his current velocity, he has mere moments before he is engulfed in flames. With his gaze directed upward, his mind is blank. When he spots a wooden platform tumbling end over end, narrowly missing him to his right, he hears it crash into the ground with tremendous force. The part of him that was on the platform collides with the other, merging the two together. He rotates in the air and slams onto the ground, landing on his chest and expelling the air from his lungs. The fire, wild and menacing, bears down upon him. Unable to catch his breath, he buries his face in his arm. He feels the heat but is not consumed by it. Looking up, he sees that he is shielded by a wall of light. A fragment of that wall breaks away, enveloping his body in warmth and the light of hope.

Get moving! You are dying!

A gasp forces air back into Colston's lungs as the nightmare recedes, only to be replaced by panic and the pain of his current situation. Tears of frustration flow; he is near death, yet he finally feels the sense of completeness he's longed for.

He refuses to let it all bleed out onto the floor. Rolling onto his stomach, he begins to pull himself toward the door. His breathing becomes increasingly labored. Aware that if he stops, he may not have the strength to continue, he winces in pain with every inch he crawls, his body tingling with numbness. He dares not pause, for he needs to see Kayra's face one last time.

He sobs, feeling his strength wane. His mind fixates on Kayra as he tumbles down the stairs. Weeping all the way, he finds himself unable to scream. At the bottom, he rests, the darkness encroaching on his vision. His heart thuds loudly in his ears.

"One last fight; get to the arms of your wife."

The emotions overwhelm him, causing his chest to tighten. Ignoring the pain and weakness, he crawls until he reaches the front door. Managing to get halfway outside, he lies there, hoping and praying that Kayra will see him. He feels the rain hitting his face, mingling with his tears.

He hears a distant sound, but he can't be sure what it is. The view of the fading gray sky and the raindrops is shielded from hitting his face when Kayra appears.

Seeing her face, he relaxes; the pain in his chest dulls to a faint quiver. He reads Kayra's lips as she urges him to hang on. The fight within him has reached its conclusion; tears fall, and he begins to see double as darkness seeps in. He barely feels the arms cradling him, but he hopes she knows how much she means to him. Locking eyes with Kayra, he feels everything fade, his chest hitching with his final breath, "I...love...you..." Colston finally, gently succumbs to the darkness and silence of death's embrace.

Chapter Twenty-One: Life Shifts

"COLSTON! NOOO! PLEASE!" Kayra screams, desperately trying to revive her dear husband.

Her hands are drenched in his blood as she desperately hopes to see his eyes flutter open, "BREATHE! BABY, PLEASE BREATHE!"

Laying her head on his chest, desperate to feel his heartbeat but met only with stillness, she cries out in a desperate plea, "DON'T LET GO!"

When the officer attempts to pull her away from Colston's body, she resists, interlacing her fingers with his bloodied left hand. As she is finally separated from him, she watches in slow motion as his hand falls lifelessly to the ground.

All sound has vanished from Kayra's world; her heart trembles, and she feels cold. She watches as a sheet is drawn over Colston, and in that moment, she loses her breakfast and faints.

It has been three hours, and Kayra gradually becomes aware of the scent of wet wipes tinged with blood. The sinking feeling in her heart intensifies as her awareness sharpens. *He can't be gone!* she shouts in her mind.

"Colston?" she dares to ask, her voice barely breaking through the darkness behind her closed eyes. Praying that this is just a terrible dream, she lies in bed beside him.

There is a shift, and then a familiar hand grasps her left hand while the other gently runs through her hair.

"Mom?" The words emerged from a constricted throat. She refuses to open her eyes.

"Yes, Ka. I am so sorry."

Kayra rolls toward her mom's hand, buries her face in the pillow, and sobs.

Her mom gently runs her fingers through Kayra's hair. Kayra opens her eyes and meets her mom's sympathetic gaze.

"My Colston can't be dead!" She sits up and wraps her arms around her mom.

"Shh, sweetheart," Kylie says gently as Kayra sobs into her shoulder.

Kayra feels the rough texture of a hospital gown against her chest as she pulls away from her mom, tearfully glancing down at herself. She notices a smear of blood on her jeans.

"Where is my shirt?" she asks.

"In a bag in the corner, it is covered in blood."

Kayra looks at her with relief, whispering, "It's his shirt."

"I'll wash it," Kylie says with care.

I held him..." she sobs, her voice breaking.

The hug from her mom is tight. "Shhh, Ka. This is going to be a very difficult road."

Kayra moves her hands, seeking comfort by fiddling with her engagement ring, anything to feel close to him. Her heart sinks when she only feels her wedding band. She raises her hands to examine her fingers, only to discover that her jade heart is missing from behind her wedding band. "Where's my engagement ring?" she asks, panic rising within her. She senses him fading from her side once again.

"It is safe in my purse until we can clean it properly."

"I want it," Kayra demands.

Kylie gives her a sad, pleading look. "Please wait until it is clean."

"Mom, please!" Kayra nearly shouts.

"Ka, quiet down," Kylie says as she reaches into her purse, pulls out a handful of tissues, and carefully opens them. Kayra's eyes blur when she sees the green heart now painted over in red. She takes the ring and slips it onto her finger, then hugs her hand to her chest as she hears the door to the room open.

"I'll answer questions later," Kayra says, folding herself into a ball.

"Sweetheart, it's us," a weary male voice says.

Kayra looks up and sees Elliot and Patricia.

Kayra and Patricia exchange a glance of cordiality in the wake of Colston's death.

"Kayra, what happened?" Elliot asks pleadingly.

"I'm not entirely sure..." She pauses, contemplating her next words. She wonders if she should simply tell the truth now that it is too late for Colston. The weight of the truth might be too much to bear. Kayra gazes into the haunted eyes of Elliot.

He drops to his knees and shuffles toward the bed, holding his trembling hands out to Kayra, "My boy lies in a morgue, killed by a gunshot to the chest. Please! Who committed this atrocity?!" Elliot sobs.

Kayra clenches his hands and holds a look of pity. The desperation in his eyes terrifies her.

After her dad died in a fall at work in 2016, Kayra and her mom discovered some stuff. Under the label, *Rhavin and Driscoll's Search of Justice.* When they asked Elliot about it, Elliot explained that he and Savion had worked tirelessly for two years to uncover the identity of their son's kidnapper. He admitted that their efforts had yielded no results and expressed his intention to stop obsessing over it in order to help his family cope with their loss. Kayra, Kylie, and Elliot decided not to inform Colston about this.

"I believe it was the man who kidnapped him," Kayra says, her heart shattering.

Elliot squeezes her hands and buries his face in the sheets, hiding his anguished expression.

"Dad!" Kayra cries.

Patricia moves forward and wraps her arms around her husband while casting a glare at Kayra. Kayra does her best to maintain civility, and she is about to ask a question when Elliot cries out, "I couldn't protect him!"

Kayra feels Elliot loosen his grip on her hands. She frees them and attempts to place one hand on each of their shoulders.

When Patricia angrily shoves her hand away, "Don't touch me." She warns.

Taken aback, Kayra huddles against her mom. She is trying not to take it personally, as she has just lost her son. However, Kayra feels compelled to address the situation; her heart is too heavy with grief to ignore this behavior. "Patricia, please, I--"

Patricia glares at her and slaps her, saying, "You fell out of love with my boy!"

"What the hell?" Kylie asks, protecting Kayra.

Kayra is too stunned to speak.

Elliot looks up.

"Oh, stop it! You only stayed with him for his money!"

"Patricia!" Elliot exclaims, "It is not the time! Our son, her husband, has met a tragic end. We should be comforting one another."

Elliot gazes at his wife, who regards him with a cold expression.

"I want you to leave," Kayra says evenly.

Patricia gazes at Kayra blankly and says, "Wow, we are just grieving our loss."

"Dad can stay, but I want you to leave. Colston would not have tolerated you slapping me, even in grief," Kayra asserts, standing her ground. However, her throat tightens with emotion.

"Come on, Elliot. Let's mourn for Colston elsewhere," Patricia says, straightening up.

Elliot remains still, extending his hand toward Kayra. She takes it, feeling comforted, and she yearns to cuddle in his arms. With his other hand, he reaches into his pocket and pulls out an object, speaking while glaring at his wife. "To Kayra, my daughter, my son, your husband told me that if anything were to happen to him, there are many things he would leave behind, but there is one thing he wanted you to have." Elliot turns and presents Kayra with Colston's wedding ring. This ring, which Colston had ordered, is made of tungsten, featuring interlacing strands of blue and gold in a diamond pattern that wrap around its entirety. Inscribed on the inside are the words, *His Kayra*.

Kayra reaches out to take it when Patricia's expression shifts from surprise to anger. "How did you get that? I thought it was with me, along with the rest of his stuff."

"I would like his wallet," Kayra says, concerned that she might attempt to access his hard-earned money.

"So you can continue living off his money!" She retorts sharply. "You're just going to sell the ring!"

Elliot jumps to his feet as Kayra hides against her mom, sobbing. He firmly grips Patricia by the shoulders and says, "You promised! For the sake of Colston's memory, put aside your personal grievances. I don't know what changed after you had Colston, but you are no longer the woman I married. You believe you are entitled to our son's things after you abused him and then attacked his wife. In my heart, I know that Colston fully forgave Kayra, and she still truly loves him.

Give me his wallet, now!"

The room falls silent under the mounting tension. Kayra's heart trembles at the sight and longs to be enveloped in Colston's arms.

Patricia does not take her eyes off Elliot. When she reluctantly reaches into her purse and retrieves a clear bag, Kayra instantly recognizes Colston's wallet and the small notepad he always carried with him.

Elliot grabs the bag, and Patricia, tearfully, says, "Don't bother coming home." Then, she storms out of the room.

"Okay," Elliot whispers, standing there with heavy shoulders.

Kayra pulls away from her mom and slides off the bed. She stands in front of Elliot, tears streaming and his eyes filled with pain. Kayra embraces him, and he immediately returns it, "I am sorry," he whispers. "We went to see him. If you want to, you can go, but I signed the paperwork, so they will be releasing him to you."

"Thank you," Kayra whispers.

There is a knock at the door. Elliot and Kayra remain in their tearful embrace as two detectives enter.

"Kayra Driscoll?"

"Yes?" She says.

"We are truly sorry for your loss. I am Detective Sage, and this is my partner, Detective Fox."

"Please tell me you know who did this," Kayra asks directly.

Detective Sage steps two paces into the room and says, "His name was Lance Vaclav."

"Was?" Elliot asks, beating Kayra to it.

The man glances back at his partner, who makes no effort to intervene. He lowers his head and, as if burdened by guilt, says, "After shooting your husband, he shot Todd Ulric before turning the gun on himself."

"Todd was there? Where was Melody?" Kayra asks.

"Melody Dakota was killed by Todd," Sage explains.

Kayra is shocked; her mind is in turmoil, but one thought stands out above the rest: "Was he behind Colston's kidnapping five years ago?"

Finally, Detective Fox interjects, "The investigation is still ongoing, at which point you will be asking Conright and Barnet."

Kayra breaks the embrace and faces the detectives squarely. "This man, I refuse to acknowledge as anything other than a cold, calculated murderer; that man is HIM! I don't want my husband's name shared with the public. I will address it when the time is right."

Kylie draws her close from behind.

"Thank you, detectives. My daughter-in-law will be eagerly awaiting your findings," Elliot says.

As the detectives exit the room, a doctor comes in, "Too many people in here. I need everyone out."

"I want to go home," Kayra says.

In the car, Kayra lies in the backseat, curled up in a ball. Colston's ring rests loosely on her thumb.

Elliot is in the passenger seat after

being left stranded at the hospital.

"Kayra," Elliot says, looking back. "I am so sorry. I shouldn't have brought her."

Kayra nods, her gaze drifting as she absently plays with Colston's ring.

Elliot reaches back and gently places his hand on her head.

Kayra grips his hand with her right hand, her eyes shifting to meet Elliot's. "I understand why; if she hadn't slapped me, she would have been fine." Her voice is hoarse.

Arriving home and stepping out of her mom's car, Kayra stares at the empty space beside her car. His voice echoes in her mind. She feels utterly lost; the silence is deafening, and the world's colors seem duller in his absence.

Before seeking solace in his studio, Kayra takes a shower to wash away the remnants of blood. As warm water cascades over her, she suddenly finds it difficult to breathe.

"Colston!" she screams.

"Kayra?" her mom calls, rushing in.

Kayra steps out of the shower and into her mom's embrace. They both collapse onto the floor.

Kylie cradles her daughter as she weeps for half an hour.

Kayra stands up numbly and gets dressed. Not a word is spoken as she enters Colston's studio, while Kylie joins Elliot in the living room.

She closes her eyes and hears his voice echoing within these walls.

That bastard stole him completely and

then followed him into death! She screams in her mind.

She picks up her phone and prepares to make the most difficult call she's ever going to make. She dials Jordan.

"Kayra, I hate to make you guys wait, but I need to finish something for Colston and I." The excitement in his voice is enough to twist and churn Kayra's stomach.

Kayra speaks gravely. "Jordan, I need you to sit down."

There is a heavy silence on the other end of the line. No doubt, Kayra has just extinguished the creative storm that was blowing Jordan's sails. She hears the strangled emotions.

"Ka----yra?" Jordan's voice comes over the line, pleading.

She just spits it out, "Colston was killed!"

She hears the phone drop and then disconnects. With trembling hands, she redials.

The phone picks up to Jordan, who is sobbing, *"This----can't----be!"*

"He was shot while up at therapy!"

"What!" There is a pause, and Kayra anticipates the next question. *"Was it him?"* The darkness and hatred that laced that question are frightening, especially coming from Jordan.

Kayra responds as quickly as she can, through sobs, "It was Lance Vaclav, and he took his own life after shooting Colston."

The noise emanating from the phone line is inhuman; the agonizing sound conveys both pain and sadness, deeply unsettling Kayra. She cries out louder, yearning to embrace him, "Jordan?"

His voice is much softer. *"I just saw him yesterday... There was so much hope."*

"JD, please, I need you."

"Kayra, I am packing up and coming back."

"Please drive safely."

"I will. See you tomorrow; stay strong," Jordan says.

Kayra hangs up and places her phone on the desk. The noise continues to echo in her mind as she walks out to join her family.

She curls up against Elliot's right side while Kylie gently rubs her back.

The air is thick with questions, but Kayra cares about only one: Why Colston? A question that she knows she will always be asking.

The next time she awakens, it is dark, and she finds herself in bed next to her mom.

She gets up, mindful of her throbbing head, and makes her way to the bathroom. She splashes cold water on her face and sips some from her cupped hands. As she gazes at her reflection in the mirror, she takes in her swollen and red eyes.

"What am I supposed to do?" she asks herself. Oh, how she wishes to be wrapped in his embrace.

She collapses to the floor, her hand gripping the edge of the counter. She stifles a scream, reflecting on the past week and a half as she watched Colston struggle relentlessly, only to have his life taken away. She screams silently.

"Kay?" The weary voice of her mom calls from behind her.

Kayra turns and falls against the cupboards. "How long does the pain last, Mama?"

Her mom sits down with her and says, "When you love someone so deeply, having them ripped away from you so suddenly leaves a lasting scar." Kylie pauses and adds, "Father died three years ago, and late at night, when I can't sleep, I cry and beg for him."

Kayra hugs her and says, "I loved him so much."

"I know, hon, this road is not going to be easy. Just remember," she says, gently adjusting Kayra so she can point to her heart. "He's there, just as you were with him."

That brings Kayra some comfort. Her mom gently lifts her head and says, "Don't feel ashamed of your grief. Releasing is the best way; just listen to your mind about how to express it."

Kayra, with her mom's guidance, returns to bed.

The enticing aroma of pancakes rouses Kayra from her slumber. Although they smell delicious, her stomach churns. Reluctantly, she drags herself out of bed.

Walking into the kitchen and taking in the sight from the hall, Elliot is cooking while Kylie is wiping down the island.

"Morning." Kayra greets them in a soft voice.

"Hi, hon," Kylie says, abandoning her cleaning to embrace Kayra.

"Morning, Kayra," Elliot says.

He glances at her and says, "I have a question."

Kayra and Kylie broke their embrace. "What?"

"Sunday. What was truly going on?" Elliot asks as he is dishing up the food and turns off the stove, his face contorted in agony.

Kayra stares at him, recalling his reaction to what they shared that night. "I asked Colston the same thing last week: if he would ever tell me the full truth about his ten-day ordeal. He said he didn't know, and that his reality in the hands of his captor was a nightmare only the two of them could comprehend." Kayra is doing her best to hold it together. "At this point, knowing the truth would not provide any comfort."

He simply shrugs and nods, "Pancakes?" he asks, tears welling in his eyes.

"Maybe later," Kayra says, turning to head into the studio.

"An hour, please. You need to eat something."

"Alright,"

Kayra walks into the studio and locks the door. She lies down on the floor on her stomach, pretending to hold Colston's hand. "Never ask me to let you go again," she says, tears streaming. "Why couldn't he just leave you alone!?" she yells.

She sits up on the floor, reaching blindly for paper and a pen, and begins to write.

Will this grief ever leave?
I ponder as I grieve
For the love I never got to express.
For the words left unsaid, causing distress.

His final farewell resonates within my soul.
Leaving me feeling broken and cold
I held him close, but now he's gone
Leaving me in sorrow to mourn

I wish I could turn back time
To tell him I love him, to make it right
But now all I can do is cry
And wonder if this pain will ever take flight.

The memories haunt me day and night.
Of the moments we shared, now out of sight
Regret fills my heart; tears fill my eyes.
As I try to come to terms with his untimely demise

I yearn for closure, for peace of mind.
To let go of this grief that's left me blind

Will this sorrow ever fade away?

Or will I be haunted by it every single day?

Will this grief ever leave?

Perhaps not, but I'll learn to believe.

That one day, we'll be reunited above.

And I'll finally get to say, 'I love you, my love.

She gazes at the words, which are both painful and true. How is she meant to do this on her own?

There is a knock on the door. "Please leave me be!" Holding the paper to her chest, hoping to hear his voice again through the words.

"Kay, please, it's me." The voice is soft and trembling.

"JD." Kayra stands up, unlocks the door, and pulls it open before throwing herself into his arms.

Jordan embraces her tightly, reminiscent of the embrace he shared with Colston yesterday.

"I am so sorry, Kayra."

Kayra remains silent.

After a long while, she whispers, "Thank you for coming back."

"I'd rather be nowhere else, and I am here for as long as you need me."

"Hey, sorry to interrupt," Kylie says gently.

Kayra and Jordan are looking at her.

"There is a detective here; he is just inside the door."

Kayra steps away from Jordan's embrace and approaches him to extend a formal invitation into her home. As she gazes at him, she is looking upon the icy demeanor of the detective who had rebuked Colston in the hospital.

Kayra envisions squeezing Colston's hand to prevent herself from taking an action she might later regret.

"Let's move away from the door," Kayra says, striving to keep her voice as steady as possible.

They stop a few feet from the door, and she doesn't offer him anything.

"What is your name and badge number?" Kayra asks straightforwardly.

"Silvester Barnet, 17175. I have what remains of Mr. Driscoll's personal effects, and I have a few questions regarding some items." He holds up a clear, sealed bag.

There is his phone, the only item belonging to Colston that hasn't been returned. What catches Kayra's eye is a smaller, sealed bag containing an unfolded piece of paper smeared with blood.

"Can I see the paper?" Kayra asks.

"Yes, that is what I had a question about. There are two sheets of paper, set back to back," he says as he opens the first bag and pulls out the second one. He pauses before handing the bag over. "First question: during the autopsy, it was discovered that there was very recent damage to Mr. Driscoll's vocal cords. Prior to his death, did he engage in excessive yelling or perhaps singing?" His words are not gentle.

Kayra gazes past the bag, her attention fixed on the side where the upper left-hand corner is drenched in blood. Only the word *Through* is readable at the top, and a lot of the first verse remains indecipherable. "No! Colston took care of his voice. Perhaps he was screaming for help!"

Barnet remains unfazed by Kayra's outburst and hands over the bag.

Kayra turns the bag over in her hands. The other side is free of blood, and the title reads, *Let Me Go.*

"What is your question?" she asks through gritted teeth.

"On the phone was a private video from Mr. Driscoll's Collective channel. While the lyrics differ, the choruses closely resemble the original in the video. Any idea what they mean?"

Kayra senses Jordan looking over her shoulder. "Jordan, is this his sword and shield?"

"I believe so," Jordan replies. "Was there any damage to the pha-- to the killer's vocal cords?" he asks, recalling the sound of Colston singing the chorus through his studio door.

"I am not at liberty to discuss that, but this one," he says, pointing at the blood-smeared paper, "contains both Mr. Vaclav's and Mr. Driscoll's fingerprints. The other one, found in Mr. Driscoll's back pocket bears only his prints. Additionally, Mr. Vaclav's fingerprints were also found on the phone. What does 'sword and shield' mean?"

"I don't know! He was trying to save himself because you guys failed him!" Kayra screams.

Jordan interjects before Barnet can continue, "Whether or not you answer my question, Kayra, I don't believe Colston's vocal cords were damaged solely from screaming for help." He wants to believe that Colston's final moments were not spent in desperate cries; "He sang for his life. Remember, his voice had broken through the killer's insanity at the house. Perhaps this was his attempt to replicate that." Jordan concludes.

Kayra found it to be both a great comfort and, at the same time, heartbreaking.

"Why are there two different sets of lyrics?" Barnet asks, only half-interested.

It is Jordan's turn to express his irritation, "I don't freaking know! I was not there!"

Kayra gently leans into his chest and asks, "Answer me this one question: Was the man who murdered Colston also behind the kidnapping?"

"We are still working on it," Barnet says as he opens a folder. "These are the release forms for Colston's body. I need your signature, and once you have made arrangements with the funeral home, we will transport the body."

Kayra is fuming as she signs the papers. "I do not want to hear the announcement of my husband's death on the news!" she reiterates.

He nods, takes the signed paperwork, and

then shows himself out.

Kayra, Jordan, Elliot, and Kylie are left staring at the lyrics to *Let Me Go*.

"This was the last thing he sang," Jordan says in the stillness.

For Kayra, life is a cycle of tears and numbness, oscillating between the studio and the bedroom. The pain and burden of her loss show no signs of leaving her mind or body. She wears his ring on a chain long enough to press it against her heart.

On Monday, the 16th, the family was able to arrange a funeral service after having the body released late Saturday. There could be no more than ten guests, and the only time the director could accommodate them was Wednesday at 5 p.m. Additionally, only Kayra could come the following day, Tuesday, to bring clothes and view the body before the service. Any form of wake must be held in a private home.

She agrees and is instructed to arrive at the funeral home by 11 a.m.

The parents leave the house at noon on Monday to give Kayra some space.

Not much is said between Kayra and Jordan. They are dealing with their loss in their own ways. Not wanting to intrude on one another, they each occupy different spaces in the house.

Jordan sits in the living room, utterly bewildered. He reflects on the mash-up, *The Dying Lament,* which conveyed hope amidst tragedy. Why couldn't it be translated into real life?

"Kayra?" he calls out.

"In the studio," she calls back.

Jordan gets up to join her because he has a question.

He finds her lying on the floor and sits in the hallway just outside the door.

"Can I ask you something? You don't have to answer either."

"Okay,"

"Has Melody reached out?" Jordan asks.

Kayra pops her head up, looking confused. Then her grief stricken mind reminds her of how little she has spoken to Jordan since he returned. "I am sorry I didn't inform you about everything that happened. Todd killed her, and after the phantom shot Colston, he shot Todd before taking his own life."

Jordan is astonished by this: "Why so much death?"

"I don't know, but all of this could have been prevented. After I tend to my husband's body, I will take action."

"I'll be right beside you," he says, still in shock.

Kayra lies back down and says, "JD, I am not ready for a life without my songbird."

Jordan is unsure how to respond to this.

Later that night, Jordan couldn't sleep, so he got up. He stands in front of the studio, hesitant to step into the sacred space. Since returning, he had not stepped foot in the room; he felt as though he would be intruding on Kayra and this place, which held great significance for Colston. Not wanting to taint that connection, he had refrained from entering. He teeters on the brink of breaking down, aside from the distress he expressed upon first hearing that Colston had been killed. He held it together for Kayra.

Taking a deep breath, he enters the studio, only to be immediately brought to his knees. Why couldn't he escape the grip of fear?

"You should be thanking me for preparing you for such an outcome." His own hardhearted voice echoes in his mind.

"Not now! Not now!" Jordan insists in a hushed tone.

Jordan crawls to the computer and turns it on. Through a cascade of tears, he navigates to Colston's channel and clicks play on a random video.

Kayra is awakened by Colston's softly singing voice.

"Cole?" she whispers.

She moves to get out of bed and opens her bedroom door. The door to his studio stands ajar, and the glow from the computer spills into the hallway. Kayra cautiously approaches the open door and peers inside. A figure is slumped over in the chair, resting against the desk.

"Colston?" Her voice is soft as she steps into the room.

Kayra places a hand on the shoulder; her heart leaps with joy while simultaneously sinking into a profound sorrow. The face that turns to meet hers is Jordan's.

His eyes are tired and red. They widen immediately upon seeing Kayra. He stands and whispers, "Sorry. Sorry."

Jordan attempts to leave, but Kayra stops him by grabbing his arm. "JD, stop," she says gently.

He attempts to pull away and responds, "No, I have intruded on his space."

"Jordan!" She pulls him back, her voice cutting through his panic.

He faces her, his head bowed like a child caught in a place he ought not to be. "I just couldn't sleep," he says weakly.

Kayra caresses his cheek and whispers, "Who are you being strong for?"

"You, Kayra. He was your husband," Jordan says.

Kayra urges him to sit back down, and he complies. She pulls up the other chair and sits, taking his hands in hers. "You lost your brother, your singing partner," she says gently. "Your grief is just as valid as mine. As for intruding, do you want the truth?"

Jordan nods, tears streaming, and his heart feels at peace.

"During the eight years that Colston owned this studio, he never invited anyone inside. If he were to collaborate with another artist, he would rent a different space. You and I are the only people he ever permitted to enter here."

This surprised Jordan, as he knew Colston to be laid-back and not particularly fussy about anything other than his voice.

"Why?" Jordan whispers.

Kayra shrugs and replies, "Don't know."

A video begins to play, immediately capturing Kayra's attention. *Tell Your Heart*

To Beat Again, Colston's first cover following the kidnapping. The struggle was painfully evident in his eyes. He was still quite weak, yet he was eager to return to work. Mostly out of fear that he might not have the strength to do so.

"It took him so long to get past the first verse without being reduced to tears," Kayra recalls. "The intense sobbing would follow, and then he would psych himself up for another attempt. I could only listen and pray. I knew he needed to do it, but at the same time, I wanted the pain to end."

Jordan leans forward in the chair and pulls her closer.

"We should get some sleep; tomorrow is not going to be easy," Jordan says, holding steady.

Chapter Twenty-Two: Was it Him?

Among the desolate, fog-encrusted streets, she walks; the only sounds breaking the stillness are her footsteps and her breathing. She feels as though she has a destination, as her steps carry a sense of purpose. There is a disconnect between her heart and mind, a rift she fears will never be mended, for much of her heart died with him. Her hand finds the ring hanging around her neck. How can this simple piece of metal bring her comfort? It was the man who wore it that was the comfort. The beating heart, the voice that could soothe the soul. Yet, she is not ready to compromise... But has she already?

Her feet have halted their forward progression, and she emerges from her thoughts. She gazes at the street clock looming above the fog; its hands continue to move as time ticks on. She scrutinizes the inscription: *Idaho, Welcoming Mountain Paradise.* The words seem to tremble and rewrite themselves. *He who for whom the clock ticks lies on the brink of death; only upon the final breath will relief from suffering come and new light dawn.*

"No one survived! Suffering still exists for those who must bear the memories!" Kayra's anguished voice fades along with the fog.

Revealing a man standing on the grass patch, dressed in a black leather jacket and dark blue jeans, Kayra feels her breath catch in her throat. The man glances over his shoulder, his brown eyes deep and vibrant, reflecting the glow that always used to radiate from him. Colston turns fully, exclaiming, "Kayra!" His wide smile shows no trace of the nightmares, memories, or the phantom who once haunted him as he runs toward her.

"Colston!" she cries, sprinting into his arms.

Their bodies immediately lock in an embrace, both sobbing. Kayra kisses him with such desperation and claws at his shirt.

"Kay?" he asks gently.

With her arms wrapped around the back of his shoulders and her ear pressed against his chest, the hollowness kills her, reminding her that this is not real. "What?" she sobs.

She feels his fingers gently playing with the ring that hangs from her neck. Looking up at him, she asks, "Did you want this with you?" Her voice is tinged with pain, but she adds, "If you want it, you can have it."

His fingers glide up her neck to her chin, and he shakes his head gently. "You keep it, but I want something to remember you with me."

She reaches up and intertwines her fingers with his. "Anything."

"I want your words," he says, brushing his lips across hers.

Slightly confused yet enjoying her husband's gentle touches, she asked, "What do you want me to say?"

"No," he whispers, kissing her ever so delicately. "I want the poem."

"Your poem?" she asks, confirming.

"Yes," Colston says. "I want you to promise that you will continue to live."

His words pierce her heart like a dagger. She gazes at him through tear-filled eyes and gently caresses his face, saying, "I will live, yes. But I am still married to you."

"Honey, don't throw away anoth--" She places her fingers on his lips.

"Colston, we aren't divorced; you have merely departed from the mortal realm. Your arms are the only home I desire."

He hugs her tightly and says, "I will be waiting for you to come home."

"Can you sing to me?" Her eyes are beginning to grow heavy.

He smiles and lowers their entwined bodies to the ground, gently beginning to sing, *"We had a melody woven across the skies, strummed on the strings of our old lullabies. Let each note linger; let the music sway. In every heartbeat, I'm never far away.*

In echoes of laughter, in whispers and sighs, I'll be your harmony, where love never dies. Though shadows may deepen and daylight may flee, find strength in the music; it's where you'll find me.

And if silence weighs heavily upon your soul, remember our stories; they'll make you whole. I'll be the echo in each sweet refrain; in laughter and love, I'll forever remain.

So dance through the darkness; let your spirit ignite; for love is a beacon that shines through the night.

So cry for me, my love, when the rain begins to play, but don't forget to dance; let your heart lead the way. Live for tomorrow; let the sun kiss the night. When I'm gone, just hold on to the light.

In every moment, I'll always be there. When the world spins, I will be in your song; just remember the love; it will carry you along."

Kayra wakes up with a bittersweet smile. "I love you, Colston," she whispers. She gets up with that song in her heart. As she opens the small linen closet, hiding in the back of the bottom shelf is an old shoebox. She slides the lid open; there resting, atop a pile of old, folded papers and small trinkets, is Colston's poem. The memory of his warm breath and the gentle brushing of his lips against hers lingers in her mind. She reads the poem repeatedly, tears welling in her eyes. Although she could simply copy it, that idea feels wrong to her.

The poem in hand, she gathers Colston's clothes and lays them out on the bed. Then, she prepares herself, her mind quiet, allowing his final song to resonate for as long as possible.

She dresses in jeans and one of his shirts, contemplating whether this is how life will be, silent and dreary. All she desires is him, not substitutes! While folding his clothes, she suddenly crumples to the floor. Her heart trembles with pain as she hears him say, *"I want you to promise me that you will continue to live."*

She buries her face in the shirt and says, "How? I asked you never to ask me to let you go."

There is a gentle knock on the door of the bedroom. "Kayra? I have coffee for you," Jordan calls through the door.

Kayra is on the floor, her legs drawn up and clutching a shirt. "Please, come in!"

Jordan opens the door and finds Kayra in her vulnerable state. He places the coffee on the dresser and sits down beside her on the floor. She immediately leans into him, and he holds her effortlessly.

"I believe the hardest thing is the absence of justice for Colston," Jordan says. He has been attempting to channel his pain, sorrow, and anger in a constructive direction. However, he finds himself unable to shake the thoughts of whether this is what Colston must have experienced.

"I want to know, but at the same time, I don't care. In the end, Colston is gone. Confirming that the man who killed him and the man who kidnapped him are one and the same is going to be maddening." Kayra pulls away. "It's almost time to go."

Jordan drives to the funeral home while Kayra sits in the passenger seat, holding Colston's Sunday best in her lap and trembling. His poem is tucked away in her pocket.

"I don't think I can look at him," Kayra

says as they approach the parking lot.

"You can simply ask to hold his hand. Do whatever is least painful for you," Jordan says, aware that nothing will alleviate her pain.

Kayra takes a few deep breaths as Jordan arrives at the funeral home.

"I wish you could come with me."

"I do too, but I'll be right here when you come out."

Kayra dons a mask and enters the building. The atmosphere is thick with sorrow and grief. She nearly collapses to the floor, struggling to accept that her beloved husband lies in this place.

"Are you Mrs. Driscoll?" the young, flamboyant man asks in a quiet, polite voice.

"I am," Kayra forces out.

"Alright, are those his clothes?"

"Yes." She hands them over with a tremor in her hand.

"Allow me to dress him, and then you can come back and see him."

"Please, I just want to hold his hand," she says as he begins to turn and leave.

The young man smiles gently back at her. "I understand. I will cover him up but leave his hand and arm exposed. You will then have up to an hour." He turns and exits through a pair of swinging doors.

Off to her left, soft piano music plays. She closes her eyes and listens.

"Mrs. Driscoll, he's ready." The young man returns about half an hour later and finds Kayra seated in one of the plush chairs.

Kayra opens her eyes and stands, but suddenly, she forgets how to walk. She looks helplessly at the young man, who offers her his arm. With his assistance, she is able to walk again.

Through the swinging doors and to the left, he stops in front of a curtain.

"He's on the other side," he says, releasing her.

Kayra slowly pulls the curtain aside. She sees the outline beneath the sheet and his right hand lying exposed. A sob escapes her lips as she immediately grasps his cold hand.

"Colston!" she cries, resting her forehead on his arm. "My songbird, I love you."

She places her hand on his still chest, pleading, "Please..."

She then feels a cold touch on the back of her hand. The shock causes her to jerk her hand away. Moments later, a familiar calm washes over her. "Colston?" she whispers, turning her palm upward as she places her hand back on his chest.

Her trembling hand is enveloped in cold. A loud sob escapes her lips as she lies against his chest. "I love you, Colston Driscoll," she whispers, feeling a chilling touch on the back of her head.

Then, light and airy, words spoken close to her ear drifted softly: "I love you too, my love."

The cold and calm fade away. Kayra's heart feels a sense of relief after their exchange. She believes she will be alright; this grief will pass, though she will always carry a missing piece, one that can never be filled by another. 'Till death do us part' No, 'Till death do we live, until we finally meet in everlasting slumber'.

Kayra spends the rest of the time lying on his chest, gazing through blurry eyes at his sheet-covered face.

Why did you have to die? This question echoes in the silence.

"Mrs. Driscoll, I'm afraid it's that time," the young attendant speaks softly from behind her.

She gently slides the sheet away from his face, revealing his peaceful expression, free from nightmares and pain. She kisses his lips softly, then uncovers him to the mid-chest to access the breast pocket of his suit. With trembling fingers, she retrieves his poem from her pocket and whispers as she places it into his pocket, "May these words keep you until I join you." She gives him one final kiss.

Her walk away from his body is the most difficult journey of her life, and her heart cries out for him. The young attendant remains close until she reaches Jordan, into whose arms she collapses while standing in the middle of the parking lot.

Jordan holds her in silence. After a moment, Kayra begins to walk toward the truck, still embracing Jordan.

"Mrs. Driscoll?" A deep voice sounds

She and Jordan turn to see two detectives approaching them. Kayra and Jordan recognized the detectives as the duo who had previously ganged up on them.

"Why?" Kayra asks, frustrated at being interrupted during such a sensitive moment.

"We would like you to come to the station. We have concluded our investigation."

"Was it him?" Kayra asks insistently.

"I'd rather not discuss it here," Conright says.

"Yes or no, that is all I want. Then we'll come."

He looks away for a moment and says, "The man, Lance Vaclav, was behind the kidnapping."

Kayra and Jordan are seated in an interrogation room, where they are offered drinks and snacks. The officer who escorted them there, while Barnet and Conright prepared the necessary materials, informed them that this would be a lengthy process. Kayra accepts the offer of water, as she has been plagued by a persistent headache that she has barely managed since that fateful day.

Jordan rejects everything; he feels nauseated by the betrayal that Colston must have experienced. Uncertain if he wants to hear more, Jordan recalls the discomfort he felt after listening to Colston's account of the forest fight that nearly cost him his life. Now, he is about to learn how this malevolent man ultimately ended his life. He remains for Kayra, determined to ensure her safety throughout this ordeal.

Kayra is still in awe of her interaction with Colston's spirit. She considers sharing the experience with Jordan, but before she can make a decision, the door opens, and in walk Conright and Barnet. Conright is carrying a box, while Barnet is carrying a thick folder. Conright sits the box down on the table, and Barnet places the folder beside it. Then, he stands with his back against the wall, arms folded.

Conright watches this with evident dissatisfaction. He sighs and shifts his attention to Jordan and Kayra. "Lance Vaclav," He opens the folder and pulls out a picture of a scrawny, pale-looking man.

Jordan and Kayra are now gazing at the man who has caused them so much grief.

"26 years old, the only legal documentation of him is a birth certificate discovered among Todd's papers in his home office."

"Wait, Todd? And he was 21 when he took Colston," Jordan says.

"Yes!" This exclamation comes from Barnet, whose tone is filled with vitriol.

Conright glares at his partner as he continues the explanation. "From the limited information we could gather from Todd's family, they seemed indifferent. Lance was the child of Todd's sister from an affair; he was essentially passed off to Todd. For reasons unknown, Lance was never enrolled in school or daycare."

Kayra and Jordan are listening to this, wondering if they will reach an answer to the main question: Why Colston?

Conright opens the box and reaches in with both hands. When he pulls them out, he holds two fists full of bagged journals.

"These contain Lance's life from the age of nine onward, in his own words. The kid was too smart for his own good. 'The Demon' left him alone in the dark because he didn't deserve the light. Although he was encouraged to improve and strive for better, the writings from ages nine to twenty primarily depict Lance enduring harsh criticisms, followed by words of endearment. This dynamic shaped him into a man with misconceptions about how to communicate with others. 'The Demon', of whom we concluded was Todd, had given Lance a laptop at the age of sixteen. From that point, we learned that Lance turned to the internet to explore hacking, trap-making, and police procedures, hoping to gain 'The Demon's' approval. The Collective Creative Entertainment platform provided him with a space to connect with others who shared similar interests. However, his lack of social skills created a barrier to forming meaningful connections. When provoked, he would respond vindictively with his words; his subscriptions numbered well over one hundred, and he was active in the comments section of each." Conright replaces the journals in the box and retrieves a stack, setting them down on the table.

Kayra notices the label on the top of the bagged journal: Colston Driscoll's Obsession Begins. Jordan also sees the title and leans back. "Kayra?" Jordan whispers.

She looks at him, noticing his hesitation. "What?" She asks, placing a comforting hand on his arm.

"I can't listen to this. This monster

documented everything! It's like a twisted memoir; I can't..."

"Jordan, I understand. You can go," Kayra says, squeezing his hand.

"I'm sorry," Jordan says, getting to his feet and leaving.

Kayra stares at the closed door, pondering whether any clarity will emerge from this situation or if she will be driven to madness by ambiguous explanations.

"Mrs. Driscoll, may I offer my input about listening any further?"

Kayra gazes at him expectantly.

"There is no closure in these journals; it is merely a descent into madness. Lance's desire to possess the voice entirely frees him from his own torment, leading him to create a justifiable reason for taking Colston. This rationale made sense to him, and he imposed it upon Colston, who resisted, ultimately provoking Lance to resort to violence. I can read some passages if you wish, but they contain detailed descriptions of everything, with Lance expressing remorse and regret each time he harmed Colston. While the war between morality and deep desire raged within his mind."

"A detailed account of the horrors my husband endured and survived." Her gaze shifts to Barnet. "You still believe it was staged! Even with the evidence and the fact that Colston is dead!"

"He didn't want to face the truth!" Barnet growls as he rushes toward the table. "Colston took advantage of what Lance lacked! Turning it into an obsession!!"

He empties the entire folder of pictures, which predominantly depict Colston's injuries. Two images come to rest directly in front of Kayra, while the rest are scattered across the floor.

The first picture depicts Colston's face, which is marked by bruises, and his lips appear chapped and pale. The second picture shows his bare chest, featuring a hole just to the right of his sternum and a deep graze extending down the right side of his chest.

Kayra gasps as she tries to push herself away from the table. She tips the chair over, "Jordan!" She screams as she presses herself against the wall on the floor.

Conright, after the pictures were discarded, seized Barnet by the collar of his shirt.

"What the hell?" he whispered sternly.

Barnet glared at him crossly, saying, "Stop playing the good boy." Barnet shoved Conright.

The door opens, and Jordan enters and hears.

"You thought the same way too!" Barnet exclaims, storming past Jordan as he exits.

Jordan briefly glances at the pictures as he walks toward Kayra.

The look of pain that Jordan sees in her eyes, he crouches down, "Kayra?"

"Colston... was... shot... twice!" Kayra exclaimed as she hugged him.

Jordan embraces her back.

Conright clears his throat. "Only one of the three was fatal." He has been picking up the pictures and has now laid out several pages in clear protective coverings.

The detective's nonchalant delivery of such devastating news infuriates Jordan. "Jesus fucking Christ! A little tact would be nice!" He stands with Kayra, who is crying against his chest.

Conright bows his head. "The two other wounds were grazes, possibly intended as a warning to maintain control. There was also a slash across his left arm, indicative of a defensive wound."

"Is that supposed to make it better?" Jordan exclaimed in frustration.

His heart breaks. Colston had fought for his life, even with the odds stacked against him. Jordan buries his face in Kayra's shoulder.

Conright continues to explain, "Something changed in the way he wrote after deciding to kidnap Colston. Amidst the ramblings and planning, this phrase is repeated for two consecutive pages: *'Means to an end; to satiate the demon; to silence the seething storm within.'*" He pauses, turning the protected page toward them.

Jordan and Kayra do not move toward the table.

Conright continues, "The next phrase appeared on nearly every other page during the ten days and a few weeks following the fire: *'The Demon never cared; the storm deepening.'*"

Kayra listens to the words penned by a disturbed individual. Words that convey pain and suffering. Yet, all Kayra feels is loathing.

"This one repeats over the past five years: *'Means to an end. Pain and misery to follow. Why bother?'* The final sentiment has dominated the last week and a half: *'Means to an end... My dearest Colston, you are the end.'*"

"WHY!" Kayra screams. "What is the point of reading those?"

Conright slams his palms down on the table. "We were dealing with insanity!"

Jordan looks at him and says, "That does not excuse your disregard for the real danger that Colston was facing." He then steps away from Kayra and approaches the table.

Conright straightens up, his chest puffed out. Jordan stands firm, stating, "You can't do your job if you already blame the victim." He then asks Kayra, "Is there anything else you would like to know?"

Kayra stands momentarily stunned by the question. She approaches Jordan and asks, "What happened in that room?" She asks thickly, "Why did no one hear the gunshots?"

"Please take a seat. Be advised that this is a forensic retelling and nothing more." The tone is unkind.

Jordan is bewildered by the indifference shown towards the overwhelming number of preventable deaths. It appears that Conright is annoyed and is deliberately making the situation as uncomfortable as possible, likely because any investigation into this matter would pose significant risks for them. By manipulating the insanity surrounding the phantom, they can deflect blame onto Colston, who was merely a content creator caught in a web of complications, thus shielding themselves from accountability.

"You staying this time?" Conright asks, gazing intently at Jordan.

He stares back and takes Kayra's hand. "Yes,"

Kayra squeezes his hand in gratitude.

Conright sighs and begins, "Melody Dakota arrived in the suite at 9:30 a.m. According to her schedule, Colston was the only client for the morning." He flips through some papers stacked behind the pictures in the folder. "Between 9:45 and 10:00, Todd and Lance entered. Melody was shot and died instantly."

Kayra tucks into Jordan.

"Colston entered the suite at approximately 10:20. Around 10:47, the first bullet grazed his right thigh. Forensic evidence indicates that he was turned away and moving toward the door. The bullet that struck him was fired from the same gun that killed Melody."

Kayra stares at Conright, water streaming. "Todd kept him from escaping?"

"Yes, the knife slash occurred when he was near the door, around 11:06. The next bullet graze happened moments before the fatal shot, at approximately 11:29. Colston punched Lance in the side of the head, but the gun must have been aimed directly at his chest. When it accidentally discharged due to the surprise attack, it grazed the side of his chest. The fatal shot was fired at point-blank range. I must emphasize that Colston's fight was extraordinary, as he should have died instantly."

Kayra's face is now nestled against Jordan's chest.

Jordan narrows his eyes at the detective, wanting to chastise him for depicting Colston's struggle to survive. He seems to share the belief that Colston chose death over confronting the truth. As he hears Kayra crying again, memories flood back of the dance Colston and Kayra shared in the kitchen while they worked. Jordan slams his fist on the table, startling the other two. "Speaking of insanity! Insanity is what you did to Colston! That man deserved a long and fulfilling life after the ten days of hell he endured!" Jordan can't contain his emotions.

His eyes scan the table, catching glimpses of words, most of which the detective had already read to them. However, he reads something that takes his breath away.

Colston was slumped over my shoulder; dead weight, useless, yet still lovely and beautiful. Fucking heavy, so I heaved him off my shoulder and onto the ground. His face was peaceful. 'Fucking bastard!' I kicked him, then dropped to my knees beside him, crying as I caressed his face. It was then that I realized he wasn't breathing. 'Colston?' I began chest compressions in a desperate attempt to save My Colston...

Jordan feels incredibly ill. Colston had died in the forest, but that maniac saved him, and it was not the last time the phantom refused to allow Colston to let go. Only years later did he kill him. Why? He looks at Kayra, the sorrow and exhaustion clear on her face, and he shares her sentiments. Although the officer is not proceeding to answer the second question, Kayra is grateful; a realization dawns on both of them. They pieced everything together, understanding that it was two against one in that room. A question lingers, the final question. This is one they are reluctant to ask, for knowing the truth would drive them mad. "Did the phantom ever plan to reclaim Colston? After five years, was the plan merely to kill him?"

Kayra stands, doing her best to hold herself together. "I have heard enough. Jordan, let's go."

"Mrs. Driscoll, wait. Here." Conright holds out a small bag. "I don't expect this to provide comfort or understanding, but this is for you. Take it with you and do with it as you wish."

Kayra hesitates to take the bag containing a rather dirty piece of paper. However, if she doesn't take it, she will be left with yet another unanswered question. She decides to take it. "I will return in two days to provide my statement to the public," she says, glancing at Jordan, who nods and stands up to follow her out.

Once outside the station, Kayra turns and collapses against Jordan. He simply embraces her, with tears of his own.

"Kayra, let's go home," Jordan says softly.

Kayra simply nods and allows herself to be guided to the truck.

Jordan has numerous questions about the phantom; he couldn't bring himself to refer to him by name. Why did he fixate on Colston? What was his motive? He refuses to accept that Colston died solely due to insanity; there must have been some underlying intent. Unfortunately, that truth is now lost to the earth, allowing negligence to persist.

"JD?"

"Yeah?"

"Do you think you could help me with something?" Kayra asks.

"Sure?..."

"When I make the public announcement, could you somehow stream it on Colston's channel?"

"I can do that."

Chapter Twenty-Three: The Finale

Kayra stands before the closed casket, dressed in a simple black dress. Behind her, the family waits patiently for her to say her final goodbye.

"I know that you are in my heart; I hear your voice echoing in the walls of my mind. The thought of you confined in a box beneath the ground shatters my heart into a million pieces." She kneels beside it. "A poem for you, my songbird: in the stillness of our shared home, from which my songbird took wing. Leaving me in solitude, longing to be folded within. Oh, Colston, your sweet melodies. Now lost. All that remains is an absence unsought. Your voice, the lullaby, to keep the monsters at bay; your heartbeat, its rhythm guiding my way. Now silent, leaving me adrift in sorrow. I search for your essence in spaces so hollow. Your absence is a void, a haunting silence in the air. I ache for your gentle care. My songbird, my companion, answer me. I'm on my knees. In the stillness, I hear it in the breeze. I hear your song, a whispered promise. Oh Colston, my songbird; within your melodies, I find solace as I wait for our reunion in a celestial palace. I love you, my dearest Colston." She stands and sits between her mom and Jordan.

The casket begins to lower as Kayra watches, the song *Gone Too Soon* by Simple

Plan playing in the background. Anger ignites in her heart; her home is gone. She screams silently in her mind, burying her face in her hands. Jordan gently holds her to keep her in the chair.

Jordan can no longer bear to watch the box being lowered. He embraces Kayra, resting his cheek against her back. The pain is nearly unbearable to have his life taken so suddenly and violently.

Kayra feels the arms of her mom wrap around her and Jordan. At this moment, she wishes to be alone.

Jordan and Kylie support her as they leave the cemetery. Kayra is overwhelmed with exhaustion. Once in the truck, she leans against the window and asks, "Do you think we could postpone the reception?"

"If you want to, honey," Kylie says.

Kayra yawned, "I would; we can reschedule for this weekend." Kayra's eyes grew heavy as she imagined being in Colston's embrace.

Jordan notices her nodding off. "She's asleep," he says in a softer voice.

"Good. I can stay if you'd like, so you can get some sleep," Kylie offers.

Jordan looks back at Kayra and says, "It's up to you."

"I am glad you are here; it means a great deal to her."

"Colston was like a brother to me, and she is like a sister. This has been incredibly difficult," Jordan says.

"He should never have left the world the way he did," Kylie says.

"No,"

At the house, Jordan carries Kayra inside. Kylie informs the family about the change in plans.

Jordan gently lays Kayra on the bed. She whispers, "Goodnight, Colston," before rolling onto her side.

This is devastating. Jordan retreats from the room, entering the studio and locking the door behind him. He stands with his hands flat on the desk, overwhelmed. He breaks completely, dropping heavily to his knees and sliding down to the floor. Gripping the handle of a drawer, he pulls it out of the desk, allowing it to fall on top of him. He remains there, sobbing.

He weeps himself to sleep.

He wakes up with an extremely dry mouth. As he shifts objects off himself, a folded piece of paper falls, revealing a bit of writing: *The Poison Within*.

Jordan picks it up and unfolds it. It is a song--the poignant words filled with sorrow yet profound desire of survival.

"Did he really think there was no way out?" Jordan wonders to himself. There was another piece of paper stapled to the back.

If this is found and I am in the house, please call me out. If I am no longer around, please continue reading. I feel light after the memory I have just shared, yet my heart weighs heavily with dread. I can't escape this deep-seated feeling that I am destined to die at the hands of the phantom. From the first moment I gazed into those voided eyes, I understood that my escape would require a miracle on my part or that he would have to be killed by other means. That being said, I refuse to give in or give up. I will continue to fight with all my heart. Kayra, you saved my life, not just over the past five years. My voice was my purpose, and when you walked into my life, you gave it meaning. I love you dearly, and I am so grateful that you chose me.

Love until the last breath,
Bloody and beaten, I will defend you.
My time grows short, but my love for you will never wane.
Live a full life with our memories cherished in your heart.
The crimson stains on my skin are a testament to my devotion,
A battle fought with unwavering resolve to protect you.
Though the sands of time slip through my fingers,
My heart remains steadfast, a beacon of eternal affection.
In the fleeting moments that remain,
I implore you to embrace the life we've shared.
Let our cherished moments be the light that guides you,
A tapestry of love that will forever be eternally woven into your being.

Your songbird, forever.

Colston

"What kind of power did that man possess to leave Colston in a state of utter helplessness?" Jordan asks the paper.

The picture depicted him as a scrawny man who appeared incapable of carrying two one-gallon milk jugs simultaneously. He recalled the voice, commanding and seemingly untouchable. Undoubtedly, it was embedded in Colston's psyche, further ingrained by the fear of physical pain. He stands with the papers in hand and leaves the room.

Kayra sits in the dimly lit kitchen,

sipping from a mug of tea. Jordan approaches her, wraps an arm around her shoulders, and kisses the side of her head.

"What you've got there?" Her voice is laden with sorrow.

"From Colston," Jordan whispers tearfully as he hands it to her while preparing himself some tea.

Kayra reads the pages, running her fingers along the handwritten words. "JD, how did he live with this?" Kayra asks. "He tried so hard to protect me from it."

Jordan shrugs and says, "He was fighting against the odds with hope."

"Tomorrow, I want to make it clear what happened," Kayra says.

Jordan nods. "I am with you."

Kylie prepared breakfast, and the enticing aroma lured Kayra and Jordan out of their respective rooms.

"Hi, kiddos," Kylie says, attempting to sound cheerful.

"Hi, Mom," Kayra says, feeling both empty and determined.

"Morning," Jordan greets her.

"Hungry?" She turns around, holding two plates of pancakes and eggs.

Both Kayra and Jordan nod as she sets the plates down. She says, "Kayra, Sunday, Elliot, and I, along with a few others, are going to help you start clearing out Colston's belongings."

Kayra is forking a piece of pancake into her mouth. Her eyes flash with betrayal as she shakes her head while chewing. With her other hand, she clutches Colston's ring, which hangs securely around her neck.

Her mom places her hand on the back of Kayra's hand, which is holding the fork, and says sympathetically, "It's not healthy to live with all his belongings."

"Mom, you said you still cry out for Dad. Having him ripped away so suddenly leaves a scar. I just buried him less than twenty-four hours ago. Why this sudden push?"

Kylie gazes into her daughter's eyes, which are filled with exhaustion, sorrow, and resentment. She sighs, "You are young, and I want you to be happy."

The betrayal is evident and remains steadfast. "Colston was and remains my everything," she says, fiddling with her wedding ring and then with Colston's. "I don't want another. I will be laid next to him when my time comes."

"Jordan?" Kylie asks, turning to him for help.

Jordan looks down, stabbing at the pancake. "Please honor your daughter's wishes. This isn't just a simple case of moving on; the last five years have been difficult. The week and a half leading up to his death was particularly challenging." Kayra places a hand on his back as he continues, "I do not want to let Colston go. So you can imagine what it is like for Kayra."

Kylie looks at both of them. "Alright."

They finish eating, and Jordan looks at Kayra, "Are you going to do this?"

Kylie gazes at them with curiosity.

"Yes," Kayra says, turning to her mom. "We are going to the police station, and I will publicly release Colston's name as one of the victims in the triple murder-suicide."

"Why can't you let someone else handle it?" Kylie asks.

"I want there to be an understanding of the pain caused by negligent police work. Mental scars are just as real, if not more dangerous, than physical scars."

Kayra and Jordan enter the police station at about 1:30. Kayra requests to speak with Detective Conright and Detective Barnet.

"I am Detective Chloe Togghill, replacing Barnet," she says. Turning to look into the busy squad room, she spots Conright in the far corner, seemingly preparing to leave. "Conright!"

He speaks without looking up. "Chloe, I said I was leaving. I have a flight to catch!"

"Think again, Detective!" a voice booms from behind the trio. Jordan and Kayra jump, while Chloe merely bows her head. The others in the room continue with their tasks, yet they keep an attentive ear tuned to the unfolding drama.

"Sir," Conright says, turning around.

His gaze immediately lands on Kayra, and a flash of anger crosses his face.

"Sir," he says, his tone slightly more whiny, "this trip took us four months to organize. Let Chloe and Oliver handle the public announcement." He returns to gathering his stuff.

The man, presumably the captain, moves past Jordan and Kayra. He stops in the center of the room and says, "If you walk out of here, you might as well make the trip permanent!"

Movement in the squad room comes to a complete halt as Conright stands up straight. Without turning around, he states, "I am entitled to time off." His voice is steady, yet tinged with anger.

"Indeed, you are; however, you took an oath to protect and serve. Some cases test us and push us to our limits, but the mishandling of this one is unacceptable!"

Conright turns to face his captain, his face flushed with anger. "Mishandled! What the hell? The evidence was clear!"

"Did you ever take a look without Barnet's influence?" the captain questions.

Conright stands there, staring, "Evidence is evidence." He says coldly.

The captain glances back at Kayra, his expression filled with remorse.

"I doubt Mrs. Driscoll would have expressed the same opinion. There is a reason for us to analyze the evidence and inject care."

Conright appeared offended by the comment. "Don't talk to me about fucking care, alright! The number of cases I have genuinely invested in. More than half, HALF! ended up being staged or faked. Do you know how disheartening that is?"

"But you still worked each case to completion; you maintained a strong sense of duty and care, as each and every case is unique." The captain says, "When you arrived here and discussions about reopening the Colston Driscoll case began, I assigned you to it not only because of your experience with cases involving content creators but also due to your tireless approach to solving these cases. Although I was aware of Barnet's biases, I hoped you could teach him a thing or two." His voice drops to a whisper.

Conright takes an aggressive stance toward the captain. "You used me?" he demands, visibly shaking. "I never thought this would happen in a small town. Yet here I am, in the hot seat after being on this case for two weeks! Barnet should take this wrap, not me!"

"You remained in it, as Barnet couldn't handle the heat. However, at this moment, you are merely attempting to wash your hands of this case. Complacency has sunk in. Colston lies dead, along with others. The aftermath now begins. Understanding, why all this death?"

Conright lowers his gaze, and the room remains still.

"Mistakes are inevitable because we are human, but in this job, such errors cannot be tolerated. The loss of innocent lives is an unfortunate consequence of unforeseen actions. However, these incidents can be minimized through vigilance and care on our part." The captain's gaze shifts from Conright to the others in the room. "When that badge is on your chest, you must protect and serve your fellow human beings. Leave bias, prejudice, and personal beliefs at the door of this establishment. Here, behind the badge, we are individuals dedicated to helping our community and upholding the law. If you cannot forgo your personal agenda in favor of your oath to the badge, then you may leave right now."

The room is silent as the captain's words sink in. Conright stares at Kayra, and his hand rises to his badge.

"You must have known something; they always tell someone because they crave the attention," he says, his voice tinged with desperation.

Kayra moves forward slightly and asks, "What is it that you hope to hear from me?" Her voice trembles.

"Some sort of publicity stunt that went a little too far? What would have made it more believable? They could have asked for a ransom."

Kayra is hurt and upset by Conright's failure to acknowledge the evidence that is right in front of him.

"Detective!" the captain exclaims, appalled.

"Detective, I implore you to open your eyes and your heart. You have been scarred by prior cases; Colston was a gentle soul who had no need for such an extreme stunt." Kayra says.

Conright lowers his hand and bows his head.

"You have two hours to prepare our statement. After that, you will be on a two-week suspension, and you can choose whether to return." The captain says, raising his finger and twirling it, "Back to work, everyone! Acarus!"

The room jumps back to life as Conright sinks heavily into his seat. Chloe is seated at the desk across from him.

"Sir?" A familiar voice calls from behind Kayra and Jordan.

They turn and see Oliver, who is dressed in a suit and wearing a badge on a chain around his neck.

"In two hours, there will be a press conference. Could you escort Mrs. Driscoll and Mr. Youngblood to a private room where they can wait? Please provide them with some refreshments and cots." The captain says, then turns to Kayra. "I am truly sorry for your loss, but Colston's death will bring about change."

Kayra nods.

"Come on," Oliver says.

He leads them down a narrow hallway at the back of the squad room. As they pass doors and cells, they turn right into another narrow corridor with a single door at the end. Oliver opens the door and allows Kayra and Jordan to enter. The room is a small lounge, furnished with two couches and a glass-top coffee table. There is a kitchenette nearby. "The bathroom is back in the hall, the first door on the left after you round the corner," Oliver explains as he approaches them. "I am so sorry for what happened. If there is anything my family or I can do to help, please let us know."

"Thank you," Kayra says as she plops down on the couch, feeling mentally drained. "I see you got your job back."

"And then some," he says, sitting across from her. "I was reinstated following the tragedy. As an apology, I was appointed to the position of lead detective in a new unit called Creative Shadow. This unit focuses on crimes involving content creators and stalking. I regret that it took Colston's death for people to start taking these types of crimes seriously."

Kayra looks at him, tears flowing, "If his voice can lift people's spirits and his death can save lives, then... I suppose I can live with that."

"I gotta get going, but feel free to help yourself to anything in the kitchen. Someone will come to get you when everything is ready."

Kayra is left within her thoughts, a whirlwind of emotions vying for her attention, leaving her trembling. Jordan sits down beside her and pulls her close.

"I miss him," she whispers into his chest.

"Me too... Me too."

She wakes up to find herself wrapped in Colston's arms, his warm brown eyes gazing at her.

"Why did you have to leave me?" she asks tearfully.

He lightly brushes her tears away with one hand. "It wasn't by choice; I had exhausted all I had. Honey, I tried."

Kayra pulls him close and whispers into his chest, "Shh, Colston, I love you."

She feels his body go limp. She squeezes him and sobs.

Jordan feels Kayra fall asleep against him. He leans his head back, his mind replaying the interaction in the squad room. Although he is angry at Conright for wishing that Colston had faked everything, he can't help but feel sympathy for him. It must be difficult to view his job as a joke only to have a real situation lead to death. He also admires Kayra for remaining calm while speaking to Conright.

Kayra begins to sob in her sleep, startling Jordan. Her eyes snap open, and Jordan wraps his arms around her. She returns the embrace and asks into his chest, "Do you remember that heavy feeling I told you about?"

"Yeah?" Jordan wonders.

Kayra swallows hard and looks up. "The moment he walked into that building, the looming heaviness lifted."

Kayra is interrupted by a knock at the door. It opens, and the captain peers in, "We are ready."

Jordan embraces her and gently kisses her on the forehead. He whispers, "There was no way to know what was happening. It is not your fault."

They stand up, and Jordan quickly rushes out to join the crowd, preparing to stream. He writes a description to clarify that Colston's channel has not been hacked: "Guys, Jordan Youngblood is behind the camera. This press broadcast will provide some insight. I will be making a follow-up video in the next couple of days. WARNING: VERY SENSITIVE TOPIC."

The captain takes the podium first, and Jordan goes live.

"I want to thank you all for being here. Today, we will fully address the tragedy that befell our town last Wednesday. I will now hand it over to the lead detective on the case, Detective Atticus Conright."

The captain steps aside, allowing Conright to emerge from the wings and stand before the numerous cameras. "On March eleventh, 2020, a horrific event unfolded in the late hours of the morning. In a place where one goes to seek help and mental relief, Healthy Minds, Better Lives became the setting for a nightmare. The air was thick with gunpowder, and blood was spilled. Todd Ulric, a very renowned trauma therapist, shot and killed Melody Dakota, an up-and-coming therapist who was covering for Mr. Ulric while he claimed to be out of town. Following the shooting of Ms. Dakota, the next client entered the suite." He glances over at Kayra, who is waiting for her turn. "Out of respect, I will not reveal the name just yet. Also present in the room was Mr. Ulric's nephew, Lance Vaclav, was a disturbed individual who used his uncle to trap the client. They share a troubled history. It appears that a verbal and physical altercation ensued, ultimately leading to Mr. Vaclav shooting the other individual, leaving him to bleed out on the floor. Mr. Vaclav then entered Mr. Ulric's office and shot him before turning the gun on himself. The events of that morning went unnoticed, as a memo was sent out to the occupants of the building. Aside from Melody, who was needed because of the client, the building was supposedly closed for electrical repairs. This was a senseless act of violence. I now turn the floor over to a family member of the client."

He steps out of the camera's view. As he passes Kayra, he casts her a glance filled with both anger and compassion.

Kayra takes a deep breath and steps into view of the cameras. "Hello, my name is Kayra Driscoll, and I stand here with a heavy heart. The name of the client was Colston Driscoll. Colston was a cover artist on the Collective platform. He struggled to cope with the torment he endured after being kidnapped and held for ten days by Lance five years ago. Living in a constant state of instability, the memories became all-consuming. He was abandoned by the system when it became clear that Lance was coming for him again. Despite this, he remained hopeful, believing he was entering a safe place, only to be confronted by the face that haunted him. Bearing a gunshot wound to the chest, he crawled from the second floor to the main door of the building. Dying in my arms, Colston fought against this menace until his final breath. I pray that in future cases where the perpetrator is as elusive as a ninja in the night, only the victim's emotional and mental scars remain. More care should be appropriated toward those suffering from the unseen battles and fighting desperately to maintain their sanity. Thank you."

Kayra walks away when someone grabs her wrist. She turns to see Conright's face, his eyes flickering between the two conflicting emotions. He gently releases her wrist and storms past her. As Kayra watches him leave, Jordan comes into view.

His eyes are filled with tears, and the sympathy is clear. Kayra rushes to him and gently places her fingertips on his lips. "No," she whispers, "it's going to be said repeatedly, becoming hollow. Let it linger in your eyes. I will not think less of you in your silence."

Jordan takes her hand and leads her to the truck. "I will be there in a while; I am going for a walk," he says, embracing her.

"Be careful," she says as she bids him goodbye.

Jordan walks several blocks away from the commotion, his phone buzzing incessantly with social media notifications. He silences the phone and turns into an alley.

His back collides with the building, and he buries his face in his hands. "Colston, I'm so sorry!"

"What are you sorry for? There was nothing that could have been done," his own studious and hardhearted voice replies.

"Shut the hell up! This should have never happened! He was fighting so hard."

He waits for a smart response, but when nothing comes, he exclaims, "What! Nothing to say!"

Jordan's chest aches. He shakily pulls

out his phone, hoping to seek some comfort from the comments. He notices a text message from Colston and opens it tearfully.

Jordan, buddy, if you are reading this, it means that I am either gone or that my forgetful self neglected to dismiss this message. I want to thank you for everything you have done for me and Kayra. Please ensure that she is safe. Jordan, I am proud of you and cheering for you in spirit. In the wake of the worst. The music must dominate; sing, JD, sing. I'll be listening.

Love your brother.

Colston

Jordan leans his head back against the wall and says, "I will sing, and with every note, your memory, strength, and passion will endure."

Kayra walks into the empty house, the absence of life made even more palpable by Colston's lingering scent. She places the keys and her phone on the kitchen island, ignoring the barrage of calls and texts. Making her way to Colston's studio, she shuts the door behind her. It was crucial that Kayra deliver the news about Colston's death to those who cared for him, as it helped overcome any doubt that Colston Driscoll was truly gone. However, she had hoped that sharing this news would bring some relief. Instead, she feels the weight of sympathy, a constant reminder of her profound loss.

Now she fully understood Colston's

silence regarding the truth of his kidnapping, as well as the meaning behind his final note. That deep-seated truth had entwined itself around his very soul.

Her gaze landed on the bag that contained the mysterious note given to her by Conright, the final question in this bewildering and surreal tale known as Colston's Phantom.

Kayra opens the bag, retrieves the paper, and unfolds the single page.

Kayra, I warned you and begged you to release My Colston. Look at what your refusal has led to! I knew how to save him; I could have, but like you, he was stubborn. I thought there might be a chance that after five years, his desire to survive and thrive would have kicked in. He spat in the face of my patience when he screamed and collapsed to the ground at our shared place, continuously showing resistance. I hoped to see him give me a sign that he was ready to leave it all behind and belong to me... he failed to save me. Unfortunately, I knew this, but I refused to accept that he'd let me fail. His eyes, his voice, and his very existence revealed the monster I am. So, I stole his life, just as he stole mine.

Kayra collapses to the floor, her world spinning and her heart pounding. The insanity makes her scream. Her throat aches from the outburst, and her head throbs. *He was not yours! HE WAS MINE!* Her mind echoes, "Colston, I am so sorry!" she cries out, feeling the struggle against the haunting memory.

There is a knock at the front door, but she makes no clear effort to get up. When the knock sounds again, this time more forcefully, Kayra heavily rises to her feet, her hand wrapped around his ring as she stares at the note on the floor. In her mind, she thinks, *"You may have held him captive with horrific memories, but I hold him in my heart with love and care."* She then walks out of the studio.

We remain in the studio as Kayra departs from Story's eye. The tale is exhausted, and it is time to move on. Still aware that Kayra has gone to answer the door, we sit in the stillness of this room, which is built on passion and love. We hear commotion, along with Kayra's cries and pleas. Frozen in place, Colston's story has ended, yet Kayra's has only just begun, waiting for Story to decide when the time is right.

We part ways for now...

SIDE STORY 198
JOURNEYER HERGENRATHER
CYCLE 15/67

Unfettered Ending

Dear Sior Asumanove,

The next part of this story is mainly for myself. Before the book took a turn during the 2024 rewrite that set the stage for Colston's death, I never intended for him to die while facing the phantom. I wanted to illustrate everything he endured without having him falter at the end. My goal was to convey hope for survival and the ability to overcome nightmares. By accepting what I call the "true ending," I was able to finish the book without much of a struggle. Permitting bittersweet notes to permeate throughout the rest of the narrative. I now feel confident in presenting my version, the "unfettered ending" You may choose to continue reading or skip to the Coda, where I will speak to you again. Thank you for reading.

Chapter Twenty-Four: Brink of Death

Colston gazes into the darkness of the eyes; the platform wobbles, the chain rips from his grasp, and he plummets toward the fire. A painful shockwave ripples through his body. His ears ring, and he struggles to catch his breath. The phantom caresses his cheek, and Colston reads the phantom's lips: "In the arms of eternal slumber, we are free. I will see you soon." Releasing the stranglehold on his throat, the phantom stands and walks out of his sight.

Colston lies on the floor, staring up at the ceiling. His world spins around him; he feels his heart pounding against his chest, numb with pain, yet he cannot draw in a breath. He has failed; it was foolish of him to attempt to escape the insanity.

The cage in his mind finally bursts open, launching his freezing, broken body backward. As he helplessly flies through the air, he tilts his head back to see where he is about to land, and that is when he catches a glimpse of a fire rushing toward him. At his current velocity, he has only moments before he is engulfed in flames. With his mind blank, he looks up and sees a wooden platform tumbling end over end, falling ahead of him. He hears it smash into the ground with tremendous force. The part of him that was on the platform collides with the other, merging together. He rotates in the air and slams onto the ground, landing on his chest and expelling the air from his lungs. Splinters from the platform stab into his chest. Unable to see the wild and threatening fire that is undoubtedly bearing down on him, his view is blocked by the large, thick platform. Struggling to catch his breath, he buries his face in his arms. He feels the heat, but it is not overwhelming. Looking up, he realizes he is shielded by a wall of light and the platform. Then suddenly, all the light breaks free from the protective barrier, enveloping his body in warmth and the light of hope.

Get moving! Your life depends on it!

A gasp forces air back into Colston's lungs as the nightmare subsides, only to be replaced by panic and the pain of his current situation. Tears of frustration flow; he is near death, yet he finally feels the sense of completeness that he has fought so hard for.

He refuses to let it all spill onto the floor. Rolling onto his stomach, he begins to pull himself toward the door. His breathing becomes increasingly labored. Wincing in pain with every inch he crawls, his body tingles with numbness.

He sobs, feeling his strength fade. His mind fixates on Kayra as he tumbles down the stairs, weeping; screaming is beyond his capability. At the bottom, he rests, the darkness encroaching on his vision. His heart thuds loudly in his ears.

"Fight; get to the arms of your wife."

The emotions overwhelm him, causing his chest to tighten. Ignoring the pain and weakness, he crawls until he reaches the front door. Managing to get halfway outside, he lies there, hoping and praying that Kayra will see him. He feels the rain hitting his face, mingling with his tears.

He hears a distant sound, but he can't be sure what it is. The view of the fading gray sky and the raindrops is shielded from hitting his face when Kayra appears.

Seeing her face, he relaxes; the pain in his chest numbs to a dull quiver. He reads Kayra's lips as she urges him to hang on. With his shaky right hand, he grips her hand, which is pressed against his chest, applying pressure to the gunshot wound. He dares to speak through his broken throat, "Please----I'm----not----ready!" Panic rises as his vision begins to blur. He watches her face turn away as she screams for help, the sound seeming distant to Colston. When she looks back at him, he reads her lips again, the ringing in his ears and the thudding of his heart drowning out all other sounds. He reads her lips, "Please, baby, help is coming. Don't leave me. I love you!"

Colston weakly utters, "I..." before drifting into the painless darkness.

Kayra experiences the full-body strain it took for him to say, "I..." and watches his eyes slide close. The rain mixing with the blood that steadily oozes through her fingers, as she applies her full weight to Colston's chest. "COLSTON! PLEASE!" she screams, hearing the distant wail of sirens approaching. Beneath her hands, she can feel the rhythm of his heart softening, yet still holding on. In that moment, she prays to God to save Colston.

It feels like an eternity for Kayra as she watches her husband battle for survival. When help finally arrives, she is pulled away from Colston, her eyes never leaving his still face. Questions bombard her: What happened? What is his name? Who are you? And are you okay, ma'am? All go unanswered. Once they stabilize Colston enough for transport, a struggle with a bullet lodged in his chest, and the significant loss of blood, Kayra tearfully pleads, "Please, he's my husband; can I ride with him?"

The youthful-looking officer gazes at her and says, "They are trying to keep him alive. I can take you; is that alright?"

Kayra pries her gaze away from Colston just before he disappears from view. "Thank you," she whispers, struggling to maintain her composure now that he is out of sight. Regret washes over her with all the things she left unsaid. If he dies without her by his side... *Please, Lord, do not take my love from me. This nightmare must end, and I long to stand hand in hand with him on the other side. Please, oh Lord, in Your heavenly name I pray. Amen.*

She is in the police car, following the ambulance, her blood-covered hands folded together. With all her might, she is willing Colston's heart to keep beating. As tears roll down her face, in the back of her mind, she doesn't know how or why. She understands the feeling of losing him to death; the hollowness and silence left in his wake are palpable, causing her stomach to churn. She shakes her head vehemently, trying to clear her mind of such thoughts because he is going to live.

Drifting amongst the desolate fog, a distant sensation of hands on his face and pressure on his chest. The burning pain gradually dissipates the further he drifts away. He has been here before, and he weeps, as he is not begging God for another chance. He has endured pain and betrayal; to die now, in Colston's mind, is far more honorable than if he had died in that bathroom. Yet, he refuses to let go because there is still a fight within his spirit. He wonders if the phantom has made it to the other side and is met with disappointment that he did not follow.

If he were to simply let go, the last five years would have been in vain. Admittedly, the circumstances would make it more understandable to the onlooker. Colston has been tested beyond normal limits as he grappled with what happened to him while attempting to open that cell. Now that the cell is open, he lies feeling a sense of completeness within the fog of oblivion. The only regret he would have if he didn't awaken is not saying, 'I love you too,' to Kayra.

His heart thunders in his ears, his throat aches, and his body burns; he is returning. This time, he doesn't have to pull himself toward it. It is a relief to have no doubt about where he is going. The darkness around him lightens, and he feels something foreign down his throat. The rhythmic beeping of machinery accompanies his pounding heart. An alarm sounds distantly, echoing in the air. He then hears multiple voices, which is disorienting, and the foreign object is finally removed from his throat, allowing him to breathe fully on his own.

His eyes refuse to open. He feels his body weakening as he struggles to breathe on his own. He longs to hear her voice; among the cacophony surrounding him, none belongs to his wife. He summons his strength, aware that this effort might plunge him back into the fog and darkness with the risk of fading away completely. Colston harbors a deep desire that he must communicate. Wetting his lips and working his jaw, he manages to utter, in a voice that is barely audible, "Kayra."

Kayra has been staring at the same spot on the floor for the past thirteen hours. She sits in shock, torn between the urge to cry out in fear and desperation and the need to remain strong for him. Due to the vastly creeping pandemic, visits within the ICU are prohibited, allowing no more than one family member in the waiting room for longer than four hours. However, given the circumstances surrounding the attempted murder, the hospital has permitted Kayra, her mother, and Colston's parents to remain in the waiting room so they can be close by in case they are needed.

The extent of injuries and internal

damage inflicted in such a short time, along with the significant blood loss, is astonishing. Kayra, along with the doctors, could hardly believe that Colston was still alive. The two bullet grazes were the least of their concerns. The swelling in Colston's throat and the bullet that had ricocheted off his ribs, nicking the esophagus before embedding itself in the right lung, were far more alarming. The surgery lasted two hours, during which he suffered cardiac arrest. Fortunately, they were able to revive him within seconds.

They have received no answers regarding who else was in the room, and Kayra is not responding to any questions posed by the family. She simply lacks the strength to speak; all she wants is to be with Colston, to hold him, and feel his heartbeat. This is the third, and hopefully final, time she will ever find him in such a state. Her heart aches, and she is afraid to breathe, knowing that a life hangs in the balance. She recalls the moment Colston spoke about the aftermath of the fight in the forest. She had stared intently at the floor, listening as he described what it was like to lie on that threshold. Now, she lies there with him in silence, hoping to impart her strength to him. The thought of him dying is a pain that would shatter her world. The idea of continuing on without him is simply too much to bear.

"Kayra, you need to eat," Kylie whispers, gently rubbing her back.

"I can't, Mom. I just can't!" she

exclaims, springing to her feet, only to immediately collapse back into the chair as her weak legs fail to support her. With her trance shattered, the tears she has been holding back cascade down her cheeks. She gazes at her mom and says, "It's been hours since he came out of surgery."

"His body has endured something very traumatic, and his mental state is also affected. The healing process will be slow and lengthy; just remember, no news is good news."

Right then, the door flies open, and a masked doctor rushes into the room. "Mrs. Driscoll?"

Both Kayra and Patricia stand, the doctor's gaze shifting between the two women. "Kayra?"

"Yes?" Kayra asks, stepping forward, feeling as though she might be sick.

"Please, come with me," he says, turning to hurry out the door.

She follows, consumed by worry, tears streaming, unable to ask what is wrong.

He guides her through several corridors, pushing open the door to the ICU. The ICU is arranged in a four-hallway configuration, with an outer corridor encircling the entire area. From the nurses' station, located at the center, the doctor leads Kayra down the left hallway, passing five doors, until they reach the very last one on the right.

The doctor pauses outside the door. "He woke up and said your name, but we took him off the ventilator to prevent him from panicking. He may need to be put back on it, but his request for the name of his wife is a great sign that he is still grounded here." The doctor then opens the door and allows her to enter.

Kayra's gaze settles on her husband, who lies still, eyes closed, and surrounded by steady beeping, telling her that he is still here. She slowly approaches him and gently grasps his right hand, being careful of the IV port inserted there.

The doctor is speaking to another physician just outside the room. Kayra allows the voices to blend with the rhythmic beeping of the machines. An oxygen mask covers Colston's mouth and nose, and the swelling in his neck is horrifying. Most of his left forearm is wrapped in a white dressing. His skin feels cold and clammy against hers, lacking any color. She kneels beside him, gently rubbing her tear-streaked cheek against his fingers.

"Colston?" Her voice is soft; she longs to place her hand on his chest, but she fears causing him pain. Gently, she runs her fingers through his sweaty hair. "Babe, what the hell happened to you?" She kisses his fingers tenderly.

"Ma'am?" a doctor asks, rounding the foot of the bed.

"Kayra, please," she says, looking up. "Is he going to pull through?"

"Kayra, I can say this with absolute certainty: Colston is going to live. If he survived a point-blank shot to the chest, crawled down one story to get help, and then endured cardiac arrest during surgery, he has a fighting chance. Of course, the risk of infection remains significant, and his pulse rate is weak. We opted for the oxygen mask after removing the tracheal tube to prevent any further damage to his throat and to preserve his ability to sing. His body is simply weak and needs time to rest."

Kayra feels a great sense of relief upon hearing that, and her heart jolts as she feels a slight squeeze from Colston's hand. She turns her head so quickly that she feels a pop. "Colston?"

The doctor appears on the other side. "Mr. Driscoll? Colston, if you can hear me, please squeeze your wife's hand."

Colston had been battling the encroaching fog, fearing that he might drift too far and be too weak to come back. He desperately hoped to discern Kayra's voice despite his suppressed and distorted sense of hearing.

The additional oxygen transforms the fight to remain out of the fog from a battle into a gentle pull, enabling him to conserve energy to heal his battered body and calm his troubled mind. In addition to hearing Kayra's voice, he needs confirmation that the phantom is either dead or imprisoned, and that Todd is also securely locked away.

He feels the hand that grips his; through the numbness, he knows it is Kayra. She speaks his name, and it echoes clearly in the space where he rests. It fills him with both comfort and sadness; she is the one who finds him in his worst states. He knows this hurts her, and he desperately wants to wake up, be with her, and hope that the phantom will not have another chance at him. He must be honest with himself in this space; if the phantom is still out there, Colston won't have the strength to play the game of cat and mouse after what has just happened. He knows he should be dead.

Kayra's voice echoes again, asking, "What the hell happened to you?"

Colston cries out into the emptiness, *"They toyed with me, drawing out the fact that the phantom intended to kill me!"* Yet, the darkness held around him. Denying him from seeing his wife. Although this is distressing, he remains calm, knowing he is in the hospital and not bleeding out on the ground. He longs to see his wife's face, relaxed and gazing at him with love. However, he cannot move toward her voice; the pain is nearly unbearable. He understands that he will have to endure it soon, but he feels too weak at the moment.

He can hear the doctor; although his voice is not as clear as Kayra's, Colston has no difficulty understanding the doctor's words. When he shifts his focus to the hand being held by Kayra, it responds to his command to gently squeeze. He simply wants to let her know that he is present and can hear and understand her.

Upon hearing the doctor's request to squeeze Kayra's hand in response to questions, Colston feels frustrated, as he simply wants to commune with his wife. However, he knows he should be grateful for his life, thanks to the medical team. So he releases his frustration, focuses, and then he squeezes Kayra's hand. He hears her tearful gasp and longs to hold her close.

He then hears the doctor speak loudly and clearly, "Colston, I understand that during your healing process, the presence of loved ones is important. With everything going on..."

The desperation is evident in Colston's increasingly tight grip on Kayra's hand, and tears leak out from his closed eyes. His heart rate spikes and then plummets to an uncomfortable level. The doctor places a reassuring hand on Colston's shoulder, "You didn't let me finish," He is gentle with his words, watching his heart rate closely. "Colston, taking your past trauma and the additional trauma from this experience, we have discussed allowing only your wife to be here to support you during this time of healing. Unfortunately," he glances at Kayra, "you are going to be isolated here. Do you think you can handle that?"

Kayra shifts her gaze to him and says, "Yes, I would go more insane being kept from him."

"No other family members are allowed to visit him while he is in the ICU. This decision has been made with careful consideration by myself and my colleagues, despite it contradicting both established and new hospital protocols. Kayra, I must ask you to stay focused and concentrate on Colston. We are currently working on a hypothesis here."

"Okay?" Kayra asks, her curiosity piqued.

"What is it that's worth risking your job over?"

The doctor appears to hesitate before deciding whether to share his thoughts. He glances at Colston with a hint of concern but quickly turns to Kayra, smiles, and shakes his head. "Trust me, everything will be fine. Let me find an escort; give me a moment," he said, starting to move toward the door.

Kayra stands, still holding Colston's hand. "Hey, what do you mean by 'escort'?" Her eyes widen with fear as she looks at Colston.

"This is merely a precautionary measure; we are uncertain if there are other individuals involved in this matter. I will find someone who can better explain."

Kayra, still not appearing any more visibly relaxed, nods and scoots closer to Colston. She rubs her thumb along the side of his hand, and as the doctor leaves, Kayra leans in and gently kisses Colston's tear-streaked cheek. "My love, I will be leaving you for a couple of hours. I will be back before dawn. Please sleep, Colston; please stay alive."

Chapter Twenty-Five: Critical Uncertainties

Kayra kneels down again, gently resting her head on the edge of his shoulder. She doesn't want to hurt him, but she desires to cradle him. She remains there for five minutes, listening to the sounds of machinery while focusing on the rhythm of Colston's breathing, which lulls her into a peaceful slumber.

A soft knock interrupts the quiet, gently awakening Kayra. She lifts her head and turns to see Oliver entering the room, masked, gloved, and dressed in scrubs. The sight jolts Kayra out of her relaxed state.

"Kayra, I apologize for this, but everything is fine; it's just a precaution. I will escort you home and explain everything."

Kayra nods, stands, leans in, and kisses Colston's cheek. "I will be back." She releases his hand and leaves the room, praying that nothing goes wrong, though her heart remains heavy.

Colston drifts back into the fog, exhausted yet relieved that Kayra can remain with him. Although he feels no pain and is warm, he continually reminds himself that this is not where he wants to be all the time, softly whispering, *Kayra, I will come back to you.*

"Doctor McDonald is in the waiting room informing the rest of your family on the situation. We will be exiting through the back to avoid any contact with anyone who may be sick."

"Oliver, why the escort?" Kayra asks.

Oliver sighs as he pushes the door open with his back, allowing Kayra to move past him and step outside into the chilly night. "I am restricted from sharing too much. However, I will say this: I was reinstated as a form of apology for what occurred earlier. Regarding the escort, you are in the red, being the closest to Colston. We are uncertain if there are other accomplices."

Kayra halts near the car and stares at Oliver tears of anger are running down her cheeks. "Now they care?!" she exclaims, feeling a tightness in her chest. "Is it because someone else was involved? Please, Oliver, tell me something. Colston was meant to die; I can see that. But when he was kidnapped and when the man reappeared, they didn't care at all!" Her scream reverberates through the still night.

Oliver steps forward and gently guides her to the car, whispering, "Three people are dead; Colston is the only survivor."

Three? She sits in the car, stunned. Were they against Colston? Did he kill? If so... how? A new wave of panic rises within Kayra's chest.

Oliver sits in the driver's seat and places a hand on her shoulder. "Kayra, what I can tell you is limited since the investigation is still ongoing. It was a setup to get Colston," he says, hoping that this is enough to answer her unspoken question: Who was it?

Kayra is reluctant to embrace the desperate relief that comes with the knowledge of the phantom's death; she wants it explicitly confirmed. However, the thought that Colston may have been the one to have killed him is even more painful. "Did Colston kill?" she asks directly.

Oliver pauses before pulling out of the parking lot. "I... don't know."

Kayra sees that he understands her plight. Tears fall as she says, "I know it was for survival, but... but..." Her voice drops to a whisper. "I don't want him to be a killer."

Oliver nods and shifts the car into drive. Kayra sits crying silently, her heart pounding in her chest. This idea is one she cannot shake.

"Kayra, may I explain a few things to you?" Oliver asks gently.

"Yes," she replies.

"Any clothes you wish to bring will be washed, and any electronics will be sanitized. Colston is vulnerable; even the simplest bacteria could pose a life-threatening risk to him. Once back at the hospital, you will change into scrubs in a private room and be tested again for the virus. When you test negative, you'll be permitted to enter Colston's room." Oliver then shifts his tone, "Kayra, are you alright?"

Kayra looks at Oliver, feeling numb once more. "He was dying right there on the ground. In the room, he gripped my hand, showing that he is still here with me. But until I see his eyes and hear his voice, this dream lingers like a veil. Oliver, I don't want him to be a killer."

"Will you view him differently if he turns out to be one?"

"No," she replies swiftly, "I am concerned about the impact it will have on him. He has endured enough already."

"I understand; I could tell from the little I observed when I walked in that he had been through a lot. Additionally, I didn't see Jordan in the waiting room."

"He doesn't know. He left for home on Tuesday." Her eyes are wide and staring blankly. There is a sense of relief in this, in the hours she spent away from Colston. She didn't immediately rush to him, as she had done after his nightmares in the past. "When I'm back with Colston, I'll call him," she says.

Oliver pulls up to the house. "Let's go."

Kayra sit in the police car, illuminated by the combined glow of the moonlight and the streetlight. Her own car is the only one parked in the driveway. Fear grips her, making it difficult to move. She had come so close to losing Colston, and the possibility still looms, which was utterly terrifying.

Oliver walks around and opens the door. "Kayra?"

"I can't go in there. I don't want to wake up and confront the reality that my Colston is actually gone." She sobs, and tremors ripple through her.

Oliver kneels on the curb and gently

takes her hand. "This is me speaking to you as a friend. Colston is still alive, and he is waiting for help to navigate whatever he is dealing with mentally. But you need to feel comfortable in order to support him."

Kayra nods, still trembling, as Oliver helps her out of the car and into the house. She steps into the dark, silent home, a stark contrast to the morning they had left together. Taking a deep breath, she leaves Oliver and heads to the bedroom. The sight of the empty bed and the vacant house thrusts Kayra to her knees. "He is still alive!" she cries out. Why can't her mind cease its torment?

"Kayra?" Oliver calls from the hallway.

"I'll be okay," she calls as she gets to her feet, repeating in her mind, *"He's alive and waiting for me."*

She packs a few sets of clothes into a washable bag, along with her phone charger and laptop. Not wanting to linger in the empty house, she grabs her two bags and returns to Oliver.

"Ready?" he asks.

"Yes."

Time is nonexistent for Colston as he lies among the fog. At irregular intervals, he surfaces to the sounds of beeping and pain. Each time, he lingers longer, pushing the limits of his body's pain threshold. His eyes refuse to open, and he can only twitch his right hand as he drifts back into the fog. Terror grips his mind as the phantom's laughter shatters the silence.

Colston's body seizes up. He takes a deep, sharp breath, causing his heart to race. Alarms begin to blare, and voices surround him. He starts to taste copper in his mouth as the mask is removed, intensifying the pain in his chest and his overwhelming fatigue. Colston vomits and coughs up blood. He feels himself being moved and desperately wishes against it.

"Colston, stay with us!"

His throat fills with blood; he needs to inhale.

"Colston? Come on, breathe!"

He feels himself fading as he refuses to inhale the blood. He throws his head to the right and forces the blood out.

"Good, Colston. Take slow breaths; get it all out."

"Kayra!" Colston groans, coughing and gasping for breath.

"Nurse, please go get her! Colston, I need you to relax. Your body can't handle this."

Colston croaks, "Nightmare."

"You are safe."

Colston feels his upper body lift off the bed, experiencing immediate relief. He takes his first normal breath and opens his eyes.

"Colston, I have you; just relax," the nurse says. "Just breathe. Hey, it's nice to see your eyes open."

"I don't know for how long," Colston says, through his damaged voice.

"Hey, Colston, it's a start. Just stay with us."

Before Colston could respond with, 'I'll

try.'

"Colston?"

He turns toward the voice of his wife, "Kayra." His voice is just a hoarse whisper.

Kayra rushes to Colston's left side and gently cups his face. "Baby," she says. She is deeply unsettled by the amount of blood around him.

Colston feels himself beginning to drift as he holds her tearful gaze.

"Sleep, babe, I'm here." Kayra can see him struggling to keep his eyes open.

The nurse and Kayra gently help Colston lie back down. Although his chest pain flares, he endures it, keeping his eyes open and absorbing the sight of his wife's face.

"I--love----you," Colston whispers as he drifts back into the darkness.

Kayra watches his eyes close while the nurse repositions the mask over Colston's mouth and nose.

Kayra clutches his left hand. "I love you, babe."

Kayra moves away from the bed, allowing two nurses to work around Colston to change the sheets and change his gown.

"May I ask what caused this?" Kayra asks.

"He said that he had a nightmare." The nurse observes Kayra, attentively watching her reaction.

"I am not surprised; nightmares have become commonplace." She gazes at her husband, who is shirtless. His upper chest is bandaged, but from the edge of the wrappings to his mid-belly, his skin is deeply bruised. "Oh, baby," she whispers, moving closer to the bed.

The doctor is monitoring Colston's vitals. "How often can these nightmares occur?" he asks discouragingly.

Kayra is assisting in dressing Colston in a gown when she responds to the doctor, "They are unpredictable." She looks up, feeling that familiar weight again, and places a hand on Colston's shoulder. "He can't have another, can he?"

"No, unless we induce a coma to facilitate healing, but that presents other complications," the doctor says.

"No, I will help him through if they come again," Kayra says, gripping Colston's left hand. "I want to know that he is here and can hear us."

The doctor looks at Kayra with concern. "I understand the importance of having your husband present, but if his life is at stake, a medically induced coma will allow his body the time it needs to heal. He requires at least a week of rest before facing another nightmare."

Kayra nods as she looks at Colston and gently rubs his head. "I won't get in the way if that time comes," she whispers.

The doctor nods and says, "I will leave you now. Would you like something to drink or eat?"

"Water and a salad, please," Kayra says. Being here with Colston has rekindled her appetite a bit.

"Alright, I will have that sent up right away," the doctor says, walking out.

Kayra slides a chair over to the bed and

sits down, holding Colston's hand.

"Baby?" she asks in a low voice. "I am here; you are not alone. I believe that the phantom is dead. You are safe." She lays her chin on the bed, gently rubbing his hand.

"He's------dead?" Colston asks, his voice barely audible, though his shock and relief are evident.

Kayra pops her head up and says, "Yes, though it wasn't said word for word. You are safe, and you must relax and rest." She watches as his eyes open--though not fully, just enough to reveal their bright hue. They are pained and fearful, but there is something else she notices, something that Kayra thought that monster had stolen. The sparkle in his eyes is stronger than ever, showcasing Colston's strength in this moment. Overwhelmed with relief, happiness, and great fear, Kayra begins to sob. "You need to rest, honey. I'm here."

Colston gathers his voice and expresses his desire to hold her, "Hon, I want to be free, and I survived a second encounter." Colston gasps for breath.

Kayra places her hand gently on his arm, "Shhh, later. Your body needs to heal." She listens to his poor voice. "Another nightmare will do you in."

"I----have----no----control." Colston breathes.

"I understand, but at this moment, he can't hurt you anymore. We can work through the past once you get better. The progress with Melody has been fantastic, and we can get back on track."

Colston shakes his head, and his eyes begin to close. Inside, he screams against the overwhelming pull; he longs to be awake and present with Kayra. "I am----sorry." He takes a deep breath, and tears begin to fall.

"Colston?" She stands, panic rippling through her as she clasps his hand. "Don't let go!"

"I'm... scared," he whispers, his voice fading. His body feels numb as he grips Kayra's hand. "I----don't------want----to------die." His eyes remain open, fixed on Kayra.

She gently rubs his forehead and gazes into his eyes, which are filled with both vitality and fear. "Colston, you are not going to die," she reassures him, her voice trembling with emotion. "Healing is difficult and frightening, but I am here for you. I love you."

"I----love------you,----too." His eyes close as he drifts off, fear swelling within him. His body feels weak, and his heart trembles in his aching chest. These words follow him into sleep: *"Relax, love, sleep. I will be here when you wake up."*

Kayra moves toward the window and breaks down in tears. She feels exhausted and terrified. The certainty she once had has faded away. His body simply needs to rest, but his mind is tormenting him. She glances at his sleeping form, feeling helpless about how to reach him. Hearing him say, 'I don't want to die.' Combining in her mind with him pleading that he wasn't ready when he laid on the ground outside the building. Compels her to give him everything she has. He has been fighting and has won many battles; now, this struggle is about overcoming the damage that has been inflicted.

She cannot bear to watch her beloved wither away on this bed due to his tormented mind. She rushes back to him and sits by his side. Taking hold of his hand, she says, "My songbird, whether you can hear me or not, it matters not. Just know that you are safe and sound. I am here to silence the fear that undoubtedly grips you."

She senses Colston's body respond to her words; another layer of fear peeled away from him. Yet, his eyes remain closed, and his hand stays motionless. She smiles, pleased with the realization that she is helping him.

"Honey, I am going to call Jordan," Kayra says, feeling at ease about contacting him with Colston right here.

Colston's hand twitches in hers. She wonders and then asks, "A good idea?"

A forced cough escapes from him, followed by an even more strained, "Yes."

"Honey, please don't try to talk." It pains her to hear him speak with a damaged throat. She would have preferred to hear him struggle to communicate when the fear of nightmares was present. "Save your strength; just one squeeze of the hand for yes and two for no. Is that okay?"

A gentle squeeze envelops her hand. He coughs dryly and lets out a moan.

"Honey, do you need more painkillers?"

Colston opens his eyes slightly and whispers, "Call Jordan."

Colston, despite his need for rest, feels a strong urge to be present with Kayra. He fears the possibility of not waking up and leaving her to witness his demise. Additionally, he wants to be awake when she calls Jordan so he can help ease the news and support Kayra during this difficult time.

Kayra gently places her hand on his shoulder. "After the call, you need to get some rest," she says, her voice caring yet firm.

Colston smiles and nods.

Kayra pulls out her phone. Glancing at the time, 5:45 AM, she thinks, *God, I'm sorry, Jordan.* She looks at Colston, noticing his tired eyes, and dials Jordan's number. She places the phone on speaker and sets it on the bed in front of their clasped hands.

The phone barely rings once before Jordan answers. His voice is subdued and confused. *"Kayra, what happened?"*

Kayra looks at Colston, her expression filled with concern. "Jordan..." Her voice is soft, tinged with sadness as she squeezes Colston's hand. "Colston is in the hospital and in critical condition."

"He's alive?!" His voice rose in volume and panic.

"Yes."

Jordan openly sobs into the phone, *"I knew it! Something was off; I should have called sooner! Are you okay? What happened?"*

Kayra wonders what he means by, 'he knew it'. But she could ask about that later, "I am... hanging in there; I'm lucky to be here with Colston."

"Colston, my brother." A sob escapes.

"JD, he is awake but can't talk," Kayra says, starting to cry as tears stream down Colston's face. "JD, we almost lost him," she adds.

"Was it him?"

"Yes," Colston manages to say before Kayra has the chance to respond.

"My God, Cole. How... Is he... What?" Jordan struggles to speak straight after hearing Colston speak. He takes a deep, shaky breath. *"The most important thing is that you are safe and still breathing."*

Colston, at that moment, lays his head back on the pillow and gives a voiceless, "Yeah," as he closes his eyes, allowing himself to drift away from the pain. He understands that he needs to drift willingly rather than simply passing out; he might never come back.

Kayra's eyes are fixed on the EKG machine, observing his oxygen level fluctuate between 86% and 87%.

"Kayra?" Jordan asks after a prolonged silence.

"Sorry, Colston fell asleep, and I was monitoring his oxygen levels."

His voice comes over the phone, low and concerned. *"How bad is he?"*

Kayra turns away from the machine monitoring her husband's vital signs and glances at the phone. "JD," she says, her voice hitches with emotion, "He was shot while up at therapy and crawled down one floor and out the front door with the bullet still lodged in his chest. His throat is severely swollen."

"Dear God... Would you mind if I came back down?" Jordan asks.

"Please, JD. You won't be able to see him, but it would be wonderful to know that you are here."

"I just need to be there for you and Colston. I will arrive early tomorrow unless something changes."

Hearing his voice, she feels safe and secure. "JD?" She picks up the phone and moves to the window.

"What? Kayra, please don't shatter the illusion," Jordan pleads.

Kayra is perplexed by Jordan's plea, "What do you mean?" She gazes longingly at Colston, yearning to be enveloped in his embrace.

"The illusion that he is fine. You said he fell asleep. I don't want to accept the painful truth that he is actually dying." Jordan gasps and chokes as his throat tightens with emotion. *"Kayra, please tell me that he's fine."*

Kayra is shaking, her hand resting on the windowsill. "He is stable; he just needs to rest."

"Mrs. Driscoll, are you okay?" An older woman's voice calls from the doorway.

Kayra is startled, nearly dropping the phone. She turns and sees Elnore, who is holding a tray of food.

"Hi," she says softly, "hold on, Jordan."

Elnore moves toward Kayra, setting the tray down. Her aged, caring eyes are filled with concern. "Could I speak to you for a moment?" she asks quietly.

Jordan, I will call you right back."

"Okay."

When she hangs up the phone, the feeling of being worried sick is nearly overwhelming. She wishes she had kept Jordan on the line; she is exhausted and deeply concerned about Colston. She doesn't know how much more she can endure.

Elnore settles Kayra down on the cot. "Kayra, your mother-in-law had to be removed from the hospital," she explains. "She was insisting on seeing her son, claiming that you don't deserve to be with him and that you don't truly love him and that you are trying to kill him. I share this with you so that you are prepared for when you leave here. Here is the card for Oliver Acarus, in case you need a guard for yourself and your husband."

Kayra looks at her, feeling a sense of inclusion amidst all the uncertainties and unanswered questions. "Thank you for letting me know," she says.

Elnore exits the room, leaving Kayra in a state of confusion as she stares at Colston. She moves to his side and grips his hand. "Babe?" she asks, her voice low and trembling. "Please, don't leave me."

Colston's hand squeezes hers, and she collapses to her knees, sobbing into the sheets. Gently placing her other hand on his arm, she shakes as she whispers, "Rest, baby."

Colston could sense that Kayra is under

immense strain. He feels powerless to help her, knowing that doing so could jeopardize his own survival. He wants to hold her and reassure her that everything will be alright. He curses the phantom and Todd for putting his family through this ordeal.

His body is exhausted, and the pain is overwhelming. He lies in the fog, crying. Helpless once more, he knows Kayra needs him, but he cannot be there for her. He struggles to force himself to be present, barely able to hear or feel. He cannot communicate his desires or provide the support Kayra needs.

He had heard about what his mom had done and was deeply upset. His world revolves around Kayra, and if she were to leave, he wouldn't survive. Her hand in his and her voice are his lifelines during his moments of weakness. She continues to save him, and she deserves everything.

He clings to her, wanting to support her until his last breath is taken naturally.

Kayra lays her head on the sheets, holding Colston's hand, and falls asleep.

She jolts awake in Colston's truck. He is gone, attending therapy. A quiet calm envelops her, but it is soon shattered. The door to the building swings open, revealing Colston lying there, his arm outstretched and blood oozing from his chest. Kayra screams and flings open the door of the truck, but as she steps out, she is engulfed by darkness. Hearing Colston crying out for her, she frantically searches and screams for him.

"Kayra, are you there?" His voice, filled

with pain and fear, pierces her heart.

"I am here, Colston! Where are you?"

"It's too late..."

Kayra wakes up screaming, but her cries are gently silenced by Oliver's embrace. "Shhh, you don't want to wake Colston. I apologize for this. Elnore is off duty, and your mom isn't allowed in here," he says softly. The hug is brief, avoiding any lingering awkwardness.

Kayra lies on the cot beside the window, where darkness envelops the outside world. She gazes in tired confusion before turning her attention to Colston, who appears to be asleep. Kayra is acutely aware of her throbbing headache and her urgent need to eat, drink, and relieve herself. However, her eyes fixate on Colston's bandaged left arm, which is stained with a significant amount of blood.

"His arm?" Kayra exclaims, panic evident in her voice.

"A nurse is coming," Oliver says.

Kayra is extremely confused about why it is bleeding so much and the fact that Oliver is here, "Who snuck in?" Tears in her eyes.

Oliver gazes at her with stern yet sympathetic eyes. "No one came in."

Kayra's confusion transforms into wonder: how could this happen? Colston is not strong enough to move in such a way as to open the wound. Her eyes widen with fear as she looks down at her own hand. She had fallen asleep with her hand on his arm. A sob escapes her lips. She brings her hand to her face, trembling and feeling nauseous. "I hurt him...again."

"You didn't mean to," Oliver reassures. "You were asleep after a long day and a traumatic experience, both of you sleeping for nearly thirteen hours. I came in here to try to wake you and saw that you were in a nightmare and what you were doing to Colston. I had to move you, but Colston will be fine."

At that moment, a nurse enters the room with a tray of tools and fresh dressing. "Ma'am, I am going to clean his wounds. I advise you not to look."

"I'll stay over here," Kayra says as she looks back at Oliver. "Any updates on the investigation?"

Oliver shakes his head. "Nothing. They are waiting for Colston to be well enough to discuss what happened in that room."

Kayra nods and glances over at Colston. Suddenly, she feels Oliver's hand on her arm. "Kayra, your phone rang at one point. I saw that it was Jordan, and knowing how close you three are, I answered it and reassured him about a few things. Jordan just arrived less than an hour ago."

Kayra smiles, "Could I leave to go see him? I know I will retake the test and change my clothes. I just need to see Jordan."

He looks over at the nurse who is cleaning and dressing Colston's wounds, "Let me go get the doctor. We need to arrange a meeting with you and the parents. There is some urgent news we need to discuss."

Kayra looks at him in panic as Oliver stands, "I'll be right back." He rushes out of the room.

Kayra is left with her heart racing.

Colston lets out a painful groan.

The nurse speaks quickly, "I am almost finished, Mr. Driscoll; just a few more minutes."

Colston opens his eyes and turns his head toward Kayra. He immediately notices the fear in her eyes; she appears so timid, "Kayra?" His voice is barely above a hoarse whisper.

"Colston." Her voice matches his in volume but is laced with fear. She is battling the urge to flee. Although she cannot bear to hear any bad news, she cannot simply stand by and watch him fade away. The fear that rises in Colston's face intensifies as she remains frozen in indecision.

The nurse had just gently retied the gown around his chest before making her exit. Colston slowly reaches out his arm and pleads, "Honey, please. I am here." He is crying and scared.

Kayra takes a step forward, her mind racing with worry and panic, tears rolling, "Colston, I am scared."

"Come here," he urges gently when she remains still. "What are you afraid of?"

"The doctor wants to meet with our families." She gasps, "Babe, are you... letting go?"

Colston hears these words and feels a surge of worry for himself. He is still weak, but the fog has nearly disappeared from his mind, allowing him to rest. However, he wonders if something is brewing within that he remains unaware of. He believes he no longer teeters on that precarious threshold. "Kayra, I am weak and in pain. Since I have survived the past and what happened in that room, I can endure this." He takes a deep breath, gazing intently into Kayra's eyes. "If I die, it will be beyond my control. I am not ready to go."

Kayra breaks down and approaches him, very gently laying her head on him, "I can't see a world without you." She whimpers into his chest.

Colston ignores the increasing pain just enough to hold her, and she moves away from him before he has to ask.

"Sorry," she whispers, gripping his hand and sitting in the chair beside him.

"It's fine," he whispers, unable to conceal the pain in his voice. He lifts his trembling hand to her cheek. "I love you."

Kayra presses her cheek against his warm skin and whispers, "I love you too."

Chapter Twenty-Six: Family Breaks

Colston falls back asleep after being awake for nearly thirty minutes. Kayra watches him drift off with a sense of ease and calm. Observing the strength in his eyes and hearing it in his damaged voice, they spend those thirty minutes simply enjoying each other's company.

There is a knock on the door, and the doctor opens the door, "Am I disturbing?" His voice is gentle.

"No," she whispers, glancing at Colston's serene face, "he's sleeping."

The doctor enters the room and closes the door. "Kayra, I have some things to discuss; I hope you are comfortable with that."

Kayra interlaces her fingers with Colston's and says, "I am ready."

The doctor nods and moves closer to the bed. "There is a growing infection, so in about three hours, we will take him for a chest X-ray to determine its location. That is the most concerning news I have to share." He reaches toward Colston's neck. "The swelling has decreased but remains at a concerning level. Other than that, he is still in critical condition, though he is on the tail end of it." He then looks away from Colston and directly at Kayra. "Next, I would like to have your mother and your father-in-law present."

"What has my mom done?" Colston asks in a light voice; his eyes slide open.

The doctor looks at Colston with a sympathetic expression and says, "You need to just rest."

"I need to know that my family is okay," he says, gasping between several words, as he squeezes her hand.

Kayra gently rubs his hand and says, "Honey, you need to rest. We will all be fine, and I promise to tell you the truth once you are out of the ICU."

Colston turns his head toward her and says, "Kayra, please, I want to hear."

Kayra looks up at the doctor and says, "I know I might be pushing the boundaries of my role here, but Colston wants to be involved. Can we find a way to gather everyone here?"

The doctor's eyes shift from Kayra to Colston as he contemplates. He then shakes his head and says, "You just need to focus on healing, Colston. You are not out of the woods yet."

Colston shakes his head. "Please, do not leave me in the dark." He is becoming increasingly agitated, and tears begin to well up in his eyes. "I was unaware of Todd's true intentions behind his desire to help." His breathing grows labored, and he winces in pain, yet he presses on, desperate to express his feelings. "The betrayal and wasted years culminated at gunpoint as he fed me to the wolf, using the guise of being taken again to make it easier to kill me. My mother is notorious for her cunning, especially when I am involved." Colston trembles, his heart racing. His body rings with pain and fear as he looks toward Kayra, who gazes back at him with wide eyes. "I should have told you everything regarding my mom."

Kayra gently places her hand on his chest, attempting to soothe him. "Shhh, babe," she whispers, wiping away his tears with her thumb. She struggles to manage her own fear as she processes what Todd did. A multitude of questions arise about what transpired in the room. "Your mom won't come near you. Not after Sunday."

Colston is struggling to regain control; his head pounds, and he feels sleep creeping in, "Please don't leave." His voice is barely audible. He despises having to say this, but he needs her.

"Colston, I will not leave you to face this alone," Kayra says, watching him struggle against sleep. She leans closer and whispers in his ear, "Rest, my songbird; I am here."

The doctor pauses to process what Colston said. "I will be right back." He turns and leaves the room.

Kayra watches him leave, refusing to let go of Colston's hand as she stares blankly at the sheets. Her heart breaks as she processes what Colston said, still reeling from his account of the fight in the forest.

She reaches up and gently runs her fingers through his hair. "Babe, you are so strong and have fought so hard," she whispers. "I am not leaving you; I am committed to you and our life together."

She moves her hand and gently places it

on his chest, feeling his heartbeat. She buries her face in the sheets and sobs. He is still alive after everything; how is that possible? A limit must be approaching, and she needs to protect him from it.

Colston begins to sob in his sleep about half an hour later, startling Kayra.

"Colston, honey, wake up," she pleads urgently.

"No... let her go!" Colston cries in his sleep. "Kayra, I am sorry."

"Colston!" Kayra exclaims, raising her voice.

Colston gasps awake, his tear-filled eyes locking onto his wife. Despite his pain, he pulls her into a tight embrace.

Kayra tries to avoid putting weight on his chest while still wanting to enjoy being in his embrace.

"I dreamed that you were held at gunpoint by Todd and the phantom." He cries, trembling.

"Shhh, they are dead. They can't hurt you anymore." She cradles his head as he weeps into her shoulder.

"I------want to--------put this--------behind------me. I----am so freaking scared------and tired. I just------want------to------go--------home." Colston gasps between sobs; his chest hurts so much that he nearly begins to wail.

Kayra holds him and pleads, "Babe, please, calm down. I am here."

"He------almost killed--me----twice!" Colston cries, tightening his grip on her.

Kayra is struggling not to fall onto him,

tears streaming down her face in fear. "COLSTON! Look at me," she pleads, cradling his face in her hands.

He locks eyes with his wife and takes a deep breath, gazing into her lovely brown eyes. There is so much fear and pain reflected in them.

"You escaped twice; yes, the mental torment will still linger. However, you can begin to heal, knowing that he is dead." She feels terrible for raising her voice at him. It isn't his fault, but he must remain calm for his body to heal, as he will need his physical strength to support his mental recovery. "You are not alone; let that thought leave your mind. I. Am. Never. Leaving."

Colston's breath catches, and his eyes widen; the cadence and desperation echo the moment when the phantom had declared. "I. Am. Your. Everything." His face was being cradled as well. The difference lies in the eyes; the genuine, loving brown eyes of his wife gaze back at him. He calms himself, allowing his heart to slow and cease pounding against his aching chest. He suppresses the urge to cough, which causes his chest to heave.

Kayra's phone begins to ring, prompting her to move and answer. She notices Colston wince in pain as he struggles to suppress a cough. Glancing at the caller ID, "It's Dad!" she exclaims and hurries back to the bed, picking up the call. "Hi, Dad. You're on speaker."

"Son? You there?" Elliott asks, his voice sounding old and weary.

"Yeah, Dad, I'm here."

"Oh, my boy, your poor voice. The doctor says that by Sunday, you should be out of the ICU and can have a few more visitors," Elliott expresses. Even over the phone, Colston could hear his dad's distress.

"Dad, what is Mom trying to do?"

Colston hears his dad sigh in defeat. "She is pulling the same shit, this time trying to paint Kayra as the bad guy... And we can't find her."

Colston glances at Kayra, who understandably appears frightened. He weakly grips her hand and says, "Dad, could you share with Kayra what Mom did years ago?"

"First and foremost, Kay, please don't blame Colston for not telling you. This happened years ago, and we had believed that Patricia was improving after years of therapy and support groups. Unfortunately, I later discovered that Colston's abuse began at a much younger age. These are merely the instances where I witnessed the abuse firsthand." He let out a sigh of guilt.

Kayra looks at Colston, who is slipping into sleep. She gently lays her cheek on his arm and says, "Don't worry, Dad. I won't be mad at him. Just so you know, your son is drifting off to sleep."

"Alright," Elliot says, lowering his voice. Kayra can hear the emotional toll this is taking on him. He takes a shaky breath and begins, "Colston was ten years old and fully engrossed in his vocal talent, not yet on the Collective Creative platform. We wanted him to be seventeen. On school nights, when he wasn't overwhelmed with homework, which was rare, he attended vocal classes or church youth gatherings. The confidence he gained from his talent helped him come out of his shell. He discovered a kind of magic in music, and he loved it, striving to share it with others. Patricia, a stay-at-home mom, began to feel lonely. I worked as a rehabilitation engineer in hospitals and clinics across the state. When I wasn't traveling, Colston and I would often arrive home at the same time. I always emphasized the importance of family time to Colston, so we would have dinner, watch a movie, or play games before bed. During those moments, we would talk about our days. One night, I was running late to get home, and Patricia wasn't answering my calls. By the time I arrived, Colston was already cleaning the kitchen, his nightly chore, which he usually did with glee while singing. That night, however, he was silent, and the stress was evident on his face. I hugged and kissed him before responding to Patricia's call from the bedroom. In the room, face to face with my wife of fifteen years and the mother of my son, I noticed a change in her that frightened me." Elliott pauses, his emotions building. Kayra desperately wants to comfort him. "Patricia did not greet me warmly; instead, she told me to sit on the bed and began to speak. She expressed her loneliness now that Colston was not home as much and asked me to get her pregnant again so she could feel fulfilled as a mother. I immediately shut that idea down. Before I could encourage her to pursue hobbies or consider working now that Colston was becoming more independent, I saw her shut down, refusing to hear anything else I had to say. I believe that was the moment that triggered the change. In the following days, Patricia became increasingly overbearing toward Colston, and I unfortunately had to travel to the northern part of the state. She tried to turn Colston against me, requesting that he stay home more to prepare for the eventuality of me leaving them. A scene unfolded when I walked through the door after returning from a four-day trip. Colston stood there, seven feet away from me, trembling. I dropped my bags and rushed to embrace him. Just before he was in my arms, he cried, 'I'm sorry.' As I held my boy, I heard my wife scream from my left side, and both Colston and I were struck by a bat along our sides. I dropped to the floor, shielding Colston, who was crying, though his cries were drowned out by Patricia screaming at me to release her baby boy. I yelled at Patricia to stop; fortunately, she didn't raise the bat again. She just stared at me and said coldly, 'I know you want to leave; why are you back? Give me Colston now.' When I let go of Colston, he moved away from both me and Patricia, looking confused and scared as he glanced between us. He ran to his room without a word. Patricia cooed after him, but I shut her down and demanded to know what the hell she was doing. That entire experience changed our family dynamics. Colston agreed to stay home after school from Monday to

Wednesday, but he could be out until curfew for the rest of the week, on the condition that Patricia attends therapy and starts a hobby. We promised never to fight like that in Colston's presence again."

"Kayra, I apologize for this lengthy explanation, but I wanted to share it with you because there was another incident that will make sense to you. Are you okay with me continuing?"

Kayra listens in shock as Colston snores softly in the background. A sense of fear washes over her, worrying that she or Colston might be in danger because of this situation. She gently interlaces her fingers with Colston's while resting her head on his arm. "Yes, Dad, I'm ready to hear more," she replies.

"Right," he takes another shaky breath and starts again. "This new dynamic lasted for five years. Colston was fifteen and did not want to spend time at home. When Patricia wouldn't relent, Colston would retreat to his room, singing or, on occasion, gaming, ignoring his mom's pleas to share how his day had gone. Colston would text me, explaining that he was tired of his mom's clinginess and felt unsafe confronting her alone. I later discovered that the last time he had confronted her, she had threatened him. I had promised to talk to her that night." He pauses in his narration and falls silent for a moment. Kayra didn't know what to expect, but she refrained from interrupting his pauses. From her years of dealing with Colston's trauma, she understood that these pauses allowed for a cohesive and tangible retelling, which was crucial for releasing trauma. "I spoke to Patricia as we got ready for bed. I approached the topic by praising Colston's good grades and his exceptional singing. To which she immediately retorted harshly, 'Your son is refusing to leave his room before you get home. I have been keeping my promise.' 'He is a teenager and needs his freedom.' 'Then give me a baby!' she demanded. 'No way!' I shouted in return. 'Then Colston needs to keep his promise.' 'You are the ADULT!' I screamed. Patricia stormed into the bathroom. I walked out of the room, left a note on the counter, and went to stay at a hotel. I wish I hadn't, or at least that I had taken Colston with me. That night, Patricia ended up ripping off the door to Colston's bedroom and had tied him to the bed, with tape over his mouth, cooing at him. Colston didn't sleep and ended up missing school the next day, prompting the school to call me. When neither Patricia nor Colston answered the phone calls, I raced home, and Patricia held a knife to his throat until I said that I would give her another child. I was then able to free Colston and get him into the car. I apologized as I drove us back to the hotel. He wasn't crying, just blank; I could cradle him, but he didn't return the gesture. I thought I had lost Colston; he had been traumatized, and I felt responsible. To protect Colston, we stayed at the hotel for a night, and I switched positions at my job to be at home. I was able to take the brunt of her outbursts." He let out a deep breath.

Kayra had listened to it and now needed to process her thoughts. However, one question stood out among all the others: "If she gets to Colston and sees him in his current condition, what will she do? Will it trigger her?"

"Yes, she's also upset because I haven't been home since Sunday, but I had to tell her that Colston is in the hospital," Elliot says. "Are you okay, Kay?"

"It is just overwhelming, and I want to concentrate solely on Colston. As far as I'm concerned, I don't want her anywhere near him from now on." She says, as Colston emits a painful grunt and arches his back. Kayra sets the phone down and gently squeezes his hand. "Colston, sweetheart, wake up."

"Make the pain go away." Colston's airy voice pierces through Kayra.

"Hold on, baby." She reaches over and presses the call button. "I'm calling for the nurse. Stay calm, honey," she says, gently rubbing his sweaty face.

There is a knock, and the door opens. "Yes?" the nurse asks sweetly.

When Kayra turns to face her, she immediately rushes over to Colston. "Mr. Driscoll, if you can hear me, I am going to give you more pain medication."

Colston continues to arch his back and bursts into tears. "Please!" he begs.

"Please remain still, sir; any movement may cause you discomfort."

"I can't breathe." His eyes open, and he looks at Kayra. "Baby?"

"Shh, it's alright." She watches him calm down as the medication takes effect; a painful smile crosses her face. It is so difficult to see him dependent on heavy drugs. "No one will hurt you again."

Colston's head vibrates, and his body resonates with pain as he wishes for a pillow to be placed over his face. He is exhausted from enduring pain, physically, mentally, and emotionally. When the numbing sensation washes over him and the fog of pain recedes to the back of his mind, it never truly disappears; it merely waits for its moment to seize control again. He opens his eyes and gazes at his beautiful, patient wife. The sadness is clear in her eyes, and he hears his father's voice in the distance. *"Colston, my son."* Kayra picks up the phone and holds it to his ear.

"Dad," he says, his voice soft and distant.

"You are strong and can overcome this rough patch. Kayra, Jordan, Kylie, and I will be here for you to lean on. I wish you had leaned on me sooner, but I understand why you didn't. Colston, you were nearly killed, and I am not ready to say goodbye to my only son. I want to be there to support you."

Kayra and Colston exchange a concerned glance. "Dad, we need to address the situation with Mom. I can't be suffocated by her; this healing process is going to be challenging. I can't endure another incident like what happened on Sunday, and your three kids are going to need you." He takes a strangled breath.

"I promise you won't see her again. I should have left her after what she did when you were fifteen. Oh, Jordan wants to speak with you." They hear the phone change hands.

"It is great to hear from you, buddy." His emotions are evident. *"I am so happy that you are still with us."*

"Yeah, thank you for coming back," Colston says.

"I'd rather be nowhere else."

"Jordan, if you need to rest, you can go to the house," Kayra says.

"This boy needs it; he looks terrible," Elliot says.

Colston smiles, and Kayra chuckles, "Honey, I'm going to sleep while the pain is away."

Kayra nods and leans in to kiss him. "Goodnight, babe."

Jordan leaves the hospital at 12:36 AM. He has to pull over because he breaks down in tears. During the entire drive back to Idaho, he had maintained a blank stare, allowing his emotions to build up. He was still in shock, recalling Kayra's voice on the phone. Over the years, he had heard fear and sadness in her tone, but that call had been filled with dread. He had been staring at his phone since around 5:34 PM on Wednesday, when his creative drive had unexpectedly vanished. As utterly terrifying as that was, the intense sadness and devastation that emerged for no apparent reason left Jordan frozen, fixated on his phone. His heart ached as if he had lost a part of himself, yet he was trying not to let his worry overwhelm him. It reminded him of the time when Kayra and Colston failed to answer the door, and he thought the worst of Colston. He trembled at the thought, but that intense emotion could only be attributed to Colston, a man who had rekindled his love for singing, a passion he was beginning to lose. He couldn't simply pick up the phone and call to alleviate his anguish; he was afraid of the truth. When Kayra's name appeared on the caller ID early in the morning, he answered, striving to remain as composed as possible. His heart shattered, and a howl began to rise within him, only to die down into sobs upon hearing that Colston was alive.

Jordan composes himself and approaches the house, eager to just crash. He leaves his bags in the car and walks up to the front door. As he pulls Colston's keys from his pocket and prepares to insert the key into the keyhole, the door suddenly swings open, revealing a person with a crazed expression. "What are you doing here?" they demand.

"Patricia?" Jordan asks, finally managing to focus his tired and emotionally strained mind on the person before him. He recalls that he needs to call Elliot if he encounters her. Pulling out his phone, he has a question on the tip of his tongue. The fact that she is in Kayra and Colston's home is deeply concerning, but the question never escapes his lips as his phone is suddenly slapped from his hand, and he is pulled inside.

Caught off guard by the speed and strength with which he was yanked, he fell to the floor near the kitchen island. The room is dark; when Jordan looks up, he sees a glint of metal reflecting in the moonlight.

"Don't move!" Her voice is hushed and frantic. "Is anyone following?"

Jordan does not recover as quickly as he would like, staring at the darkened figure looming over him. His mind is convincing him that this is merely a dream, as he is asleep in the uncomfortable chairs of the waiting room.

"HEY!" Patricia barks.

Jordan's attention snaps back to the dark room of Kayra and Colston's house. Streaks of moonlight cascade across Patricia's face, illuminating her frenzied expression in a nightmarish manner. Jordan's skin crawls with fear as she drops to her bony knees. "Jordan, you were not meant to come here," her voice is low and cunning as she shifts her gaze from side to side.

"Who was?" he questions in a shaky voice.

She pulls away sharply and stands. "NOT YOU!" she screams, slamming something solid onto the counter. Jordan jumps, nearly in tears from fear, as he struggles to compose himself. The alarm bells in his head ring loudly, but his body remains unresponsive. "On your stomach, hands behind your back!" she orders.

Jordan can neither fight nor comply; he is paralyzed by fear.

"How pathetic!" his own hardhearted voice roars, barely ripping through the paralyzing fear. *"Wake the fuck up! Fight, or your friends will be in danger!"*

"What?" This escapes Jordan's lips as he is shoved forward, his chin striking the tiles. He rolls to his right, knocking over a stool in the process. As he begins to climb over it, he feels Patricia's fingers grasping at his shirt.

She is shouting at him to remain still.

"NO! Why are you doing THIS?" He asks, scrambling over the stool and regaining his footing.

When he turns to face her, she is pointing a gun at him. The crazed look in her eyes is the most frightening thing he has ever seen. "Whoa! Hey, put that down. There's no need for that." His hands are held out in front of him, trembling uncontrollably; he honestly doesn't know how he is still standing.

"It is necessary because that money-grubbing harlot is standing by my son's side solely for his money!"

"What? Kayra? No, she freaking adores your son!" Jordan yells, his mind in a state of panic, hoping to wake up soon.

Patricia narrows her eyes. "You claim to be Colston's friend. How can you not see it? No kids, and yet she stays home on HIS dime!"

"No, she does her own thing. She's just not as open as Colston is." Tears fall, and his knees threaten to buckle.

"What are you getting out of this?" Her eyes suddenly widened. "You're here to steal something, aren't you?"

"No!" Jordan screams. "I am here to sleep. Kayra and Colston are like family to me."

"Enough! I am tired of talking. My son needs to be saved, and you are going to help me."

Jordan feels his heart race. "Colston needs time to rest. If you go to him, you are putting him at risk." He is trying to appeal to her, just enough to create an opportunity for him to escape and call the police. However, his voice lacks strength. *"Come on, JD! She is going to get Colston killed! She's a woman with a gun; the pain of a gunshot is far better than the loss of Colston or Kayra!"* His own voice screams at him. Jordan stares at Patricia and the gun, paralyzed with inaction.

Patricia shakes her head. "Years of excuses for why I couldn't see my only son. He was kidnapped and now nearly killed; I CAN PROTECT HIM! People like you, Kayra, and Elliot just sit idly by, benefiting from his suffering. Poor little singer boy, struggling through the horrors brought on by his chosen life path. When Colston needs to withdraw his voice from the world to save himself, I can show him that hiding will prolong his life." She stares at him sternly and speaks with unyielding authority. "Get on your knees and put your hands behind your back. Don't make me kill you, Jordan."

Jordan could feel the intensity of the fight, the deep-seated desire to protect. It had burned brightly over the past week and a half, but now, when it could make a significant difference, it was stifled. *"Because you are all talk,"* his voice taunts him.

Patricia advances on Jordan during his moment of hesitation. She presses the gun to his head and whispers, "Get on your damn knees!"

Jordan complies, silently crying as a zip tie restrains his wrists behind him. Patricia speaks with glee, "I don't want anyone to get hurt who doesn't deserve it. Let's go get my boy."

Jordan could argue that they won't get anywhere near Colston before being intercepted. He knows that this will lead to her imprisonment, preventing her from seeing Colston for a long time. Ultimately, he remains silent. He is compelled to exit the car; Patricia ensures she stomps on his phone while keeping the barrel of the gun buried in his back. He is then placed in the back seat of his own car.

She presses the gun to his head. "Make a sound or attempt to run, and I'll kill you."

Jordan nods in understanding; his ability to speak is overshadowed by his overwhelming fear. He gazes into the eyes of loveless possessiveness. *I am failing by permitting this.* The door slams shut in his face.

Patricia gets into the car and merges onto the road. "Now, Jordan, I need you to listen and listen well," she says, her voice reminiscent of a schoolgirl attempting to assert control over a situation she doesn't fully understand. "At this early hour, people are practically dead on their feet, and security consists of just one person. I know where they have stashed my boy--"

"Stashed?" Jordan asks, his hands bound

behind him, and the gun no longer pointed at his face. For some reason, that terminology finally ignites his fighting flame. "He is in the ICU with a gunshot wound to the freaking chest! Not stashed; they're saving his life!"

Patricia turns in her seat, grabs the gun, and slams the butt of it down onto his thigh. Jordan howls in pain and collapses over in the seat.

"He shouldn't be there if the right people gave a shit!"

"That I agree!" Jordan exhales sharply. "But what's done is done, and he is alive!"

"Shut it! He's alive within a lie. Don't you see it?" Patricia glances at him in the rearview mirror.

"You are delusional," Jordan says, at a loss for words.

"THAT IS WHAT EVERYONE SAYS!!!" she shrieks, contorting her body to bury the barrel of the gun in Jordan's chest. "Jordan, you are my ticket to Colston with little to no bloodshed." Then she remembers that she is driving.

Jordan can still feel the hard steel pressing against his chest, and the warning reverberates in his mind. He is uncertain about what to do next.

Patricia then continues to explain the plan, saying, "Once in the room, you will control that harlot, and I will convince Colston of his next step." She finishes, sounding pleased with herself.

Jordan sits up straight as she pulls into the empty parking lot of the hospital. She parks in a darkened corner, exits the car without turning off the engine, and moves around to Jordan's door. As soon as the door opens, the gun is pressed against his head. "Do as I command. Just think about how this will affect your career if you get many people killed."

Jordan is paralyzed with fear as he is yanked from the car. A bony hand grips his right arm while a gun presses against the center of his back. His legs give way beneath him, and he collapses to his knees.

"Jordan!" she whispers into his ear, the gun pressing against his spine, while his hands fall free. "Think of the pain Cole would feel knowing that this life led to his best friend's death. Now stand and move!"

Jordan perseveres through the pain. Her bony fingers grip his right arm, guiding him toward the front doors. The lobby is quiet, and Patricia urges him down a corridor that leads to the ICU.

"How? How?" Jordan struggles to comprehend how this situation can be unfolding. Colston needs a respite from those who are eager to exert control over him. Jordan limps along, desperate to encounter another person, hoping to serve as a buffer for Colston, as he is useless. He is smashed against the doors, forcing them open with his body, and now they find themselves in the outer hallway that encircles the entire ICU.

He gazes down the hallway toward the nurses' station before being abruptly pulled to the left and out of view. His heart sinks when he realizes that no one is there.

"God, are you trying to let Colston get

killed?" Jordan screams in his mind.

He stops in front of the door, where the label beside it reads, **Driscoll, Colston.**

"Open the door!" she whispers.

He grips the handle and turns it until the latch clicks. Patricia pushes him through the door.

There is a dim light to the right and moonlight filtering in from the left, allowing Jordan to see just how bad Colston looks. His pale skin and swollen throat are alarming; the oxygen mask fogging up with each breath Colston takes overwhelms Jordan's heart with guilt.

Patricia's fingers flex on his arm as his gaze shifts to meet Kayra's. She lies in a cot beside Colston on his left, holding his hand. Noticing Jordan's look of distress, she can safely infer that a threat looms over him or that a weapon is involved.

"Don't move!" Patricia whispers as she sees Kayra attempting to sit up.

Kayra moves slowly and carefully to avoid disturbing Colston's rest. She is determined to protect him no matter what. "You can't be here; you're putting Colston in danger!" she says in a fierce whisper.

Patricia pushes Jordan toward the right side of the bed, halting just before the foot. "It's all because Jordan crumbled so easily at the sight of a gun. There's no instinct to protect others when self-preservation takes over." Her mocking tone pierces Jordan's heart like a dagger. "Now, release my son!"

Colston's decision to sleep while pain-free allowed him to experience a dreamless and restful slumber. Perhaps holding Kayra's hand is helping to calm his mind. He begins to feel dull pangs of pain in his chest, but he remains grounded and centered within the idea of months of healing. Although this prospect is still daunting, he feels prepared to push through, which in turn lifts his spirits. As the pain gradually pulls him from sleep, he becomes aware of Kayra's increased heartbeat through their clasped hands; she must be having a nightmare. He squeezes her hand gently, hoping to provide her with comfort so she can rest peacefully. When he hears her light, startled gasp, his damaged body instinctively tightens. "Kayra?" he asks, opening his eyes.

The scene that greets him as he opens his eyes makes him pray that it is just a dream. At the foot of the bed stands Jordan, with Patricia right behind him.

"No, please, let me wake up! I can't endure another nightmare!" To his horror, this dream does not fade; instead, it escalates as Patricia gazes at him.

"Everyone, quiet!" she whispers as the gun buried in Jordan's back is aimed over his left shoulder at Colston. She pulls Jordan to the right, nearly causing him to stumble. "Do that again, and I might accidentally pull the trigger. Now turn off that machine; I don't want anyone alerted."

Jordan gazes tearfully at Colston as he reaches up to turn off the vital signs monitor. Patricia then scoots them back.

Colston removes the mask and exclaims,

"Patricia, just kill me! I can't take any more of this!"

Patricia's expression tightens. "I am your mother! You are going to live! Under my care, you will thrive! These people have made you wish for death, and if you continue down this path, you will either end up here repeatedly or, worse, dead!"

Colston can't believe he is once again staring death in the face. Begging doesn't even grant him the final bullet; he is going to have to push, reaching deep within himself, asking himself if he is actually ready to die after having already escaped it. Being kept on the brink of death solely for people to torment him with entrapment is not the life he wants. "Life you have given me, but my mother you are not! I lay here too weak to move, barely able to speak, and yet you have a gun aimed at your only son!"

She throws Jordan aside and rushes at Colston, pressing the gun against his right shoulder as she thumps her fist on his chest. He grits his teeth; he closes the fingers of his right hand around the barrel of the gun and drags it across himself, tearing the paper gown and causing the utmost pain as it moves across his chest, until stopping it in the center.

Patricia's eyes widen as the gun is moved; her head slightly shakes. "No, Cole." Her voice is quiet, yet her hand remains on the gun, and her eyes shine with intent.

"There, my heart beats under." His voice trembles, and he is very much aware of Kayra's hand in his. "I am not a freaking piece of property to be kept for one's amusement."

"No, son. This hussy is doing that to you, living off your money and pretending to love you!" Patricia growls.

A wave of panic washes over him when he feels the gun press harder against his chest. He is in too deep to pull back now; with tears, he presses on, "My wife is not the one pressing a gun to my chest! Patricia, you hold my life in your hands!" He frees his hand from Kayra and places his hands on Patricia's shoulders, pushing her away. "The choices only benefit me," he declares. He forces himself upright, the gun still firmly set, asserting, "Put a bullet in my heart! Or leave me and my family alone! I never want to see you again!" He is nearly sitting straight now, feeling wetness trickling down his chest. Colston sees betrayal and hurt flash across Patricia's face, and the gun trembles. He readies for a flash of pain, then the nothingness of death. He feels the buzzing starting to take hold; his breathing becomes harsh, and again, here he was begging to be allowed to let go. The eyes of Patricia stare at him, unblinking and apathetic. He senses with his fading awareness that Kayra has moved from his side. "Kayra! Jordan! I love you!" Colston cries out, feeling Patricia push back against him.

Suddenly, Patricia's cold glare flashes with surprise as she is grabbed from around the waist and is spun away from Colston by Jordan. She shrieks that she is being attacked as she presses the gun to Jordan's left side and pulls the trigger.

"JORDAN!" Colston and Kayra scream in tandem.

Kayra delivers a punch to Patricia's face, knocking her to the ground. She follows her down and prevents her from getting up. Patricia is shrieking for her to get off while yelling that Kayra is harming her baby boy.

Kayra screams back, fueled by overwhelming fear and anger, "Wake the hell up and listen to what my Colston said! He is done! Done with being controlled!"

Jordan has never experienced this level of pain before; he falls backward, landing on Colston and knocking him completely back onto the bed.

"JD------stay------with------me!" Colston gasps, his chest heaving as he struggles to breathe.

"I am sorry; I love you," Jordan says, fading into unconsciousness.

The door swings open, and a doctor rushes in alongside Oliver. "What the hell?"

Colston feels his body buzzing, his heartbeat slowing within his chest. A tear trickles down his cheek as he allows himself to drift and continues beyond the point of no return.

"I NEED SOME HELP!" the doctor calls out.

Oliver has placed Patricia in handcuffs, while Kayra stands up and observes the doctor administering CPR to Colston. Jordan lies across Colston's lap, his blood soaking the sheets.

"I need you to apply pressure to Jordan's

wound!"

Kayra reacts numbly, gazing at the two men who hold her world together. They hang in the balance as she clutches the corner of the blood-free blanket and pushes against Jordan's side. The absence of any response, not even a groan as he lies still, is a troubling sign. Meanwhile, the doctor behind her continues CPR, cursing the sluggish response time.

"CODE BLUE!!!" he screams, then curses under his breath about who turned off the vital signs monitor. Moments later, a team of doctors rush in with a crash cart.

"ABOUT TIME! QUICKLY GET JORDAN AND PREPARE THE DEFIBRILLATOR! WE ARE NOT LOSING COLSTON!" the doctor commands.

Kayra is relieved from the duty of holding pressure on Jordan's side and is left to painfully watch, eyes fixed on Colston. His voice echoed in her mind, recalling his desperate request for Patricia to end his life. He had reached the limit, and it was crossed.

"He is not strong enough to breathe on his own!" the doctor yells.

"Please, keep him alive," Kayra whimpers; she cannot let go.

Chapter Twenty-Seven: The End

Colston is sitting in his studio, typing out lyrics for his original music. His excitement and nervousness are palpable. After a five-year odyssey, he is coming to an end, breaking free from the confines of being merely a cover artist, a transition that will not be easy. The challenge is exhilarating, almost to the point of driving him mad. Despite his happiness, he finds that some of the lyrics are difficult to digest. Themes of death and misery permeate his work; should he take these into account and explore their deeper meanings, or is he merely juxtaposing ideas to subvert his listeners' expectations? He can only hope that wherever these lyrics originate, the lid is tightly sealed so that these thoughts do not overwhelm him... again.

There is a knock at his door. He leans back in his chair, rubbing his eyes. "Come in," he says warmly.

The door opens, and suddenly, arms wrap around him, gliding down his chest. He lowers his hands from his eyes, tilting his head back to see Kayra's smiling face looking down at him. She kisses him, then lays her head beside his and whispers, "Ready to go."

"Of course."

Avoid the darkness.

The truck is packed for a few days' trip to Jordan's place.

It waits to take you.

These have been a common occurrence ever since he began writing the album. He never gave them much thought; instead, he viewed them as warnings while he treaded the darker waters to create the songs.

"I thought you were completely finished with the album?" Kayra asks, glancing at the screen as he lowers his arms, and they break the kiss.

Colston gazes at the screen, making no effort to conceal what he has written. The lyrics are to the song *My Life's on the Line*. He is reworking it with a much softer and more succumbing approach, contrasting the grittier spirit that appears on the album.

"I am done, for the most part," Colston admits. "There is one song that I have not written down yet."

Kayra nestles her head into his neck. "Why not? And how? Don't you have the music all laid out?"

Colston gently guides her around and sits her on his lap. "Recording will start once we return. However, there is one song for which I have not yet been in the proper environment for it to emerge in its complete form."

Kayra gently rubs her hands on his face, cradling it. "Where do we need to go to help you release that song?"

Colston releases a breath, his heart swelling with pure joy. This woman shares in his passion so effortlessly that the moments he can offer her make it all worthwhile. "We are heading there, creating quite a poetic ending."

"How so?" Kayra asks, running her fingers through his hair.

Colston, with his left hand, grabs the mouse and opens a picture. It is the back cover of the album, featuring a lantern resting on a light wooden table. Beside the lantern, on its left, is a list of songs. "When we did the three-night stay at the Stark Night Experience, during the serenity of the first night, you had gone to bed while I remained awake at the old wooden table. The light from the lantern danced, oblivious to its impending extinguishment, producing illumination that allowed for sight and instilled a sense of calm amidst the suffocating darkness. The flame was beautiful yet threatening if mishandled." Colston fights back tears as he speaks with such passion. "I knew I had to capture that moment. We had taken a vacation to immerse ourselves in three full days of darkness, with the only source of light being an oil lamp. It was a light survival simulation, and I found myself weary at the table, staring at the flame. My mind settled; I shut out the world, aware of the dwindling oil. Instead of refilling it, I chose to work with it. I felt present, happy, and calm during that first session. I had fully written *A Song to Start* and had begun *Light Wasted, Darkness Holds*. In the two subsequent sessions, I started *My Life's on the Line* and *Cold Waves* and *Hearts Beat, Untied*. While here, I finished the songs I had previously started, along with *The Poison Within* and *Wake UP!*. However, the song *Means to an End* refuses to be written here. I envision myself crafting the lyrics as I sit on the beach, bathed in the light of the sunset." He takes a deep breath, gazing at the titles of the songs. In a trance-like manner, he says, "Inducting the end of a long, arduous journey, the contrast between the vastness of the ocean at the end to the suffocating darkness at the beginning." He looks up at Kayra and gently pulls her face close. "It is all worth it." He kisses her.

Colston begins the drive out of state around midday on a Tuesday, and the roads are mostly deserted. As he heads west, he listens to Kayra discuss her plans to redecorate the sunroom to reflect her creative style. Responding to the abundant creative energy in the house, there was something truly majestic happening when Colston started exploring original music.

Kayra has witnessed his passion truly soar when he performed a cover. He embodied the story or character, making it his own. As he crafted his own narratives and composed the melodies, he didn't need to adopt a persona, as these stories were authentically his. This release, though daunting at times, was a remarkable experience to behold. Colston carried himself with a sense of self-identity that made Kayra smile and fall in love with him all over again.

Colston pulls over at a rest stop along the La Grande-Baker Highway, marking the four-hour point of their journey. He steps out of the truck and stretches, noticing that the sun has just dipped behind the trees.

Kayra approaches him from behind, wrapping her arm around his waist and ducking under his raised arms. As he lowers his arms to embrace her, her hand rests on his chest. "I'll take over driving; you know how your body reacts at this time of day," she says gently, gazing at him caringly.

Colston sighs, "Yeah, I guess, but don't you find that strange?"

"No, darling, it is just you," she smiles. "Your discipline is extraordinary, and that is why your passion shines."

Colston smiles and kisses her. "I'm going to try to fight it to write the song."

"Just don't resist to the point of hurting yourself." Her voice is sharp and warning. "Let's get back on the road." She shifts back to a lovely and kind tone.

Colston moves to the passenger side of the truck, still feeling the impact of Kayra's words. He cannot explain how or why, but it just wasn't his wife. Climbing into the truck, he hides the fact that her words are hurting him. She pats his arm and pulls out of the rest stop. Before Colston can attempt to stay awake, he finds himself enveloped in a dreamless darkness, accompanied by the pile of undulating dross that has lingered in the corner, though it is beginning to fade. For as long as he has been working on the album, this pile of dross has been present; however, he cannot recall if there was something else before the Stark Night Experience, the moment the album was born. Whenever he gets within ten feet of the undulating, shapeless mass, he is struck by immense pain and overwhelming sorrow, from which he immediately recoils. Now he stares, his mind reeling with lyrics, his only comfort. Yet, he is filled with fear because he does not understand the source of the pain he has infused into the album. He feels somewhat inauthentic, as his purpose as a singer is to elicit emotions from the listener, facilitating connections: music to singer, music to listener, and singer to listener. How does that translate when the singer does not comprehend the emotions he is meant to convey? Tears fall at that thought; has he grown numb? Has his passion begun to fade, transforming into a mere job? A sob escapes his constricted throat.

"God, have I forsaken thee!" He cries in fear.

He gazes at the pile and realizes that this is where he is drawing from. He whispers, "I must understand." He shifts and positions himself just outside the influence of the pain and sorrow. Before he lies down in preparation to immerse himself in it, he hears voices, too faint and distant for Colston to discern, yet his heart twists with anguish.

The dark space rocks violently, sending Colston tumbling away from the pile.

His eyes snap open as Kayra's arm rests across his chest, the forward momentum propelling him toward the dashboard. Tires screech, and horns blare in the chaos. Colston quickly turns to Kayra, his eyes still heavy with sleep as they adjust to the light of the new dawn. Kayra stares at him in panic, gripping the steering wheel tightly with one hand.

"Honey, are you okay?" Kayra asks, breathless.

Colston nods and places his hand on his chest, gently patting Kayra's arm, which is blocking his hand from resting directly over his heart. The twist of pain he felt in the dark lingers. The question now is whether he should draw attention to it. He recalls the tone Kayra used last night; her words now contradict his issue; he must fight it or it will hurt him. He decides to keep this struggle to himself until he can comprehend it better. He looks ahead and notices they are stuck in a traffic jam. "Are you alright?" he asks.

"There is a gas station half a mile away; do you think we could trade?"

Colston intertwines his fingers with hers. "That's fine," he says, noting that they are nearly at Jordan's, less than an hour away. "When we stop, I'll call Jordan." He kisses her hand before releasing it and turning to reach into the cooler. "Want a water?"

"Please,"

Colston pulls out two bottles of water; he opens Kayra's first and hands it to her. Then he opens his own bottle, intending to take just a single sip. However, the moment the cool liquid touches his tongue, his body reacts as if it has been deprived of water for days. He chugs the entire bottle until it is empty. Breathless, he stares at the bottle and asks, "I was asleep for a single night, right?"

"Yeah..." Kayra replies, placing a hand on his forehead. "Are you feeling alright?"

"I'm good," he lies, though he feels like crying if he is honest with himself. He is fearful of what comes next, or the lack thereof, once he finishes writing the final song.

The Driscolls arrive in Washington's coastal town of Dryad's Cove at 8:20 AM. He rolls down the window, inhaling the blend of salt air and the aroma of Dryad's Cove's famous Seawater Donuts. As he turns off the main street toward Jordan's and crests the hill, the sea comes into full view, prompting him to pull over. A wave of sadness washes over him.

"Cole?" Kayra asks, her voice filled with concern. She places a shaky hand on his shoulder. "Honey, look at me," she urges gently.

Colston meets her gaze, his expression somber and on the verge of tears. "I am scared," he breathes, gripping the steering wheel tightly, his chest leaning forward. He breaks eye contact and looks back at the sea. "What if there is nothing after this album?"

"What do you mean?"

"Have you not noticed a difference in this creation process?" Colston asks, gazing at her with a pleading expression.

Kayra stares at him, drops her hand to his arm, and lets out a sigh as she breaks eye contact. "I have noticed a difference, but I didn't mention it because you seemed to have it under control."

"What is that?"

"Hollowness," she says. "There is a distinct lack of wholeness. While there is undoubtedly love and compassion for what you've created, it seems that the emotions conveyed in the lyrics belong to someone else. This may be acceptable for covers, but these are words that you have woven together; the emotions should resonate within you as you release them into the songs."

Colston breaks down in tears, saying, "I don't understand. How can I be driven to create something that holds so much meaning? Yet, I feel so disjointed from the emotions expressed in the lyrics." He begins to breathe heavily. "I feel that this is the end."

"Whoa, Colston. Take a breath." Kayra gently rubs his arm. "Don't give up on yourself. As difficult as it may be, perhaps this is the album's way of protecting you from its content. After working on something for so long, you might become susceptible to the emotions it evokes, which could harm you mentally."

Colston absorbs this information; it makes sense, yet he despises the lack of connection. He would prefer to feel emotions rather than exist as a hollow vessel.

"Perhaps once you have written that final song, understanding will follow," Kayra adds.

Colston takes a moment to gather his thoughts before continuing on to Jordan's house.

Colston turns onto the private driveway, which is lined with trees that obscure the view of the sea. Following the final bend, the stilted house comes into view, set against the backdrop of the ocean. On the screened-in porch, Jordan sits with a mug of coffee, smiling and waving as Colston drives up.

Kayra hugs Colston's arm and says, "I am so glad we are here."

"Me too." He puts the truck in park as Jordan leaves the porch and begins to descend the stairs.

Stepping out into the refreshing air, he feels the lightness fill his lungs. A heavy twinge of sadness grips his heart, but he is soon enveloped in a warm hug, which momentarily alleviates his sorrow.

"I am so unbelievably proud of you," Jordan says as he pulls away but keeps a hand on Colston's shoulder, tears welling in his eyes.

"JD?" Colston places a hand on his shoulder. "Thank you; you have been a tremendous help."

Kayra appears, and Jordan hugs her. "JD, how are you?" she asks, releasing him and intertwining her fingers with Colston's.

"Great! Come on, let's get you guys settled. Today, we're going to take it easy..."

Colston's mind drifts away from the conversation, drawn by a new and unsettling pull. So desperate, it fills him with terror because it leads to nothingness. Yet, there is a faint sense of familiarity. Could that be the source of the pull? He wonders, but before he can delve deeper into this thought, Kayra's voice interrupts his spiraling reflections.

"Huh, what?" Colston stammers, glancing at the worried expressions of his wife and best friend as something clicks into place within him. A chill washes over his body. "Sor--sorry, I just zoned out."

Jordan's and Kayra's faces relax. "Come on inside and take a load off; you deserve it." Jordan says, as he leads the way up to the house.

Kayra walks a few steps ahead of Colston, then turns to cast him a look that takes his breath away. The intensity of the warning in her eyes lasts only a moment before they soften. All he can do is smile back, as the words echo in his mind, but this time there is one other.

Avoid the darkness.

It waits to take you.

Fight, and cracks shall appear.

Colston feels an urgent desire to write the final song, but the pull is urging him to wait for the desired time.

"Colston, buddy, come on," Jordan calls from the porch, his calm voice tinged with annoyance.

Colston turns his head to look up at Jordan and see Kayra is standing halfway up the stairs gazing at him with concern.

"No, no," he whispers, shaking his head as his hands fly up to the sides of his head. "Something is wrong." He then glances at the other two, feeling dizzy, and his heart begins to race. "Is this real?" he asks before collapsing onto the driveway.

In the darkness once again, yet for the first time, he finds himself unable to hear his own thoughts. Distorted voices filled with panic and pleading echo around him. He glances toward the corner where the pile has always rested, but it is no longer there; instead, shapeless fragments are scattered about, surrounded by pockets of undulating inkiness. Overwhelming sorrow trapping him, *WHAT IS THIS? WHAT DID YOU WANT?* Colston screams, tilting his head back as tears flow. The ground trembles slightly beneath his feet, and the weight of sorrow begins to dissipate, leaving only a lingering residue. A slow, steady beeping sound reaches the edge of his hearing. Above him, the darkness fractures, allowing a dark, brilliant blue light to filter in. Strands of shimmering gold slap over his shoulders, crisscrossing his chest. As they gradually tighten around his chest, he remains standing, gazing toward the crack above. The floor transforms into a shimmering gold color, while the shapeless masses emit the deep, brilliant blue light.

A voice of resonate power reverberates through the space, and the words pierce Colston's soul: *"Caught betwixt, pain and sorrow equate to what was known, whilst the promise of fearlessness equates to dubious means. Time runs low; one must become priority. Upon the right choice, the singer's heart beats on; follow the wrong guidance, the singer's heart will cease. Was the mark left too great to bear? Is this mark free life worth it all?"*

The space instantly shifts back to its familiar state, dark and with the pile of undulating dross in its corner.

Colston drops to his knees, his eyes feeling heavy. Before he falls forward, he mutters, *"As your songbird, I flit within the shine of your eyes."*

Colston awakens, gazing at the unfamiliar ceiling of the guest room in Jordan's house. His mind echoes the aphorism, and he can still feel the strands of gold encircling his chest. He rolls his head to the right and notices a large window overlooking the driveway and the trees. Colston realizes that it is nearly his golden hour. However, there is one thing he must do before he ventures out to sit on the beach.

He sits up and swings his feet over the edge of the bed. Planting his socked feet firmly on the hardwood floor, cementing in the clarity gained, the next step will be the hardest of his life. He walks into the short hallway that turns left into another, slightly longer corridor. This leads to the living room and kitchen. Beyond the kitchen, a spacious sunroom offers a breathtaking view of the sea.

Jordan and Kayra are lounging on the sofas in the living room. Jordan is the first to spot Colston emerging from the hallway. "Well, look who decided to wake up," Jordan offers in a playful tone.

Colston's posture is heavy-shouldered,

with his head bowed. "I am sorry about that. I believe it is the combination of the sea air and the release of stress from the album."

"Darling, come and sit down," Kayra says warmly. "JD is going to start the barbecue in a moment."

Colston lifts his head, meeting the gaze of both of them. Their eyes flash momentarily with the golden hue. Colston nods slightly, then casts a sideways glance toward the sea, where he observes the blue color dancing along the horizon.

"It is the golden hour," he says, rushing to the front door to put on his shoes so he can retrieve his notepad from his truck. However, as he slips on his shoes, he hears the sound of heavy furniture sliding across the floor.

Colston is pinned against the wall, with Jordan pressing firmly against his shoulders, palms flat. "Colston, you are not going to go through with your plan. This is all going down the fucking drain," he says, applying even more pressure with his hands at the last line.

Colston calmly reaches out and places his hands on Jordan's shoulders. "This is not real."

"Cole, wake up! Feel this." Jordan grabs one of Colston's hands and places it over his own chest. "There!" Tears begin to flow. "Dammit! You are alive, Colston. Please, you are young and healthy. Why?"

"Colston," Kayra says, standing there with a meek expression. "I told you never to ask me to let you go again." Then, a flash of gold ignites in her eyes.

Those words struck him deeply, but the circumstances behind the reason that those words were spoken are lost to Colston.

Colston gently moves past Jordan, wrapping his arms around his wife's waist as he gazes into her shining eyes. "That sensitive phrase is meant to confuse me, keeping me here, free from pain and sorrow, stemming from an event I cannot recall. I only know that because of that event, every breath tasted so much sweeter, every moment spent with loved ones was cherished, and every note I sang was a gift. I am ready to awaken; please let me go." Colston releases his embrace and steps away from Kayra, whose figure flickers.

He leaves to go to the truck.

Armed with his notepad and pen, he strolls down to the beach. A quick flash crossed his mind: his wrists and ankles were bound together. He does not shy away from this as he walks; although it is frightening, he feels that this is where the mark was made. After surviving such an ordeal, life takes on a much sweeter tone.

He settles down in the sand. The sound of the waves crashing against the beach calms his hectic soul as the two separate lives begin to align. He pens the title at the top of the page: Means to an End. Looking up at the setting sun, the song becomes clear... well, more like two songs. There are two versions... Duet?

He sees Jordan and Kayra beside him. The

shimmering gold strands once again crisscross over his shoulders and chest, wrapping around his belly.

"Stay here and live worry-free." Kayra is resting her head on his shoulder.

The strands are not tightening; they are merely adding uncomfortable weight.

"Death comes for us all; you have the opportunity to be free from pain," Jordan murmurs softly.

"I would rather die in sorrow and pain than live feeling lost. Let me be reborn and start anew," Colston proclaims, gripping his pen as he feels the strands working down his arms. The first verse emerges:

From covers to creations, empowered by the night's embrace
Is it a façade or a guiding light, leading me astray without a trace?
An emptiness, a void within; is this the end before I even start?
Through borrowed tunes and self-made melodies, I pour my soul and play my part.

Colston forces himself to drop the pen. "Stop!" he cries, overwhelmed by immense pressure. "Let me go! Let me control my own fate!" He gazes at the horizon, where the sun hangs just two inches from touching the horizon. He has been staring for over a minute, yet it hasn't moved.

"Please, think about this," Jordan pleads.

Colston takes a deep, constricted breath. "The temptation is alluring, but I know it is merely an illusion in my mind. For reasons I cannot recall, my body lies somewhere, heavily injured."

"Will it be worth going back and enduring the healing process, only to find yourself in the same place again at a later date?" Kayra asks, clinging to his arm.

"I won't end up back here; I would rather let myself die than face this reality. I can't live a life trapped in my own mind, knowing that my true loved ones are suffering." Colston says, gazing into Kayra's eyes. "I can only create a version that mirrors my real wife," he continues, running his fingers through her hair. "You can never replace her."

Kayra appears hurt and dejected as she looks around Colston and meets Jordan's gaze. "I guess we'll stop trying," she says in a tone of cold finality.

Jordan sighs, "All this work goes to waste. Sad, really." He says, holding out his fingers and snapping them.

The sound is deafening, at its echo, within the sudden absence of the world's sound as the sun touches the horizon.

Colston, still under the pressure of the strands, feels his mind flooded with memories of the torment he endured at the hands of the phantom. Helpless and terrified, he stands defiantly recalling the anguish on Kayra's and Jordan's faces as they watched him suffer. With the sun halfway set, Colston is suddenly struck by blinding bodily pain. He is thrust backward into the sand, his breath stolen away as the sky darkens to the deep shades of blue.

"Baby, you still have time," Kayra says, looming over him.

Colston turns his head and vomits, tasting blood.

"You are dying! Please, Cole! Let us get you inside and into the light," Jordan pleads.

"I'm not dying," Colston says, his voice strained. "I am recombining with myself." He coughs.

Kayra leans in and kisses him before standing up. Jordan kisses him on the lips and then rises to his feet. Kayra walks around Colston and takes Jordan's hand. They turn and stroll down the beach, and as they walk away, the strands around Colston unravel and follow them, taking the last remnants of light with them.

Colston feels himself choking but remains calm as he fades. Under his trembling hand, new words appear on the pad.

~~From covers to creations, empowered by the night's embrace~~
~~Is it a façade or a guiding light, leading me astray without a trace?~~
~~An emptiness, a void within; is this the end before I even start?~~
~~Through borrowed tunes and self-made melodies, I pour my soul and play my part.~~

Bound by chains of destiny's cruel hand,
A singer's soul betrothed to an unforgiving fate.
Forced to sing for his life, he became a pawn.
In a twisted game, of which there is no escape.

Epilogue

Slowly, his awareness begins to grow, and signs of life start to emerge. He hears a doctor say, "Welcome back, Colston." They begin to poke and prod him, and he shows a response. "Can we get his wife in here? Tell her Colston is back."

Colston forces his heavy eyes open. His vision is blurry; he blinks slowly once, and when he opens them again, the blurriness has diminished. This allows his beautiful wife, who is standing in the doorway, to stand out among the multiple white shapes moving about.

Tears flow; his comfort is present, and he knows that he will be alright. He cannot speak with the tube down his throat, and he wants to reach out but can only manage to slide his hand along the bed sheet.

"Kayra, he is back, but not completely. In a day, once his strength improves, we can begin running the tests to determine if we can remove your husband from the ventilator. After conducting the cognitive and breathing assessments, and once the tubes are removed, we will place him on supplemental oxygen."

Kayra nods, overwhelmed with happiness that she still has him. As the doctor and Kayra approach the bed, Colston's vision clears. Kayra immediately grips his hand as she gets close enough, her eyes shining with tears of relief.

"Colston, we are going to conduct some tests to ensure that you can manage without the ventilator. I need you to stay calm and relax. I will be moving to the other side of you; could you follow my movement with your eyes?"

Colston effortlessly follows the doctor as he moves to the left side; each time he blinks, he struggles to open his eyes. He then feels two fingers resting in the palm of his left hand.

"Can you squeeze my fingers?"

He numbly curls his hand around the fingers, attempting to squeeze, but he lacks the strength.

"Alright, it's okay. You have been in a coma for three and a half weeks."

Colston's eyes widen in surprise as he shifts his gaze to Kayra, sorrow evident in his expression.

"Oh, Colston," she says softly, leaning against his shoulder. "Please don't feel bad. You're back, and that is all I ask for."

"In all honesty," the doctor begins, "you should not be here."

Colston senses Kayra tense up, so he gently wraps his fingers around her hand in an attempt to provide comfort.

She looks at him, tears welling in her eyes. Then her gaze shifts to the doctor. "Please, my Colston is here. I can't bear to see him with tubes down his throat any longer."

"I understand that this sight is distressing, but we have seen him be fine and then decline. We are taking extra precautions to ensure his survival. Colston, please squeeze my fingers if you are in any pain."

Colston curls his fingers but fails to grip. Frustration rises within him.

The doctor nods, recognizing his frustration. "Colston, I understand that not being able to speak is incredibly frustrating, but it is necessary. Are you experiencing any pain in your chest?"

Colston blinks slowly.

"Try to squeeze my fingers," the doctor says.

Again, he cannot squeeze his fingers; tears are welling up in the corners of his eyes.

"Alright, Colston, I'll let you rest. When you tore the stitches in your chest, an infection blossomed at the site. We have been combating it with antibiotics. So far, it hasn't reached your heart or lungs, nor has it entered your bloodstream. While it is not completely resolved, it is close, and now that you are awake and alert. We will work on a pain management plan."

The pain that Colston is experiencing is characterized by occasional sharp sensations that cause an irritating tingling to spread across his entire chest and upper back.

The doctor walks out, and Colston glances at his wife. There are so many things he wants to ask and say, yet he finds himself once again robbed of the ability to speak, feeling trapped and unable to offer comfort or seek relief.

"Please stay calm; I know this is frustrating. Soon, they will remove those tubes, and everything will be fine," Kayra says, resting on his arm. "Just please stay with me."

Colston feels the wetness of tears on his arm; his heart aches because he cannot hold her or sing to her. He gazes at the ceiling; he allows his eyes to close in rest.

April 8, 2020: two days after awakening from the coma, Colston Driscoll is removed from the ventilator and can confidently squeeze fingers. Speaking is still not recommended, as his throat had swollen following the removal of the tube. He is placed on supplemental oxygen to help him for a day or two and is also transferred from the ICU to inpatient care.

Colston lies at a slight angle, with Kayra gently resting against him. He is consumed by the fear that he may no longer be able to sing as he once did. He still hasn't received clear confirmation that the phantom is dead or even who he was. He clings to the horror of what transpired, waiting and yearning to release it.

There is a gentle knock, and the door opens to reveal his dad's kind, weary face.

"Dad," Colston mouths, lifting his hand a few inches off the sheet.

"My boy," he says quietly so as not to disturb Kayra.

Elliot rushes over to him and takes his hand. "It is so good to see you."

Colston nods and gazes into his dad's eyes, which are glistening with tears.

"First, that maniac nearly takes your life twice, and then your own mother almost kills two of my children out of possessiveness."

Kayra stirs and awakens.

Colston mouths and occasionally gets out vocally one half of the words, "Is Patricia in jail?"

"She's in a psychiatric ward after being escorted out of your room. She began begging to see you again, insisting that she could save you. Oliver bluntly told her that she might have just killed you, which sent her into a downward spiral." He rubs Colston's forehead. "You don't need to worry about her, son. I am divorcing her, something I should have done years ago. Please forgive my foolheartedness."

Colston motions for a hug, and his dad gently embraces him. Whispering in his ear, he says, "I love you, son." He kisses Colston on the cheek as he pulls away. Looking at Kayra, he adds, "Thank you," before breaking down in tears.

Kayra, feeling concerned, gets up and approaches him. "Dad, hey," she says, wrapping her arms around him. She catches Colston's worried glance over his shoulder. "I don't know what you're thinking me for."

The hug breaks apart, and Elliot looks between the two. "Hearing about what happened in that room and what Todd did for the past five years, you stayed." He moves and takes Colston's hand. "You undoubtedly saved him from the brink. I can never thank you enough for that."

Kayra gently rubs Colston's leg from beneath the sheet, "It was a combined effort from Colston, Jordan, and me."

"Where is Jordan?" Colston gets the first word out audibly.

Kayra looks at Colston sadly. "He's at the house."

Colston looks on with curiosity and concern, "Is----he----okay?" He asks breathlessly, with only 'okay' being fully audible.

"Honey, he is struggling to cope with what Patricia did and how he nearly got you killed," Kayra says.

"Call----him." Colston says.

There is a knock at the door. All three turn to face it as the doctor enters. "Good afternoon, Colston. How are we?"

His cheerful demeanor is somewhat irritating to Colston's somber disposition. "Fine," this is not audible.

The doctor frowns, "Have you been able to speak any words?"

Colston concentrates a little harder. "Yes," he replies audibly.

"Any pain?"

Colston nods, his eyes quickly shifting to look past the doctor. He spots two detectives, recognizing one from his previous stay in the hospital. A grip of fear begins to take hold of him. What does he have to fear? In the grand scheme of things, the worst has already happened, and nothing these detectives could do will change that. "What do they want?" he asks, his voice low and crackly, but he manages to articulate the full question.

All heads turned toward the door at Colston's question. The doctor turns back, saying, "They have a few loose ends they wish to tie up."

"I want Oliver and Jordan to be present. I wish to only say what I need to say once." Colston speaks clearly; he thinks that this might be the only time as it is painful and overall exhausting.

The doctor nods, "I can get a hold of Oliver."

"I can reach Jordan," Kayra says, already on the phone.

The doctor turns and exits, closing the door behind him.

"Jordan, Colston wants to see you," Kayra says in a pleading tone.

His dad releases his hand, gives him a reassuring pat on the shoulder, and leans in, saying, "I'll leave now."

"No--Dad, stay," Colston says.

"You sure, son?"

"No----more------secrets." Tears of pain begin to stream from Colston's eyes, and the level of raspiness in his voice gravely upsets him.

Elliot leans down and embraces him, "Colston, it is going to be okay."

"Honey?" Kayra places a hand on his shoulder. As the hug breaks, Colston looks at her, and she replies, "Sorry, but Jordan doesn't want to come."

Colston can see that she is still on the phone. He swallows hard, "Let-me--talk--to----him."

"Take it easy," his dad warns.

"Jordan, here is Colston." She places the phone on speaker mode and gently lays it on his chest, as per Colston's request.

"JD,----buddy, what----is----wrong?" His voice is as calm and warm as he can muster.

Colston can hear Jordan struggling to maintain his composure, which robs him of the ability to speak. "Whatever happened, I----am not----mad----at you. It----was out of----your con----trol."

"I froze!" he exclaims into the phone. *"I couldn't fight back, yet there you are, bearing wounds and scars of battle! I let your mom get to you."*

Colston is about to respond when Elliot interrupts him, saying, "Jordan, please don't compare yourself to others. Everyone copes with challenges differently; the most important thing is that you are still alive. Now, Colston is on the mend and needs the comfort and support of his brother."

The room is silent as Elliot's words linger in the air, unchallenged.

Then Jordan speaks after a moment, his voice low, *"Dad, could you come pick me up?"*

"On my way," Elliot says, hanging up. He gently kisses Colston, gives Kayra a hug, and then heads out of the room.

The silence lingers a moment longer as Colston reaches for Kayra's hand. With a sense of longing, he asks, "Is the phantom dead?" The mere mention of the name unleashes a torrent of memories that flood his once still mind. He neither fights nor ignores these recollections, as he seeks clear confirmation of the man's fate.

Kayra looks at her husband and speaks with confidence, "Yes, the phantom is dead.

According to the timeline constructed by the detectives, Todd shot and killed Melody before you arrived. Then the phantom, after shooting you and leaving you to die on the floor, entered Todd's office and shot Todd before turning the gun on himself."

The expression that spreads across Colston's face is not one of immediate relief; rather, it is one of fearful confusion. This startles her, but before she could ask about it, there is a knock on the door. Oliver peeks in. "Are you all set for the detectives?"

Colston coughs several times, wincing at the pain in his throat and chest.

"Waiting on Jordan." Kayra replies.

Colston speaks in a hushed tone, barely above a whisper, "Just you, come in. Please."

Oliver does so, shutting the door behind him.

"Hon, promise me that after meeting with the detectives, you'll rest your voice," Kayra pleads.

Colston nods and looks at Oliver. "I--want--them--to--know," he says, closing his eyes in an attempt to gather himself. "I know what happened; I will not entertain being berated or made to look like I had a hand in this." Colston lets out a harsh, dry cough and groans.

"I understand. I'll go inform them and wait for Jordan," Oliver says as he prepares to leave.

"Wait, can you please help me give him water?"

Oliver smiles and moves back to the bed.

Kayra takes the water and, with Oliver's assistance, supports Colston's head just enough for him to drink. The water, slightly cool, provides temporary relief from the pain.

Colston lies down once more and closes his eyes for a moment. Eventually, he falls asleep.

About twenty minutes later, Kayra gently shakes Colston awake. He stirs and peers at her with a smile, saying, "Hi, love," though his voice carries no volume.

Kayra smiles back and runs her hand through his hair. "Baby, I'm sorry to wake you," she says, glancing to the other side of him.

Colston feels a hand gripping his right hand. Shifting his gaze in that direction, he meets Jordan's tearful face. "JD." Again, it is not audible.

"I am so sorry, Colston." He leans down and buries his face in his arm.

"Jordan," Colston gets out audibly. "Please, remember what my dad told us. JD, don't hide how you feel about what happened that night." Colston squeezes his hand. "You were always there for me and Kayra during those nightmares. I------want------to------be------there------for--------you."

Jordan nods, "Alright, bud."

Oliver then peeks in. "Colston, ready?"

Colston looks at his father, Jordan, and his wife, takes a deep breath, and nods.

Jordan, with the aid of Colston's cane, moves to the other side of the bed, standing beside Kayra while his dad stands at the foot.

Oliver enters with Barnet and Conright. Conright displays an expression of indifference, while Barnet lingers behind both Conright and Oliver, wearing a look of disgust.

Colston begins, "What are you going to ask?" his voice is low. "But first, what was his name?" he asks, though it will not replace his personification of the man who nearly killed him.

Barnet scoffs, "Don't play coy about your partner in crime." He whispers, causing Conright to shoot him a sideways glance. Barnet stands moodily with his back against the wall.

"His name was Lance Vaclav... Mr. Driscoll," Conright says in a monotone voice as he faces Colston. Now tasked with addressing Colston about the incident, Conright struggles to formulate a question that wouldn't imply it was staged. After a moment of contemplation, he finds his direction and presses on, "What is the significance of these?" He sets a folder down on the bed and pulls out a clear sheet containing two papers back to back. One of the papers has the upper left-hand corner soaked in blood.

Colston takes a deep breath. "Lyrics," his mind whirls with the fear that resurfaces as he recalls standing before the phantom, preparing to lay everything bare. "I unknowingly saved myself the day of the house fire in the woods. I sang unprovoked and without prompting while lying on the dirty floor, sick, beaten, and freezing to death. He heard me, and it prevented him from killing me that day. I knew we were going to meet once I found that note at the house, and I knew that I was going to face him alone." Colston pauses, swallowing hard. "Those lyrics tell two stories: one is mine, a plea to reach him, to convey that I and my voice were not his. The other is his relentless conviction that he knew best and could save me from myself. Placing us in this unwanted duet, my hope was to break him so he would let me go. It worked, but Todd chased that hope away, transforming him back into the monster, realizing that the only way forward was death."

Barnet steps forward and exclaims, "That is a load of bullshit! You really expect us to believe that he willingly sang with you?"

Oliver holds him away from Colston, whose fear is mounting in response to the aggressive advance. His body braces for pain, and his mind threatens to collapse once more. However, Colston shakes off the dread and says, "Look at me, detective. I'm lying in a hospital bed, having narrowly escaped death at the hands of that maniac. I had to save myself in the only manner that made sense to me. I didn't ask for any of this." Colston's body trembles.

Conright turns toward Barnet and orders, "Leave! I'll finish this!"

Oliver forces him out.

Conright clears his throat and continues, disregarding Colston's evident distress. "Now, there are journals documenting Lance

Vaclav's obsession over you. Would--"

Colston interrupts him sharply, saying, "There is documented proof of what he did! Yet, I am being treated as if I had a hand in this."

"The fact that you are the only survivor and had lyrics prepared indicates premeditation."

Colston is astonished by this.

"Is my son's strength and will to survive this monster going to be held against him?" Elliot interjects, unable to remain silent.

"Sir, we are simply doing our job. We are exploring every avenue to gain a complete understanding; however, some circumstances just don't sit well," Conright retorts sharply.

"You----guys----have----a time------line of----that----day, with------my explanation--of the----lyrics." Colston pauses, taking a deep breath. "Only I and the phantom will truly understand what happened. It may have seemed planned or unorthodox; I know what I faced and will continue to endure as a result. I have nothing to hide and have been cooperative with you after both incidents. Now that he is dead, I can move on with my life, though I will forever bear that mark on my soul." Colston looks up at the ceiling and closes his eyes.

He hears a defeated sigh, followed by the sound of the door closing, leaving an uncomfortable tension in the air. Colston is left to regain control of his breathing; even the airflow over his throat brings tears to his eyes.

He feels a hand on his arm. "Cole?" This is Jordan, and his voice is somber.

Colston opens his eyes and meets Jordan's gaze, "JD?" He feels his heart leap in anticipation of bad news, news he is uncertain he can handle at this moment.

"The day before I left, we shared a moment of profound honesty. Accepting what was to come, you fought valiantly and achieved victory. A week into your coma, I received a text message from you."

Colston immediately flushed with embarrassment. "I was not awake to dismiss it," he says, looking at Kayra. "There is a note and a poem for you in my office. I wrote both after the last session with Melody. I had a way that I could possibly escape, but deep down, I knew I was going to die." He glances at himself and then up at his family, tears blurring his vision. "When the phantom pressed the gun to my chest, both of us crying, slinging words of hatred and pleading for understanding, driving him to the edge... pushing him to end my suffering." He lets out a sob and closes his eyes.

More silence envelops the air as Colston's words sink in; there is nothing left to say. This is yet another horrific memory he must endure. All the others can do is listen.

"There is something that scares me to my core," Colston says, his eyes still closed.

Kayra places her hand on his shoulder and asks, "What is that, babe?"

Colston opens his eyes. "The phantom had me pinned, his hand nearly robbing me of breath, and even after the shot to my chest, he left me alone. He could do everything else to me, but he could not bear to watch me die. I don't know why that chills me so."

Jordan speaks, "You were his everything, his 'means to an end' as it were. Keeping you close to death meant he could still save you, no matter how angry he became. Your survival gave him a sense of purpose; the moment that bullet entered your chest, he must have realized that a line had been crossed. Watching you die would mean he was watching himself die. Even the most deranged individual would experience that 'come to Jesus' moment; he couldn't confront the reality that his life was slipping away."

April 27, 2020, at 1:20 in the afternoon. Colston has been out of the hospital for a week and a half. He is on light pain meds and at a much greater threat of heart failure, yet his voice, though a bit on the rough side, is still intact, just one more constant reminder of that desperate push to save himself when all other avenues failed. He and Kayra are in the process of moving to Dryad's Cove, where they found a small house near the beach and not far from Jordan's place.

Colston sits in his barren studio, sitting on a folding chair with his laptop resting on a TV tray. The haunting memories of his kidnapping still linger, now coupled with the unsettling scene that unfolded in the therapy office. However, the grip these memories once had on him are fleeting, leaving Colston merely startled by them, but what he truly despises is the sensation that washes over him whenever he sings. He feels the phantom's presence, and difficult as it is, he recognizes that this is now his new reality. His only job is to ensure that it does not spiral out of control.

On the screen of the laptop sits the revised version of The Poison Within. The moment he found out that the phantom was actually dead, the song called to him. During his final days in the hospital, he added the sound of a flatline and then the sound of him coming back from the brink of death. He ends the song with strength and hope, whilst acknowledging that the influence of the phantom will linger.

He reached out to a man known as BLUEJAY, a music producer, songwriter, and vocalist. Colston was new to songwriting; he could re-lyric but even in that he didn't hold much stock in his ability. BLUEJAY and he corresponded over social media, and luckily BLUEJAY was unaware of what happened because he lived in Oklahoma. So it was Colston just asking for help reworking a song. He, with the help of another lyricist, Brutsie, was able to get him a rough draft by the time he was released from the hospital.

He has the full song two weeks later and is truly thankful for the speed and the dedication that was shown. He absently runs his fingers over his wrist. "As complete as I feel, the lasting mark burns within, forever a reminder of the hell endured, making every breath thereafter so much sweeter," Colston says to the room.

"Colston! Babe, we're getting ready to go to lunch!" Kayra calls out.

Colston smiles easily, "Coming!"

Colston Driscoll exits the room, simultaneously departing from the ever-watchful gaze of Story. His narrative has been shared, and now Story turns its attention to the next. Rather than gazing longingly at the door, let us focus on the song.

The Poison Within

VERSE 1

I sip from the cup of venom
And swallow down the poison from his lips
From his lips

Trapped by my fate's intentions
I can't escape from this preordained end
Preordained end

VERSE BRIDGE 1

I yearn to take control
Freezing as I reach for stability

VERSE 2

My hope consumed by dread
Leaving me with faith that's torn and worn
Torn and worn

Now I am left for dead
My tortured mind can't take this anymore
Anymore

PRECHORUS

My courage is suffocating from the tightness of this chain
I must escape from destiny's pain

CHORUS

These flames may try to engulf me
And the cold may try to encase me
But I must stand and fight back fate's relentless toll

(BACKING VOX: YOU CAN'T DEFY YOUR FATE)

But the poison lies inside me
And it destroys the faith within me
As this blackened fate begins to bring me down

[SOLO]

VERSE 3

My breath begins to fade
I'm still a pawn within his twisted game
Twisted game

So now I must surrender
As I lie in death's embrace forever more
Forever more...

I am sorry to the ones I love
But I've grown tired from this fight
This is my final breath...

(Flatline)
(Beat silence: ACCEPT YOUR FATE/DEFY YOUR FATE)
(Gasp, cough, rhythm starts up again)

I reject the cup of venom
As I push away the poison from my lips
From my lips

And God's light begins to shine
This faith and hope surrounding me is real
It's all so real

My heart beats steady
Each breath tastes sweet
I'm unbound, I am alive
Now free from the poison within!

CHORUS

My soul forged in the final crucible
My body's been steeped in blood
My mind's been wrought with terror
My heart's been on the line

Yet I survived and now I'm in control
My life belongs to me
And although I'm deeply marked and scarred
I now have a song to sing

A song for the ones I love
A song for this brand new life
For I have survived fate's stranglehold
I have survived

The poison within!

Song by: Colston Driscoll
Produced by: BLUEJAY
Additional lyrics by: Brutsie

Coda

Hello, Dear Sior Asumanove,

You can finally release a deep breath; you have just finished reading Colston's Phantom: Brink of Death. As for me, I can breathe deeply knowing that I am writing this after finalizing the entire book for you. I feel a strong sense of pride mixed with a twinge of sorrow. I take pride in the fact that it is complete and ready for the next step in the publication process. I feel sorrow because it's finished, and I hope the lessons learned while crafting this story will carry over into my future projects. Writing is a profound experience offering something unique for both the author and the reader. In the past, I tried too hard to give my stories depth, which often resulted in them falling flat in conveying what I wanted to share. However, that was not the case with Brink of Death. I had a solid foundation from the very first breath inspired by YouTuber and singer Caleb Hyles, to whom I have dedicated the book. If I hadn't, I would feel remiss, as whenever Colston Driscoll sings, I hear Caleb.

Regarding the theme of the book, it is something I often lost sight of amid the chaos in previous projects. The desire to feel complete and to have control over one's own life remained clear throughout, making my heart sing as I wrote, seeking those wants not only for the character but for myself as well.

I could talk endlessly about this book, but I won't take up any more of your time. And of course, my biggest thanks to you for reading my work!

Colston Alex Thief
11:04 PM 03.05.25
4:01 PM 11.20.25

Caleb’s Channel: @CalebHyles
BLUEJAY’s Channel: @BLUEJAYMusic1994
CG5’s Channel: @CG5
Brutsie’s Channel: @brutsiethegutsy
My Channel: @DarkCold Laboratories

www.ingramcontent.com/pod-product-compliance
Lightning Source LLC
LaVergne TN
LVHW090544110826
845146LV00001B/8